Beyond the Yew Tree

Whispers in the courtroom.

Only one juror hears them.

Can Laura expose the truth before the trial ends?

Also by Rachel Walkley

The Women of Heachley Hall
The Last Thing She Said

Beyond the Yew Tree

Rachel Walkley

Spare Time Press

Published by Spare Time Press
Copyright © 2020 Rachel Walkley
All Rights Reserved
ISBN: 978-1-9996307-5-1

For Roz

* * *

"There are two kinds of guilt: the kind that drowns you until you're useless, and the kind that fires your soul to purpose."
— Sabaa Tahir, *An Ember in the Ashes*

"No guilt is forgotten so long as the conscience still knows of it."
— Stefan Zweig, *Beware of Pity*

"New love is grand. Savor all the crazy, muddled might of it."
— Eli Easton, *The Mating of Michael*

* * *

Day One

Monday

MONDAY MORNING, OR DAY ONE, as Laura dubbed it, began with a brief frisk of her arms and legs followed by a thorough search of her handbag. Satisfied that the Thermos flask contained nothing explosive, the guard directed her to an airless room with cheapskate chairs and an overindulgence of cork noticeboards. Forty strangers waited there, corralled into an unsuitably small space, each one trying not to make eye contact. The awkwardness was akin to the unnatural quietness of a doctor's waiting room.

She was surrounded by the restless and frustrated; keen to start and eager for the finish line. Some had brought newspapers and paperbacks. One young man with wireless earpieces hugged a laptop sleeve to his chest and dropped into a chair with an ingrained expression of boredom. In the corner, the vending machine was stuffed with crisp packets and confectionery, its unhealthy contents an incentive for eating out at lunchtimes. Laura regretted leaving the puzzle book and obligatory apple at home.

The first morning of jury service involved watching a short information video and completing the necessary tedious bureaucracy. Waiting for something to happen, Laura stared out of the window at the rugged stone walls of Lincoln castle. The sense of entrapment intensified. None of this was her choice. Nothing ever was, it seemed.

A black-cloaked usher swept into the room with a pile of papers balanced on one winged arm and spoke to the collected with her flittering eyes partially hidden by purple-rimmed spectacles. The greeting was a scripted welcome delivered in a happy-all-the-time tone. The reason was obvious – this was a normal working day.

A typical morning for Laura began with a Sudoku and eating the worthy apple. Crosswords were too whimsical and nuanced for her taste in puzzles. She completed both activities on the bus ride into the city. Then, after an essential caffeine fix (robust black Americano), she logged on to her computer and checked her emails for anything significant, as in important to her projects rather than office tittle-tattle politics. Laura preferred a predictable, uneventful day to exciting unplanned crises or emotional meltdowns. No surprises, no sudden happenings. At least a trial was structured and carved into a pattern as old as the castle. With luck, she'd incorporate the disruption into her life with as little fuss as possible. Managing disruption had been an unfortunate trend ever since Marco had extended his trip to Italy.

'Please answer your name,' the usher said, rearranging her papers. Names rattled out of her mouth, then, 'Laura Naylor?'

'Here.' Laura collected her handbag and flask.

The middle-aged woman next to her chuckled. 'It's like being at school again.'

'Beryl Savage?'

Laura's neighbour stuck up her arm, exposing loose folds of flesh and a red-mottled scar. 'That's me.'

More carefully pronounced names were called, their owners identified among the crowd. Having completed the roll call, the usher tucked her files under her arm. 'Please follow me.'

They formed an orderly procession through the courthouse. Somehow, they would be whittled down to twelve. They were herded along corridors and stopped outside an oak door where the word "silence" was embossed in brass.

'Let's hope they don't pick us,' Beryl whispered. Close up, the chestnut recolouring of her hair was obvious; the roots were honey grey.

Laura was thinking the contrary. She had no wish to sit around waiting, nor be told to reappear each day to be dismissed after a couple of hours. How would she spend that wasted time? More Sudokus? A book? She reserved reading for quiet evenings.

Beryl clutched her bag. 'I mean, what if it's a murder?'

'Unlikely,' Laura said. 'Let's hope not.'

'One of my cousins was stabbed to death outside a pub.'

Laura, startled, nearly tripped over her own toes.

'Second cousin, twice removed, or thereabouts,' Beryl said. Hardly riveting; Beryl appeared equally disappointed.

Murders were rare according to the statistics; Laura had checked. Would gruesome photographs and distressed witnesses bother her? There was no way of telling. Would she prefer a lengthy case or oddments of criminality in bite-sized trials?

'It could go on for weeks,' Beryl said. 'I can spare the time. Retired, myself. Tough on you young people, though, isn't it?'

Laura appreciated the young remark: she wasn't wearing any make-up.

The usher coughed loudly. 'Please remember to be quiet. Just fill the seats at the back of the court.'

Laura followed Beryl into the courtroom. The floorboards creaked, as did the unwelcoming benches. She was surrounded by solemn wood panelling that covered the walls and partitioned the court into boxed sections. The echoes of travelling voices were uninterrupted by the jurors' arrival; from barrister to barrister, clerk to judge, the mash-up of words lost their meaning long before the sounds reached her ears. The room was alien, almost unnatural, like a film set. She half-expected a cameraman to leap out or a director to shout, 'Cut'.

The judge, wigged and gowned, cleaned his spectacles, waiting for the newcomers to settle into their seats. Laura's attention immediately fell on the man in the dock: middle-aged, hunched, and eyes downcast. His smart smoky suit matched the colour of his hair. Laura couldn't picture him as a pub brawler or burglar. He blew his nose on a handkerchief. He wasn't going to softly sob his heart out? Surely the victims cried and the defendant remained grim-faced? He stuffed the hanky back in his jacket pocket and glanced up to the public gallery. A solitary woman, similar in age, elegantly dressed, nodded and offered him a wobbly lipped smile. When he didn't respond in kind, she redirected her attention to the judge.

The introduction was a list of reminders, things to do, and more specifically, what not to say outside the courthouse. The task completed, the judge allowed his gaze to travel the length of each row, eyeing his potential jury with a neutral, somewhat bland expression.

'Ladies and gentleman, I should warn you this case could last three or possibly four weeks.'

A collective gasp greeted his statement, prompting mutterings about the expected two weeks of service.

'That's it. He's a murderer,' Beryl said, bright-eyed.

Laura trusted statistics.

The prosecuting barrister rose and faced them. 'Before we select the jury, does anyone here know Craig Brader?'

His question was met with silence.

Craig Brader. Laura thought hard. Had she seen his name in the newspapers, on Facebook? Anywhere? Nothing sprang into the void. Pleased, the lawyer nodded at the judge.

'I bet it's his wife who's dead, and that woman is his lover.' Beryl uttered her condemnation without fear of her surroundings.

'Hush.' Laura pressed her finger to her lips. 'That's your name they've called out.'

'Oh, is it?' Beryl rose and entered the jury box.

Four more names, and each person moved forward to the segregated area.

'Laura Naylor. Juror seven,' the usher said.

Laura's legs were already stiff. She took up position next to a man with chewed fingernails and corduroy trousers.

Straightening up, the wary defendant watched the jurors occupy their seats, his sharp eyes perched above pinched cheeks, sandwiched on either side of a long nose. He wasn't crying. He wasn't even upset.

What had Craig Brader done that required three weeks of scrutiny?

After the prosecutor had finished his opening remarks regarding the thirteen indictments that covered an eight-year period, the jury filed into the secluded deliberation room. The usher closed the door and warned the jury they would be summoned back in less than fifteen minutes. Deflated by the realisation that Craig Brader's crimes were hardly going to raise her pulse, Laura selected a chair in the farthest corner of the poky chamber and waited. The room fulfilled its design requirements: uninspiring whitewashed walls, gravel-grey carpet, and bars across the windows. The furniture amounted to the obligatory twelve chairs, long table, and a gurgling water cooler with thimble-sized plastic cups. She poured a cup of coffee from her flask. One person dispatched an envious glance in her direction, a few others sniffed longingly. The aroma of arabica was unfortunate.

In the coming weeks, whenever they shuffled in and out of court number one, the oldest in the building, this sad room would be their prison. The tallest man – Number Twelve – cocked his head to the two adjacent toilets.

'At least we've en suite facilities. His and hers; no hanky-panky.' He rocked on the balls of his feet, grinning from one droopy ear to the other at his humourless remark.

'No kettle.' Beryl sighed. 'I fancy a cuppa.'

Laura left her flask on the table. 'It will be safe here, won't it?'

'Sure,' said the man in the corduroys, who'd sat next to Laura in the jury box – Number Six. 'It's not as if the criminals get to see this side of the courthouse.'

The chairs weren't especially comfortable; a room without a leisurely purpose. A few of the other jurors circled the table, incessantly restless; most chose a seat and hung their coats or bags on the back of it.

Something, an irritating insect, invisible and unseasonable, buzzed around her head. She swatted the air and struck nothing of substance. The windows were sealed shut. Trapped like the jurors, the insect must have taken up residence.

While Number Six stared through the bars at the grey skies, Number Twelve stood with his legs planted apart and folded his arms across his chest. Laura wasn't a fan of his booming voice; the room failed to absorb it.

'I'm Brian. I run a canning factory. We might as well get to know each other.'

Laura kept her mouth shut. She'd prefer not to reveal her job title. Having heard the indictments – several counts of defrauding a charity amounting to tens of thousands stolen – she'd wondered if the barristers would consider her presence on the jury fortuitous or disadvantageous. Theft was theft, and while she understood the numeric intricacies of embezzling and possessed the expertise to decipher it, the human perspective was a novelty. She dreaded the word "guilty" being tossed about in a careless manner, but persuading people needed the kind of confidence that would likely elude her. Best if she let the others interpret the evidence and she'd only offer her opinion when *absolutely* necessary. Jury service for most people functioned as a break from work, a respite, but her experience might be dangerously close to a busman's holiday without the recreational aspect. She wouldn't be obstructive, merely observant and introspective, which was her preference. She was required to give a verdict, nothing else.

Beryl happily divulged her name.

A woman in a jacket the shade of buttercups and wearing lashings of indigo mascara introduced herself next. 'Jodi. I teach. I also write poetry. So, he's been fiddling the books. Why does that take weeks to prove?'

'Numbers are complex.' The speaker was a young man with walnut-coloured eyes. He didn't provide his name.

'He's not a trained bookkeeper,' Brian said. 'He's the finance director of a charity, a position that gives him access to money. You heard the barrister; he's been at it for years.'

The man opposite Brian had a dour face with a head topped off by a shiny bald pate. 'He's innocent until proved guilty.'

'Naturally, naturally,' Brian said. 'Didn't mean to imply otherwise. That's what we're here for.'

The unenthusiastic introductions ended abruptly. The usher returned and despatched them silently into the courtroom.

The defence's opening rebuttal was swift. The charges were false, and Craig Brader was the victim of a malicious conspiracy orchestrated by a third party yet to be divulged.

Brader's gaze remained transfixed on the floor of the dock.

Without an explanation, the judge dismissed them for the rest of the day. Laura retrieved her flask from the retiring room and screwed the cup tightly on top. The buzzing was back. Less like a fly, more of a long exhale or the sighing hiss of a snake. It followed her out of the room. The noise seemed to belong entirely to Laura; nobody else mentioned it. The jury dispersed with an urgency that evaded her. There were a few hours of daylight left, a regular bus service, and no need to rush home to an empty house.

She stood in the shadow of the building and surveyed the broken walls of the castle. The expanse of the inner bailey, which in medieval times would have been a bustling hive of activity, was now an open area housing two key buildings: the crown court and an old prison. On previous visits, she'd ignored the courthouse with its classic architecture and ivy-clad walls because it wasn't of interest unless you had business there. As for the museum housed in the prison, that too was a miserable reminder of the less fortunate. She'd not stepped foot inside; it was probably milling with tourists. She favoured a walk around the reconstructed ramparts and bought an annual ticket. It was likely for the duration of the trial she might use the walls to escape unnecessary conversations. She needed her fellow jurors to focus on the charges laid against Brader and not dwell on the particulars of the defrauded charity's beneficiaries. She could stomach the former, but the latter was bound to bring up upsetting memories of that fateful day.

Coiling her scarf tighter around her neck, she followed the guided walk, keeping her eyes on the horizon rather than below to the castle's interior. Lincoln was built on an escarpment, an ideal location for a domineering castle. With the Gothic cathedral next door, its sky-high spires and frontage easily beating the castle's diminished towers, the two great structures, twinned by their age, looked down on the city below. Laura searched the scene and failed to pick out the council offices where she worked. Geography was not a strong point, nor was she blessed with any sense of direction. The low sun dogged her, and she shaded her eyes with her arm. The streets below were squished into a maze of patterns and, between the grim shades of grey, greenery poked out. In the distance were the ploughed fields of the Lincolnshire farms.

She walked briskly through the Lucy Tower, chased by a flurry of amber leaves. Sheltered inside were grisly gravestones, memorials to those who had had their necks snapped by the noose

– she loosened her scarf in an act of faintly unconscious sympathy. Thank goodness she wasn't expected to condemn anyone to that fate. She had poor knowledge of modern prisons, but she was sure they were better than the Victorian gaols. She paid no heed to the headstones and continued her trek.

The blustery circuit was a distraction both from the disappointment of the court case – how humdrum the next few weeks were going to be – and the realisation that going home offered her no respite from her worries. What had she expected? For over a decade her life had been shaped by mundane events, the most recent encapsulated by her cousin's wedding in a tiny parish church somewhere near Nottingham. A truly miserly affair with a pound-a-head buffet and a no-hats policy. Her cousin, who masqueraded as a vegan while secretly spreading butter on her bread rolls, was quirky and dull in equal measure. The groom wore an ill-fitting morning suit and danced most of the evening with the chief bridesmaid, a pencil-thin girl in a cerise dress with a festoon of ribbons (and bows!). Definitely something fishy there, Laura had thought as she'd consumed the fizzy prosecco (bitter-sweet) that her aunt had declared was expensive champagne. Laura danced with nobody.

Marco's absence had hit her hard. She'd really believed he could have made an effort and returned for the wedding. With his excuses given – busy, couldn't possibly leave his father in the lurch – she sent back the invitation with one name, not two. Her aunt and uncle knew better than to comment, but her cousin had swooped down on her at the church, offering commiserations.

'He's a sod, isn't he? Can't be arsed obviously,' she'd said far too loudly; heads had turned.

Laura's cheeks had flushed with embarrassment, and she'd retreated behind a pillar.

With her tour of the castle walls completed, Laura had no more excuses to delay her journey home. The sun had sunk below the highest aspects of the horizon, and its departure triggered a drop in temperature. She hurried to the bus stop.

Letter number one – reward points – spend fifty pounds and get back three. Twenty was Laura's weekly budget for non-essential things. She scrunched the voucher into a ball and tossed it into the waste bin in the far corner of the lounge. Letter number two – interest-free credit on transfers. She only had the one credit card and avoided any temptation to collect them. She manufactured a paper plane out of the sheet, threw it, and missed the bin. Letter three was another familiar variety – please give us money. Why she'd signed up to the cat rescue charity's mailing list was a mystery. She was allergic to cats and suspected a scam. She would check if the charity existed, and if they didn't, she would report them. One of the virtues of working for the county council was she was well versed in how to file reports.

She salvaged leftovers from the fridge. There was a choice of soap operas on TV to watch while eating. She liked to flit about from one to the other. The habit, which annoyed Marco, stopped her becoming too involved in the lives of unreal people who made awful decisions. However, paying some attention armed her with sufficient information to join in conversations at work with those who cared what happened to their favourite characters. Laura didn't believe in the fake empathy, but she gorged on the daily shows in a comfortable bubble and successfully ignored the hypocrisy of her reasoning. At nine o'clock she switched over to watch a documentary (fluffy tiger cubs) and read a book at the same time (unknown celebrity animal rights activist). Words (fur being one) wafted around; she mixed up those she heard and those she saw and began to nod off.

Her phone beeped. She jerked and scrambled around the cushions to find it. Feverishly, she swiped the screen and held her breath. But there was nothing from Marco. The notification was a reminder to make a packed lunch for jury service. She deflated into the scatter cushions.

Things were getting ridiculous. It was three months since Marco had stuffed a heap of designer-label clothes into a rucksack and gone to Italy to help his father look after his sick mother.

'Tesoro, just a few weeks during the holidays. I'll be back at start of term,' he'd told her. 'He's in up to his neck in shit.' Marco liked English idioms, scattering them liberally into his speech. Not all of them made sense.

The so-called "shit" was not clearly defined and probably was to do with his father's business. Throughout their year of living together, Marco had gone out of his way to avoid his family's pleas for him to visit. Then, out of the blue, he was on a plane to Naples and rapidly breaking a string of promises to Laura. The first promise – I'll text you every day – slipped from every few days to an occasional message at the weekend. Emails dried up, too; they hadn't exactly provided much information anyway. His Facebook account had never been a source of personal news; he shared music videos and football pundits' voiceovers; that was about it for social media. One month later, that stream had dried up, too.

At the beginning of October, genuinely worried, she'd called him. He'd answered on the sixth attempt.

'I'm fine,' he'd told her with the kind of impatient tone he reserved for fools. 'It's taking longer than I thought.'

'What's taking longer?' she'd asked.

'Stuff,' he'd said, utilising his Italian accent.

'Stuff?'

'Sì.'

'What about your studies?'

Marco was supposed to be studying for a master's at the university. That was how they'd met, not as fellow students, but at a business skills event hosted by the university. The council had sent her as a representative – she was supposedly skilled – and embarrassed she might not be, she had hidden in the corner of the room with the equally shy Marco, a mature student with hazel hair and a gold chain around his neck. The pair of them had quietly sipped on cheap wine for half an hour before plucking up the courage to talk to each other.

'It can wait.' Marco had shrugged off her concerns about his unfinished degree.

'And me?' she'd asked. 'When will you come and see me?'

'Soon. And one day, I give you a lovely holiday here—'

'But you live here, don't you?'

A long pause. 'I live here, too,' he'd said, a touch haughtily.

The question had to be asked. 'Is there somebody else?'

'No,' he'd said with a surprising amount of passion. 'No, no. I... my father...'

'Oh?'

Marco's father was supposed to be an important businessman in the town, and he'd once been a councillor or something political. As for Marco's mother, she was a mouse. If she happened to be present during a call, she said something in Italian – no English – and slipped away silently.

'It's very difficult. Family stuff. You know.'

She didn't. Her family were fragmented and few in number, easily accommodated in and swiftly out of conversations. Marco shunned talking about his numerous relatives, cloaking them in unnecessary secrecy. Laura knew all about keeping a secret, especially the guilty kind. Eventually, after several weeks of dating him, she'd told Marco what had happened years ago, but he'd never grasped why the unfortunate accident upset her so much; probably because she had syphoned off a distressing detail and kept it to herself.

'Do you still love me?' she'd asked.

Another unnecessary pause. 'I do. I'm sorry. This isn't fair on you, I know. We're treading water.'

Sinking was more accurate. 'No, it isn't fair. Text me, please. I can't stand the silence. It's ridiculous. It doesn't cost you an arm and a leg to send a text.'

'I try,' he'd said feebly.

The conversation had left Laura in a quandary. Why hadn't she dumped him and ended it all there and then? Her mother had cheerfully offered this advice. But Laura hadn't been able to bring herself to do it by the end of the summer, and she still couldn't a month later. Marco was her boyfriend, and while she might not be with him, he held that title. Things had been good between them until he'd left for Italy. Her romantic needs were small scale; she wasn't impressed by flowers or chocolates, although a decent bottle of wine ticked a box, and a peppering of frivolous conversations was fine as long as they entertained. Measured doses of kisses and cuddles certainly helped (more than helped if she was honest). Years of solitude had ended that night at the university, and she was damn sure if things came to an end it wasn't going to be because she'd given up trying. A piece of Marco was still lodged in her heart; likewise, she hoped she was in his.

All the same, what she felt was an overwhelming sense of emptiness brewing. She ditched the phone on the cushions and made sandwiches for the next day's lunch, slapping butter onto the bread in a careless manner. Usefully occupied, she rallied. The fracturing relationship was Marco's fault, not hers; she had done nothing wrong.

Day Two

COURTROOM NUMBER ONE WAS FREEZING. If icicles dangled from the ceiling, they wouldn't look out of place. Laura buttoned up her jacket and hunched her shoulders into a shelter. She glanced at her watch; only fifteen minutes had passed since the last time she'd checked. The prosecution barrister – she'd decided to call him Mr Waverly as he had the tendency to wave his hand in the air in a melodramatic way when hammering home a superfluous point – had provided the jury members printouts of a spreadsheet and was reading aloud every line. The defence lawyer scribbled notes. Behind him, Craig Brader slouched with his chin on his chest.

She stifled a yawn. The vivid elements of last night's dream lingered on, and they didn't help her concentrate, nor did the incessant hissing which undulated around her. Through it all the lawyer droned on. She recognised the numbers and words as basic summations of the charity's latest financial reports and nothing that warranted detailed analysis. Others, unsure of what was significant, made their notes. Scrambled notetaking wasn't how her brain worked; she couldn't listen and write at the same time. Finally, the last page of figures was entered into the court records, and the judge wisely called a break. The twelve of them converged on the retiring room.

'Jesus,' muttered a muscular man with mud-crusted Nike sneakers. He paced the room, eyeing the window as if hankering to escape. It was a hellishly boring case.

She dispatched him a sympathetic smile and immediately regretted it. She wasn't there to make friends.

Numbers Man, the quiet one, wrote neat columns on a piece of paper. Beryl fished out a magazine from her handbag. Most of the jurors switched on phones with a collective sigh of relief: the world outside was still there. Nobody spoke for a few minutes. Laura ignored her mobile. She doubted anyone had sent a text; she'd left strict instructions with work about disturbing her.

'He's falling asleep,' Brian remarked, throwing his voice into the stillness. 'Brader. He's nodding off.'

'Don't bloody blame him.' Mister Fidget scratched his chin. 'What if he does? He might get a bollocking from the judge. What if he started snoring?'

'I don't think it matters if he falls asleep. If we did, then that wouldn't go down well.' Brian had become the de facto guru. Within the space of one day, he had assumed the role of the knowledgeable one without ever having his knowledge put to the test.

She wondered if he had understood the facts presented so far. Surely the boss of a company would know how to interpret a balance sheet?

Brian rocked on his heels. Only he and the fidgety man had declined to sit out the break. 'Somebody must have brought a complaint against him; how else would he be in court? A board member or police officer?'

Laura had already constructed a plausible explanation in her head. She'd concluded it wasn't appropriate to speak about her assumptions. The complaint, or accusation, was likely to have begun life innocuously. An internal audit, perhaps, handled by the charity's regular accountant might have flagged up something odd with the accounts. After several discussions by the board of trustees, a forensic accountant had probably conducted an investigation. At this point, Brader, if he was guilty, would be hoping that the money he'd squirrelled away was safely out of sight. The tax inspector would want to know what was going on, and then the Charity Commission would have been contacted. What had started out as an act of diligence would have snowballed, leading to a bandwagon of interested parties flagging up discrepancies and, finally, the police would have stepped in. How long ago was that? Laura tried to recall what the barrister had said in his opening statement. Two years?

'Do you think the Feydons are in on it, too?' asked the mousy woman, with letterbox spectacles, who sat opposite Laura.

Laura whispered to the woman next to her, 'Feydon?'

Her mute neighbour shrugged off the query.

What had Laura missed?

'Feydon is the family behind the Seeside charity.' The explanation was provided by Beryl. 'I've crocheted blankets for guide dogs for the blind and I remember they're linked to Seeside because they both help the blind. If Brader is the charity's finance director, he must know the Feydons.'

Laura hoped Beryl would continue to surprise them all with her little snippets of information. It would put Brian in his place. As for the Seeside's beneficiaries, the visually impaired, they would hopefully appreciate Laura's innate diligence when it came to handling numbers. She tried hard not to think about them, who they were, as it clouded her mind, and she had to stay decisive. There was no reason for anyone in the courthouse to know about her emotional baggage.

They returned to the courtroom to listen to more balance sheets. Mr Waverly had several years of financial history to present. The only thing Laura noted was the charity had a cashflow problem and, although the donations were healthy and steady, a lot of money had been spent over the years. The charity operated lean, maybe too skinny.

She shivered, and her teeth clattered. Tomorrow she would wear a thicker jacket and woolly socks. Why had nobody else commented on the temperature? And how had that irritating buzzy thing managed to survive the cold? It pestered her, like a tiny mosquito, always there, whining away, but never visible. She was starting to doubt what it was she was hearing. The sound was static, focused around her, and clearly appreciable by both of her ears. Perhaps she was developing tinnitus.

Day Five

B Y FRIDAY, she had gleaned the names of her fellow jurors, except Number Six, who sat on her left in the jury box. He had switched from corduroys to cosy jeans. His profession couldn't be inferred from what little he said or wore (Brian sported a platinum suit all week). Mr Fidget's actual name was Haden, and she wasn't surprised to learn he worked at a fitness centre. For some reason fit men didn't appeal to her (Marco was flat-footed). Maybe she wasn't the best judge of people on the basis of their appearance.

There was slight Amil, the physics student who wrote lists on scraps of paper. Pauline with the letterbox glasses; she worked at a post office. Deborah was a dentist and counting down the last few weeks before she retired. Two nondescript men shared an apparent mutual dislike of Brian; they rolled their eyes at his posturing and formed a sub-committee. The awkwardness was unfortunate; she shoved their names to the back of her mind. Brian was fine. Perhaps not his unnecessarily abrasive voice that smacked of authoritarianism, but he held doors open, poured drinks from the water cooler, and offered anyone a mint whenever he had one himself. Laura liked Jodi, who had an infectious laugh and spent a few minutes each break composing a few lines of poetry.

'Not about you lot,' she said, when Brian raised a wary eyebrow. 'Not allowed, is it? No, I'm writing about the castle. Don't get into Lincoln very often, so it's nice to make the most of it.'

'What about the castle?' Laura asked.

'I try to imagine it in the dark of night after everyone has left. The city humming in the background. The moonlight...' Jodi dropped the small notebook inside her handbag.

'I don't have much of an imagination.'

'Oh, I disagree,' Jodi said empathetically. 'We all have one. I mean, it's just something you utilise unconsciously. I tell my pupils, imagination will find you, so be creative.'

Laura frowned. 'I'm not really creative either.' Art had eluded her at school. She manifested a distinct clumsiness whenever she came into contact with paints, brushes, or glue.

'Creativity isn't about covering a blank sheet of paper with ideas. It might be working with things, seeing something differently to how everyone else sees it, or hearing it, if you're that way inclined. Look at this guy in the dock, he's pretty creative with money, don't you think?'

He certainly had more money than his job had paid him. The evidence was in his bank accounts and the assets he'd acquired over the last few years – four-bedroom house, a BMW in the driveway, and a holiday to the Maldives. However, he had also inherited a poorly defined amount of money from overseas relatives. Lucky man, if that was the truth. Laura wasn't sure she'd heard enough to decide beyond reasonable doubt whether Craig Brader was honest or not. The presumption of innocence kept her from rushing to any conclusions, and she cautiously maintained the illusion she was ignorant of accountancy matters. In the meantime, the evidence drip-fed by the prosecution needed to flow faster.

'Financial acuity doesn't require the same skills. It's not the same as words. Or pictures,' she said to Jodi.

Amil, with his dark locks and elfin features, lifted his gaze away from his phone. 'You can see patterns in numbers.' He returned to tapping his mobile as if he never expected anyone to follow up his remark. A man of few words and fewer expectations.

'The only thing being creative with me,' Laura said, rubbing a bleary eye, 'are dreams.' The delirium of strange images pestered her sleep, while during the day, the quirky noises (clucks or tuts, and other odd stabbing sounds) whispered close by, distracting her from time to time as the evidence mounted. It was only outside the courthouse that tranquillity returned.

Nobody else mentioned voices, and she wasn't going to embarrass herself by asking.

Jodi wasn't listening. She'd picked up a conversation at the other end of the table. The usher rapped on the door and summoned them back. Time to squash into the jury box.

When the judge adjourned the court at three o'clock, Laura scrawled two notes on a sheet of paper and left it in the jury box – nothing left the security of the courtroom until the judge delivered his summing up.

Printing invoices.
Raffle tickets.

Satisfied those two jottings would jog her memory when the trial reconvened on Monday, she walked out of the courthouse and into a downpour.

The umbrella she carried for the anticipated deluge kept her dry down to the knees but, as she dodged the puddles, her ankles and feet were quickly saturated. The castle precinct was emptying fast. Most tourists had given up exploring the exterior walls of the castle, and only the hardiest persevered. She wouldn't join them today. Dashing along the path to the gatehouse, she spotted a man running between the prison block and heritage centre. He held aloft a wad of folders, using them as a makeshift umbrella. He ran with his heels kicking out, like a horse. By the time he made it to the side entrance, he was drenched. The door was locked. He cowered under a dripping gutter and delved into his pockets. His failure to juggle the things in his hands resulted in the folders landing on the gravel path in a heap.

Laura hated to see disasters involving neat piles of paper. She was the one at work who kept the filing cabinets tidy and badgered others into maintaining orderly in and out trays. She hurried over to him and scooped up the folders.

'Dammit,' he muttered. 'Fu... shit. I mean, sorry. Thank you.'

'Let me hold them while you find your keys.' Laura shuffled the folders around under the shelter of her umbrella and shook off the drops of rain. A yellow leaf had stuck to one purple cover. She peeled it off.

The man patted down his pockets. 'I thought… got it.' He fished a single key with a fob out of his trouser pocket. 'Thank you so much.'

She handed him the files. 'No trouble.'

She had a good view of his face now and the wet dollop of nutmeg hair. Rivulets of rain streaked down his cheeks, under his square chin, right into the hollow of his neck where the water seemed to have pooled. He wasn't wearing a tie, nor was the top button of his shirt done up. Given the dusting of bristles on his face, he'd not shaved that day and he probably wore glasses, because she spotted red dints on the bridge of his nose. The fleeting examination was over – he turned and slotted the key into the lock.

'Thanks again,' he said over his shoulder.

Laura's Good Samaritan moment was over, and it had left her with a warm glow in her chest. Her mother liked to say, "Just be nice, and the world is nicer back."

That evening, her mother had plenty to say when Laura rang for their weekly catch-up. Angela Naylor wanted to know about the court case, and Laura's refusal to divulge anything frustrated her.

'It's not a murder. Rape? Oh no, that would be awful—'

'It's nothing violent,' Laura conceded, tired of the battery of unanswerable questions. The last thing she wanted to mention was that Seaside was a local charity providing holiday homes, caravan parks, and tailored excursions for the blind. Her wily mother would immediately ask if Laura was on the verge of a panic attack. She wasn't; she hadn't had one for years, and Seaside was surely irrelevant to the events of her past.

'That's all I'll say, Mum.'

'Marco?' Another tentatively presented query.

'A text. He's in Rome.' It had arrived not long after she'd got home.

He hadn't answered her reply – *When are you coming home?*

'Rome?' The problem with geography extended to Angela, too. 'That's where the Pope lives, right?'

'It's where a lot of Italians live.'

'I know you don't want to hear it, love, but really, he's not—'

'You're right. I don't want to hear it, so please don't.' She shot across her mother's negativity with a display of pique that surprised her.

Marco should have a future in Lincoln. But it seemed two years of studying wasn't worth coming back to, never mind her, his girlfriend… supposedly.

'He's not the kind of man to give up on things. I should know,' Laura said. The lie stuck in her aching throat.

Her mother said nothing. A wise decision, and shortly afterwards, they ended the call.

Laura folded back the duvet on her bed and plumped up the pillows. She'd brought up a hot chocolate and planned to read a chapter of a biography she'd chosen from the library. She preferred real lives to fictional ones, although recently she'd come to doubt that people told real stories. The revelations in the tales of an ex-soap star were harder to believe than the fictional character portrayed on the television.

The purpose of the quiet time before switching off the lights was to try to mitigate the return of that dream. She'd suffered four consecutive nights of nearly identical nightmares. Recurring dreams of the unpleasant kind, typically involving shattered glass and screeching tyres, had once been a speciality of hers. But she believed she'd shaken them off and had never mentioned them to her mother. Sometimes she needed Angela to be like other mothers, sympathetic and soothing. Unfortunately, Laura wasn't sure her mother understood those needs, and dreams were hardly the best way to communicate her apprehensions. In the past, when insomnia had plagued Laura, Angela had suggested everything from sleeping pills to hypnosis. Laura had rejected any offer of outside intervention, especially from strangers. She'd waited, and eventually the flashbacks had fractured into tiny slivers of panic that were easier to ignore.

What her recent dreams alluded to was vastly different to those of the past, and they were obviously something to do with the castle and its history. Current events had awoken evocative thoughts and, along with the persistent noises she heard in the courthouse, Laura suspected something was going to happen that was bound to upset her inner, delicately balanced karma. It wasn't a pleasant feeling. Jodi was right; Laura had more imagination than she realised.

Laura had a fever, possibly Pauline's cold. It had to account for the rise and fall in body temperature and the uncomfortable degree of perspiration. She tossed aside the duvet and blinked hard, trying to wipe out the imagery of bulging eyes and protruding tongue that had precipitated her abrupt awakening and heralded a wave of shudders, gulps of cool water, and a lengthy period with the lights switched on. It was the fifth night in a row she'd dreamt of the same woman with the grotesque facial distortion. Laura wasn't sure what a hanging might do to a person, but somehow, she'd conjured up a realistic depiction of an executed woman — the angry marks strangling her neck were especially conclusive.

The dream began with Laura waking up in a prison cell on an unyielding bed as narrow as a coffin. An unearthly coldness infiltrated her bones — she was unaware of her clothing — and the cold was painful, assuming pain was what she was feeling. The rough brickwork was covered in flaking plaster, reminding her of hardened gruel. There were thin vertical lines scored into the grain of the wooden door. Dried, bloody threads. Somebody had attempted to escape and failed. The floor was strewn with sawdust, dirt, and torn paper; not shredded like the machine she used at work, but ripped into pieces.

There was one window, so high up it was a skylight. Barely any light seeped past the bars, and as she reached up, with alien alabaster hands and nails crusted with congealed blood, she spotted a figure in the gloom. At this point, a lucid Laura should be screaming herself awake, but she was trapped.

The woman, bonnet-topped and unadorned in her grey gown that hung limp around her slender waist, emerged from a corner, walking backwards. Just before she bumped into the bed, where Laura was now curled into a ball, shivering uncontrollably with fright, the person swung around in slow motion, which quickened Laura's pulse, and thrust her gnarled hands out. Tainted by bloodshot eyes, blackened lips, a twisted tongue, and that god-awful putrid line around her neck... the strange apparition opened her mouth to speak...

Laura had woken up, breathless, heart thumping against her breastbone. The unnatural images remained embedded in her waking thoughts, unlike normal dreams, and they saturated her emotions with horror. But the experience wasn't quite like a paralysing panic attack, not in the way she remembered those bad spells. The bizarre scene belonged in a theatre or cinema, played out for her, an audience of one.

The dream, always the same, like an episode repeating itself on a loop, was too vivid in its details to forget, so it lingered on and became part of her memories. She lay there, fatigue defeated by the rigours of adrenaline, and convinced that if she managed to doze off again, the nightmare would rematerialise. What bothered her the most was that, throughout the macabre scene, she had heard noises like the ones in the courtroom – hissing, tiny squeaks, and a high-pitched whine. However, she now knew they weren't anything to do with a fly or any other small creature. She was hearing a voice: distorted, quiet, and infantile; the incomprehensible whispers of a young child, possibly a girl.

Shivering feverishly, she pulled the duvet up to her chin and stayed stiff until dawn, then she got up and dressed. The aching diminished during breakfast. She hadn't sneezed or blown her nose, so she ruled out a cold. She moved around her house, avoiding the things that were Marco's, and came to the conclusion that she needed a major distraction. More importantly: how to escape the dreams?

She'd go to Newark. She had an open invitation to visit an old school friend, and it wasn't too far on the bus. The alternative plan was turning up at her stepbrother's house, gritting her teeth and asking for a bed for the night. Fingers crossed, Amelia was home and free.

The First Saturday

AMELIA LIKED STRIPED SOCKS with snug individual toes. Laura admired her friend's forays into the world of eccentricity and wished she had the courage to do something different with her appearance, although dyeing her hair pink was a step too far. On weekdays, Laura stuck to her sober twin set of black trousers and jacket with a variety of muted shirts. At the weekends, she preferred jeggings and baggy sweatshirts. Amelia had opted for torn jeans that seemed all the rage and a logo-splattered hoodie. Unfortunately, Amelia needed to lose about ten years to look the part of rebel teenager. What she lacked, she made up for with an indefatigably joyful personality. It might be hard for Amelia to believe that Laura had and always would envy her, but she did, and the ungracious jealousy was probably due to a hankering for memories of a happier Laura.

There wasn't an obvious reason why Laura liked Amelia's company. They had little in common. What kept them together was the fallout of broken families. Their parents divorced in the same school year when they were about ten years old. Probably because it meant they were often caught up in the middle of arguments and bitter custody battles, they preferred each other's company, and the companionship continued even after their respective fathers moved on to new relationships. They both subsequently shared the mutual mistrust of suspicious stepmothers and avaricious step-siblings.

For most of the evening, while Amelia's boyfriend was at his bowling club, they caught up on news (besotted Amelia had firm ideas of what Laura should do about Marco) and ate sloppy noodles out of takeaway cartons. Laura found solace in Amelia's warped sense of humour, and by the time Jordan was home, they had drunk a good quantity of wine.

'I'll make up the spare bed,' Amelia said.

'I can do that.' Laura jumped to her feet and swayed. She giggled. 'I'm a little tipsy.'

Amelia rubbed her eyes. 'Ha. Don't blame me. You brought the bottle.'

'I did.' Laura had impulsively purchased it on the way to the bus station. 'It was on offer.' She didn't mean to sound stingy, but she always had to watch the pennies.

Marco had his own money, and although its origin was a little unclear, he'd never failed to help out with the rent or bills... until he'd left her in the lurch by going to Italy. Now that she was alone, stern frugality had set in.

Amelia shrugged off the excuse. 'Good plonk doesn't need an expensive label.'

The bed was a sofa in the spare room. Amelia lay a sleeping bag along its length. She apologised for the mess: cardboard boxes, an exercise bicycle, and several charity bags stacked in the corner. 'We're having a clear out.'

'That's fine,' Laura said sleepily. 'I'll cope.'

She squeezed between the junk and wriggled out of her clothes. The damp sleeping bag rucked around her waist, and the old sofa was lumpy. Hardly ideal sleeping arrangements, but she remained optimistic that she'd be safe from the horrors of the recurring dream. She shut her eyes and drifted into sleep on waves of restlessness.

This time the tormented woman touched Laura's arm, and Laura woke up screaming. The dream had followed her. A scantily clad Amelia ran into the room, convinced Laura had seen a burglar – there had been a spate of them recently on the housing estate. Sporting underpants and an uncovered tattoo of a dagger on his chest, Jordan searched every room armed with a sixteen-weight bowling ball. Laura's pleas for him to stop only elicited more embarrassment.

'Sorry, I'm so sorry,' she said, struggling not to cry. The dreadful dreams had become intrinsic to her deepest sleep and perversely mesmerising. 'It's just a bad dream.'

Amelia handed her a glass of milk. 'You're white as a ghost—'

'Please, don't use that word. I'm not seeing ghosts. It's just ever since I've started jury service…' She stopped. She didn't say the courtroom was in a castle with a long and violent past. The unnerving intrusion, the whispering, troubled her more and more. It had to be linked to the nightmares, but how?

Amelia's eyes widened. 'Is it a murder?'

'No.' Laura wished it was as it might justify the nightmares; bad dreams in her experience needed a trigger, a connection to the real world. 'Nothing gruesome. Something else is bothering me. Look, forget it. I'll be fine.'

Laura had never spoken of the other nightmares, and Amelia was only vaguely aware of the accident; she'd been at university in Portsmouth when it had happened.

'Sure?' Jordan appeared over Amelia's shoulder, the bowling ball gone.

'Yes. Sure,' Laura said firmly and wiped her eyes. She plastered her usual prosaic face over the troubled cracks that Amelia and many others failed to spot, except her mother, Angela, and Marco, who had, on the odd occasion, nearly seen past them.

She burrowed into the sleeping bag. Coming to Amelia's had been a mistake. She'd brought along something evil, and it had tainted her friend's house. The details of the dream persisted, cementing themselves deeper in her waking memories: the cell, the marks around the woman's neck, the pleading tone of strange whispers, coming not from the prisoner's mouth, but originating within Laura's head, just like at the courthouse. Any hope of detaching herself from the fear they created had to lie waiting for discovery in the castle. She remembered hurrying through the creepy graveyard. If there were clues, they might be within those stone walls. She should visit the Lucy Tower and take a closer look at the names engraved upon the headstones. If Brader's trial was dull, at least the intervals between sessions might provide answers to her dreams and a cure for her affliction.

Day Six

Monday

L AURA ARRIVED PROMPTLY, as requested, in the jury waiting room at ten o'clock.

'There's a delay. We'll be starting at eleven,' the usher announced.

Unlike their retiring room next to the courtroom, this one they shared with other jurors, and consequently, they had to limit their conversation. Discussing their case wasn't appropriate, not that Laura had anything to say on the matter of Brader vs the Crown. Craig Brader was the last thing on her mind.

She had an hour before they reconvened. She left the claustrophobic waiting area, exited the building, flashed her annual ticket at the attendant, and climbed the steps up to the wall walk, then hurried along to the tower.

The morning mist had dispersed, leaving a dull sky heavy with potential rainclouds. Magpies harried the squirrels with caws and swoops. Their cries, as well as the cold, penetrated her skull, taunting her headache. By the time she reached the entrance to the craggy tower, she was breathless and preoccupied with the information she'd absorbed.

The Lucy Tower, according to the previous evening's research, was built on a motte, an artificial hill. Lincoln Castle was unusual in having two mottes and towers. The square observatory tower by the east gate provided the best view of the city. In the early part of the nineteenth century, a turret had been added by a prison governor who had an interest in the stars. The Lucy Tower was possibly older. The geometrically angled walls, ruined and roofless, were open to the elements and home to an untamed yew tree and graves, similar in some respects to a church graveyard, except the corpses of the executed were not spending eternity in hallowed ground.

On her last visit, buffeted by the chilly wind, she'd paid little attention to the headstones. Today, she hoped they might reveal a woman's name, something to explain her dreams. With the still air marred by the odour of rotting leaves, she approached the first row of low stones. They stood no higher than her knees and were partially hidden by the dew-laden grass and mulch. The rain had turned the ground soft beneath her sinking heels, and she had to walk on the balls of her feet, kicking the leaves to one side to uncover the identities of the buried. The gravestones were marked with the initials of the nameless souls above their death dates. Crouching lower gave her a better view of the cuts in the stone but no additional information, only the initials. She pursed her lips, disappointed by the degree of anonymity afforded the executed.

What kind of people was she treading upon? If they had been hanged then it was likely they were the worst kind of felons: murderers and rapists. She hoped that was the case. They needed to be wicked to justify an execution. There was a finality to capital punishment. What if those in judgement made a mistake? Now that she was on a jury, she appreciated how easily people could be swayed by gut instincts and emotional influences. When it came to Craig Brader, she would concentrate on the facts.

She gave up the unfocused hunt. There was nothing on those lichen-covered stones to explain her nightmares. Last night she'd slept better, probably because the woman had given up trying to communicate with Laura and stayed in the shadows — only her wretched rasps were audible — and consequently, Laura had begun the day feeling refreshed and less fearful. Why had she assumed a connection to the graveyard? Her theory was ill-conceived. Acting irrationally was something she would not condone in others. A better explanation was fatigue in combination with an over-stimulated mind — Beryl's chatter about her dead cousin had started it all.

Laura left the shady enclave, returned to the courthouse, and submitted to the fruitless search of her bag. Rules were rules, something she'd usually considered important, but away from her working habitat the rules of others seemed overly officious. When she went back to work, and her colleagues baulked at the minor constraints placed upon them by the management team, she might not be so hasty to nit-pick at their complaints.

In the cool courtroom, the prosecution barrister, the grave Mr Waverley, continued to build his case against the beleaguered Craig Brader. The next witness, a forensic accountant with nasal tones, plodded through a batch of dubious invoices, pointing out the dates and amounts, and the quantities leaving the charity's bank account and going where exactly? Examining a sample invoice, Laura appreciated the point he was making – there were discrepancies with payments. Under cross-examination by the defence lawyer, the accountant admitted there was nothing to imply Brader had printed any of the suspect invoices himself. Brader folded his arms across his chest and smirked at the woman in the public gallery. She smiled softly in reply. His bravado waxed and waned according to who was asking the questions.

Laura added an extra comment to her curt note about invoices. Little things were important when it came to spotting anomalies. She wondered if everyone else saw things the way she did. During the break, Brian talked at length about how his accounting system crashed regularly, implying his experiences explained the dodgy invoices and payments. Laura squirmed uncomfortably at the premature deliberations. She said nothing and stuck to her decision to stay out of mid-trial discussions. None of the court officials expected a juror to be an expert witness; her role was to judge, not create bias. So far, the consensus among her fellow jurors was the prosecution case was loosely held together and not making a great deal of sense. The jury were taken in by the defence's counter arguments; sympathy came easily.

'Too much paper,' Derek the dustbin man lamented, stroking his bald patch. 'That's the trouble with the world. Cut it all out.'

Laura preferred paper to electronic filing systems. There was a rainbow of colourful tabs stuck to her folders and an index to where everything was in her cabinets. Her boss, Michael, wanted her to shun paper, but she insisted on printing things off. She often spotted discrepancies that she'd missed on the computer.

After lunch, an auditor took the stand; an external one appointed by the Charity Commission. He dawdled through his evidence, and the lack of pace proved unfortunate. She noted the air around her had cooled significantly, heralding a spell of distraction. The hissing nonsense was back in abundance, along with grunting; nothing porcine in nature, as it was too high-pitched. It had a human aspect, almost child-like, reinforcing Laura's suspicions that the sounds and dreams were connected to where she was, the courthouse, and its surroundings.

She stuck a finger in her left ear and wriggled it. Number Six dispatched a bemused expression.

'Earache,' she mouthed.

However, the insidious noise had taken up residence. It wasn't tinnitus; she'd looked that up. She removed her finger and tried to concentrate on the auditor's monotonous drawl. Something about a bonus payment... did employees of charities received bonuses? That surprised her.

The little voice interrupted. *Listen*, it said.

The clarity of the voice was markedly different, less juvenile, and it penetrated her conscious mind, sharpening itself; accompanying the gasped word came the unambiguous fear of losing control and betraying herself. The courtroom dimmed. Light collapsed towards a distant point. Laura rubbed her blurry eyes. She felt ill and dizzy, close to panic. She grasped the pencil and contemplated stabbing the point into her thigh. She done such things before when she tumbled down there... If she fainted... *You won't be able to see me.* The distant voice stretched words from one end of the sentence to the other. More followed, delivered slowly, breathlessly, pained and notably youthful in pitch, its gender veering to the feminine. *You need to follow me.*

Who? Laura looked around – somebody was playing tricks on her. The others in the court were watching the man in the witness box, listening to the exchange between him and the lawyer, and oblivious to Laura's messenger. The pencil slipped out of her fingers just as a wave of nausea hit the back of her throat; this was panic, the kind that once assailed her whenever she approached a car door. She wished there was space in the box to lie down for a few seconds.

The gasping whisper clearly enunciated a word: *Bronte.*

Abruptly, Laura's cloudy vision sharpened, and the tunnel vision widened. The courtroom was bathed in an unusual luminescence that dazzled. Gone was the intrusive voice and the associated ache behind her eyes, and in its place was a strengthening quietness. Embarrassed, she glanced at her neighbour – he held out her pencil; she hadn't noticed him retrieve it from the floor. She mouthed a 'Thank you.' Being clumsy was better than being crazy. He retained a quizzical expression. It was nice of him to worry, but unhelpful. Her uninvited whisperer was the problem.

The auditor's monotonous commentary recaptured Laura's attention. Her swift brush with insanity was over. She slowed her breathing and jotted another note on the paper with a shaky hand.

Missing Builder.

The witness left the box. The ambiance stagnated, and it fell silent once again.

Why me? If she alone heard things, then wasn't that a privileged position, something special? Or maybe the impairment was a delayed reaction to the accident and the whispers had triggered some psychic break. She hoped not. Her mother simply wouldn't cope with more trauma. She couldn't be unhinged. She fought so hard not to be. Silly Laura, she clucked to herself. Why not treat it all like some game, an adventure? Giving up wasn't in her nature, or why else was she still waiting for Marco to come back?

The recurring dream required an answer, and she hated mysteries. Calm logic was the antidote, and it had always sufficed when reasoning suffered. There was a story out there, and it wasn't about herself. The clues left in her subconscious were caricatures, mimicking something real perhaps, and nothing, obviously, to do with the trial. She decided she was approaching things the wrong way. The graveyard was where her nightly visitor had ended up, but the ghoulish effigy might have been incarcerated in the prison prior to her demise, and the secret of her identity might belong in those walls. When she next had an hour or so spare, she'd visit the prison museum. She was in possession of an additional clue, a possible name: Bronte.

Day Seven

Tuesday

THE JUDGE provided the opportunity for Laura to visit the prison the next day by way of other pressing matters: the jury wasn't needed until after lunch. Overnight, the inclement weather had fled over the North Sea, leaving in its wake a pervasive dampness in the air, the kind of chill that assaulted the joints of both young and old. She wound a scarf around her neck, stretched her fingers into the tips of her leather gloves, and strode along in her soft-soled shoes. While the other jurors stayed away from the castle precincts, she entered the museum at ten o'clock, wondering how onerous prison life would have been compared to the Victorian slums or the hardships of the workhouse.

She read all the information boards on display, soaking up the details as if revising for an exam. The women's prison wasn't bleak in the way she'd anticipated, at least the décor wasn't. She'd expected grimy cells, and although they were boxy, the rooms had been sanitised with whitewash and light bulbs, tricking the eye into believing there was space enough to house an individual comfortably. The illusion was dashed in one cell by the sight of a scrawny hammock strung between the walls – even a diminutive woman would struggle to squeeze herself into that contraption. Laura's erstwhile ignorance was further debunked by the manner of the prisoners' containment – total segregation. The "separate system" ensured no prisoner came into contact with another: a captive in constant isolation. Prisoners and wardens were forbidden to speak to one each other, and to prevent any inmate communicating with another in the exercise yards, their faces were masked.

From the descriptions she deduced the purpose of solitary confinement wasn't to augment the punishment but to bring about a metamorphism in the prisoner. By forcing the prisoners into silence, the founders of the system expected a transformation born out of reflection and penitence. Advocates believed the cocooned criminal would emerge from their prison chrysalis as a reborn, upstanding individual. The reality was harsh, and segregation was later abandoned.

Laura tolerated the hustle and bustle of incessant city life, but existing in solitude for hours and days at a time would frankly drive her to the edge of reason. A monk or nun might choose to close themselves off from human contact, but in her opinion, to inflict such a mind-numbing practice on a prisoner would only further unbalance them. The religious overtones riled Laura; where was the godliness in stripping away the dignity of a person, numbering them, hiding their faces and eliminating their past lives?

'How awful,' she muttered. Nobody heard her remark. She hadn't encountered any other visitors. Like the past inhabitants, she, too, was experiencing the claustrophobic quietness, and nothing broke through the thick walls, neither birdsong nor distant traffic; only her footsteps on the cracked flagstones provided a soundtrack to her progress.

Remembering the purpose of her visit, she stuck to reading each panel, noting the prisoners' names, searching for any that might have gone by the name Bronte. She drew a blank, which was no surprise. She wasn't convinced any longer that Bronte was the correct interpretation. Perhaps she had imagined hearing it. But imagination wasn't her thing. For example, if somebody was following her now, wouldn't she know the difference between real footfalls and the illusion of the mind? Not wishing to test her theory, she hurried out of the cell block accompanied by the clatter of her own heels. Echoes, not phantom noises, and they reassured her.

The final part of the visit was the chapel, a well-known exhibit, and she believed in savouring the best until last. Facing the eagle's nest pulpit was a honeycomb of tiered wooden cubicles in the form of four crescent rows of individual pews, each with their own divider and no view other than the pulpit before them. Plain and simple, the chapel was a tidy construction that ensured each prisoner never saw another; they were loaded into the row at one end and kept in a perpetual state of isolation until the service ended.

Laura entered one such lidless crate and shut the door. There was only space to stand or sit upon a hard bench. She tucked her elbows in and perched on the edge of the seat. Opposite her was the high balcony. What kind of sermon would the prisoners have heard? Hellfire and damnation, or redemption through salvation? Either way, the congregation in their tiny upright coffins had no choice but to listen. The layout reminded her a little of an amphitheatre. Was there about to be a real-life performance? She glanced up at the overhanging pulpit. Empty, the towering box seemed to loom over the pews, casting a long shadow. Had the prisoners quaked in their boots or dozed off in boredom?

She stood, swayed slightly, aware of a cooling brush of air against her face. Then a noise close by. A cough? A sneeze?

She turned, cocked her ear, and focused on the sounds slipping by her. Shuffling, or scuffling shoes? The direction was clear: somebody was in the cubicle next to her, and probably seated as the crown of his or her head wasn't visible above the partition. The unnerving discovery meant her neighbour had been there since she'd arrived in the chapel – how else could a person be barricaded into a miniature cell when she blocked their exit? Holding her breath, she leaned towards the wooden partition. Should she say a little 'hello' or clear her throat?

She opted for a gentle cough. The response was visceral: the temperature dropped a notch. Coldness burrowed through her clothing, and, with icy tendrils, touched her skin. She perceived a shadow darkening the painted panels, turning them from warm curative cream into a bleak grey. Outside, which was visible through the high windows, load-bearing clouds had blotted out any hope of sunshine. An explanation of sorts, and it calmed her teetering nerves, pulling them back from the brink of dread. The creaking had ceased, too, and her next-door neighbour was eerily quiet.

'Hello?' Laura said cautiously.

How rude. The other person could reply, say something. Maybe they were deaf? Best ignored, she decided, as was often the easiest option when dealing with awkward so-and-so's. She'd seen everything she wanted to see. As she turned, her elbow caught the door panel leading into the other cubicle. Slowly, it swung open, egressing into her limited space. Squeezed, she pressed her legs against the narrow bench. The adjoining cubicle was empty, and the next one – the door to it was open, too. Beyond was the wall; nobody could access the pews from that direction.

Laura's pulse quickened, and goose bumps pricked the nape of her neck. Walking backwards, appalled by the discovery that her imagination had permitted her mind and hearing to be so cruelly tricked, she nearly fell out of her cubicle into the aisle. The door had moved soundlessly, as if on oiled runners. She scrambled up the steps to the main entrance and collided with a solid body.

The man was vaguely familiar.

'Hello again.' He smiled for a second, then, catching her elbow, steadied her. 'Are you okay?'

Laura's trembling knees refused to lock straight. 'Yes,' she said breathlessly. 'I think.'

He chuckled. 'You look like you've seen a ghost.'

Amelia had said something similar.

Laura shook her head. 'It was nothing.'

He lowered his arm, freeing her of his gentle grasp. The dangling lanyard was decorated with the logo of the museum. Now she remembered: the man in the rain with the umbrella of folders. His grin had vanished. Two expectant bushy eyebrows lifted; something about her answer had intrigued him.

'Nobody ever does,' he said.

'What?'

'See anything. They feel it.' He shrugged. 'I've not and I work here. So I guess—'

'Feel what?' She looked over her shoulder at the deserted chapel. There were others like her who could perceive something unnatural in the midst yet still appear otherwise lucid?

'Oh. Stirrings. Just silly stuff. It only takes one person to say they've seen a ghost, and suddenly, you've got a haunting.' He opened the door for her.

He meant well; there wasn't a trace of mischief on his face. She peered at his name badge. Sean – curator. A council employee like herself. Could he help her solve her little mystery about Bronte? She jerked her head towards the pulpit.

'I suppose if anyone is going to see anything, it's from up there,' she said.

'You'd have thought so – a captive audience.' The soft smile returned.

Laura followed him out of the chapel. 'Is it just this place that's haunted?'

'Oh, the castle supposedly has a few. Given its history, it's hardly surprising.'

It probably was an added attraction to have ghosts. People might visit the castle especially in the hope of seeing one. Should she tell him what she'd felt, what she'd heard – did the museum keep a keep a record of ghostly encounters, strange sounds, and whispered names?

'And do the ghosts include prisoners? I mean, the executed ones?' she asked.

Sean scratched a spot behind his ear. He had chestnut hair, cropped short, and flattened ears. There was something dainty about his features in amongst the details of masculinity, the fashionable stubble, wisps of nostril hair, hedgehog eyebrows, and a prominent Adam's apple. She focused on his lips, which were thin and puckered. He was treating her question seriously – was it possible he actually believed in such stuff?

'What happened in there?'

She pulled her coat tighter around her shoulders. 'I thought I was alone, but… I'm on jury service,' she said, tossing out the fact, and he picked it up with a bemused expression.

'We get a few come over from the courts. Jury service, eh? Interesting?'

'Not really. Lots of waiting. So I've been walking around the castle… hearing things.'

'Ah.' He pointed the way to the exit. 'Tell you what, I'm on my lunchbreak now. Why not come with me to the café, and you tell me what you want to find out.'

How did he know her true purpose? No matter. The offer was good, though. Useful.

'You don't mind me hijacking your break?'

'I owe you for rescuing me in the rain.'

What a sweet smile. She fashioned one on her own face. Since Marco had left, she'd forgotten the art. Handling men was a skill that she had yet to master, otherwise, Marco wouldn't be in Italy, incommunicado.

She waited while he went to fetch a jacket. He returned wearing a navy knitwear piece that covered the museum logo on the breast pocket of his shirt. Sean was going off-duty. He insisted on buying her something. She agreed to the hot chocolate but declined his generosity when it came to the soggy salmon and cream cheese sandwich and bought it herself. She preferred his knowledge to a sandwich. The corner table of the café had a wobbly table leg and he wedged a piece of discarded cardboard underneath it. A practical man, too. He didn't rush her either. The space was welcome. She had to reclaim that achievable calmness, the calmness that everyone who knew her recognised. Talking about ghosts didn't come easily.

With Marco, the initial conversation that had sparked an interest in him was his planned career in business management, the subject of his master's. He also had a fascination with cartoons. His studies had provided an easier talking point than his comical drawings of football players. Still, it didn't matter that they had little in common; he'd that magical Italian accent and vibrant eyes that arrested her attention every time she looked at him. Sean wore glasses, which he'd fished out of his jacket pocket; frameless spectacles that pinched his nose and magnified his pupils. He had green eyes and a few freckles around his cheeks. His age was indeterminate: though so was hers.

The commonality continued. Both of them worked for the city council, and the subject enabled them to avoid talking about the court case, which she assumed he understood was not an appropriate topic.

'So,' he dragged the sound out slowly, letting her finish the last mouthful of sandwich, 'you heard or saw something?'

'Heard. In court—'

'Court? You were haunted in the court?' His verdant eyes lit up brighter.

She was left with the impression that most days he wasn't excited by life in the castle precincts.

She started to peel an apple with a blunt knife. 'A childish kind of whisper. At first, it was like a fly buzzing by my head. Now its tone has shifted.'

'And in the prison?'

'Shuffling. I was convinced somebody was in the cubicle next to me.' The apple slipped out of her hand and rolled across the table, the still-attached peel trailing after it. She giggled at both the silliness and her embarrassing inability to eat with a modicum of dignity.

He nudged the apple back in her direction with the tip of his finger. 'What do you think you're hearing?' He glanced up, and a flicker of something passed across his face.

'Oh. Nothing… Just thought I'd heard a name.'

He picked up his coffee cup. His lower lip hovered close to the rim without touching it. 'Really? You know, if you remember it, I could check the records. We have some info about the prisoners, things we collect for the exhibits, but most of the good stuff is held in the county archives.'

Laura wished she hadn't chosen an apple. The pale flesh was bruising quickly; it smelt odd, unappetising. She sliced it in half, then answered him.

'Bronte.'

He blinked. 'Come again.'

'Like Charlotte and Emily. The Bronte sisters. But the weird thing is, it sounded like a first name. I know, it's just crazy. Forget it.' She bit the slice in half and crunched on it. The dry tartness blended with the smoky salmon. Why were her senses so acute? Ever since the court case had begun, it was like she had gained some extra senses while her existing ones were magnified: bright lights hurt, her taste buds were shrewd, and her flesh shivered with the slightest drop in temperature.

'Unusual. Just Bronte?'

She nodded.

Sean wiped his hands on a napkin and pushed the rimless glasses back up his nose. 'I'll have a look. Can't promise anything. There's nothing else?'

Why would he ask that? Was she transparent: as thin as tissue paper? She'd not mentioned the dreams, yet it seemed he had an inkling she was on the cusp of wanting to reveal more.

'I… you know, my mother would tell me not to talk to strange men about personal things until at least a dozen dates have gone by,' she said abruptly.

Her mother had said it after Laura's commencement of her relationship with Marco. Laura was sure her mother's humourless quip actually referred to her father's swift affair more than her daughter's love life.

'I think I'm in danger of breaking her rules, because I do want to say something, but I don't want you to run away like I'm crazy.'

'Crazier than seeing ghosts?'

'Hearing them, I think is more accurate. But at night, I do see things in my dreams. Usually I only remember snippets, and by lunchtime, puff, it's all forgotten, but this dream…' She pushed the half-eaten apple to one side, her appetite lost in the coils of peel.

Sean's unremarkable face softened into gentle reassurance. He had an attentive gaze to go with his flattened little ears. Without saying a word, he encouraged her to continue, and she told him about her recurring nightmare set in the prison cell; the grotesque features of a hanged woman; the paper strewn across the floor.

He pursed his lips and arched his thick eyebrows. 'Wow, some dream. You think this Bronte is the same person in your dream?'

She shrugged. 'I only started having them when the jury service began. It's a bit of a coincidence, isn't it?'

'It's unique. The accounts I've heard of don't mention dreams, but visitors come and go, their incidents are fleeting episodes, and those of us who work here seem immune to such tales. Unbelievers, I suppose.' He dropped his chin, hiding his eyes from her.

Was she detecting a hint of envy on his part? He wanted the distinction of being different to his colleagues. It didn't make sense:

he was a curator, a purveyor of facts. However, she needed an ally, one who could overlook the macabre and seek out the truth.

'So… assuming I'm not…' She omitted saying crazy. 'Can you find out anything?'

'If this Bronte was hanged in the castle, the execution would have to be no later than the mid-nineteenth century.'

'Why?'

'Because after that, hangings were carried out at Lincoln prison, not here in the castle gaol, which closed in 1878.'

'And women?'

'Not many. I can check the names, if you like?'

'Could you?'

He patted his pockets. 'Got a pen? I'll write down your email address.'

She dug into her handbag and extracted a piece of paper and pencil. On it she wrote her personal email address and handed it to him. Her sleeve slipped up her arm, revealing her wristwatch.

'Oh my God, the time.' She hastily gathered up her coat. 'I'm due back in court.'

Sean jumped to his feet. 'Of course, I'm sorry. I've kept you—'

She hadn't wanted an apology. 'No, no. My fault.' She turned back to face him. 'Thank you. I must seem like a right nutcase—'

'No, you're not,' he said. 'I think it's fascinating.'

She checked the time again. Ten minutes before the court resumed. 'I must dash.'

When she reached the stiff door and pulled on the handle, she risked a glance over her shoulder. Sean was standing by the table, watching her while he swept the debris of their lunch onto the tray. He nodded, acknowledging her, and in doing so she was sure a blush was colouring her face. His expression was neither one of bemusement nor pity, it was something else, and harder to define.

The heat of the blush she carried across the grounds of the castle, through the security checks, and into the jury room.

Beryl smiled. 'Hello. You look as if you've run a marathon.'

'Have I?' Laura said breathlessly. 'Just forgot the time.'

'Oh, don't worry. Usher has just said it will be at least another half an hour. Judge is hearing another case.'

Laura dropped into a chair and folded her arms across her chest. The inconsistent workings of the court were unlike how she operated, and now the frustrations of the day seemed to lodge themselves right in the pit of her stomach where the apple should be resting. In addition to the delay in proceedings, she'd just given her email address to a man who'd heard her harp on about nightmares, ghoulish voices, and hangings. He must think she was off her trolley. If he had any sense, he'd chuck the paper in the bin. No wonder he'd been giving her funny looks.

Her father liked to bark, 'Pull yourself together,' whenever her mum had lost her cool over something trivial. But it was always the best attitude to adopt. No more of the ghost nonsense. She had Craig Brader's future to decide, a living person who might end up in prison or possibly not. The feeling she was getting was that the other jurors were definitely shifting to his side.

The postcard was wedged between a letter from her bank and a clothing catalogue. She ditched the catalogue in the kitchen bin, ignored the letter, and feverishly examined the postcard. The vintage black-and-white photograph of the Coliseum sealed her interest.

Marco's cursive handwriting, full of loops and italic slants, covered the back of the card. However, the number of words was small. Dropping her handbag on the kitchen worktop, she braced herself for the inevitable disappointment.

Dearest Laura,
I'm so sorry.
I wish I could write more.
I should be back soon – two weeks?
Juggling too many balls.
Sorry xxx

No name. Not even "love" from him. The postmark date was three days ago, and Marco hadn't added a date at the time of writing: two weeks from when exactly? All the modern tools of the information age, and he sent a snail postcard.

Juggling balls? His mum was ill, she understood the necessity for the visit, but the protracted stay had not been adequately explained. What on earth had possessed Marco to write such a superfluous message and not back it up with a meaningful phone call or text? Rome wasn't at the end of the world, yet he seemed intent on convincing her he was staying in Outer Mongolia.

She huffed and sighed her way through her evening meal, her emotions unprepared to deal with Marco. Upstairs, after a shower, she suddenly remembered she was waiting on another man – Sean's email.

Back in the lounge, she fired up her iPad and checked her sparsely populated inbox. Nothing. He'd either not found anything or had had no time to look. She swiped the screen away and lay the iPad next to the postcard on the small coffee table. Time for the soaps, the incongruous world of artificial people and their daily changing relationships. The television programme chattered away in the background, neither winning nor losing her attention.

She closed her eyes, dozing almost. The iPad bleeped, and she snatched it up.

The message came from PringleSN21. Sean Pringle. She couldn't help thinking about crisps.

Hello, Laura.
So nice having lunch with you.
Afraid I've not had much luck with your Bronte. Nobody of that name, first or family name, mentioned in our records. The only woman hanged was Priscilla Biggadike in 1868 for the poisoning of her husband. She was the first woman to be hanged in private, as previously public executions happened on the roof of Cobb Hall. Her trial lasted seven hours! Very circumstantial evidence. Poor woman.
Sorry for not being much help.
If you think of anything else, just ask. I'm happy to meet again for lunch or dinner.
Sean

The awkwardness was there in the limp sign-off. Two communications: two apologetic men. However, if one of them had achieved anything positive beyond the obvious disappointment of failing to provide her with useful facts, it was Sean. While Marco frustrated her with woefully inadequate information, Sean had at least tried to be helpful.

He was happy to meet for lunch or dinner. If she was expecting a subtle hint of wooing her, he had blown that out of the water. He'd come out and said it – he wanted to see her again. She doubted she needed to come up with much of a request to initiate the next stage. As for Marco, was he slipping away? She wanted to remain loyal, but three months on, it was impossible to know what to think when he refused to engage with her. Marco was in danger of losing his special status even with his stuff in the house.

She checked her texts. Nothing, again. Prodding the touchscreen with stiff fingers, she composed a curt message.

Thanks for the postcard. So glad you're okay. Would it be too much to ask for you to ring me? Can't take much more of this silence.

No kisses. No emojis. Just the truth.

With her heavy eyelids warning her of impending sleep, she made a decision. If she had another nightmare, she'd arrange to meet Sean.

A light flickered outside, probably a fading streetlight, and the strobe effect turned her bedroom into a disco. She lay in bed in the pose of a plastic doll; weary but unwilling to venture into sleep and dreams. She'd thought the nights of panic-induced dreams were done, that she'd conquered the need to relive those few seconds of her life that always replayed themselves in excruciating slow motion. Dreams, she concluded, were fragments of a disturbed memory that needed to find peace, preferably wiped and forgotten. With a great deal of effort, she dragged herself away from those morbid memories.

From the image gallery on her phone she opened one of the last photos of Marco. He was grinning inanely at the camera, his big eyes brimming with laughter, his flashy white teeth glinting. If there was a reason for the smile, she couldn't recall it. He was relaxed and happy. Three days later, a radically different Marco, pale and agitated, was gone, his backpack stuffed with clothes, a laptop sandwiched between two shirts, and his passport in his jacket pocket along with the ticket for the flight.

Laura touched her cheek, the spot where Marco had pecked with his dry lips before climbing into the taxi. The cab had taken him all the way to Leeds airport, an extravagance given that he normally used public transport. All the little signs that something was seriously wrong now coalesced into one stingy postcard. The truth started to emerge: it had to be another woman, and he simply couldn't end things with Laura until he was certain he had a future back in Italy. All the stuff about his family needing him was a pack of lies.

Cheating wasn't Marco's style, though. He was honourable, decent and honest about things. If he was off gallivanting with somebody else, why not simply come out and say so? And what about his business studies? Next to her in bed was Marco's space. He'd not occupied the spot for weeks and weeks; she kept it free and refused to sleep in the middle of the bed. She missed his soft breathing and murmurs. He always slept in his boxers, even in the winter months, and when he dozed on Sunday mornings, she'd often tickled his chest hairs and teased him awake.

Was she about to lose her first substantive boyfriend? She'd never judged her previous flings as significant, those interludes of genial friendships, initiated by mistake and forgotten as quickly as they'd begun. Dotted over the years, each one of them had ended either abruptly, as if somebody had discovered some dark secret about her, or the relationships had fizzled out due to inertia. Her quirky mannerisms and inability to shake off a rigid approach to scheduling her life was probably the reason she lacked appeal.

With Marco, things had been different from the outset. He'd simply brushed aside her habits or worked around them. He neither laughed at her nor took her too seriously. He seemed to want her structure to balance his lackadaisical attitudes and had demonstrated to Laura how a natural introvert could turn into somebody pleasingly normal and sociable.

The contrast between their approaches stuck out sometimes.

He laughed softly – teeth slightly bared and eyes sparkling – at other people's jokes; she generally smiled politely and struggled to identify humour. She preferred wit to sarcasm. He nodded sympathetically when told something sad; she pursed her lips and offered a solution, which was usually met with a look of disapproval. If he stayed up all night to study and write, he slept through next day, which she considered bizarre. What was the point of turning days into nights?

His explanation had been insipid. 'Because my brain seems to get on with it the moment a deadline hits.'

'That's cramming,' she'd retorted. Merely thinking about careless time-keeping gave her a headache.

Insomnia wasn't something new to her, except during the past week she'd discovered it had a different impact. The fatigue, far from sapping her, focused her mind. Lying awake, unhappy at the prospect of another night of delirious dreams, she had the opportunity to appraise her life choices. Marco had certainly helped her develop as a person. Even before she'd met him, she had never been shy or afraid to speak her mind, but Marco had softened her acerbic tongue and shown her that it was possible to exercise one's opinions and stay mellow. Given more time, she'd master warm geniality and gentle persuasive language. Unfortunately, she'd lost his influence at a critical moment when her knowledge might be advantageous: a fraud trial with an indecisive jury.

There were moments since Marco had gone back to Italy that she also craved his physical presence: the intense furrowing of eyebrows as he concentrated on reading a heavyweight textbook; the clatter of his pointed shoes as he charged up and downstairs because he'd forgotten something or mislaid an object of little significance – the tiny huffs of annoyance amused her. And she missed his charming gestures, so Italian and vivacious. He literally signed his way through a conversation, even when speaking on the phone. The only time those hands stilled was at night. They lay resting on her, a conduit for her pulse, and he must have felt the energetic beat of her heart through his palms because he responded with a kindness that she appreciated. He called her pretty, and she believed him.

Meeting her family had been an awful chore for them both. Angela had called him, "colourful" – he did dress rather stylishly; her father labelled Marco a "chatterbox", which she put down to nerves because with most people her boyfriend was taciturn.

Margery, Laura's other mother, the one who'd managed to foist on Laura two stepbrothers, described Marco as "okay". Just that. What the hell did it mean? Was that okay, but could do better, Laura, or okay, that's as good as you'll probably get?

Amelia added "fit" to the repertoire. Sometimes "sick", which Laura hated. She hadn't the imagination to go with those trendy words. He was kind of good-looking and well-structured, but not like Michelangelo's statues. Italian men weren't all God's gift on Earth, which once upon a time had been her stereotypical view, and unfair. As for his appealing mind, Marco was sharp, a razor if he put his thoughts ahead of his emotions.

He had to come back or else he'd duped her, and how would that help her ongoing transformation into a resilient member of society? Jury duty had demonstrated, at least to herself, that she was neither eccentric nor woefully forgettable compared to any of the other jurors. They were what every trial expected, a dozen strangers flung together, making small talk while fully aware than in a few days they would need to discuss in great depth the guilt or innocence of another stranger. What a weird world she'd been thrown into with little preparation.

Her colleagues at work had never outwardly implied she was awkward or gauche. From what she could glean from how they operated as a team, they preferred to work around her than through her. Yet, if they really needed her expert opinion, they came knocking on her door all fired up and injured by somebody else's criticisms. Laura was good at sweeping aside the emotional nastiness of work and focusing on the issues of "getting things done". Even Marco had admitted it was something he found useful when he lost track of time.

Perhaps that was the reason behind his absence. He had lost months of time because she wasn't around to set him straight. She had to change that attitude of his. Unless he answered in the next twenty-four hours, she should seriously consider ending their relationship.

Day Eight

Wednesday

A DRIZZLY GREY MORNING further sank Laura's already meagre spirits into a deepening abyss. During the bus journey into the city, the weight of mist flattened the urban landscape and hid the treetops and buildings. She arrived in the jury waiting room with leaden feet and an inescapable sense of futility. She poured herself a coffee from her flask. People slowly congregated for each of the separate jury boxes of the courthouse. Beryl rested her handbag on her lap and sighed. Her face was drawn down, weary like Laura's. It took several minutes for Laura to pluck up the courage to ask why.

'It's this case,' Beryl whispered. 'I don't like to admit it, but I don't understand things. I thought it would be about one big sum of money, not all these invoices and cheques. No wonder it's not clear-cut. Do you find it hard to follow?'

'Sometimes,' Laura said. But mostly not. She omitted the last part for Beryl's sake. 'But I knew it wasn't going to be straightforward. Fraud never is.'

'I suppose.' Beryl plucked a tissue out of her handbag and blew her nose. 'Everyone seems to have caught this cold. You look a bit peaky yourself.'

'I'm fine. Just a bad night's sleep.'

The haunting dreams continued unabated by Sean's assertion that Bronte didn't exist. Laura had spent the night incarcerated in a phantom cell with an agitated woman whose muted activity amounted to repetitively sweeping up the scattered pieces of paper on the flagstone floor. Strangled sighs accompanied the brush of her arms. Regardless how alien the dreams felt, Laura needed to ignore the macabre episodes and focus on Craig Brader. While Beryl fretted about her competence to judge, Laura preferred the lucid analysis of Brader's trial to her incoherent adventures in dreamland. She needed grounding in reality. Things could all change once the defence started its rebuttals, opinions might swing in a different direction, and she might have to agree with Beryl: there was no clear-cut verdict, and arguing otherwise was a waste of time.

'Poor you,' Beryl said. 'It's horrible having all this responsibility. I didn't ask for it. Who does?'

Laura flinched at "responsibility". She wished Beryl hadn't mentioned the weighty word. 'Well, he's not going to die in prison if we find him guilty,' she replied.

Beryl's eyebrows knotted above the bridge of her nose. 'I should hope not. He's a thief, not a murderer.'

Laura briefly closed her eyes. She hadn't intended to belittle Beryl's concerns.

Jodi dropped into a seat opposite. 'Mornin'.'

'How's the poetry going?' Beryl asked.

'I'm working on something else. Feel like I've run out of steam on the castle. Too much time here.' She laughed joylessly.

'Know what you mean,' Beryl said.

Laura was side-lined as the two women batted back and forth this and that, stuff that was as interesting as the pages of a women's magazine. She would have to try harder at talking inconsequentially, but not today. She was too consumed with distractions to engage in humdrum conversations – someone in the room was crunching on a carrot stick. And why the excessive use of zesty perfume?

The usher summoned Laura's jury to the door and counted their heads as if they were on a school day trip. A beaming smile greeted the last number.

'Excellent. All present and correct. Let's go, shall we.' She bounced out of the door with her black gown flowing behind her.

'Oh joy,' said somebody behind Laura.

Brader was already there, eyeing the floor with his hands clasped together. The barristers were chatting in the manner of old friends, which they might be for all Laura knew. The moment the judge entered, they returned to their respective seats and donned seriousness, an expression they seemed to wear with magnificent ease. She was slightly jealous of their ability to switch in and out of modes. Laura had one all-round *modus operandi*.

The morning dragged phenomenally slowly. There were points of order, requiring the jury to shuttle in and out of court. Brian huffed each time but said nothing. Haden eyed the heavy mist outside the window and drummed his fingers on the sill. Small talk prevailed. Nobody wanted to risk saying something relevant to the case, which was perfectly understandable. Deliberations came later, and by then, they might know what it was that would decide Brader's guilt or not. Currently the general mood reflected Beryl's earlier concerns. At least the unsettled proceedings kept Laura occupied. The whispers, tiny bleats of desperation, were ignorable. However, there was no escaping the fear she harboured; if the noises continued to harass her, she would have to consider the inevitable and more traditional route – a trip to the doctor's.

The judge released them for lunch with a sympathetic smile. 'Back at two, please.'

Two o'clock meant more than an hour's lunch break. A few applauded the extension and planned to dash off to the shops or the pub. Brian opened his laptop and switched on his phone. Sitting in the communal area, Laura retrieved her messages. Michael wanted to speak to her. She rang him, listened to him ramble on about some file he was missing, then the latest issues with the project she should be handling.

'Okay?' he boomed, realising she might have slipped away.

She jolted. 'Yes,' she said impatiently. What did he want her to say? She wasn't feeling guilty about missing work. It was something of a relief not to think about it. She recalled the missing file and pinpointed the fact he sought.

'I knew you'd remember,' he said gleefully. 'Thanks, Laura. Can't wait for you to get back. So much to catch up on.'

She finished her sandwich in silence, pleased that nobody else had stayed in the waiting room. Even Brian had disappeared in search of food. With lunch consumed and her coffee flask empty, Laura appraised the gloomy skies and decided to venture into the

Lucy Tower again. There was one grave that she should visit: Priscilla's – P.B. – the sole female occupant of the graveyard, according to Sean. The B just might have something to do with Bronte.

The stone steps were slippery, and she held the icy railing. With no wind to chase it away, the mist had settled inside the Lucy Tower and thickened. Laura walked among the headstones and nearly stumbled over the root of a tree before identifying the right grave.

P.B.
Dec 28
1868

There she lay, under Laura's feet, Priscilla Biggadike, murderer.

Overwhelmed by the prickly sense of cold, Laura shivered and stepped sideways. As she navigated around the headstones, a horribly familiar combination of feelings emerged; a dreamlike state coupled with a peculiar sense of detachment from her surroundings. She wanted to run. Instead, she was spellbound, and acutely observant; her senses were sharpened, hyper-aware. The turbid mist swirled around the gnarled trunk of a yew tree, dancing in and out of the bowers and branches, but it wasn't the suspended dew that held her attention. An obscure shadow grew out of the nearest gravestone, and the densest part seemed to hug the tree. With her heart in her mouth, transfixed by the strange undulations of darkness and unable to respond with any sense of urgency, Laura rooted to the spot. Without the presence of sunshine, she couldn't fathom how the shadow had taken form. Like windswept grass, the blackness pivoted and swayed, and from the midst of it, a thin white line – an apparent stream of light – reached out, and the point of it touched the lonely headstone.

A gasp of breeze shot through the ruins for a second. The shadow, bleeding out of the earth into the tree, was now conical and losing substance. Slowly, it sank into the ground and vanished. Only then did it strike Laura that she hadn't heard a thing since she'd entered the tower: no distant traffic or squawking crows. An awful swell of panic followed the encounter. She scrambled backwards and tripped over the very root she'd just avoided, landing on her bottom with a spine-juddering thud. With her nerves jangling and her lunch threatening to make a return journey, she swallowed hard.

'Dammit,' she said, loud enough to know she wasn't living in a dream. She rose to her feet and wiped her dirty hands on her coat.

She hauled her handbag strap over her shoulder and marched up to the grave under the tree. The withered branches hung lower than she'd anticipated, which meant the moving shadow had been child-sized. She hunted for footprints, but the grass was undisturbed with no obvious marks on the ground. The chosen gravestone had a sheen to it and was scrubbed of lichen, almost polished. Crouching, she brushed aside the fallen leaves hiding the lettering. The capitals and numbers chiselled into the marker were precisely impressed as if freshly engraved. In any other graveyard the headstone might be a new addition or a replacement, except the base was firmly embedded in the ground, and its style belonged with the other markers in the graveyard.

Laura traced the carved letters with her fingers, letting them slip in and out of the etched initials.

E.H.
1872

There was something deeply satisfying about feeling the characters, as if she was performing a peculiar emotional homage to a long-lost soul, somebody with a forgotten past. But whom? And if this deceased person wasn't the woman in Laura's dreams, then who was haunting her days and nights so persistently? As the ground lightened, the world outside encroached once more through the medium of a wailing siren down below the castle walls. She turned away from the tree and stone, closed her eyes for the briefest of seconds, and regrouped her frayed senses. Now and again she felt as if she'd lost ownership of them. A silly idea, perhaps, so she dismissed it quickly. What she needed was an independent opinion, and preferably from somebody who had an open mind. She hoped Sean's offer of help was genuine – he seemed both pragmatic and approachable, and who else could she turn to?

Back in the waiting room, she checked her phone and composed a reply to his email. She asked him if there was any chance, *please*, that he might have missed something.

And could they meet for lunch again.

Day Nine

NUMBER SIX STILL LACKED A NAME. He'd not divulged it, and Laura and her fellow jurors were too polite to ask for it. The corduroys were back in the form of a khaki-brown shade with worn knees and threads sticking out of the seams. There was dirt under his fingernails. A keen gardener, Laura guessed, or an outdoorsy type. Given his age, he wasn't a candidate for retirement, so perhaps he was unemployed or resting between jobs. Or maybe he was a professional gardener. The guesswork led her nowhere. The occasional words spoken by the man revealed nothing. There was something about him that kept her speculating. At the start of the next session, he folded his arms and sighed through puffed lips. Frustration affected them all.

'What?' she whispered, glancing over to the judge.

The proceedings hadn't started yet. The usher was handing out documents to the jury.

'He doesn't look well,' Number Six said.

It was true: Brader was huddled on his seat and blowing his nose. His pasty cheeks sagged under his red-rimmed eyes and their painfully grey shadows. He rubbed his neck and croaked a response to a question. It barely reached Laura's ears.

Laura checked her notes, the couplets she'd written over the previous days. They'd meant something at the time of writing, but today, given the distraction of nightly dreams and boyfriend issues, she wasn't sure if they represented either concrete facts or biased opinions. She folded the sheet over, wrote the date in the corner, and prepared herself for a smattering of evidence dished out alongside procedural legalise. The morning was supposed to be the final session of the prosecution's case. A batch of phone messages from Brader's mobile were to be read into the record. Next to her, Amil licked the tip of his pencil; his notes were unsurprisingly copious. Everyone practised a different style of notetaking, twelve individuals epitomising various memorising techniques. Or maybe jotting things down helped fight the tedium. Laura preferred to listen. She was good at listening.

Abruptly, an hour into the session, Mr Waverly ceased reciting text messages and glanced at the judge, who removed his spectacles.

'Mr Brader,' the judge asked kindly. 'Do you require a break?'

Brader was leaning against the wooden panel of the dock; his lips had turned a strange shade of puce. He shook his head.

The transcript of calls, which mainly featured text conversations between Brader and his wife, hadn't exactly raised eyebrows. The references to depositing money in bank accounts and picking up deliveries lacked detail: no amounts, account numbers, or names of recipients. They didn't give anything away; Mr and Mrs Brader were adept at codified exchanges. The brevity of messages, seemingly innocent in nature, was only suspicious in light of the charges. Not one of them revealed why money had moved around. Laura chose a handful of texts to aide her memory and wrote them down on her notepaper.

The usual deposit today. Hopefully more next week.
Printers called. Getting angry.
I'll deal with it later, don't worry.
Envelope waiting for collection. Usual stuff.

And so on. If Mrs Brader was involved, why wasn't she also in the dock? She wasn't even in court. Perhaps that was why Brader finally chose that moment to keel over and disrupt the proceedings. Mr Waverly was plainly annoyed. The defence barrister rushed over to Brader.

The judge puffed out his cheeks and turned his wigged head to face the jury.

Laura scribbled two new couplets.

Cash payments?
Tax evasion?

The jurors filed out, initially to the retiring room, then when it became apparent Brader wasn't playing games, the usher escorted them to the waiting room. There they erupted into a hubbub of fretting and agitation.

'This better not delay things,' Brian said.

Inevitably, it did. The usher returned. 'Sorry folks, he's sick, and the judge has adjourned. Ring the office number at five for an update on tomorrow.'

The collective sighing represented a near unison chorus of frustration. Laura was secretly pleased. She'd arranged to meet Sean for lunch and, instead of rushing it, she now had the luxury of a free afternoon. The longer the court case dragged on, the more time she had to solve her own little mystery. When would she have the opportunity during her busy working day?

'Poor man,' Beryl said unsympathetically and collected her handbag. Even Beryl's patience was stretched thin.

'What are you going to do?' Laura asked.

'Service in the cathedral. Although it will mean exchanging one hard pew for another.'

Laura grimaced. The court needed a makeover and comfy chairs.

'I'm having lunch with a friend,' she said and scooted out the door without Beryl; she hadn't intended the announcement to sound pretentious.

The new friend had emailed her that morning, responding to her request to look up "E.H.". Laura was delighted that Sean hadn't only acknowledged her email promptly but had promised to check that morning and meet her for lunch. Such attention was elucidating: Sean was interested in her.

She waited for him in the entrance lobby of the museum. He was late. She paced, checking her watch. There wasn't any real hurry on her part, but his tardiness brought on a nervous knot in the pit of her stomach. What if he had changed his mind and wanted nothing to do with her or her silly enquiries? Or, of course, he might have simply forgotten.

He appeared, slightly red in the cheeks, from a side door.

'Hello,' he said. 'Sorry. Telephone call.'

'That's okay.' She absorbed the apology, along with her excuses for his lateness. She was taking up his time; he had every right to push her down the list of his priorities. 'Thanks again for meeting me.'

They walked to the café, and she lost the gentle argument when he insisted on buying her a sandwich and drink. She chose a ham salad and a different table without the wobbly leg – her own were behaving skittishly. Annoyed with herself, she felt like she was giving in to doubts. She was a functioning adult – with a few issues tucked out of sight of normal human observations. Her dream ghost might imply she had psychic abilities to connect with the departed, but Sean had no such magical access to her inner anxieties, and he would only see what she showed him. After they'd torn open the packaging and sipped a few mouthfuls of their drinks, to her relief, he broached the subject of the gravestone. Her nerves were close to tatters.

'I've had a good look in our files and I can't find anything related to a prisoner with the initials E and H. Male or female. The date doesn't match either.'

'Oh.' The small exclamation replaced a much louder "Oh" in her head. It hadn't crossed her mind that he wouldn't find anything.

'Are you sure you remember the letters right?' he asked, digging into his BLT with a snap of his teeth.

She waited until he finished chewing. Her appetite was dallying, as uncertain as her meandering thoughts. 'Yes.' She pictured the smooth stone and etched letters. 'There was quite a shadow. The yew tree, I suppose.' She constructed a plausible excuse for his benefit; her eyesight was fine, as was her hearing, and hypothesising wasn't the same as outright lying.

'Why don't we go up there after lunch and double-check?' He smiled. The offer was sweet, the kind that a gentleman made; he'd suggested a way out that saved her embarrassment.

'Sure.' She bit into her sandwich. She'd show him the headstone and he'd see it for himself. As for his records, files weren't always reliable when it came to documenting events. She'd learnt that much during her day job, and the trial had reinforced that opinion.

'If you don't mind me asking,' Sean said. 'How are the dreams?'

'Oh.' This time the nuanced exclamation didn't signal disappointment, merely confusion. 'More of the same, but different.'

He raised a solitary eyebrow like Roger Moore, except on Sean it created a lopsided expression and nothing suave. Marco had two neat lines that sat above his chocolate-coloured eyes. Sean's eyes were blue, almost transparent. His gaze was glued on her face and refused to budge. He wasn't bored or spinning out the conversation: she really was the centre of his attention.

'I thought the dreams were repetitive, which they are, but they're also progressive. Rather like a slow-moving story. Each time something different happens at the end. The woman, my companion, if you like, is less gruesome. I suppose I'm getting used to her. Last night, I picked up the pieces of paper and put them on the bed next to me. They look like a puzzle. I think I can piece them into a document.' She hesitated; that wasn't all of it.

Sean licked his fingers. 'And?'

'Can you feel in your dreams?'

He shrugged. 'Like pain?'

'Touch. Like texture?'

'I don't really remember my dreams. Can you feel something?' he asked.

'Emotionally, I feel almost numb, like I'm on the sidelines waiting. The paper felt substantial in my hands. Rough. Embossed?'

'No writing?'

She shook her head. 'Anyway, I started to fiddle with these strips, trying to line them up. Then I woke up.' The abrupt awakening had infuriated her. For the first time since the dreams had started, she'd wanted to stay asleep.

He grinned. 'Sounds intriguing. I wish for once I was a psychologist.'

'I'm not sure I'd want to see one. I don't think it would help me.' Those who had tried had never truly helped her move on, barring one perhaps who'd approached her problem from a different angle.

'I just meant there might be something going on that you're blocking out, like a bad memory or trauma.'

She prayed she wasn't blushing and ducked her head a fraction, inspecting her half-eaten sandwich. 'I don't think so. Nothing terrible has ever happened to me.' She glossed over the lie with breathless haste. It hurt, lying. 'It's more like I'm intruding in somebody else's episodic dreams.' Haunted ones. She chewed on the bread and, for a while, they ate in silence, for which she was grateful.

Unlike the previous day, when a blanket of grey had sat heavily over the castle, the clouds were a thin gauze stretched across the sky. They climbed the steps to the front of the restored Lucy Tower, Laura leading the way – Sean had access to the gate at the top, avoiding the longer walk of the southern curtain wall.

'Before my time, but I gather renovating this twelfth century tower was a nightmare. Turns out, the Victorian prisoners did a botch job of reinforcing the walls with iron clamps. Who'd have thought robbers made such poor builders?' He chuckled. 'The embankment was also overgrown.'

Once inside, she pointed to the far tree. 'Over there, just under that branch is where—' She squinted, then hurried off the path.

The ground was littered with dead leaves, sparse grasses, and the yew's fallen needles. The bareness sent her head into a spin, as did the nearest gravestone to the tree, which was covered in bird droppings and lichen, the carving chipped and weatherworn. The initials were visible, and definitely not E.H.

'It was here.' She tapped her foot at the space between the tree and headstone. 'I know it was here.' She circled the tree, then the stones.

Sean crouched next to one and traced his finger along the carvings, just as she had done.

'I can't see… Maybe it was a different one…' He floundered. The excuses weren't for him to make.

Tears gathered in her eyes, and she wiped them away quickly, before they fell. They were hot, angry tears of embarrassment and fear. She was losing her mind. There had been a stone, a newer one, not like the others, and now it was gone.

'I saw it,' she said weakly. It had had substance; she'd felt it with her fingers. If it had been an apparition, why hadn't her fingers slipped through it?

He examined the spot by her feet. The ground was irregular, but undisturbed, and presented no evidence that a gravestone had been recently removed. And it would have gone overnight – who would steal a headstone out of the blue?

She steadied herself against the trunk of the yew, her stomach churning with unfettered and savage nausea. 'I'm not crazy, am I?'

Sean stared at her, then the row of headstones, counting them with a nod. 'You're not crazy.'

'I must be,' she said pitifully. 'I work for the council, for the finance controller. I'm good at what I do. I'm a rational, level-headed person who does things by the book. I'm reliable and... fastidious. People don't like me because I pick things apart and tell them what I think.' She caught her breath, refusing to let any tears fall. 'I can't explain what I saw.'

'You don't have to.' He scratched the back of his head, then lifted his shoulders to his ears in a persuasive shrug. 'I believe you. Let's just leave it at that. Something was here, and now it's gone. And perhaps, like your dreams, it's somebody else's memories, and as realistic as the sounds you hear. Everything is connected.'

Another person's memories? An odd premise. She liked the idea of being a memory vessel because it meant she was just a convenient conduit and there was nothing sinister linking her to the past. 'Then what should I do? Do I just carry on as if nothing is going on? I can't stand not knowing.' She straightened up, ignored her uncertain knees, and moved out of the shade of the tree.

'The records we keep here aren't complete. A while back there was an exhibition about the prisoners, those hanged, including Priscilla Brig... the woman. It happened before I came along. Most of information comes from the research done for the exhibits. So perhaps there was a headstone here and it's gone, and so are the records.'

She wished it was that simple. He'd kindly made up something to placate her. He couldn't possibly believe she'd seen a phantom tombstone rising from the ground to taunt her, then sinking back into the earth, swallowed up, leaving nothing but dirt and leaves.

'Sounds far-fetched.' Like her nightmares and ghostly voices and eerie sounds. She hadn't even mentioned the strange line of light that had pointed out the gravestone.

'When I'm next down at the archives, I'll check.' He held out his hand, not for her to take – they were several arms' length apart – it was a gesture of encouragement. He beckoned. 'Come on. I have to get back to work. But don't worry. We'll get to the bottom of this.'

Hearing child-like voices that failed to communicate was several notches below disappearing objects in spooky graveyards; this ghostly shadow had to be another attempt at badgering her into accepting she was experiencing something supernatural. Believable or not, she was haunted, just her, and nobody else. And what was she expected to do, call up a paranormal society and demand an investigation? Sean was right. She wasn't going to be defeated by it, whatever *it* was.

She followed him towards the steps. 'You don't have to.'

'Tell you what.' He pivoted on his heels, nearly colliding with her. 'Why not come out for dinner with me? Somewhere away from the castle, and we'll talk about other things. Take your mind of it all.' His cheeks flushed pink: tinged by embarrassment or shyness?

She wasn't sure if he was continuing his quest to humour her. She hadn't said anything about Marco, and he'd not mentioned anyone either. Was this a date a "take me out to dinner and get me drunk" kind of date? Or a "let's be friends and I'll help you" sort of date?

'Dinner?' she croaked, her mouth paper-dry.

'Sure. Just a chat, nice food. Better than those sandwiches.' He grinned. He dallied by the open gate, his fingers twitching nervously.

A cold blast shot through the gap, and a flurry of leaves rustled against her boots.

'Where?' She thought for a moment that the buzzing was back. It wasn't, though. Blood was pulsating against her temples, threatening to start an almighty headache.

He suggested a restaurant the other side of the city. Thankfully, it wasn't Italian and was within walking distance of a bus stop she used. She wasn't prepared to explain why she hadn't a car. The time, half-past seven, suited her.

'Good,' he said pleasantly.

She followed him down the steps. There was a bounce to his feet. Hers felt a little leaden, uncertain. Her tumultuous emotions were in flux again; she wasn't in the right state of mind to determine their exact origins. Either she was upset because the headstone had vanished without trace or because she was giving up on her boyfriend. Both were the likely cause, and horribly emotive. Sean deserved the truth. She'd have to explain to him at some point that she wasn't entirely free. Although she'd made no promises to Marco and neither had he to her, they lived together. His clothes were in the wardrobe, his books piled up on a table, and no end of other things that didn't belong to her littered the place. He hardly counted as a housemate. He had a purpose in her life, and until a few weeks ago, she was steadfast in her need for it.

'Okay?' Sean asked.

She had not noticed the pause in her steps. They should part company; the path forked.

'Yes,' she said clearly. 'Quite all right.'

'Until Saturday?' He raised that crescent eyebrow once again.

'Yes.' She smiled, somewhat feebly. 'Looking forward to it.'

He turned and walked away without glancing back in her direction. She risked a snatched look over her shoulder to the tower above. A lone crow flew up, squawking and flapping its wings. Sean was right about one thing – she had to escape the castle and regroup her thoughts.

By the time she'd reached home, she'd resolved not to feel guilty about meeting Sean. A mini-date would test the waters, and why shouldn't she make new friends, male or female? It was her choice, and if Marco was frolicking with his friends in Italy, then she was entitled to have a life of her own.

'Bugger it.' She'd missed his message. The text had arrived on the noisy bus.

I'm sorry. You're right. You deserve an explanation. There are loose ends to knot. Explaining in person is better. Love M.

Love. Why did he have to throw that into the message? The solitary word once might have aroused her, now it annoyed. Loose ends? What was he alluding to – their relationship or his father? She wasn't going to treat him to a reply. Marco could stew.

She remembered at five o'clock to ring the court, to check in as requested by the usher. The automated reply informed her, as a juror for court one, that the trial was postponed until Monday. Brader was still ill.

Tomorrow, rather than mooch about, she'd go into work and have a normal day. She'd ignore the inquisition about jury service and focus on the tendering reports. Hopefully, by Saturday she might have shaken off all the pervasive doubts and try to give Sean a nice evening out. She was confident she had the ability to deliver the necessary practicalities of a first date: a touch of soft eyeliner and lip gloss, a reasonable pair of shoes that gave her a little extra height – not that Sean towered over her – and a few practised smiles when he talked, especially if it was football or rugby, one of the two was usually the case. With luck, she might find out more about him. She was resolute that, unlike with Marco, she would delve into Sean's background thoroughly and ensure there were no secrets tucked out of sight. One elusive man in her life was enough.

The Second Saturday

HE WAS WAITING outside the restaurant, one of those chains that always had burgers, salads, and pizzas. And chips. It also sold fish, which Sean pored over, smacking his lips.

'I love bass, don't you?'

She tried out a small neutral smile. She wasn't fond of fish; fishcakes were fine, but she couldn't stomach a whole fish, the needle bones and metallic eyes staring back at her. 'I'll probably have a burger.'

'And fries, of course.'

She appraised him, trying hard not to judge. He'd chosen a faux-leather jacket, which was perhaps too heavy around his shoulders. It crowded him, dwarfed his neck. Thankfully, he removed it.

'Bit chilly today, isn't it?' He kept up the small talk for a while.

She nodded, saying yes and no appropriately.

With their order given to the waiter, including a bottle of red wine, he settled with his elbows on the table. Laura shifted back in her seat.

'Are you okay?' he asked.

Should she mention Marco? The guilt gnawed a little more than she'd like. Upon hearing about him, Sean might squirm uncomfortably, hurry through the meal, unprepared to deal with the consequences of competition, even if that competitor was abroad. Or he might shrug, reveal that he, too, was involved with somebody, and offer her the chance at a vengeful, illicit affair, something sordid and conducted in the quiet hours of their lives, and she'd have to learn to cover it up. It might actually be exciting but leave her feeling grubby and used. Was she prepared to be the other woman? Angela would be suitably aghast if she ever found out.

Sean, his cheeks flecked with warm red spots, his tidy lips drawn into a bemused downturn, wasn't showing signs of Casanova influence; he was no Don Juan. 'Laura?' he nudged with his kindly voice and immediately pushed her concerns to one side.

'Sorry. I'm fine.'

The smooth skin of his face wrinkled into a smile, and she replied in kind. There was something about him – what it was, she wasn't sure and couldn't put a finger on the right descriptions or feelings. It seemed unfair to project her insecurities onto him. Sean had an aura, that was it, a positive vibe thing that she wanted to latch on to and use. Maybe that explained why, when he smiled, her heart raced a little. She unfolded the napkin and smoothed it over her lap.

He closed the menu. 'I know we weren't going to bring it up, but just to say, sorry, no chance to check with the county archive yet.'

She waved a dismissive hand. She hadn't expected an instant service; this wasn't a work-based relationship.

'And,' he continued, 'the dreams…'

Yesterday, she had read reports at her desk. A familiar landscape and one that grounded her. Michael was delighted to have her outside his office, and he interrupted her constantly with updates and demands. For once, she didn't mind. It was restorative, being wanted and excelling at something. Then, both on the Thursday and Friday nights, the progression of dreams continued. Nightmares no longer, she wasn't waking in a cold sweat or screaming in her head. What they were was a sequence of clues ploughing her onwards. She pursed her lips; was she sitting opposite a fellow detective? How far would he be prepared to go to help her solve her mystery?

She opened her mouth to answer, only to have to deal with the arrival of the starters and the wine. She dipped a nacho in the sour cream and crunched her way hungrily through several more before realising Sean was talking about something else. He wasn't a pushy man with an agenda. Why did he have to be so likeable?

'Do you like Christmas? I'm not a fan. We have to put up decorations in the museum. It's not as if we have many…' He dropped an olive onto his tongue.

'I usually don't bother. The office has a tree. My mum, she has this artificial one that sheds needles, and the cat chews them. Dad prefers to put up a real one in a bucket. Margery insists on outside lights—'

'Margery is your sister?'

'Oh.' She paused. 'No. My stepmother.'

'Ah, that makes sense with the two trees.'

Laura blew out a tiny stream of air between her salsa-flavoured lips. She hadn't intended to reveal the intricate details of her family. Her plan was to get him to "open up". This was a good place to start.

'And do you have… a family?'

He wiped his mouth with the napkin. 'Sure. Parents.' The tips of his ears went pink. He stopped looking at Laura's face and examined some spot in the distance.

'Mine are divorced,' she said. 'When I was ten. Dad remarried, Margery, and I have two stepbrothers. Both older than me. I don't like them.'

Her honesty wasn't a gift specifically for Sean. She always told people the same thing. Marco had, when thinking about it in retrospect, seemed taken aback by her bluntness. He adored his mother, worshipped her, if that word was an appropriate thing for a son to do. As for the father figure, he was just that. A cut-out family member with no substance who rarely communicated with his son and preferred to dote on his daughters. Marco should have been more sympathetic towards Laura. Hindsight had revealed a different take on his reaction.

'Still married?' she asked Sean.

'Me?'

'No, your parents?'

'Yes, yes.' He swallowed half of his glass with one swig. The blossoming redness in his cheeks matched the colouration of the wine. The line of his shoulders had gone rigid, shaping him into a boxed frame.

She realised what he'd skipped over. 'But you're divorced?'

He lowered his glass and sighed. 'We were students.'

She'd finished the nachos. The main course was several minutes away. The opening was widening.

'Where?' She prodded him onwards, pleased with her progress.

He fiddled with his cutlery. 'South. Reading. She got pregnant. It wasn't planned. We're not sure what went wrong, but it happened. It wasn't her fault any more than mine. You know, it's not one hundred percent reliable.'

She nodded, uncertain if he was talking about the pill or the condom. She liked to use both; collectively, they were more reliable and ensured a shared responsibility.

'So. We married. Maisie came just at the end of the final year. And then we realised we both wanted different things in life. She wanted to live here, me there. My career was a slow start, hers was a fast burn. Maisie was stuck in the middle.'

'Sorry,' Laura said.

A twitchy smile this time, with a fragility to it. 'Don't be. We broke up amicably. We're still friends, but she lives down there, and I'm up here. She married again, has two boys, and Maisie visited in the school holidays.'

Laura sensed a but, or some tragic ending.

'Visited?' She held her breath, preparing herself for an accident. Laura knew all about the tragedy of the unexpected.

He poured more wine into his glass, filling it to the brim. Laura declined. Hers was only half-empty.

'She's twelve, really more like a teenager. Wants to spend her holidays with friends, riding her pony, shopping. Stuff I can't really do with her. So she doesn't visit much anymore. Hardly at all.'

Relieved nothing tragic had occurred, Laura spontaneously touched the back of his hand. He didn't flinch. In fact, he turned it over and held hers, and acknowledged it with a squeeze.

'Thanks,' he said quietly and released her hand. 'Just taking some adjustment. She's got two fathers, and I'm not the one she calls Dad anymore, at least when she's with her mum. I accepted her request to drop it because it was getting confusing for the boys. Now, I'm the man with no title. Just Sean, I suppose.'

Margery was always Margery. But then, it was different for Laura. She'd lived with her mum, who'd never remarried or even dated much. There was only one Mum.

'That's tough. I didn't live with my step-mum. They don't live too far away. I saw Dad at weekends, holidays, too. But we don't get on. He met Margery while he was still married to Mum.'

The bitter truth had meant giving her father a suitably hard time. Had she been right to do so when she wasn't exactly sitting comfortably herself? No, she mustn't compare. Her father's affair with Margery had lasted two years before he'd owned up and asked for a divorce. Her mother had taken anti-depressants ever since. Laura folded her napkin and realigned the untidy cutlery. Little things always worked magic on her troubled thoughts. She was sure Angela's therapist would have told her to do those kinds of things when distracted by anger or guilty feelings.

'Maisie likes us all, both of us dads, but she wants her own life, too. I have to respect that.'

The arrival of the waiter with the main course relieved Sean of further explanations. The fish had been decapitated, the bones removed, the fillet shiny grey and smelling of the stall in the market, the one she hurried past.

Laura disassembled the contents of her burger and ate each component separately. 'Not so messy,' she explained.

Sean laughed politely. He'd a nice, wholesome laugh.

She remembered a conversation with somebody at work whose grandchildren lived in South Africa. 'This might sound odd, but have you thought about recording a video diary for her. Chat to her about life, and then... I know, it's a silly idea.' She stabbed the burger.

He stared at Laura, his blue-tinged eyes brightening into pinpricks. 'Actually, I think that's a wonderful idea. She does watch videos of celebs. I just need to chat about something we both like.'

'Football?'

Another smooth rumble of laughter. 'No. She's got two brothers for that. She likes tennis. I used to play quite a bit at uni. Almost made the squad. I'll think about it. Thanks, Laura.' It was his turn to reach out and pat her hand.

She managed not to flinch or squirm. He relaxed, loosened the top button of his shirt, and his stiff shoulders shed an invisible burden.

By the time they were scraping the plates, she'd decided to answer his earlier question.

She inhaled deeply. 'The dreams—'

'Yeah?' The quizzical eyebrow rose.

'I've worked out what's on the paper. It's been like a puzzle, doing it in my sleep. She watches, says nothing, like usual, but when I stroke the paper, she smiles.'

'How macabre for you,' he said sympathetically.

The fear was gone. She'd accepted her nightly companion as non-threatening; Laura had misinterpreted the spirit. The tormented woman remained a lonely figure. Hopeful, too. Something about the patience of waiting in the dim corner with her hands crushed together had softened the caricature. Even the gruesome details of her neck and eyes were less obvious in the shadows, as if her face was devoid of features altogether. Laura, in the dream, had focused on the paper fragments and woken to a small epiphany moment.

'It's braille.'

'Braille?'

'Sheets and sheets of torn up braille.'

'How weird is that.' He eyed the stack of menus in the wooden stand. 'Fancy dessert?' Food was an easy distraction for Sean.

She envied his ability to lighten the mood. 'I'm full, thanks. You go ahead if you want...' It gave them more time, which felt surprisingly important.

He patted his stomach. 'Probably best not to. Do you know much about braille?'

'No. Nothing. Never touched it before. It's all those dots. I had to feel them. Then, I woke up.' But she wasn't in any doubt.

'I wonder what will happen next.' He waved at the waiter.

Tonight, she'd find out. She wasn't at all comfortable with the idea she was being haunted by a blind person. It was an unwelcome complication, and so was the court case involving a charity for the blind. If she told Sean why, would he understand? It didn't matter;

she wasn't ready to divulge the reason. She'd taken months to tell Marco, and then she'd left out bits because saying them was like a dagger cutting into her heart. He'd been surprised by her confession, then his sudden departure had overtaken the shame. She'd never found out if he thought she'd got off lightly.

'I'll get a book out of the library,' she said instead. But when? Monday she'd be back in court, and from then on, she assumed the case would rattle to a timely conclusion.

'There's a museum somewhere,' Sean said, scratching his chin. 'A private one that specialises in the blind... I'll look it up. Maybe they might be able to help you.'

He seemed pleased with himself. She wished he wasn't keen on that particular idea. But, there again, she needed answers, and fast.

Bronte

1844 - 1862, Lincoln

A T THE AGE OF TEN, and probably in secret, my mother taught herself to read. She fell in love with Mr Rochester and Heathcliff, cherishing the well-worn books of the three Bronte sisters. From that young age she chose the name Bronte, refusing to answer to her given one, which infuriated her mother and aunts. She hid the books under her pillow. (Near the end of her life, she confessed to me that she'd stolen them but never said from whom.)

Bronte was twelve years old when she'd first seen him pass by. She lived in a neighbourhood avoided by many, so his appearance was a stark contrast to the usual pedestrians. He wore a velvet tall hat and long coat with two swishing tails and, as he strolled along the street, he swung a stick back and forth. It had a brass knob, very smooth and rounded, like a pebble on a beach. Bronte's viewing point was advantageous; she pressed her nose against the warm glass of the bakery window and fixed her gaze on his spiky whiskers and dapper cravat. The vivid recollections of that first scrutiny lived on with impressionable Bronte; the consequences of her misconceptions were long-lasting and terrible. The romantic hero of her books failed to materialise in real life.

Escaping her mother's wandering attention, Bronte followed him and discovered where he lived – a house with sunburnt bricks and four front windows. Four windows, not two, like hers. Even though Bronte's mother gave her a clout for running off, she kept returning to the house and, from behind a tree trunk, she mastered the art of spying.

He had another admirer, one who called upon his house too regularly for Bronte's liking; a woman with straw-coloured hair and a parasol. A carriage would drop her off and pick her up a few hours later. She had a loud laugh that carried across the street to the tree and she had a sway to her hips that offended, although none but Bronte would understand the exact nature of that offence. Bronte struggled to contain her bitterness, and the accompanying avarice weakened her kindly nature. Having reached nineteen years of age, he was too old for Bronte and he would never wait for her. There was nothing she could do to upset the courtship other than hiss a curse and hope the rival fell over into a puddle and broke her delicate ankle.

After the wedding, he stopped walking down Bronte's street and left the red-bricked house. She failed to locate where he went to live with his bride.

Bronte's mother preferred the coal merchant's son. He had knobbly knees and a bowed back. Bronte resisted his orchestrated overtures and refused to accept the sooty hand he held it out. Many nights she argued with her mother until a festering wound formed between them that refused to heal. When Bronte was seventeen, she spied her man again, taking the very path he'd walked five years earlier. Except, she noted, he held his walking stick stiffly and wore a blanket of black from his hat down to his boots.

She followed him, and he led her not to the red-brick house, but a smaller one with three windows: two upstairs, one downstairs. A mourning wreath hung off the front door knocker. He opened the door, and a small boy barrelled into him, sobbing and pounding on the man's thighs. He swung him into his arms and carried the child into the house. The door slammed shut behind him.

All these things Bronte remembered clearly, never faltering in her recollection. The man never knew she had marked him as hers from such a young age. She waited, impatiently, for his mourning period to pass, then she boldly knocked on his door.

She carried a basket of buns and gingerbread covered by a linen cloth. He shook his head and began to close the door.

'No callers,' he barked.

'Sir, they're a penny.' She lifted a gingerbread man to her nose and inhaled. 'A child would find this most delicious and rewarding.'

The crack widened. She thought he was even more fetching than from across the road. Bronte had done her best to improve her looks, which I have on good authority were of excellent repute. Her eyes were icy blue, her powdered cheeks soft like cotton, and her combed hair silken and flowing. The line of her thin lips was augmented with rouge, and a woollen scarf, arranged like a halter, was usually draped around her narrow neck – its thinness would later serve her well, the noose snaps such a neck swiftly. Her intention had remained unchanged since she was twelve years old, and she was determined not to miss a second chance.

He stared at the offering she held aloft. 'Ha'penny.'

Bronte sighed. She had taken the basket and goods without telling her aunts, who preferred her to work at the front of the shop since Bronte had a good understanding of numbers and reading orders. If she didn't return with money, their trust in her would be broken, and she would once again have to do hours of backbreaking work that left her hands aching.

'Why not all for a shilling?' She had picked the finest collection of buns from the early morning batch.

He scratched his chin. Close up, Bronte was a little disappointed by the missing button on his jacket, the threads hanging from his sleeves, and the uneven length of his whiskers. Clearly, he needed a wife back in his life.

'Would not your wife—'

'I have no wife,' he snapped.

Bronte stiffened. 'I meant no disrespect, sir. I assumed—'

'I recently lost my wife.'

She lowered her eyes demurely. 'I offer my most sincere apologies. I am sorry for your loss.'

He snorted. Ten years later, when Bronte told me of this encounter, she reinterpreted this derisory nasal exclamation for what it was: amusement at her misunderstanding. At the time, she believed it was an acknowledgement of her sympathy. The details of this memory, I swear, are accurate, as with all things she said. She had a wonderful way of drawing pictures in my mind.

Bronte arranged to call on him at least once a week with her custom delivery. These visits continued after her eighteenth birthday, and with each one she managed to creep farther into the house: the hallway – narrow and echoey – the parlour, sparsely furnished and, at the back, a grubby kitchen with a blackened range. There in front of the heat sat the boy, his son, James, playing with two dice.

Upon the sixth such visit, he poured her tea and invited her to sit. They shared a bun. The black stains on his fingers and occasional smudges on his cheeks turned out to be ink. He worked at a printer's. Bronte was delighted. He set the type for notices and pamphlets, penny dreadfuls and, occasionally, books. His speciality was wanted posters for the local constabulary. The irony of that haunts me today. The house he grew up in – the one with four windows – belonged to his grandfather, and he had passed along Bronte's street by way of travelling to and from work. Once married, he'd diverted his route to his new home.

As her confidence grew, Bronte stayed sufficiently long enough to wash a few dishes or stir something in a pan, anything that conveyed to the handsome man that she was interested in him. She bought his son a shadow puppet.

He showed no hint of his true nature, his appetites. He lulled Bronte by instigating a visit to the shop, providing him a good opportunity to meet her mother and aunts without arousing unnecessary suspicions. Bronte probably blushed; her cheeks often burned hot when she was either angry or ashamed. When I had placed my palm to them, if she had permitted me to do so, the raw heat seemed to singe my flesh.

Her plan achieved fruition when James turned six. A small page boy, Bronte recalled without malice. Her mother, initially angered by Bronte's furtive meetings, quickly mellowed when she saw the large house and the decent wage he brought home each Friday. She tried to tax her daughter in whatever way she could, as if she was owed a debt, but Bronte was never one for unnecessary charity and gave her no more than a few pennies from time to time.

What her mother did not know was behind those three sparkling windows, Bronte was suffering the consequences of a terrible mistake. While James hid under his bed clutching his dice, his father ensured Bronte was never left alone, keeping her by his side every hour he was home from work. And if she did stray out of the house, he questioned her at length as to the purpose of her trips. Just visiting the bakery to buy bread might cost her a bruise or two.

'You tell Bill,' he would snarl, 'or else I'll take my belt to your back.'

The handsome, gentlemanly William vanished. The stick he swung, she realised too late, was not for the purposes of keeping him upright when drunk, it was to bend her to his will. As for James, although he was left untouched, he learnt many evil deeds from his father and later practised them on me instead. The spoilt child, made in the semblance of his saintly mother and ruined by the malicious spirit of his father, ordered Bronte around as if she was a servant and not his stepmother. When Bronte shouted back, James smirked and threatened to inform his father. There was little she could do but suffer the consequences of James's meanness. William's cruelties were harsher to bear.

I arrived ten months after the wedding. I was not welcomed. According to William, what I harboured within me was the curse of the Devil. James's spots had been so numerous they covered his scalp and neck. Bronte nursed him – William refused to enter the bedroom – and consequently, she, too, had succumbed. I, invisible to the world, hidden inside her belly, also suffered. The disease that tainted my birth left Bronte barren. She bore the news well, I am sure. She never wanted another child spawned by the man she'd so foolishly married.

The midwife who attended my birth confirmed that I had no sight. My milky-white eyes attested to that diagnosis. What she also told my parents was that I could not hear either. William believed this to be true. Bronte was less convinced. For years she whispered into the void while William slept, and every word of her regrets and fears reached my ears. What she said tearfully, as if in agony, should not be heard by a child. My innocence was shattered at a young age. To protect myself, I remained mute, and William inferred that to mean I was genuinely deaf. With my uselessness confirmed, he had no one to witness the harm he inflicted on my mother.

Day Ten

Monday

THE NEW BATCH OF JURORS dispersed themselves among Laura's mob, disrupting the routine of morning with their form-filling and requests for pens, and foolishly they battled with the vending machine with an eagerness many had lost days ago. Conversations hurtled back and forth between court one's jury, who paid little heed to the newcomers in much the same way final year students might ignore freshers.

'Good weekend?' Beryl asked.

In the past, Laura hadn't been afraid to say no to such a question. When once she'd rebuffed the query at work, an awkward pause ensued until somebody had plucked up the courage to ask why not and then regretted hearing her reply. It turned out to be an excellent way of removing that particular question from the Monday morning set of greetings.

She had, overall, had a good weekend. She'd succeeded in not having a "date" with Sean but an enjoyable meal out instead. She'd also spent Sunday reading up on braille, which proved fascinating.

'Yes, thank you. Productive and nice.' Laura reevaluated the whole greeting thing; was it that hard to make up something positive to say? Everyone seemed able to do it, and given Beryl's satisfied expression, the response eased the tension that came with the beginning of a new week.

'And you? Did you have a good weekend?' Laura asked, discovering a chirpy tone was also achievable.

'So lovely not to have to come here on Friday. Had an extra day to catch up with the laundry. My husband took me to Scarborough. Bit blustery; I do like the sea air.'

Laura had gone to Scarborough as a child. During the summer holidays, they'd stayed in a caravan (florid green décor; strange smell). Her parents had bickered constantly, causing no end of grief because there was nowhere for Laura to hide in the confined space. Every inch of the interior was jam-packed with things. The claustrophobic setup had triggered the argument, something about him not "getting it enough", which stuck in Laura's head as an odd thing to say because he ate *all* his dinner and snored *all* night long. On the last day, when "it" was shouted again across the tiny expanse of the caravan, she'd slipped out, wandered off to the beach, and caused panic amongst the small community of holidaymakers. She'd played with seashells on the beach until her father scooped her up into his arms – she was five and easy to carry. She remembered he breathed heavily into her hair, tickling her ear, then told her to drop the shells she'd collected. She'd clung on to them, though, and at the caravan where her mother waited, clutching a sodden tissue, crushing Laura in an embrace, they cut into her palm.

'You need to give him enough,' a pained Laura had whispered into the knots of curly hair. She'd kept the shells for a few years until Angela discovered them in a shoebox and threw them out. None of them wanted to remember Scarborough, and they'd never gone back.

The old hands of court number one offered advice to the new jurors in the form of a relay. Brian, Beryl, and the other talkative ones handed over the baton of useful information that the ushers and introductory video hadn't provided, especially the part about two weeks feeling like an eternity. The camaraderie was infectious.

Laura saw only an illusion of friendship. Nobody had an inkling what went on in each other's lives once they left the building. They kept personal matters to themselves, dodging the awkward questions with deflections and digressions. The game suited Laura. The forcing together of twelve individuals was unnatural, and risky, and it pleased her to think that at the end of the trial, the small group would have no enthusiasm to keep up the pretence. There were no friendships developing, although she wasn't spotting enemies in the making either. Everyone was polite, eager to stay neutral in conversations to the point where it was cringe-worthy listening to the kindness of strangers played out for the benefit of other strangers.

The one person her jury wanted to know more about was Brader. Laura wished she'd had his biography to read and that the writer had packed it full of personality and insights. Instead, they were scrutinising a man based on scant information. The facts of the case were unsullied and sanitised, disseminated clinically and only questioned in a limited fashion. Who Brader was remained a mystery. Faithful husband? Kind-hearted? Humorous? Devoted to his kids? None of these things had been elucidated, leaving Laura with the impression that Craig Brader was a cardboard cut-out with no personality propped up in a dock. He really needed to come alive and project something across the court, or else she might believe he was giving up the fight.

The usher summoned them to the court. Now it was the defence's opportunity to change her perception of Brader.

Number Six waited for Laura to sit before lowering himself onto the bench. 'Looks better, doesn't he?'

She concurred. Brader was alert, upright, and for once not sniffing noisily into a handkerchief.

The defence barrister, Mr Calm – another one of Laura's pseudonyms – cleared his throat. 'The defence will be calling Mr Steven Feydon.'

Beryl's less-than-subtle 'Ooo,' echoed around the court.

The middle-aged Steven Feydon (copper hair, tramline lips, three-piece dusky suit with handkerchief poking out of the breast pocket) strode into the witness box, swore himself in on the Bible, then clasped his hands behind his back. He rocked on his toes. He looked straight at the defence barrister, who cocked his head at the jury. Feydon realigned his focus right onto Laura's row of jurors. As for Brader, the avoidance of eye contact between the two men was blatant.

This man, a member of a family who should have lost all faith in Brader, was a defence witness?

'Please tell us what you do for a living, Mr Feydon,' Mr Calm said.

Feydon began with a gruff introductory throat clear. 'I'm director of the charity, Seeside. I oversee fund-raising and the spending of money on worthy causes supported by the charity.'

'Seeside is the charity that employs Mr Brader?'

'Yes.' Feydon rocked harder on his toes. His mouth twitched, humourless.

'You've known Mr Brader for some years?'

'Many. We went to school together. I asked him to join the charity when he was made redundant from his previous job.'

Laura leaned forward. Here were some of the blanks in Brader's employment record. However, Mr Calm provided no follow-up question. And as the questioning progressed, it seemed the chipping away at Craig Brader's stony façade wasn't going to happen. Feydon firmly answered that as far as he was aware, the operations conducted by Mr Brader had been ship-shape. Nothing had come to attention until the accountant's report, and only then had he reluctantly contacted the Charity Commission and realised the serious nature of the accusations. The narrative of events was the same sequence as described by the prosecution, except this time it lacked any wrongdoing. It merely illustrated an investigation orchestrated and controlled by Feydon. There were hints of suspicions from the various auditors, and the police's involvement had changed the nature of the probing.

'Seeside has suffered. Our funds are down. Nobody trusts a charity that can't look after its own affairs.' For the first time he glanced over to where Brader sat with his arms crossed. The exchange was brief and lacked both animosity and poignancy.

What degree of loyalty was needed among friends to support the lack of evidence? It bugged her that it wasn't obvious in their demeanour.

'So as far as you're concerned, Mr Feydon, Craig Brader has done nothing wrong?'

'He's always been honest with me.'

'And you have faith in him?'

A pause, the slightest of hesitations, interrupted the flow between the two men.

'Yes.' Steven's gaze dropped to the usher's table between the jury box and his station.

Laura heard a lack of conviction. She fixed her attention on Mr Waverly, the prosecutor, who was scribbling over his notes.

Mr Calm checked through his list of questions. 'You are satisfied that Seeside has not been the victim of fraudulent activities?'

'None that I can discern.'

Feydon was walking a tightrope of non-committal answers. He wasn't forthright, but neither had he condemned his friend. Laura made a note.

Friends first.

Beryl, during the short toilet break, was relieved by the witness's personal knowledge.

'Thank goodness he's said something positive about Craig. I was beginning to think it's all about spreadsheets and audit reports. Isn't it nice to finally get to know the man in the dock?'

Laura stared, first at Beryl, then across to Jodi and the others on the opposite side of the table. The collective relief was obvious. They wanted the emotional overlay as much as Laura, the difference was they were going to use it to Brader's advantage. Laura had planned a different outcome. Now she wished she'd made those copious notes, ones that weaved persuasive intricacies into the sparse facts she'd taken down. She wasn't capable of presenting hard-nosed factual evidence to an emotionally charged group of strangers. She poured herself a cup of lukewarm coffee with a shaky hand. She wished Sean was sitting next to her offering his intuitive thoughts. He would surely agree with Laura's perspective.

The next session worsened her anxieties. Feydon was led through some of the evidence presented by the prosecution in the previous two weeks. Mr Calm selected the least contentious things, and Feydon searched his memories, pausing frequently. The spreadsheets, notes of meetings and recollections of phone calls, spanned many years; consequently, Feydon merely confused the jury with an oblique lack of clarity.

Mr Calm picked highly selective points, things that Brader might have done. Feydon, fidgeting with the tip of his tie, shrugged off most of them.

Feydon referred to a builder who no longer worked with the charity. 'I wasn't aware of anything remiss with the contract.'

'So, nobody in Seeside issued these bogus invoices?' Mr Calm asked.

Laura couldn't decide who to watch – Brader or Feydon. Brader's eyes darted everywhere, while Feydon stared at some point on the other side of the courtroom.

'I can't explain where those invoices came from. They must have been printed by another company.'

'By another company,' Mr Calm murmured.

The implication was the builder was responsible for the deception, which to Laura made no sense. Unless, of course, there should be more than one defendant in the dock.

Feydon's frustration at the line of questioning ended the tie fiddling. He straightened his back. 'We're just a charity, relying on the goodwill of employees and volunteers. Charities are easily picked on by bigger players, people who think they can milk us. Underhand stuff. The people who suffer are the ones who benefit from what we do in the wider community – the blind.' Feydon addressed the jury, the punch in his voice obvious. 'The longer this drags on, the harder it is to attract donations.'

This, the trial, was dragging on, there was no arguing with that verdict. The judge dismissed them for lunch.

Laura avoided the other jurors. She hadn't received an email from Sean, nothing to indicate he'd made any progress with the gravestone. If she popped over to the prison building, she might be able to catch him during his lunchbreak. Just a quick chat and update. She'd not told him about the history of braille or the other stuff she'd read about on Sunday. She'd just... what? She wasn't sure what else she wanted to say to him.

The woman in the ticket office of the museum smiled. Laura had no plans to revisit the museum. Sean could take her to lunch in the café; an agreeable proposition.

'Is Sean Pringle around?' she asked.

The woman's eyebrows knitted. 'No. He's off site today.'

The reason was logical. 'Of course. He's at the county archive.'

'He's not there.' The curt response was a dismissal. She wasn't going to provide any more information about a colleague to a stranger.

Laura walked into the café and sat. Dragging her chair closer, she collided with the table, and coffee splashed over the brim of the mug. She picked at the sandwich, managing only half of it. She was tired of thinking but couldn't stop the flow of anxious thoughts heaping up on top of each other.

What a fool she'd been to think she was Sean's sole project of interest. He had a job; she respected the diligent worker. Expecting him to waltz off to hunt down a missing gravestone, something that only she'd seen, was far-fetched and selfish. He'd shown her kindness on Saturday, and she should have left things there and stopped pestering him. Why should he follow through? His interest in her was based on nothing more than rumours of ghosts in the castle. She'd inflated things by telling him her sad dreams and giving them far more credence than they deserved. After all, she hadn't dreamt of the cell or the woman last night. She'd gone somewhere else, a room that was almost empty, and the only thing in it were little building blocks stacked in the middle of the floor. And a child's primitive doll. That was it. Hardly a haunting and unlikely to induce a cold sweat.

A small part of her was disappointed the nightmarish prison was gone. But its departure meant that she was moving on. Not once today, as she focused on Mr Feydon, had there been a single hiss, whisper, or grunt. So, she was free of the affliction, and it was time to drop the silly theory of a story to unravel, a past that didn't belong to her or anyone else. Sean probably thought the same and had immersed himself in work, and if he still intended to approach a museum about the braille, it was unnecessary. She'd send him an email, apologise for all the fuss she'd made, and hope that they could stay friends in another capacity, one based on normal day-to-day things.

Slumping in the seat, she sensed a "but" developing. Was she capable of forging a simple friendship with Sean? Bothered by the implication the answer might be no, she abandoned the sandwich and swallowed the dregs of the coffee. She went back to the courthouse recommitted to her jury service. It was the prosecution's turn to question Steven Feydon.

'Mr Feydon, you attended the same school as Craig Brader? A private school?' Mr Waverly asked, the tip of his pen poised by his notes.

Feydon's hands were hidden behind his straight back. 'Yes, until we were eighteen.'

'And then you left to attend… Durham University?'

'Yes.'

'And Mr Brader went to… Exeter.'

'Correct. We stayed in contact.'

'Naturally. You're best friends.'

The tiniest hint of red crept into Feydon's cheeks.

'So,' Mr Waverly drawled. 'You went on to work together?'

'After graduation? No.'

Mr Waverly examined his papers. 'Mr Brader had various jobs, mostly in construction and civil engineering, which is what he studied, but not finance. You went on to work as a stockbroker, hedge fund manager, company director, and also… a printworks.'

'That's a brief summary of my career to date. The printworks belonged to my family. I only had a cursory interest in it; it's highly specialised and run by a dedicated and independent team.'

'You owned other businesses, yes?'

The tinge of pink stretched over his nose. Laura stiffened. The prosecutor had hit on something.

'Yes. Over the years. I admit, they weren't always successful.'

'Successful?' Mr Waverly raised his eyebrows. 'I'm right in thinking they failed, did they not?'

Feydon's voice lowered. 'Due to the recession. My employees all received full redundancy packages. It was unfortunate that the economy slumped.'

Laura shifted her gaze to Brader. He was flushed, and not this time with illness, but embarrassment. He was ashamed of the line of questioning. He'd put his friend in an awkward position. At last, Brader was demonstrating something redeeming – empathy.

'The charity, Seeside, then passed into your capable hands.'

Feydon winced. 'It's a family enterprise… I mean, commitment. We're all committed to making Seeside work.'

'And then you employed Mr Brader, your friend from school, whom you'd not worked with previously, correct?'

'Yes.'

'He'd just been made redundant. Another unfortunate redundancy.'

'Yes.'

'The charity's secretary, who stood in that very dock last week, told us that you had not interviewed him formally nor asked for references.'

'I've known Craig—'

'Not exactly the actions of a reputable company director. In fact, it seems you have a tendency to break things, Mr Feydon. Hardly the Midas touch. You paid no attention to Mr Brader's financial activities, and you were happy to leave everything in his hands while you attempted yet again to carve a career as a hedge fund manager. How often were you in the offices of Seeside during Mr Brader's tenure as finance director?'

The bloom of red was now a sea of crimson. Feydon blustered and muddled up his dates. Mr Waverly, sensing he had Feydon on the ropes, battered him with numbers and numerous records of his absence from meetings – the apologies were minuted by the secretary. Feydon was rarely in the office. Mr Brader, it seemed, was running the show on his own.

Laura was pleased. Not for Feydon, who for whatever reason had not come across as the diligent director of a charity, but because Brader looked like he wanted to be swallowed whole by the wooden floor. If Feydon had failed to keep an eye on his friend, then, surely, all the testimony of the morning when Feydon had happily accepted that Brader's actions were above board was meaningless.

'Mr Feydon, after the auditor raised their concerns, the police were invited to investigate. Who instigated that request? You?'

'No. It was another trustee. Mrs Sharpness. She didn't consult with me.'

'I wonder why…' Mr Waverly's remark was nearly sotto voce and was rebuked by a warning stare from the judge.

Mr Calm rose to his feet to cross-examine again.

'Mr Feydon, are you the sole member of your family with responsibility for Seeside?'

'No. My Uncle Anthony assists. My father passed away some years ago.'

'And has your uncle expressed any concern about the running of the charity by Mr Brader?'

'He was assured by me and, given his health…' Feydon paled in the midst of his pause. 'We gave the police complete access to everything. Tony was pretty hands-off, though.'

'Because Mr Brader has his confidence?'

'He has the confidence of both of us.'

'And to reiterate, you have never had any concerns over Mr Brader's bonus payments, his involvement with local companies, or his relationship with property developers?'

'None. While Craig worked at the charity, the donations increased.'

A fact that Mr Waverly had not mentioned. Laura shot him a glance, expecting something of a flinch, but the barrister was placid, unperturbed by the information.

'And as far as you are aware, Mr Brader's personal financial situation is accounted for by his own family's circumstances.'

Feydon paused. 'I'm not party to his family's situation, but Craig had a number of relatives with property abroad. He always told me he expected to inherit a decent sum. I assumed he had.'

Mr Calm smiled. 'Thank you. There's no further questions, Your Honour.'

The judge removed his glasses. The dismissal was swift.

Laura smoothed out the crease in her paper. What to write? There was only one point of interest that stuck. Something that she should have given more attention to the previous week when it had been mentioned in another witness's evidence.

The old schoolboy network had deep roots.

She left the castle precincts, drawn away by an incomprehensible lure. It was as if she was hooked on a fishing line and was slowly being reeled in from a great distance. From out of the background thrum, she picked out the renewal of the soft voice and curiosity encouraged her to go farther afield; it was easier to play along than resist, and bridling her fear brought her a degree of respite. The whispering had a hypnotic sweetness and lacked discernible words, but the lyrical tone also flowed like a language. A foreign tongue or a child's undeveloped one? Laura wandered down the steep hill, and when presented with a choice of direction, she was guided by either a tonal rise or fall, a delicate yes or no, or alternatively the subtle hint of feet rustling leaves in the gutter. She needed to fine-tune her hearing to pick up on the sounds and combat the noise of modern streets. Eventually, she came to where the city met the river. Battling the chill of an autumnal evening, with winter keen to make its entrance, she explored the lower streets, as if she, or her companion, was hunting for a specific location or house. All there was were shops and car parks, which were greeted with tiny huffs of frustration – Laura agreed, modern cities had lost their appeal.

As she walked, the imaginative part of her mind, which she had thought inadequate for the task, was transported to somewhere with no diesel fumes or solid blocks of concrete. The countrified scene smelt sweet (honeysuckle or roses) and lush (weeping green leaves formed a curtain – a willow?). There was even a moment when pins and needles (thorns?) pricked the fingers of one hand, the one not clutching her handbag strap. She shook her arm, and all the phantom sensations vanished at once. Her fuzzy vision cleared, and she was swiftly reacquainted with the dull street.

It dawned on Laura that Sean's idea wasn't entirely ridiculous: she might be a receptacle for somebody's memories, and they manifested as dreams in her sleep – the ghostly woman trapped in her cell was a key player but not the guide. During Laura's waking hours, somebody else, apparently a child, had planted in her mind the need to roam, and that same subtle spirit had created the unusual levels of curiosity that she normally reserved for finance reports and not historical clues.

What kind of person infected the mind of another and turned them into a vessel? A guilty or remorseful one? Both. And plainly the ideal emotions to haunt Laura.

Her teeth started to chatter uncontrollably.

Walks

1865

MA TOOK ME FOR WALKS nearly every day. I gripped her hand and stumbled over the unfriendly cobbles. If I tripped, she hauled me back up onto my feet and chided my clumsiness. She guided me away from the horses' hooves that clipped the loose stones, past the salty fishmongers, along by the church chimes and down a steep hill until we reached a river.

The park was the best place: quiet and thoughtful compared to the boisterous streets. There, under the rustle of leaves and birdsong, Ma educated me.

'Hold out your hands.' She turned my palms upwards, and I held them so like a bowl for her to use.

Leaves. Wet and as big as my palms. Prickly twigs that snapped. Pointed thorns on rose stems. And bark.

'That's rough, and wrinkly,' she said.

The worms wriggled. I dropped their slimy tentacle-like bodies and squealed.

'Hush. They're better than maggots.'

She scolded me for lowering my hands. They trembled, fuelling my anticipation. I was wary, because of my ignorance, but trusting. Ma never allowed anyone else to touch me.

Stones are jagged. Pebbles from a stream, though, are smooth. Coal is filthy and heavy. Back at home, bathing my hands in a pail of water, she told me about ice (teeth chatter) and snow (powdery flour). When she made bread, which she often did, she sometimes let me carry the flour in a paper bag all the way from the bakery.

If Grandma was there, she'd give me a currant bun. 'Just for you,' she'd say, tickling a spot under my chin. I never said thank you. I maintained the illusion of my deafness even for her.

Ma mixed the flour in a bowl on the kitchen table. I sneezed.

'Dust is similar to flour,' she said. 'Ash, also, but learn the difference.'

Ash is hot. Red-hot and burns, like coals in the fire. Another dip of my hands in the water. My poor hands bore the brunt of Ma's lessons.

I sniffed things, too. She'd hold them to my nose. Petals; they are sweet, which is the taste of sugar, a treat for good girls. Whereas nettles are a reminder the world is a dangerous place for a blind girl. My favourite smell is lavender. Ma put it in a bowl on the windowsill.

'It's purple and grows like grass,' she said. 'Straight up and sways with the wind.'

Purple meant nothing to me, but green grass did, especially the smell of cut grass. I learnt that purple and green are partners, happy playmates.

Mud stinks. The putrid waste under my boots that reeked and spread from house to house, never washed away by the rain. Ma tried to steer me past the puddles, but often as not, I walked through them and drenched my stockings.

'Look,' she started to say, then sighed heavily. 'You'll have to get used to wet feet. I can't show you puddles.'

Puddles and mud are brown, and I quickly formed a dislike of brown. But not coffee beans, which Ma said is also a muddy thing if ground and mashed. I loved the smell. Walking past the coffee houses, I loitered, inhaling the pungent aroma, until she dragged me on.

Blood is red. It oozes, smears itself if free to spread. Warm, too, when fresh. I thought sometimes it had a particular smell (later I called it grief). Ma bathed by the fireplace in the kitchen and grumbled about it. Father called it evil, a woman's curse, and every month he harped on about it, that it was not right that he had no more sons.

When he was angry like that (speech slurred and breath foul) I squished myself under a stool.

If sunshine could be held in my hands, then it was my favourite thing. In the park on warm days, I lifted my arms above my head, reaching for the heat, and spun around.

'What a sweet child.' People said those kind of things to my mother as we walked in the park. 'Bless her.'

Ma said nothing. I was not blessed at all. The sunshine was the only thing that I really wished I could see, more so than the petals or feathers (light and ticklish). I wanted to buy a yellow dress and be sunshine, so I could warm my house on a winter's night, heat the buns in the oven, and melt the icicle spikes that hung outside the windows.

Father told Ma to dress me in black, the dirty coal colour, because I should not be seen. Ma sewed the dress with a needle (spiky) and thread (fine, it slips through the fingers). I stuck a thimble on the end of my thumb and licked it – metal tastes bitter.

'Don't,' she said. 'It's precious. If you swallow it...'

The thimble disappeared from my thumb. That was how I saw the world at three years old. Things came, then disappeared, and in between when my hands were empty, I felt nothing.

Day Eleven

Tuesday

THE EMAIL DROPPED IN HER INBOX the next morning. Laura read it during the bus ride into the city.

Apologies for missing you yesterday. Niamh told me somebody was looking for me, and going by the description I assume it was you. She's very sorry not to have asked for your name.
The archive is closed on a Monday. I had to attend a tedious series of meetings elsewhere. I'd much rather be helping you!
I was thinking this should be a joint effort. The archive is open on Saturday. If you can meet me there at ten o'clock, then we could search the records together. Suggest newspapers as a good place, or the census records. What do you think?
Sean

She read it through twice, especially taking heed of the exclamation mark. The surprising flutter in her chest was palpable, as was the pang of regret at her hasty conclusions. He hadn't forgotten her. If she wanted to keep the spark between them alive for longer, she'd have to put more effort into cultivating a friendship and not cheapen it with churlish criticisms. The bus rattled over the potholes, and she composed a reply with a prudent digit.

Sean.
I can meet you on Saturday. It's a pity my jury service prevents me from meeting you earlier in the week. Maybe I could pay for a dinner out this week. Wednesday?

She'd have to dip into her savings if they went somewhere nice. Twenty pounds wouldn't stretch far...

I had a different dream last night. A bit odd, and shapeless. It left me feeling empty rather than fearful.

Too much information. She deleted the last sentence.

I also went for a walk down to the river. I wonder if the archive has old maps of Lincoln. I'd like to know more about the streets.

The request would stand out as odd, but until she could make sense of it, she wasn't going to explain it. As an afterthought, she added her mobile number.

It's fine to use this, if you like.
Laura. x

Amelia added one or two little kiss crosses – Laura had taken to copying her friend. Marco was granted three, so was her mother. Dad got none. She removed the single cross from the draft email; she was jumping ahead with her presumptions. She'd only met Sean a few times and she wasn't sure what the tactful protocol was for a non-date. If Marco turned up next week as promised, then she'd have a deep and meaningful conversation with him, put things straight, and decide whether to work things out or not.

Waiting for Sean's reply, she clutched the phone in her hand. The plans she concocted in her head had a tendency to fall apart. She should know that by now.

Her phone beeped.

Laura.
I'm sure the archive will have maps. I assume you're interested in the mid-19th Century. I'll send them an email request to prepare the way for our visit.
Wednesday is possible. I usually chat to Maisie on Wednesdays. If we could meet at eight, then I should be able to schedule both. Been thinking about your video idea. Tried it on Sunday. Wish that I could just talk to the camera. It's harder than it seems.

Where do you fancy eating? I could recommend The Pie. Do you know it? It's a gastro pub. Serves really great food.
Sean

The answer was swift, and reading it through, she couldn't help noticing he was letting her into his confidence faster than she'd anticipated. Her advice on father-daughter relationships would need to be substantially edited and offered up with caveats. It was possible, though, to say nice things if she cast her mind back to those early years of her life. Yes, she would try to stay positive.

Tuesday was a disaster for the court case. The usher's cloak hung limply off her harangued shoulders. She spoke with a heavily laden apologetic tone. The initial delay was due to the taxi service. They'd forgotten to pick Brader up. Lincolnshire was a big county, and the jurors themselves had come from all over, the farthest from the outskirts of Grimsby.

'Jesus H Christ.' Haden folded his arms over his chest. 'Doesn't he drive? Who doesn't drive these days?'

Laura bit down on her lower lip, silencing herself. Living in a city had always been the excuse she gave for not owning a car, and the answer rarely led to further enquiries. But curiosity in a courthouse was part of the proceedings and unstoppable. The questions zig-zagged across the room. Where did Brader live? Did he get expenses paid by the court?

'Perhaps he's lost all his money in legal fees,' Brian said. 'Can't be cheap.'

'He's rolling in it. That's the whole point of this trial. He's got more money than sense.' Haden sucked in his chest and blew out a balloon of gum until it snapped.

They were left in the waiting room for an hour while another taxi went to collect him. The usher slipped in with a beleaguered and wary expression.

'Sorry. Today's witness is probably stuck in traffic. Big accident. Everywhere is snarled up. Another hour or so.' She dashed out.

Haden sprang to his feet. 'I'm going for a coffee. Anyone joining me?'

Laura was left with Beryl, Amil, and Number Six.

'Gosh,' Beryl said. 'A mass walkout. Do you think they'll come back?' She giggled.

'Wonder who the witness might be.' Number Six stood by the window and stared across to the outer wall. There were wisps of grey in his short hair. He was impossible to age. A handsome man with square shoulders and a straight nose, of all the jurors, he presented the saddest face, carved by a worldly weariness and impenetrable eyes. Whatever occupation he practised remained a mystery. 'Probably a character witness,' he said.

'As long as it's not another boring auditor. They do drone on.' Beryl offered them all fruit pastilles.

Amil declined. 'They've got gelatine in. I'm a vegetarian.'

'Have they?' She perused the packaging. 'Didn't know that.'

Laura sucked on her choice: orange and sickly sweet. She preferred spearmints.

'It's got to be somebody with a counter theory,' Amil said.

'Counter theory?' Beryl screwed up her face. 'What do you mean?'

'Brader needs an enemy, somebody who's stitched him up.'

Number Six slumped into a seat. 'Hardly somebody the defence would call.'

Laura could see Amil's point. 'Then what about a person who's prepared to point the finger at somebody who's maliciously set up Brader.' Seemed a little far-fetched. 'Trouble is, I don't think he has any friends who know enough about his job to speak up for him.'

Amil blinked. 'I'd not thought of that. Maybe this witness is his mother.'

It turned out it wasn't his mother but his sister-in-law (canary-yellow jacket, skin-tight leggings, and knee-high leopard-print boots). The apology to the judge for her tardiness was ill-conceived. 'I should have left earlier. Didn't expect so much traffic. I'm not usually up at this time of the morning.'

She winked at Craig, who shrivelled in his chair and shot his solicitor a wide-eyed stare of alarm. The defence solicitor tapped Mr Calm's shoulder and whispered into his ear. The barrister shook his head. The list of questions on his notepad, which was in Laura's line of view, was extensive. It was nearly lunchtime, and her stomach was already knotted with a blend of hunger and fatigue.

The witness made an affirmation to tell the truth, then in a shrill voice and without any prompting, launched into a speech. 'The auditor, the one brought in by Steven Feydon, was in love with Craig's ex-wife. His first wife. He stitched Craig up, and that's—'

Laura rolled her eyes to the ceiling. The witness was living in a soap opera or one of her celebrity biographies.

The defence barrister's ears went pink, and he held up his hand to stop the tirade. 'Can we start at the beginning, please.'

The beginning was ten years ago and required an hour of repeated questioning and interruptions from the judge to clarify the points before anyone had a clue what she was wittering on about.

Laura picked up her pencil and added a couplet.

Bad acting.

Amil scarcely wrote a word during the testimony. He merely stared at the yellow jacket as if caught in headlights. The judge, to the relief of everyone – staff and jurors – called for the lunch break. They filed out of the court. Beryl was the first to start chuckling, followed by Jodi.

'She's seen too many TV shows, like *Judge Judy* or something,' Jodi said. 'It's like she expected a confrontation.'

'It was a very entertaining interlude.' The comment was from one of the other men who rarely spoke.

'Waste of time,' Brian said stridently. 'Hardly added anything to the case. Brader squirmed throughout. Can't think what the defence was thinking, calling her.'

'It's the stage effect,' Beryl said, offering one of her pearls of wisdom. 'Couldn't help herself. Probably thought it was her fifteen minutes of fame. Except there wasn't a journalist in the court, and the judge looked ready to toss her out.'

By the end of the afternoon, after the prosecution had finished stripping apart the sister-in-law's theory that Craig had been stitched up by the jealous auditor who'd had an affair with Brader's ex-wife, a woman Brader hadn't been in contact with for six years, the witness had lost her shrill tone. Brader's ex-wife wasn't putting in an appearance to back up the story, and without her testimony, there was no reason to believe the auditor would act maliciously on her behalf. Brader offered his sister-in-law a kindly acknowledgement at her failed attempt at a conspiracy theory. Laura caught the sweet smile out of the corner of her eye, and she added another note.

Desperate measures.

And pointless, although it had added an engaging spell of frivolity to the proceedings that Laura found oddly gratifying. She'd felt no cold blasts and heard no charmed whispers; it was as if the trial had gained precedence and what happened outside the courthouse was now more important. The session ended at three. The judge cleaned his glasses vigorously as he dismissed the jury. The progress of the case was unsatisfactory. The answer to Brader's guilt surely lay in the numbers and not in affairs of the heart. Emotional entanglements were what Laura faced with her evening out with Sean.

The moment she exited the building, her invisible, humming companion directed her to wander north, to the streets behind the castle and cathedral – the child seemed neither happy nor sad, and eventually, the singsong voice died away to be replaced by a different sound. As Laura wrapped her scarf tighter around her neck, a flurry of snowflakes swirled about her. The grey sky was heavy with the anticipated fall of snow, encouraging pedestrians and drivers to leave for home early. The buses would be packed. Laura decided to catch a later one. It wasn't as if a blizzard was due, just a light dusting.

While the shop signs were lit up, the dull streetlights waited for the appointed hour of their awakening. White freckles dotted the premature darkness, and an icy chill blasted her ankles, shoving her along. She hurried, choosing what she thought might be a sheltered side street. A sensible person would have gone home, but her empty house was uninviting. Common sense deserted Laura, as it had done on several occasions since she'd frequented the castle.

She listened. Her breaths faltered; she wasn't alone. There it was – the semblance of footsteps. She tried to ignore the patter of shoes that tracked her and failed. They, for it might be one or two pairs of feet, moved in a sprightly way. Laura glanced over her shoulder and confirmed there wasn't anyone there. She hurried, tripping on the cracks in the pavement, challenging the footsteps to keep up with her. Were they following her or harrying her along? The voice in the court had asked her to follow – dare she?

Laura stopped. The treads whooshed by her, sending her heart briefly into her throat and an arctic shiver down her spine. An echo stayed, a pathetic whine and childish in nature; it lingered in her ears. Her companions were eager, hastening to somewhere ahead. Trepidation transformed into excited curiosity; what possible harm could they do to her? The sprinkling of footfalls led the way, like the Pied Piper, and always within earshot. She kept pace, emboldened by a sense of purpose, and ignored the bitter cold in the hope of discovering another clue – a destination of some sort.

Abruptly, whether because the traffic noise had increased or because her hearing had lost that strange acuteness that had begun in the precincts of the castle, the pattering ceased. Laura halted. She was outside a twinkling café, the bay windows draped with lace curtains. A hot drink might rid her gloveless hands of numbness. The small, two-storey establishment, which hosted no more than a dozen round tables, was red-bricked and in need of better signage. The white-dusted roof tiles were as uneven as the cobbled streets, the window frames askew, and the inside walls bare-boned without plaster or paint. A guidebook would call it bland. Laura was generous enough to see warmth.

The banner over the window, written in archaic text and peeling in places – *Ye Olde Bakery*.

Pausing to listen, she concluded she'd either reached the destination of her escorts or the limits of her ability to hear them. There was time before the next bus for a quick mug of hot chocolate and a muffin. She chose a table at the back of the shop, away from the draughty window and door. Sitting there, reading the laminated single-sided menu, she uncoiled her scarf. The room felt like an oven in temperature and brought with it the delicious aroma of fresh bread at a potency that triggered a rumble in her stomach and a salivating mouth. She licked her dry lips.

A young woman appeared from the back of the premises: rolled up sleeves (unremarkable tattoos) and a white apron (badly creased but spotless). She pulled out a notepad from her back pocket (dog-eared) and hovered by the table. Laura was left with the impression the waitress had been abandoned on her own. She smiled, hoping to inspire some enthusiasm.

'We're closing in an hour,' the woman said jovially, without looking at Laura. 'It's the weather.'

Laura hid a smile; English weather was both convenient and inconvenient, depending on perspective.

'It's very cold out,' she agreed. 'Lovely and warm in here, though. Do you bake bread every day?'

The woman blinked. 'Sorry?'

'I can smell it.'

She laughed. 'We get the bread shipped in from a big bakery every morning. Haven't made bread in this place for nearly a hundred years. The owner likes the authentic look; she's getting on a bit herself.'

Laura sniffed. The smell had gone, replaced by roasted coffee and a musty something emanating from the floor. The tired café was limping on, relying on antique oddments and dried flower displays, stained linen, and old photographs of Lincoln in crooked frames. There was no sign of muffins on the counter.

It didn't matter, the place was open, and Laura still fancied a drink. 'Just a hot chocolate. No cream.'

'Chocolate sprinkles?'

'Please.'

It arrived five minutes later, and she drank it quickly. The milk was frothy, the chocolate sweet. It warmed her insides and spurred her onwards. It was time to go home. There was nothing for her here, just another fruitless exploration of the past. She hadn't found anything that linked an executed woman to braille and certainly not to an old bakery. Either she lacked the imagination to see a connection or there was none. Sean was her only hope for making sense of things.

Writing

1867

MA PUT SOMETHING between my first finger and thumb. Small, tubular, dense; a stubby carrot? I raised it to my mouth, ready to bite, but she tapped my hand away.

'Not food.'

She moved my chair closer to the table and held my hand in the canopy of hers, the skin scaly and raw, slowly transforming into bark, which saddened me. She shaped my fingers around the thing in my hand.

'Pinch it.'

What is it? I never say my words, just think them. Or I grunt; Ma understands.

'Chalk.' She placed my other hand on a smooth surface. 'Slate.'

She guided the chalk over the slate. It scratched and squeaked, and I flinched. But she would not let go; over and over she repeated the swirls and patterns, all the time whispering in my ear.

'Circle. Like an apple.' She left me to practise on my own before taking my hand once more and moving my wrist back and forth, jerking it in different directions.

'Careful, your sleeve is smudging it. Keep your arm off the slate.' She raised my elbow. 'Triangle.'

I had no idea why Ma wanted the chalk to move this way and that, but my efforts pleased her.

'Good girl.' She patted my head.

Father was out. We only played those games when he wasn't there to witness my most rudimentary education. Later, when I had learnt letters, she gave me pen and ink, and I secretly wrote my name, perhaps hundreds of times.

EMMA

I never saw a single scrawl.

One evening, Father found a scrap of paper with a crude alphabet. Ma had forgotten to burn it on the fire.

'You can write better than this, boy,' he said to James.

'It's not mine, Papa.'

He clouted James, who crashed into the table. 'Don't lie. Whose is it then?'

I sat very still, like a statue, as I often did when William prowled about the house.

'Her?' He laughed. 'She can barely hold a spoon.'

'I don't know, Papa. It isn't how I write.' James snivelled.

Father snorted. The oh-so familiar sound. I hated it as much as his belches and farts. Ma's vision of a handsome gent in top hat and sleek jacket never fitted with what I heard come out of him. He was ugly, scruffy, foul-breathed with ripe feet. His clothes were coarse and heavily stitched. The ink stains bothered Ma. She scrubbed his shirt cuffs, bemoaning that he never wore sleeve holders.

'Where does the money go?' she'd lamented. He had refused to buy them or a new shirt.

I stayed on my stool in the corner, listening to James contest the accusation, praying that Father would not find the slate hidden behind the coal bucket.

'Mother must have brought it home in one of her baskets. They use old paper for wrapping bread.'

Father scrunched the paper. The fire crackled and spat. After that day, Ma never gave me paper to write upon. The slate eventually cracked, and the chalk shrank until it slithered away between my fingers.

'There has to be a better way,' she said.

William sent her to work in Grandmother's bakery because we needed more money.

'But what about Emma?' she asked.

The worry in her voice frightened me.

'She can go with you. Tie her to a bench or something.' He left for work, his stick clattering on the flagstones.

'Come on,' Ma said, taking my hand.

Grandma wouldn't let Ma work in the shop at the front of the bakery as she was too tired to be trusted with handling coins. She worked every weekday from four in the morning to lunchtime, then went home to cook, wash, and clean for Father while he was at the printworks and James at school.

I had a stool in the corner of the bakery where I listened and sniffed the air. By the time Ma arrived the dough was already kneaded and risen. The moist air swam with the rich aroma of frothy yeast, hot metal, and sweat. Grandmother's bakers spent hours in the middle of the night pummelling the dough with their fists, sometimes their feet, before retiring to sleep. When they woke, the rested dough was removed from the warm trough and shaped into loaves and buns. If they had any, dried fruit was added. Grandma put a few pieces in my hand and let me eat, staunching my ravenous hunger.

Ma had to help with the ovens. She lifted the tins in and out of them, shook out the hot bread, and filled the tins with more dough. Other times, she rolled the dough into a Coburg loaf because there were not enough tins. If Grandma was out buying flour, Ma stood me on my stool and let me poke my fingers in the dough or roll out my own loaf. She whispered instructions into my ear. So I learnt to bake bread, but nobody knew. Mostly, I was in the corner, waiting, choking on the blooms of flour that perpetually floated on the warm currents of air.

The heat was unbearable. I tore at my sleeves, cooing for fresh air, and was ignored. Everyone was too busy to notice a silent child's tantrum. The windows, all open, seemed to offer nothing but a constant stream of noise and foul smells. I covered my mouth, feeling dizzy, and wishing the morning gone. Then, when a distant church clock rang the hour, the heat cleared. The oven doors clanged shut, and the fires dampened down. The sweet taste of dozens and dozens of cobs and loaves filled the shop; I licked the air, my tongue darting this way and that. Customers dropped their pennies on the counter, and the bread was wrapped in cloth or paper.

'Two of these.'

'Ha'penny.'

'A dozen buns.'

'That's a shilling...'

And so on. By late morning, I was asleep, propped against the cool brick wall, my floury thumb in my mouth.

Ma nudged me awake. 'Come on. Time to go.'

Grandma laughed. 'She can't hear you, so why do you talk to her?'

Ma wrapped a coat around my shoulders. Outside was brittle with the cold, nothing like the sweltering bakery.

'No reason not to, is there? She's not loopy, only blind and mute.' Ma hurried me out of the door. She had not lied. She'd merely omitted the truth. I could hear everything.

Day Twelve

T HE MAN IN THE DOCK was introduced to the jury as Mr Ben Cardwell, an independent auditor and chartered accountant.

Beryl's moan was appreciable; she was saying aloud what everyone else was thinking. Laura, even with her head for numbers, dispatched a sympathetic pout along the line of sluggish jurors. Beryl folded her arms across her chest and examined an old water stain on the ceiling, praying perhaps that the roof might leak and save them. How many auditors were needed to determine fraud? The evidence was there, as far as Laura was concerned, and it might be convoluted and difficult to frame, but the links were established: the money went out of the charity's accounts and into another's, then out again probably several times, and then there was the obvious lack of explanation for Brader's disinterest in Seeside beyond the money.

'Mr Cardwell,' the defence barrister told the jury members, 'has been given access to the evidence, and he will be providing an independent view of the records. You may consider him an expert witness, rather like a forensics or medical expert.'

Mr Waverly wasn't paying attention. He was whispering to somebody in his half of the court, a woman in a trouser suit who'd come into the court armed with a stack of papers and a stressed expression. The two of them were having a muted, slightly heated exchange.

Laura listened, which she still believed was key to the trial process, as Mr Cardwell provided a dry appraisal of why a pension top-up was affordable, as Mr Brader hadn't had one since he'd started working for the charity. The bonus he'd been awarded was in the trustees' powers to award, and the rules clearly stipulated it should only be paid if the funds were growing, which they had been doing. As for writing cheques to himself to cover cash payments, he agreed that it wasn't best practice, but there was no actual direct link that Mr Brader had used his personal account for receiving payments.

'From what I can see, all the work commissioned by the charity on their properties, the holiday homes and caravans, are well documented and corroborate Mr Brader's records.'

Mr Cardwell's hands were trembling. His body language seemed at odds with his carefully delivered statements. Every now and again, he glanced not at Brader or the defence lawyer, but the opposing barrister, who was now wading through documents, searching for something, it seemed.

The matter of the cheques was concluded, and Mr Calm turned his attention to the invoices. Laura was keen to know what Mr Cardwell thought of the excessive amount of invoicing that had occurred, especially in connection with a builder based in Lincolnshire.

Mr Calm, the defence lawyer, checked his notes. 'These invoices were issued to—'

'Your Honour.' Mr Waverly scrambled to his feet, clutching a document. 'I apologise for interrupting, but a matter of some importance as been brought to my attention by the prosecution clerk with regard to Mr Cardwell's independence. It may not serve the defence to continue questioning Mr Cardwell in light of these findings.'

The exasperated judge lowered his spectacles. 'An issue of disclosure, I assume?'

Mr Waverly's shoulders sagged a little. Mr Calm lost his calm exterior. The colour drained from Brader's face, and Mr Cardwell appeared relieved the questioning had ceased.

'Members of the jury, due to this unforeseen matter, I must ask you to leave while we discuss this.' The judge pointed his pen at the lawyers. 'Where is Mr Brader's solicitor?'

In the jury room, Brian rubbed his hands gleefully. 'A bit of drama, eh?'

Beryl slammed her handbag down on the table. 'I've had enough. I don't understand a thing. It's pointless going on when nothing makes sense.'

'I disagree,' Haden said. 'It all made sense until the defence started. And that's the point, isn't it? Throw a spanner in the works and tie us into knots. It's all about doubt.'

Haden leaned against the wall, his long legs crossed, his pose confident. He'd made up his mind, Laura realised. He had it clear in his head what Brader had done and he was sticking with the decision, and until they started deliberating, he had no plans to divulge anything, one way or the other. Maybe she had an ally, or a foe.

An hour later, they filed back into court. The judge, peering over the rim of his half-moon glasses, waited for them to settle.

'I'm going to ask you to set aside Mr Cardwell's expert opinion. Due to a late disclosure by the CPS – and this was not helped by the defence only being presented with their witness's report yesterday – the defence was unaware of a conflict of interest. Mr Cardwell cannot be considered independent, and you must strike any comments or notes you have relating to his evidence. We will move on after lunch.'

Number Six joined Laura in the jury area for lunch. He'd brought sandwiches. There were other jurors eating, but none from their court. For most, the need to escape, even if it meant trudging along icy pavements, was preferable to that room. The snow had laid down a gauze of white on the roads, which the cars had since trampled into slush, but the ice-sheathed pavements remained precariously frozen. Laura preferred the safety of the courthouse. She wasn't going to venture out onto the cobbles of Steep Hill, especially as she wasn't sure if somebody, or something, might follow her. Unwittingly, she carried a burden on top of everything else that came with a trial, and other than Sean, she had no means to shift the weight from her shoulders.

Laura had nothing to eat. She wasn't especially hungry; she anticipated eating a calorific gastro meal in the evening. Huge quantities of chips. Pubs weren't her thing, especially in the summer. She preferred a coffee shop with pastries and a reward card.

'Why do you think that happened?' Number Six asked, peeling the cellophane off his homemade sandwich.

She contemplated the question. Her theory was that the witness, expert or not, had some connection to another company that the charity had dealt with in the past.

Number Six finished chewing a mouthful. 'Perhaps Brader and the other guy know each other. They were taken by surprise by something.'

She thought that unlikely, but there had been a mutual reaction of some sort between witness and accused. The level of incompetence required by the defence to miss the obvious was unworthy, and doubtful, unless Cardwell had lied to Brader's solicitor, which was a very risky thing to do. Perjury was a serious offence. She offered a different appraisal.

'If that was the case, the defence wouldn't have used Cardwell in the first place. More likely, he's done some work for one of those companies Seeside use, and perhaps the parent company has a different name or he's worked for a different subsidiary, and it only came to light when the defence issued the report he'd compiled.'

'So, the prosecution forgot to mention the name of a company Seeside worked with, and bingo, there's a conflict of interest. Sounds tenuous.' He bit into his sandwich.

'That's the judge's decision. But now the defence has lost an expert witness, one who was happy to excuse the claims of fraud; so what else does Brader need to help prove his innocence?'

Number Six shrugged. 'A miracle.' He stared at her over the squished corner of his sandwich. He had hairy hands and no rings, but the nails today were immaculate. When he lowered his head, he revealed a perfect tonsure of baldness.

His reply was too harsh to ignore. It was time to overcome the embarrassment of asking. 'I never caught your name,' she said.

'Didn't you?' He looked perplexed. 'I don't suppose I've said it. Wasn't intentional, it's just… I used to have a generic title.'

She waited; he still hadn't said it, and he might be weighing up the reasons why.

'I'm Iain. MacDonald. I'm not Scottish. Grandparents were.'

'And the title?' she asked.

He lowered his sandwich, and his voice. 'Father.'

A priest. 'Used to have?'

He smiled. 'I can see that nothing much gets past you, Laura.'

She'd only offered up her name a couple of times, and it had stuck somewhere along the line. 'You've retired?'

'Do I seem that old? Heavens, I must be losing my looks.' He patted his cheeks playfully.

She laughed. 'You have a very nice face.'

He bowed his head. 'Thank you.' He sighed. 'I'm no longer a priest.'

She leaned over the low coffee table that bridged the gap between them. 'I'm so sorry. Getting defrocked—'

He chortled. 'Good grief. Not like that. No excommunication. I voluntarily handed in my dog collar.'

'And ring.' She pointed at his naked hand.

'Lowly priests don't wear ecclesiastical rings.'

'What went wrong?'

The skin paled behind his grey-flecked stubble. 'You don't mind asking awkward questions, do you?'

'No.' She never had and she thought the approach worked particularly well with men. Except her father, who'd slapped her across the face when she'd asked him why he was a cheating bastard.

He cocked his head at the room's occupants. 'If you don't mind, I'd rather not say. It's not a suitable environment for a confessional.'

She wondered why he'd picked that particular word. Criminals weren't allowed on jury service. 'I'm sorry. You're right, it's none of my business. Do you have a new occupation?'

'No, I'm like an actor. I'm resting.'

'How nice. I wish I was resting some days.'

'What do you do, when you're not here?' He was on the offensive now, and it was only fair to answer.

'I'm the assistant to the county council's finance controller. I do the leg work. My work experience is diverse.'

A smile spread across his face, a soft one that implied amusement at her predicament. She wished she'd conjured up a different job title. He quickly changed his expression when she didn't return the smile with one of her own.

'My turn to apologise. You don't want the others to know. I understand. It will probably come out once we start deliberating. You can hardly hide your experience.'

She sighed heavily. 'I know.'

'And?' He raised two heavy eyebrows as weary as hers.

'I don't think I can do it. Persuade them, that is.'

'Well, I do, Laura. I think if you speak up honestly, then they'll listen.' He checked his watch. 'I'm going to risk breaking my neck on the ice and go for a walk. Join me?'

She nearly went, but she had one non-date on her agenda, and a second one was too much to manage. 'No, thank you. I'll wait here. Where it's quiet and warm.'

A tongue clucked in disappointment. It wasn't his.

Laura looked over her shoulder and shivered at the empty corner of the room. She just wanted to be alone.

'Possession? You think you're possessed, is that it?' Sean shook out his napkin and draped it over his knee.

Laura's mouth opened and snapped shut. Had she implied mind control? It wasn't the intention of her self-deprecating comment. Possession wasn't so organised or kind, surely; her ears only heard, the dreams only saw, while her mind was free to think.

'No. I feel like somebody is directing me with their memories or dream-like memories. But, no, I'm not possessed.' She laughed half-heartedly.

'Of course you're not,' Sean said swiftly, a worried look on his usual hearty face. 'I wasn't suggesting it.'

She should stop the conversation there; batten down the hatches, as her mother liked to say, and enjoy the dining experience. She inspected the glossy menu of the popular pub. Nearly every table in The Pie was occupied. Fortunately, the music was unobtrusive, and the diners weren't packed together like sardines. She was okay.

Sean lowered his menu after a cursory glance. 'I'll have the fish pie and chips.'

'You like fish quite a bit.' She ran her finger along the options, ticking off the possibilities. She was famished, and even things that normally didn't tempt her were worth considering.

'I don't get it much at home. Fish stinks the place out. So, yeah, I do go for it if it's on a menu.'

He'd ordered a bottle of beer, and while she dithered, he poured it into the pint glass. He waited patiently.

She sipped on her sparkling water. 'I'll have... the... Hunters Chicken. With chips.'

Sean intercepted a passing waiter, and the order was registered.

'Hopefully not too long,' he said, toying with his cutlery. 'You were saying that you've been having different dreams.'

She settled back in her chair. Sean had a white moustache from the froth on his beer. She pointed at her top lip, and he followed her directions, chortled, and wiped his mouth with the napkin. She noted his comfortable laughter. Neither of them wanted to crush the impetus of their friendship with pessimism. Again, she wondered if likeability was a genuine thing. The nuances of humanity depicted in the trial were facilitating her perception of Sean's demonstrable niceness. An unexpected benefit.

She lowered her glass. 'Yes, it's becoming episodic.'

'And you're not in the cell, but a room?'

'Yes.' Sparsely furnished and undecorated, but not a cell. No pictures, just a threadbare rug, which she'd sat upon. 'There aren't any bars on the windows. The door isn't locked. I feel small. Forgotten.'

'And the woman?'

'No. I can't see her. I can't see much actually, just these little blocks on the rug. Tiny, almost too small to pick up.'

The background music transitioned, leaving his voice exposed and loud in its musing. 'Interesting.'

Was it? What would Sean be doing if he wasn't dining out with her? The very thing she'd be doing: eating food off a lap-tray, alone in front of the television. The thought was comforting. Familiarity should be built on commonality. She wasn't averse to changes in routine, but life was easier when it moved seamlessly from one day to the next, avoiding the unforeseen. It made her an odd choice for a haunting.

The gentle interrogation continued. 'And a doll, you said?'

'Stuffed with straw. Old.' The doll had been held many times and needed repairing. It rested on the girl's lap. 'I'm... She's wearing a pinafore dress.' Which reminded her of infant school and sitting in assemblies while the big people talked using grand words and kept hushing the smallest children whenever they piped up with silly noises. Nobody was hushing her in the dream. Why was she, the girl, silent?

'Actually, thinking about it, you're the one possessing somebody else. Aren't you inside her? What else do you see?'

'I don't see the braille or sheets of paper,' Laura said. 'Can we skip over the possession thing. It's not what I'm feeling.'

He blushed and muttered an apology. 'So, whoever this is... the memories you're borrowing—'

'Oh, I like that. Borrowed memories, yes—'

'They belong to this person; a child, and she's lent them out. What do you think?'

'I've not a clue. But the noises I'm hearing around the castle, the little child's voice, she's the one in the dream, I'm sure of it.' Laura's palms were clammy. 'I'm quite aware this is all very odd, and you're been very kind listening to me.'

Sean's blush deepened. 'I've never met anyone like you, Laura. So open and honest—'

'Open?' She had to think for a second how to take that. 'Everyone who knows me thinks I'm difficult because I either say the wrong thing or don't say the things they want me to.' They sniggered sometimes at her answers or frowned. Neither exactly positive responses.

'That's not what I'm thinking. I meant open, as in approachable. Charmed, too, as if filled with something special. Magical.'

She crushed her hands around her napkin. The Pie was hot, the tables now were too close together, and she wasn't sure she liked the music; it lacked a melody. She swallowed a mouthful of icy water.

'Is that why I'm... haunted?' she asked quietly. 'It only happens when I'm near the castle. At home, nothing.' She corrected herself with a small shrug. 'Except the dreams.'

'And when we sleep, we are at our most receptive. Vulnerable.'

The frisson of a shiver moved down her spine. He held up his palm. 'Sorry, I didn't mean to scare you.'

'I'm not scared,' she said indignantly.

'You've gone a little pale.'

She touched a cheek. 'I feel damn hot.'

He covered his mouth with his napkin as if to mop his lips again. But he wasn't quick enough; she caught sight of the whimsical smile.

'Are you laughing at me?' It would be disappointing if she was misjudging him.

'No, sorry. You seem so cool, then say you're hot... never mind.' He sat back.

A large plate arrived on his place mat. The pie steamed, misting up his glasses. He removed them and dried the lenses with his napkin, rubbing briskly, perhaps a little embarrassed by the silly remark about body temperature – abruptly she understood the undertone rippling beneath it. Had his wife not liked his little mannerisms, the way he picked up on subtle expressions? Laura appreciated perceptiveness. Anyway she shoved his diversionary comment to the back of her mind; it wasn't appropriate with Marco still... what?

'It's just... it must be unpleasant having these recurring dreams,' he said.

It was best to keep the subject from wandering again, for both their sakes. 'It's disconcerting, especially as I seemed to be,' the word he used stuck, 'opening up during the day. I went for a walk in the snow yesterday evening, quite why I don't know. Everyone else was heading home.'

The chicken breast was smothered in a sticky BBQ sauce. She teased the bacon off it, setting it to one side. The cheese was too hot to eat. She nibbled on a chip, a crispy thick-cut one.

'It snowed quite heavily for a bit,' Sean said. 'I was stuck in traffic.' He put his glasses back on. They perched on the bridge of his nose, and as he leaned forward over his plate, they slid down.

'You should try contact lenses.'

'I did. I kept losing them. I'm not very good with little things. Big fingers.' He waved one of his hands. The fingers came with broad knuckles and a multitude of creases in his palm. An old hand on a young man. Did it imply wisdom, too?

'So you went for a walk; brave of you,' he said.

'I was followed. Then led by someone. One or two possibly. I heard them walking right next to me. But nobody was there. No footprints in the snow. I ended up outside this café, rather dingy inside. It was once a bakery. I could smell,' she paused to remember the wondrous aroma, 'fresh bread.'

'Good smell.'

'Except, according to the lady who served me, they hadn't baked bread there for decades. I was the only customer. I think she was about to close the shop, and I turned up.'

'A bakery?'

'You could see into the back room where the ovens would have been in the brick walls. Quaint. Shabby.' She frowned. 'Do you think it's possible to find out more about the place?' She told him the name of street.

'I've never been down there. Never knew there was a café.'

'It could do with better signage.' And friendlier staff.

'Yet, you were summoned there.'

'Taken there. I am possessed, after all.' The sigh was heavy, and unintended. She wasn't good company.

He shook his head gently. 'Don't think that.'

Her lower lip trembled. The chicken was still a slab on her plate, the sauce too heavy for her stomach. She wished she'd had the lasagne; Marco made lasagne with fresh pasta layers and a homemade tomato sauce. It took him hours, but it was worth it. She closed her eyes, angry at the intrusion.

'Laura?' Sean said.

She blinked. 'Sorry. I'm thinking about somebody.'

'A friend?'

'Yes. He's abroad. I don't know if he's coming back. I started out missing him, needing him. Now, I'm not sure.'

'Must be very confusing for you. If I'm making you uncomfortable, I could—'

'No,' Laura said firmly. The no-date policy was entirely of her making. She wasn't going to ruin things with Sean by implying she had no control over her own affairs. 'It's not like that. Not anymore.'

The words stung, saying them hurt. Why couldn't she live with guilt? What was it that forced her to hold on to the emotion, carry it with her wherever she went, then unload it onto somebody else? A disastrously bad habit.

Sweating slightly, and obviously enjoying himself, Sean had eaten most of his fish pie between sporadic words and sips of his beer. He demolished food with a relish that she envied. She was too fussy and easily distracted. What did he like about her then? Perhaps the obvious: they were both unabashed by their mutual curiosity in each other.

He waited for her to catch up before broaching another subject. 'How's the court case going?'

Yes, mutually inquisitive, and the deflection from dreams was also welcome. Unfortunately, the topic was self-limiting.

'The defence is presenting character witnesses, work colleagues from previous jobs, that sort of thing.' A portrait of insipid flattery that lacked much evidential substance. The prosecution showed little interest in cross-examining, preferring to push on. 'Hopefully we'll be sent out by the end of the week. I sense there may be trouble ahead—'

'*But while there's music*,' he sang back, then stopped. 'Excuse me. I used to sing in a church choir.'

There was still much about him that was unknown. As much as she didn't know about Marco, really. 'That's not a church hymn.'

'No.' He grinned. 'I like Frank Sinatra. The church was my mother's idea for keeping me on the straight and narrow path.'

She couldn't picture Sean on a bendy one. He was too comfortable in himself to be a rebel.

'I wasn't always this nice,' he said, picking up on her silence. 'Terribly bad mannered at the dinner table. Then, I was always running away from home—'

'To where?' Had he a beach, too? Somewhere that he went when things got bad?

'The sweet shop.' The smile broadened. 'Weren't you a troublemaker sometimes?'

'Yes,' she said simply. 'But not on purpose. It happens to me by accident.' The word cut across her tongue. She brought her knife and fork together. 'That's me done.'

She insisted on paying using the cash she'd taken out of her small savings account.

'Oh, I forgot to say,' Sean said, fishing a few coins out of his pocket for a tip. 'The braille, you're still interested in it? I found out there's this little museum in Gainsborough. A private collection of braille publications and printing stuff, right from when it first appeared.' He nervously scrunched his soiled napkin into a ball. 'I wondered if you'd like to visit. We could go on Sunday?'

Marco might turn up on Sunday.

Damn Marco.

'Yes. I'd love to join you. I'm not sure what I'm looking for…' She shrugged. 'It will be fun getting out.'

'Excellent. I'll pick you up at eleven?' He raised an eyebrow.

It meant giving him her address, which was fine. Nothing was going to happen. They hadn't even kissed. Or held hands.

Talking

I SCREAMED IN THE NIGHT, hoping it might stop him. I screamed too loud. She called to me, her words reaching across the bedroom to where I was huddled under a heap of scratchy blankets.

'Shut up,' William said. 'She can't hear you. Why do you bother?'

But my cries stopped him. I used those noises to protect her until Father threw me out of the bedroom.

Ma gathered me to her soft chest. 'She's still a baby.'

At six years old, I was not a baby in spirit or mind, only helpless in body, still depended on somebody dressing and bathing me, preparing my food. Bringing a new object into the house was a risky adventure if I undertook to explore it on my own. I needed a safe space.

'She can sleep in the attic,' he said, amused.

James laughed, too. He had finished school and gone to work at the printer's as an apprentice. He always had his own room.

'The attic! Bill, we have the other room upstairs—'

'The attic,' he said firmly.

I was shoved up the ladder with his big hands around my waist. I hit my head on a beam and whimpered.

'She's too tall,' Ma said. 'Please. Don't.'

Terrified of the emptiness and the rain hammering on the roof, I wept inconsolably. James called me horrible names. The more I cried, the louder James shouted up the hole.

'Oh, damn the lot of you. Have your way. Move her bed into the other room.' Father stomped downstairs.

Ma helped me down, guiding my foot from one rung to the next. She wiped away my tears and sighed heavily. She dragged my truckle bed into the corner of my new bedroom – the smallest in the house and never used for much other than storing typesetting blocks, trays of them taken from the old printer's. Father had hoarded them for some unknown purpose. When he sorted the letters, ordered or arranged them in the trays, he was easier, less ferocious in his anger. The inky blocks of letters calmed his mind.

'There's your pail,' Ma said. 'The jug of water, the soap and towel.'

She held my hand, and I touched each object in turn.

James practised his father's snort. 'Don't know why you talk to her.'

Ma squeezed my fingers. 'No harm in it.'

I reached up and found my mother's face. I traced her lips round and round with the tip of my finger. I wanted to speak. I was tired of silence.

People sing in church, and sometimes on the streets. The women in the bakery sing as they knead the dough. I tried to copy them, quietly. (*Sotto voce.* The Latin phrase is perfect and exactly how I spoke for years). Alone in my bedroom, I hummed and waggled my tongue around my mouth.

'La-la.'

I flicked my teeth with the tip.

'Ta-ta.'

Father only ever heard my grunts, moans, and squawks. I made sure he had no inkling of my secret sounds. Even Ma was not party to them. Because she was forbidden to leave his bed to check on me, I had the opportunity to whisper to myself, have my own private conversations with my straw doll, Betty. The other night time noises were dimmer but the same in nature. The thumps and crashes reached my ears, but not her whimpers or sad, lonely sighs nor his rumbling snores that once kept me awake. Those things stayed in their bedroom. I was spared them. However, I slept badly still, knowing she was unhappy.

I wanted to tell Grandma what I heard but dared not. Being blind is a misfortune, deaf a doubling of disability, but mute is a suitable occupation for a young child. I was not expected to speak, especially to grown-ups, who knew better than me. By not talking, maintaining the illusion that I was born totally incapacitated, I kept a part of me back from those worldly adults who invariably know so little of the world. I decided that only somebody special would be permitted to hear my words. I waited for them in the hope that they would listen and understand my fears.

Sometimes, in hindsight, I regret my simple logic. Perhaps if I had spoken up and warned Grandma, she might have intervened on Bronte's behalf. However, that optimism was rightly unfounded. For when Bronte needed her mother and aunts, they did not come to her aid. They stayed away and abandoned both of us. The shame was too much for them. So, if I had spoken, used my ill-formed words, then Grandma probably would not have believed them. For how could I, a dumb girl with no sight, hear those things and yet choose to live in silence? I was not to be trusted.

As the years progressed beyond my infancy, I was left for long hours alone in my bedroom. Ma considered the room safer than by the kitchen hearth. Father preferred that I was out of his sight. James occasionally entered, kicked me or poured water over my head, then giggling at his cowardly bullying, left me be.

I explored every nook of that room. I learnt the location of the cracks in the walls, the loose threads in the rug, where the mouse ran in and out, and how to unlock the chest of drawers. Father left the key in the top lock. After turning it, I opened each drawer and ran my hand along the letter sets. The familiar curves and lines of the chalk patterns returned to my fingertips. I traced each typeset, recalling the sounds Ma made when I drew them.

I had insufficient information for reading or constructing proper words, however, I was able to make up my own form of writing using combinations of letters. Alone, and happier there than in the scorching heat of the bakery, I arranged the blocks on the floor and wrote things, my sounds, and nobody else's. I giggled, softly, so only Betty and the mouse could hear. Ma, exhausted by work and housekeeping, had less time for tutoring me. James spent longer hours at the printer's or drinking beer with his friends in the taverns of Lincoln. Even Father forgot his metal blocks. He was troubled by the establishment of a new printworks with modern machines. The competition was fierce. His income declined dramatically.

Ma took to praying on her knees.

Day Thirteen

Thursday

'GO AWAY. I CAN'T DO THIS. I'm not the person to help you.'

Laura pressed her palms against the gnarled bark of the yew tree. She spoke softly, clearly, and out loud. She waited, alone, breathing rapidly, wondering if there'd be a response of some kind: a hiss or grunt. Maybe, she hoped, the gravestone would resurrect itself and rise from the dirt. If melodrama was necessary, she'd use it. However, there was nothing to see or hear. The dank air was still; the walled enclave quiet. Her message to the underworld had, unsurprisingly, fallen among the dead leaves.

She sighed with a hollow chuckle thrown into the exhale. Hugging a tree was a somewhat ridiculous morning exercise, the kind born out of desperation, the willingness to try anything that was a detour from the path to the equally cold courthouse. She'd arrived promptly at the museum's door at ten o'clock, surprised the woman on the desk with a flash of the crumpled season ticket, then she'd dashed off to Lucy Tower.

The dirty snow had melted from the streets but left a patchwork of white spots here and there where the warm tendrils of the sun had failed to reach. Winter's false start had ended prematurely. However, in the enclosed Lucy Tower, the frosty grass was lily-white and scrunched under her feet, and at the base of the walls, the brittle snow lay determined, the flakes twinkling in the frail light. The headstones stood boldly, as they had done for over a century, and as many winters had come and gone, the markers had continued to watch over the unhallowed ground and the tortured souls buried below the feet of the careless visitors.

Talking to a tree, the proxy she'd identified as the conduit, was an act of futility. But she hoped that by relaying her message, she'd feel more in control of her despair, which was the main purpose of her visit. The previous night's dream had scared her. She'd skipped breakfast, her appetite wasted on muddled thoughts, which left her burdened with wrongness in every muscle and joint, similar to a fever of body and mind.

'Please leave me be,' she whispered, the tip of her nose tickled by the bark. She stepped back from the silent tree and turned to discover she wasn't alone in the tower. She'd hoped to avoid sharing her uneasy private tree conversation; it was why she'd beaten a fast track to the graveyard.

Under the shadow of the wall, wearing a bulky jacket and a woolly hat pulled down over his ears, he emerged and waved. 'Sorry, didn't mean to startle you. I thought I might find you here.'

She walked towards him, weaving between the graves. 'How could you possibly know to find me here? Did you see me arrive?'

He shook his head, and the nutmeg strands sprinkled dewdrops onto his shoulders. He, too, had come straight to the walls. 'Just a hunch. This place calls to you, like a siren.'

'And you?' What supernatural intuition had brought him to her side? Had he come to the Lucy Tower because in secret he was hoping for some vicarious adventure?

Sean pushed his hat back, revealing pensive lines in his generous forehead. 'I'm not following you, if you think I'm a stalker.'

'No,' she said. 'I've one of those already.'

The elastic creases on his forehead vanished. 'Sorry. That's an unkind reminder.'

The frost creaked under her boots. 'I haven't much time. I'm supposed to be in the courthouse for a ten-thirty start.'

He held out his arm. 'Come on then, I'll walk back with you.'

'A siren,' she said, musing on his choice of word. 'I'm not feeling the poetic call of a seduction, more like a harbinger of fate. Something terrible happened to somebody buried here, and it's making me feel anxious.'

'The nightmares are back?' He touched her sleeve briefly, then dropped his arm. 'Careful of the steps, they're slippery.'

'The fear is. Last night I was somewhere dark, no windows, and crouched, as if I was in a box. I thought I was in a coffin underground.' She – the child – had scrambled around in that nasty place, hunting for a way out, and only when she'd stilled to catch her breath had Laura heard it: somebody was sobbing; it echoed in the confined space. But whose voice? Dreamscapes were fraught places to analyse, awake or asleep.

'I was trapped there, couldn't get out. I woke up screaming and covered in sweat. It was horrible.' She held the icy railing, and her hands renewed their trembling.

Sean waited at the bottom of the steps. 'Is that why you came here today?'

'I thought… everything started here, so maybe it will end here, too.' The idea had come to her on the bus.

'You don't want to find out who's buried in the grave? Or about the braille?' He wasn't wearing his glasses. His eyes were clear, an opalescent combination of colours that searched her face for clues. It was a pity the reflection of his glasses normally hid those fetching irises.

What could she offer him in return? It had to be more than mutual likeability and rudimentary appeal. She'd be the first to acknowledge she was hardly a masterpiece of femininity (angular elbows and knees, iron-flat hair, freckles – mirrors never accentuated the positives); she easily burdened herself with many faults.

The admission of defeat stung him; his lips dropped into a crestfallen frown, a charmingly boyish one, too. She understood why, but exploiting a tenuous mystery was only going to lead to disappointment for both of them. She wasn't free to extend her investigations beyond the length of the court case, and that was close to ending.

She walked along the wall; the crenulations provided them with a stuttering shelter from the gentle breeze. He kept pace with her, loping slightly from side to side, kicking up the frost-free grit with his hefty boots.

She glanced across to the murk of the city horizon. 'I don't think it's a good idea anymore. I'm making this happen to me.'

Even with his hunched shoulders, he was still taller than her by several inches; a bear of a man compared to Marco, although Sean wasn't heavy or overweight, the bulk was evenly distributed. Marco was a tidy package – perhaps too contained. They were nearly at the end of the section of the wall; exiting meant walking through the observatory tower. She'd paid little attention to the exhibits on the way through.

Inside the building, he stopped her with another subtle touch of his hand on her swaying arm. 'Mysteries have to be solved, like your court case. Whether you believe or not isn't the issue. It's not about blind faith. It's trusting the facts, and there are facts out there. I'm sure of it.'

Blind faith in people was a well-practised discomfort, and under normal circumstances she'd agree with him. After all, he was a historian interpreting the past through the records of those who'd lived and breathed once upon time, and she preferred the absolute clarity of numbers in columns. Both relied on facts.

'I'm using my instincts, though,' she said awkwardly. Circumstances were far from normal. 'Sorry, I'm going to be late.'

She hurried away from the curtain wall, but instead of diverging, they remained side by side. Sean was persistent.

'So, let's go back to the evidence, and don't let the ghostly stuff bother you. The archive on Saturday, this museum in Gainsborough on Sunday. If there's something to find, then let's find it.'

His dismissal of her "stuff" wasn't helpful. 'Will those trips really resolve my dreams, or the memories that I'm borrowing, as you put it?'

The quirky smile was soft and brief. 'Somebody wants a resolution,' he said seriously. 'In court, they tell you a story, yeah? A sequence of events, and you have to decide if they actually happened. This is no different. I think you're experiencing something similar. The prison, the grounds, were the start because, as you said, that's where you feel a presence strongly. But bear in mind the chapel, what you felt there, has been experienced by others. Give yourself some credit; only you have pieced things together.'

She guffawed. 'Have I? I'm not sure I know what's going on; it's not a story I understand. We haven't proved anything – the hanging, the missing grave, the braille. What's she trying to tell me? The child? The woman? The pair of them, perhaps? What's the point of it all?'

He snapped his back straighter and tried to push up the invisible glasses then remembered they weren't there, so he scratched his wrinkled nose. His cheeks were flushed and, even with his longer strides, he was breathless and as agitated as her, but in a different way.

'The braille is the story,' he said. 'We have to find that document, the one shredded on the floor of the cell. I think it's real, like a message from the past. Something tangible and discoverable.'

She admired his optimism. 'You think that's possible, don't you?'

'I'm that kind of guy. Even after the divorce, I wasn't going to give up. Last night, Maisie and I had a really good chat. She's coming up for Christmas. She wants to spend time with me.'

The flush glowed, brimming with enthusiasm; she'd mistaken it for embarrassment. Laura realised his excitement wasn't entirely due to her but had been born out of that conversation with his daughter. He had another life, and so did Laura, and it might be on hold, but it was waiting for her attention. Everything that had occurred over the last fortnight was an interlude. But he was right. They had to follow the clues, and while she was stuck in court and preparing herself for the gruelling spell in the jury room, she would give Sean the opportunity to prove that her strange instincts might be founded on facts. She wasn't crazy, but she had come to rely on blind faith too much in recent weeks. What Sean couldn't possibly know was that diminishing faith had nothing to do with ghosts or dreams, but the slow decline of a relationship that she'd created out of a need constructed for a selfish purpose. But although it was crumbling, she couldn't contemplate the final throes of losing Marco, especially as he wasn't there to explain himself.

A group of schoolchildren in fluorescent-yellow jackets trooped past them in a column of pairs. They held hands and squealed, laughed and chatted loudly. Sean turned his back on the teachers escorting them and grimaced.

'Loads of schools visiting over the next couple of days. I won't be able to meet you for lunch. Sorry. It's all hands on deck. I'm going to get them to dress up as prisoners and try and teach them about segregation.'

He'd assumed lunch was a given.

Thinking about it, so had she. 'That's a pity,' she said with genuine disappointment.

'So, I'll meet you at ten on Saturday at the archive? Yeah? Beat the doors down. I've a plan of action.' He tapped his temple.

Laura smiled. His kind enthusiasm was infectious. The fear she'd woken up with was abating. Nobody was actually harming her and, frankly, and against her better judgement, she remained intrigued. A real-life document, something written in braille, might be plausible. Why, she couldn't fathom. Logic wasn't featuring heavily in her dreams, and that being the case, she had to keep the trial segregated in her mind, to ensure Brader received a fair appraisal.

'Good. I'm relying on you to have one.' She glanced at her watch. 'Oh, drat. I'm going to be late.'

She set off at a brisk pace, forgetting to say goodbye, and only when she was outside the courthouse on the far side of the expansive bailey did she reconsider her precipitous departure. She pivoted and squinted in the low sunlight. Sean was chatting to one of the teachers lining the children up outside the prison.

He spotted her, raised his arm, and waved vigorously, nearly walloping the teacher.

Laura laughed. The relief at his acknowledgement almost brought tears to her eyes. Amazed and embarrassed by it, she charged into the toilets and rescued her flushed face with a splash of water.

When Craig Brader moved over to the witness box, he was tracked by a dozen pair of eyes belonging to a jury of keen listeners. For the occasion he'd chosen an elegant slate suit with a black tie and an ivory shirt. His hair was swept across his crown where pink scalp met grey roots. Middle-age had probably crept upon him, loosening the flesh under his chin and eyes, and stretching his waistband. However, he wasn't pensionable. A man in his forties had plenty of life ahead of him. He reminded Laura of Michael, who was reliably managerial and existed on a diet of bullet points and snappy decisions.

The oath reverberated around the court, a baritone, deep-seated but not booming, and articulated without a slip of the tongue unlike many of the witnesses who had stumbled through the wording. If he was nervous, it wasn't evident in his voice. It would serve him well. She could imagine it charming somebody on the end of the phone or at a charity fundraiser. Compared to his usual hunched position in the dock, Brader had taken heed of somebody's advice, probably Mr Calm, and given some thought to his appearance, and perhaps his confidence was increasing. He might have lost the support of Mr Cardwell, and suffered a little under his sister-in-law's warbling chatter, but he had benefited from other less garrulous friends. Those who had given evidence the previous day now sat opposite the jury in the public gallery.

Laura ignored them; her focus was on Brader. She'd composed a list of priorities, especially things that were too vague, and she assumed that the defence would resolve those weakest charges first, saving the more controversial ones for later. If things went Brader's way, by lunchtime, a few of the indictments wouldn't survive any further scrutiny. She'd placed those, including the pensions and bonuses, into one column. Nobody on the jury was likely to argue those benefits infringed the charity's rules, and although excessively generous, they were achievable for an honest person.

And what makes a person honest? Until recently, she'd thought she knew the answer to that question.

Mr Calm was meticulously going through the charges, one by one, and asking Brader if he had committed the offences. The replies were forthright, verging on the aggressive. Brader was rightly angry, and the bitterness was conveyed in his every denial.

'Did you write cheques to yourself for the sole purpose of raising cash for yourself?'

Brader screwed his hands into white-knuckle clasps. 'No. I refute that. I always used the money to make payments. In any case, they were small amounts. It was an inconvenience for me to cash those cheques—'

'Yes.' Mr Calm keenly halted Brader's divergence. 'Moving on to the invoices for the print designs and brochures. Did you take a cut of the money paid to these printers in return for tendering them the business?'

'Again, no,' Brader said, exasperated. 'The printing company refute this, too.'

The printers had not been called as witnesses for the defence. No comment was made on this, she noted.

The weakest of the charges laid against him related to events that had happened eight years ago, and Brader had left hardly any paper trail connecting him to the printers. The threads of guilt were thin and snapping under pressure. What the defence had managed to do was throw doubt on all the little transactions, things that were small in amount but added up over time. And, according to the prosecution, Mr Brader had been up to no good for years, carefully spreading out his wrongdoings to avoid detection. Heaping them together had been the prosecution's approach, and Laura had thought it was a good one. Now, she wasn't so sure. She reevaluated her list. The leftovers were significant in their seriousness but amounted to fewer instances.

The confident replies continued as the details were dissected. Mr Waverly for once had a pensive expression. Far from crumbling in the box, Brader seemed at ease with his performance. He rambled, perhaps excessively, by expanding on answers, which forced his barrister to intercede to stop him losing track of the original question. The defence lawyer's eyebrows knotted each time Brader inflated his responses with unnecessary information. His star in the box was enjoying the role of the denier too much.

Mr Calm was decidedly not calm.

Iain stirred. He leaned forward, gazing intently at Brader. As a priest, he'd heard the confessions of many worried souls hoping for forgiveness. Laura wondered how he interpreted the repeated denials of Brader and his slightly sanctimonious tone. Brader frequently reminded the jury that he had not been under suspicion until the auditor's report. Somebody had stitched him up and set the wheels in motion. He provided no explanation as to why he was facing so many charges, when any one of them on their own might have resulted in him losing his job, which had finally happened when the police had charged him. But Laura couldn't remember who had fired Brader. It wasn't Steven Feydon, who'd seemed at a loss to explain why his friend was in the dock.

Laura was itching for the cross-examination. Mr Waverly was, too; he was writing copious notes.

The jury's pendulum of indecision was likely swinging the verdict from guilt to innocence, and she could understand why. Brader's fervent denials fractured what was once concrete evidence. Facts were splintering into plausible excuses. However, Laura detected exasperation with the line of questioning, not desperation. He needed to lose the arrogance and gain something else — sympathy for the charity's good name, or was that gone along with his loyalty? She wasn't expecting pleading or anguished tears, but he portrayed too much bravado.

The judge called a halt. He lay down his pen and asked for them to return promptly at one-thirty for more testimony from Brader; the defence was determined to hear out every denial of wrongdoing.

Laura scrawled a quick couplet on her notes. Iain caught a glimpse of it and smiled in agreement. She had one ally on the jury.

The text from Sean arrived a little before six o'clock, after she'd emerged from the shower and decided on a cheese toastie.

I've requested access to maps and newspaper archives on Saturday. Hope you had a good day. Sean

She prepared several slices of cheese then answered. She nearly wrote *missed you at lunch* but decided that was inappropriate for the level of their friendship.

Busy listening to key witness. Things progressing. Survived yours?

He sent a laughing face.

Just. Ears still ringing from schoolkids. Good for museum. Too quiet some days.

Which, given the building's history of enforced segregation, was unsurprising. She tapped her thumb on the keyboard, then hesitated before hitting send. What the heck, she thought. It's only a text.

Looking forward to Saturday.

There, she'd sent it.

Me, too. I'm sure we'll find something to solve your mystery.

Ever the optimist. The toaster flashed, and she tipped the hot sandwich out onto a plate. What was he doing? Eating? Watching the telly? She wanted a mental picture.

What are you doing?

There was a lengthy pause.

Sorry. Mum called. We chat most days for a few minutes.

What was it about sons and mothers? Marco had chatted to his mother regularly, initiating his calls with an air of filial resignation. Was he driven by respect for his mother or encumbered by duty? Laura wasn't sure if there was a difference. It wasn't unusual for him to pace around the house while he talked, his lyrical tone rising and falling, the Italian incomprehensible to Laura. She picked up on the nature of those calls by referring to his body language. They spoke in rapid-fire exchanges, and he generally waved his arms around when his mother's voice lifted in volume or impatience. Laura detected a streak of melancholy in some elements of what was said. Occasionally, he'd been very still, almost akin to a mausoleum's statue. Marco had rarely relayed the topics of conversations, and Laura could never fathom if they left him happy or sad, or simply homesick.

Sean, on the other hand, gave her a quick summary of his conversation with his mother in an entertaining text. She'd had a run-in with a bolshie neighbour; his mother had won the dispute, and the neighbour had skedaddled back home with "his tail between his legs".

Laura, though, was at a loss at what to say. She had nothing from her repertoire of family anecdotes to compare. Her mother wasn't a comedian with witty ripostes. Laura relied on Margery for the preposterous stories, which Laura assumed were embroidered to impress. Maybe she'd been unfair in her judgement. Margery had only been trying to bridge the chasm, and Laura, in retrospect, treated her attempts as derisory.

She left the dirty plate in the washing-up bowl.

Half an hour had passed, and the message thread was still there, spun out between them. It was increasingly obvious why there was reticence on her part. Moving things forward required Laura to acknowledge that Sean was demonstrating the behaviour of a boyfriend, and more so than her current one.

She picked up her phone and composed a new text, but not to Sean.

Are you still coming home next week?

By the time she was in her pyjamas, she'd given up on receiving a reply, and instead she sent a message to Sean.

Goodnight.

The same featureless room with shuttered windows and stale air laden with misery and argumentative birds who scuffled on the outside windowsill. Surrounding the same figure, and arranged in lines, were the blocks. In a blurry dreamscape, where nothing is in focus, the clues are devious. Something was embossed on each cuboid; tiny raised marks that weren't visible. The girl felt them, one at a time, noting some were the same, others were different. A pedantic task conducted effortlessly. All the time, she listened and waited.

Somebody tapped her shoulder—

Laura kicked off the duvet, sat bolt upright, and clutched her chest. Pounding heartbeats climbed higher into her tight throat, and she strangled an embryonic cry. Other than a sense of foreboding, the dream gave her nothing. The girl with her straw doll and tiny blocks was biding her time, and so must Laura. She'd take a leaf out of Sean's book of optimism: everything happening to her, all the separate strands that had chosen those few weeks of her life to tangle themselves into a tortured knot, would resolve themselves.

Praying

1870

WILLIAM RARELY LET BRONTE out of his sight on Sundays. When he did excuse himself elsewhere, often with James, my mother strapped a bonnet on my head and took me to the cathedral on the hill. The most regular visits occurred the year I reached the height of Bronte's bony shoulders. My own lanky legs propelled me along, keeping pace with her, and the grasp of her hand was unyielding, especially when we mingled with the crowd gathered in the nave.

The great church introduced to me a wealth of new sounds, including formal music. My first excursion was almost too much to bear. The echoes of stout shoes on stone floors, the boom of the organ pipes, and the crescendo of voices raised in praise, intimidated and overwhelmed me, and I couldn't picture my surroundings. Accustomed to confined spaces, I had no means to imagine a cathedral's construction or purpose. Aware of my reluctance to visit, Ma tried a different approach the next time. We walked by the rough-hewn walls, from west to east, then back to the transept, and she described the scale of the building – how many houses might fit into its nave, the trunks of columns, the expanse of glittering stained glass, enough to cover the width of the street outside our house. I stroked the carved hooked noses on the ancient tombs of forgotten bishops and knelt on the cold brass memorials, tracing my fingers along the etched letters.

Coaxed by Ma, I reached the choir and finally embraced the vibrations of those vast pipes and the pure tones of the boys' singing. The words were meaningless and archaic, but the harmonies of man and boy, bass and soprano, shrank the imposing chasm to a level of intimacy I had not thought possible. The congregation's responses were mumbled until the dean's sonorous call for prayers cut through the throng waiting for their slip of bread and taste of wine. The organ fell silent.

In those moments, I felt calm, and sad, for Mother said her prayers aloud and spoke of her regrets.

'Lord, forgive my humbleness, my improper ways,' she said, her body lowered onto her knees. She dragged me down beside her, so that only I could hear her strained whispers.

'I pray for my husband, William, that I may find in him a kinder man, one who has the strength to love and be loved.' She sniffed. 'I do confess I was blinded. For my passion was not for him, but his appearance and his occupation, and the wish that he might find words to print that would cure a callous heart. Perhaps, Lord, you might find a way to help him.'

She spoke for my benefit, of that I am now sure. For what use was it to pray to God for something that was impossible? William never would print those books, the tales of romance that Bronte loved. He sold bitterness, the fliers and pamphlets of politicians, magistrates and troublemakers. He preferred posters that sold goods or notices that warned of penalties if laws were broken. As a child, Bronte had wished for leather-bound books and poetry, not sticky dough and sweltering ovens, and after marrying William, her request was met with a snort of laughter. "Books don't make money."

Each visit ended the same way. Herding me to a quieter spot, away from the departing congregation, who seemed content to sing hymns and then chatter about inconsequential things with each other, my mother chose one of the side chapels offered for those in need of quiet contemplation. It suited us both.

There were candles, unscented, thin and made from the cheapest tallow. We had a penny between us to light one. I held the lit taper, the warmth of it brushing against my fingertips, and she presented the wick to it. Holding my hand, she guided the candle onto its holder and wiped the trickles of wax off my sleeve. We knelt, side by side, on a long cushion of worn stitches, and she spread out my fingers, reminding me how to press my palms together and hold them thus, by my nose, and shut my eyes, as if my broken irises were an affront to God.

The prayer was always the same.

'Dear God and Lord Jesus,' Ma said in a tremulous voice, 'look after my daughter and give her sight, so that one day she might look upon this great sanctuary of yours and know you better and be a good servant to thee. Amen.'

My prayer was never said aloud; instead it remains bound to my heart.

Dear Lord, pray for my mother. Give her the courage to leave him and live a long and happy life. Amen.

My heart breaks when I think of that prayer now.

On our last visit – for William, of course, discovered the nature of our absences and banned Ma since she was too sinful to be in such a hallowed place – I was braver and let go of my mother's hand. Somewhere between the pillars, I bumped into a figure of heavy cloth and smothered candle scent.

'Child, are you alone?' he asked without rancour.

I backed off, hunting for my mother's skirts with an outstretched palm.

Bronte took my hand. 'Forgive her, Father, she can't see.'

'Our Lord healed the blind, did he not?' He breathed softly and level with my face. 'Keep up with your prayers.'

'She has no speech either.'

'Ah, a great pity for her. For she has a remarkable countenance, a sharpness to her features.' He rose above me and rested his hand on my head. 'Bless you, child.'

'Thank you, Father.' Bronte led me away, out of the sanctuary. A few streets closer, she stopped abruptly, drew me to her breast, and hugged me, whispering into my hair. 'Don't forget what the priest said. You're remarkable, and I know it to be true.'

From then on, I was more determined than ever to learn to speak and say my special prayer aloud.

Day Fourteen

Friday

IN THE COURTROOM, the trial picked up seamlessly from the previous day. The case against Brader was finely balanced; Laura hoped that Mr Waverly would knock Brader off his pedestal and give the jury a glimpse of the real man in the silver suit.

'Mr Brader, you worked many years in various companies as a civil engineer. Correct?'

Brader nodded. 'Yes. Mainly bridges, their design and construction.'

'And you had good contacts with the construction industry?'

'Naturally.' Brader directed his answer at the jury.

Laura narrowed her eyes, staring at him in an intensely focused manner. What did he make of all the faces homed in on his every word? In his shoes, Laura would dissolve into a state of panic. Speaking in public was not her thing, but she wasn't a quitter either and according to Amelia, Laura had a nice voice, kind of fruity but restrained. Amelia's was caustic and sharp, her laughter infectious. Laura paid more attention to the subtle layers of people's voices than she did their faces.

'But you never had any role in the finance departments of those companies?' Mr Waverly said in a slick delivery of enunciated words.

'No.'

'Or as a director?'

'No.'

'In fact, you didn't really have much involvement with the administration of the businesses. You designed bridges. Your primary job was structural engineering.'

'Yes.' Brader rose onto the balls of his toes. 'I can see where you're—'

'And yet, you were given access to Seeside's finances and funds without any accounting experience.'

'Mr Feydon didn't object. He suggested the job. Of course I know how to do accounts. I sat in on budget meetings and wrote cost-benefit reports—'

'So, you have a firm idea of what things cost when it comes to making things. But the actual process of payments, including cash and invoicing, was new to you?'

Brader flinched. Laura's eyes widened. A crack had opened up, a fleeting breach in his armour. She pressed her palms together.

'Yes,' Brader replied, regrouping himself. 'I received full support from the admin staff—'

'None of whom testified in your defence.'

A withering look of annoyance swept across Brader's speckled face. Laura squinted. He'd cut himself shaving. The tiny red scab was there on the line of his hard jaw. His hands were shaking – with anger at his humiliation or fear of defeat?

'Let's talk more about your relationship with Seeside's staff, a number of whom, when they pointed out errors on your part, were given short shrift by you.'

Amil flicked back through his extensive notes. Laura didn't need them. Brader's assistant, a young woman, had given evidence in the early days of the trial. She'd been gently interrogated by Mr Waverly, and spoken in her mousy voice of her concerns, but other than what was already on record, she'd been unable to verify anything with reproducible facts. There were no personal emails or memos that backed up her theory that Brader syphoned off money by creating false invoices. Mr Calm accused her of making stuff up after the auditor's report was written, and since she feared losing her job, she'd painted Brader in a poor light, making him out to be a bully, when in fact, she despised working for him. Laura remembered how she'd disintegrated under the cross-examination, freely admitting she didn't like Craig Brader and the way he "looked" at her, "talked down to her", made her feel small. Unfortunately, by the end of her stint in the box, she had shrunk, her head hung low, and she'd lost any credibility with the jury. Yet, Mr Waverly was resurrecting her opinions with renewed vigour.

The barrister, unwavering in his dusty wig, kept coming back to the invoices and cash payments, especially the lack of evidence that Brader had paid the suppliers.

'You don't seem to have receipts for these cash payments. Why is that?'

'I did. As I explained yesterday, somebody in the office mistakenly threw out paper records. I only picked up on it after the auditor—'

'An auditor brought in by Mr Feydon to satisfy the Charity Commission, who offer guidance on the responsibilities of the trustees. You're not a trustee, so you were not made aware of the commission's involvement before these files supposedly went missing?'

Brader clenched his hands into one balled fist. 'No. I was not told. Somebody made me look an idiot.'

Mr Waverly smiled, so softly, it was almost an illusion. Mr Calm examined his notes, his face a masterful pose of neutrality.

'Let's move on to the printer's, a company you used multiple times over the years to make raffle tickets, amongst other items. The defence made little mention of this yesterday, but am I correct that during your tenure, only one raffle was held annually?'

Mr Brader swallowed. The hue of red in his cheeks blanched. 'One, generally, unless there was a special event.'

'You arranged the printing of thousands of tickets, way in excess of your assistant's advice.'

'I was optimistic—'

'And what happened to these excess tickets? Did you collect the money raised by selling these tickets, money collected in cash, entirely for yourself?'

'No.' Brader slammed his fist on the edge of the witness box.

The judge cleared his throat.

Brader backed away from the front of the box. 'No. I kept a record of the number sold and told the trustees.'

'A record... kept by you alone?' Mr Waverly asked.

'Yes.'

'Whose honesty is in question.'

Brader's lips transformed into a snarl. 'But I bet nobody has come forward complaining about the money made from these raffles.'

'They were sold for special draws, two of which, according to the calendar you submitted in your evidence, were delayed due to poor ticket sales.'

'Which happens—'

Mr Waverly turned over a sheet of paper. 'Let's move onto the builders you used for renovations…'

Laura's wasn't sure why she was annoyed. The prosecutor was skipping over so much, missing out obvious questions – what happened after the raffle draw was delayed? In his shoes, there were questions she would ask. His haste led her to believe the trial had overextended its remit. Some other villain was waiting to be tried, and possibly convicted. Brader's guilt was looking doubtful, and unless Mr Waverly had a rabbit in his hat, he wasn't putting much effort into the cross-examination.

She searched the courtroom, the familiar shadowy nooks, the rows of the public gallery, the elevated platforms of the witness box and dock, the judge's dais with the emblem of the crown hanging behind his head, and it suddenly all felt like a pantomime set. She'd taken it seriously, as had most of the jury with their diligent notetaking; many of them had collapsed into bed hours earlier than normal, suffering with fatigue, yet none of that effort mattered if things floundered. The case had probably been decided days ago when all those little pieces of evidence failed to stitch together into a bigger picture of dishonesty and corruption.

Brader unclenched his hands and took a sip of water, and the fire in his cheeks was quenched. Although he had lost his coolness in the last exchange, he wasn't disintegrating under pressure. He maintained the denials with laudable consistency and introduced just enough doubt into the proceedings to maybe engineer his acquittal. Laura had believed only a few days ago that the case was sewn up. Now, she wasn't so sure. Standing between Brader and a prison cell was a dubious relationship with a builder.

'Mr Brader, Seeside, for the last few years that you worked for them, generally, almost exclusively, used one company to make renovations and alterations to their holiday homes?'

'The company is an expert in providing low-cost facilities for the disabled.'

'A company run by a friend of yours?'

'I know many builders.'

'A good friend of yours?' Mr Waverly persisted.

'Yes. We've known each other for some years.'

'So you didn't bother with a formal tendering process?'

Brader paused, and his gaze danced around the room, his eyes uncertain where to focus. 'No. As I said, they had the expertise—'

'But not with the blind? Previously, they only provisioned homes for wheelchair users and the infirm?'

'They have good contacts, subcontractors, and all the renovations they made are well documented. The paperwork was presented here, to the court.' Mr Brader's voice rose sharply.

'It was. The jury have an inventory of projects, the associated costs and sample invoices. Some were very expensive, and the invoices were billed to various addresses, different addresses to the contract, why?' Mr Waverly's stern eyebrows were in tune with his voice.

The impressive question was one that Laura had anticipated.

Brader stumbled. For the first time, he had no answer. 'I... don't know why. I assumed he operated out of several locations. As I said, there were subcontractors.'

'You didn't question the discrepancy?'

He went white. 'No. I should have done, but... I didn't.'

'Because, Mr Brader, you don't like putting friends in awkward situations. These false invoices from the subcontractors were never passed on by the builder, but only ever existed in your office, where you kept them, thus enabling you to make the payments to yourself using fake accounts.'

The rebuttal was swift. 'No witness has corroborated this accusation.'

'No, they haven't. We're referring to builders that Seeside ceased using two weeks before your departure. Why was that?'

Brader shook his head slightly and rolled his eyes to the ceiling. 'The contract was terminated.'

'By whom?'

'Mr Feydon. Mr Anthony Feydon, the chairman of Seeside's trustees.'

The trustees' faith in the legal process depended on more than the auditor's report. Something had triggered the charges, something personal and embarrassing to one or more parties involved, and Laura doubted it was going to be revealed in court.

'Mr Anthony Feydon, Steven Feydon's uncle, sadly, suffered a stroke and cannot give evidence.'

'He would have told you that he ended the contract for no other reason than to discredit my role. It came as no surprise that I lost my job two weeks later. You have nothing proving what I did was dishonest.' The imperious edge had returned.

For over an hour, Craig Brader had struggled to contain his dignity; he'd loosened his tie, breathed as if jogging on the spot, and throughout the bombardment, he'd fought off the worst of the accusations with his customary gravitas. Nothing was going to budge the jury if he held out for the rest of his cross-examination.

Laura made a note. The last of the day.

Blind faith.

Mr Waverly continued. 'Unfortunately, we can't provide an answer to the jury because the company in question filed for bankruptcy last year and have been liquidated. Your friend has conveniently left the country on an extended holiday. The company's accounts were found to be inadequately kept, and no taxes had been filed for two years, nor annual reports submitted, which—'

Mr Calm scrambled to his feet. 'This information is not in the documents submitted by the CPS.'

The judge sharpened his gaze, then turned to the jury. 'I'm afraid this is one of those matters of discussion that doesn't require your attention. If you'd kindly leave the court, we'll adjourn until after lunch.'

Laura hurried out of the courthouse and the calamity of the trial. There was no justice to be had when the towering decks of evidence collapsed in on themselves. As if in sympathy, a deep sigh shadowed Laura. She slowed, unsure if she wanted her companion to lead her somewhere, to places that made no sense (nonsense, too). A frigid breeze penetrated her gloves and coat; the ice blanket of the previous days had melted, but its memory clung to Laura's skin, and she responded with goose bumps and a flurry of shivers. She contemplated the warmth of a building, any shelter, except the courthouse.

The bakery café? Wait there with the whispering voices or go down the hill and explore the riverside? Maybe she'd end up at the house where the girl played with her blocks. There wasn't enough time to walk that far. She pinched the lapels of her coat under her chin in preparation to go in the direction prescribed by the determined spirit.

Two mysteries were running in parallel, and her overactive mind flitted back and forth between them, bearing down on her. One was a contrivance of her mind and equivocal. Jodi was right – Laura had a potent imagination, except while Jodi's was poetic in nature, Laura's was a sensory nightmare. If the trial ended soon with a swift jury verdict likely on Monday, would the haunting continue or stop? What if she couldn't find the answers and the dreams prevailed nightly, and indefinitely? A haunting in perpetuity frightened her. The answer had to be buried in the archives. That repository of the past might help by painting a picture of the historical context.

In the dreams, the child was tactile, and her limited experiences sharpened by acute senses. She projected sounds, smells, and even textures into Laura's mind, but visually she provided little detail, as if she was blind, which fitted with the braille. The dead woman, the original starting point of Laura's dreams, had to be the girl's mother, and the trip to the bakery, and possibly the river, seemed to have involved both; there had been more than one set of footsteps. The grave, therefore, belonged to the mother. What was the crime committed that warranted that dreadful execution? What if the child was the victim…? No, no. It was an icy dagger in Laura's heart just thinking about it.

Seeside was a charity set up to help the blind – was that a plausible connection between her mystery and the trial? Was that why she'd been chosen? The question bothered her because she wanted the answer to be something other than the obvious link to the accident. Laura closed her eyes. The only thing that might bring rest to a troubled soul was justice, the righting of a dreadful wrong. If the hanged woman was innocent, and the whispering child was pleading on her behalf, then it was Laura's job to identify the guilty person, and in doing so, the woman and child could find peace.

She opened her eyes. That wasn't going to be easy. If the evidence in Brader's trial had proved difficult to find, then a hundred and fifty-year-old case with a missing headstone and no records was nigh on impossible. While she might have the tenacity to try, Laura was pragmatic; at work she wouldn't persevere with a failing project, and she'd discourage her colleagues from doing so, too. But away from protocols, the expectations of her boss, she had the freedom to choose.

She had to make a choice about Marco, too.

She'd never told Marco the whole story about the accident.

'Hello,' a familiar voice said. 'Fancy a walk. My legs are stiff.'

She turned to face Iain. 'Sure. Where should we go?' Visible company was a welcome relief.

'Let's amble over to the cathedral.'

Side by side, the church and castle dated back to a time when both held sway over people's morals and enforced the laws that had in some shape or form trickled down into the modern era. The archaic rituals of both were a poignant reminder that forgotten things were entitled to be rediscovered.

Iain walked at her pace; he possessed loping strides and huge feet. Sitting in the jury box must be a test of his endurance. She followed him through the Exchequer Gate and into the open space of Minster's Yard. The cathedral exhibited impressive frontage with two towers and rows of empty plinths where saintly statues once stood to welcome the worshippers. She dallied to look up at the weatherworn stonework, the volume of the sheer structure rising above her head into the sky. Laura wasn't a churchgoer and usually stuck to admiring the aesthetics. Time today was precious, though. Iain walked through the cathedral's open door, and she hastened to keep up.

'If you don't mind, I want to light a candle and say a prayer,' he said.

The reason was sufficient to circumvent an entrance fee. He murmured something to a cloaked attendant and slipped past the queue. Joining him, Laura felt like a cheat.

The vast space of the nave echoed with an eerie chorus of tourists, which was too noisy, ruining the sacred silence observed by a handful of visitors. A toddler screamed somewhere, hushed loudly by a parent. There was no clergy or organist present; the service was later in the day, Iain had told her. Laura wasn't interested in the rituals of the prayerful. Instead, she wondered why Iain wanted her company.

'I thought you weren't a priest anymore?'

'I've still got my faith.' He knew where he was going – a small chapel where there was a stand for scent-free candles and a donation box for the twenty pence.

He picked up a lit candle. She expected kneeling and genuflecting, but he was subtle with his prayer, merely giving a nod to the stone altar. He touched a flawless wick with the lit one and held it until the flame (a golden peardrop) took hold, dancing a little in the draught. Whoever, she assumed as opposed to whatever, he was thinking about wasn't going to be divulged; she preferred it if he didn't, anyway.

He stood by the altar to pray, hands gently clasped before him, face downcast, and, feeling awkward, she hunched her shoulders and closed her eyes. Her heart picked up its pace, mirroring the modicum of excitement that heralded what was to come. There was some joy to be found in a place that offered respite from the outside world, and while her extrasensory perceptions held sway, for once she wasn't afraid to let them in. The temperature dropped; she shivered and hugged herself. Voices converged around her and, among the hum of chatter, she discerned distant singers chanting in harmonies accompanied by a pipe organ (toots, soft and caressing). There was no service ongoing, but there was an echo of one lingering, and it had to be from the past and not now because she was drifting again in a haze of uneasy greyness, neither afraid of her surroundings nor at rest. Dizzy, possibly swaying, she expelled frosty air in sharp exhales, tilted her head to one side, trying to extract meaning from what she heard, to distinguish anything other than her thumping heartbeats.

Close by her – Laura was sure of the presence; the energy created tingled in the roots of her hair – was her diminutive companion, her amiable ghost. Laura waited, seconds ticking like hours, until she extracted something meaningful. The girl whispered one word, and immediately the chorus evaporated, and the organ ceased. Laura straightened, determined as the child suggested, to be brave and shake off the unnatural turbulence in the cool air. She opened her eyes; it was Iain who was standing next to Laura, a quizzical expression on his face. He pointed at a candle, offering her the opportunity to follow his example. But prayer wasn't what she was thinking about. Warmth returned abruptly to her hands and feet, and her face, which flushed with relief that he'd chosen to ignore her baffling episode, the second in his company.

'I don't go to church.' The statement of fact came across like a confession.

He was in no hurry to leave and he suggested sitting on one of the long wooden benches, which were uncomfortable and packed tightly in front of the altar. There was more breathing space in the jury box.

'I know we can't really talk about it. But the trial has made me question what honesty is. Or dishonesty, I suppose,' he whispered and leant towards her.

The trial. It was what Iain expected her to be worrying about, so she responded in kind. 'I know what you mean. The intention of dishonesty, as opposed to its accidental achievement.' She recalled the prosecution's explanation for fraud and the intent of dishonesty, rather than through incompetence or lack of knowledge.

'I'm not a fraud, but I feel like one,' he said.

So he'd lost his job due to inappropriate activities. It made sense. 'I'm sure you didn't mean to,' she said.

'Oh no. It was entirely intentional. I knew I was lying.'

'You stole from the church—'

'What?' He jerked upright.

He chuckled for a couple of seconds, but not at her expense, she thought.

'Sorry, I haven't made it very clear, have I? No, that's not the reason I left the church. I haven't stolen a penny. They probably own me money given how often I forked out for my parishioners. That's where it all went wrong.'

'What?'

'Empathy. Feeling sorry for people. Prayers aren't enough, nor are good deeds. Sometimes you can't do anything but watch and listen as people's lives fall apart. Grief and loss, the burden of poverty. I witnessed it all... And in the end, I had a breakdown. Just couldn't cope. I wanted to help but...' his voice fractured. 'Being a priest is very lonely when so many come to you for advice and support. I felt useless.'

Priests had much in common with social workers and psychologists, except for one thing. 'Shouldn't God be helping you?'

He laughed again, then he covered his mouth. 'I'm sorry, that's awful of me, laughing at that. God is here.' He pressed his hand to his heart. 'But not always here.' He pointed at his head. 'The mind needs love, too. I lost it when I took up the priesthood. I gave up my lover and her world, for this.' He waved around him. 'Well, my version of this.'

'That must have been difficult.' She crossed her legs. His little flame was still burning, but many others had gone out, leaving metallic empty shells waiting for collection. Tomorrow there'd be a fresh batch to burn.

He hugged his knees, his tall back hunched into a curve, seemingly overwhelmed by the holy surroundings. The strangeness liberated Laura. She had no allegiance to something she couldn't understand.

He spoke softly to the pillar opposite. 'My act of dishonesty was on the form I sent back about jury service. I should have declared my mental health issues.'

She leaned away from him. 'Oh?'

Iain seemed perfectly normal. It was ironic given that she was the one who was probably losing her mind, especially if the voice of the child refused to rest. Frankly, she was known for being a bit off kilter with her opinions sometimes, and she'd always believed she wasn't the sort of person people came to when in a crisis; her advice usually lacked empathy, which many considered more important than practical solutions. So why was she becoming a listening channel for others? Maybe she'd misjudged herself. Was that why the ghosts had targeted her? Had she that aura that told them she was an open conduit for the troubled mind? Even Marco said she was a good listener, although she also asked awkward questions. Perhaps he meant active listener, as opposed to kind.

She accepted that those things she heard were all in her head, and more importantly, that what affected her was purely spiritual and intangible. This was where the child had come for comfort, and perhaps for hope and kindness, and courage, the word she'd whispered to Laura. If it wasn't to be found in a courtroom or the cell of a prison, she'd sought it here in a spiritual sanctuary. Was that why she and the child needed to unburden themselves of troubles, of insidious guilt, and was this the right place to find forgiveness?

Iain rubbed his hands along the ribbing of his corduroys. 'I suffer with depression. I had a spell in hospital. I'm much better but still on medication. I should have said on the form submitted to the jury service people, but I didn't.'

She barely remembered the form. She'd filled it in and sent it back weeks ago. 'Why hide it?'

'I want to be of some value again. Since I left the church, I've lost my way, my worth. This jury service is one means of finding out whether I've the ability to cope… with people.'

'What if it had been a murder or something ghastly? Wouldn't it have upset you? You can't walk out of a trial.'

'I know. I was foolish, which is why, I suppose, I'm unburdening myself in here to you. You won't say—'

He'd roped her into a lie. But nobody would have guessed his problem from what little he'd said in the jury room.

'No. It's the stigma, isn't it?'

He nodded. 'Anyway, the honesty thing made me realise how easy it is to do something dishonest and hide it from yourself, to deny it.'

Laura said nothing for a few moments. Iain, having set a different kind of example, waited patiently. He seemed to know she was on the cusp of revealing something.

She took a deep breath. 'Guilt does the same thing to a person. You hide it, refuse to face it, then it comes back to bite you. I didn't have a breakdown; I don't think I did. But maybe something else happened that I've kept to myself for years.'

'You don't have to tell me. This was my little confession. It's compulsive; once you're a Catholic, you have to confess now and again to somebody.' Pressing down on his knees, he began to stand.

'No, actually, I do want to tell you.' She touched his sleeve, and he returned to his seat. 'You see,' she steadied her breathing, 'when... when I was nineteen, not long after I passed my driving test, I knocked somebody over crossing the road. I killed a man.'

He had the wide-eyed look of surprise. It was familiar, along with the pity; both usually came together, which was why she'd stopped telling people.

'I'm sorry, Laura. How awful.'

'He struck the bonnet. and his head hit the windscreen, and he had fatal injuries. It's the white stick I remember; it bounced off. A white stick.'

It wasn't her fault. A blameless accident, the coroner concluded. But it took months of waiting before reaching that verdict. She was in shock for a good spell of it. The police had been thorough in the investigations; a fatal accident warranted it. They'd put out an appeal for witnesses. The man had walked right out in front of her at a pelican crossing. The light for her was green, another car coming in the opposite direction verified that, and she was doing the correct speed – just. Later, a campaign reduced the speed limit further. What the police couldn't fathom was why he'd stepped out.

'It wasn't suicide,' she explained to Iain. 'Nothing to suggest he was suicidal at all. So it took time to piece things together.'

'And?'

Snippets, fragments of the day lingered in her memories: the windscreen wiper had been manic, vehicles weaved, the confusion of parked cars. 'It was raining. The traffic was noisy, the wind blustery and blowing away from him, towards my car. A truck was reversing near to the crossing, reversing into a side road. It made that bleeping noise—'

'And he mistook it... how sad.' He pivoted to face her. 'But it wasn't your fault.'

His expression lacked pain or any anguished priestly empathy. He blinked a few times, processing, like she had done with his admission of dishonesty. Not everyone wore their emotions on their sleeve. Laura's mother didn't; she had her own methods for coping.

'Doesn't stop the guilt. I couldn't drive.'

Simply sitting in the passenger seat brought it rushing back: the head impacting the glass, his dark glasses shattering, the horrendous thud as the windscreen absorbed the force. He'd ended up on the road but left behind a few tufts of hair in the fractured window. And a smudge of blood. Her mother had collected her from the police station in her car – a journey home that heralded her first panic attack. Angela had struggled to understand why. She'd been more concerned about the legalities. The police had breathalysed Laura (negative) and eventually, having determined nothing malicious had happened, the officer stopped calling her. She sold her damaged car and used the bus.

'It became a habit, catching the bus. I forgot how to drive and when I looked at the cost of insurance, it was extortionate. I'm perfectly happy with the bus and trains.' She still had a driving licence somewhere in the house.

The pause in the conversation opened up a flood of unsettling memories. Angela had been with her every step of the way through the interviews and managed the mountain of paperwork from the insurance company. Margery had sent flowers to Laura. Her father had provided her with an expensive solicitor, which in hindsight was generous and what he was best at doing, but at the time, she felt he'd ignored her emotional trauma.

'They wrote to me, the family of the man, via my solicitor, and forgave me. That was the hardest part, because the coroner cleared me of blame, but the family still had to forgive me.' Tears pricked her eyes, and she gazed up at the stained glass. Beautiful pictures fractured into pieces and brought back together with lead and glue.

Iain kept his voice low, like hers. 'I understand. The guilt eats at you. Doesn't matter if it's not your fault, you feel culpable because you're human and decent.'

Yes, culpability was a familiar state for Laura, and it had created a joyless void in her soul that once contained her gregarious nature, and the emptiness left her easily satisfied by simple things. She bestowed upon others a carefully constructed placidity, and relied on an uncomplicated emotional relationship, which now appeared to be going wrong, too.

She inhaled deeply. 'I killed a blind person.' She'd said it, sent it out to where God's judgement presided. She would never know if that mattered or not to anyone; she judged herself daily.

He checked his watch. 'Crikey. Let's get moving.' He rose. 'Well, now you have a chance to ease that conscience.'

'How?'

He cocked his head to the candles. 'Shine a light on Brader. If he's found guilty, he'll have to pay back all that money to Seeside. Retribution, don't you think?'

She hadn't thought about how Brader might be punished. If the money went back to Seeside, then the blind would benefit, soothing her guilt a little. Money could never replace a person.

'It's probably not a good idea to go into the jury room with that reason in mind,' she said as they exited the cathedral.

'Of course not,' he said hastily. He wrapped his scarf tighter around his neck where once a dog collar would have proudly been on display.

She changed her mind. 'Who did you pray for?'

'You're not afraid to ask things, are you? You're going to have to use that in the jury room, you know. Bashful yet unafraid. The quiet ones are often ignored. Amil needs to speak, too. My prayer was for my lover's sake. She's happily married now, but I still like to pray for her soul, her good fortune. I owe her that.'

They passed under the gate. Rain spotted her nose, and they picked up their pace. They didn't speak again until they were close to the courthouse. On the first day of the trial, she'd paid little attention to the building, and now that she was immersed in history, she noticed the courthouse was both akin to its surroundings and at the same time, out of step with the castle ruins: neoclassical columns, square chimneys mimicking mini towers, and tall windows with gothic arches, and just like the cathedral, none of those things had a purpose; it was what went on inside that defined the building.

'Thank you for taking me,' she said. 'I've only limited experience, but I think you're still a very good priest, you just need to believe in yourself again. What about working for a charity?'

He laughed jovially. 'You know, I've been thinking the same. I should thank you, Laura, for keeping my secret. Don't feel guilty about that, will you?'

'I won't,' she said, holding the door open for him.

The jury filed back into the courtroom, and the judge waited patiently for them to be seated. The explanation for the delay was frustrating in its lack of detail.

'The situation has been resolved. The defence has no objection to continuing.' He nodded to Mr Waverly, who rose to his feet and restarted the cross-examination of the accused.

Laura was perplexed and struggled to regain her concentration. Brader's mood had changed, too. He answered the questions without elaboration and in a quieter voice. The denials continued, accompanied by an occasional exasperated huff of annoyance, but he wasn't fighting as hard.

The defence had either let him down or the prosecution had gained the upper hand. It wasn't obvious which of the lawyers was winning; both continued to operate dispassionately and professionally. However, the raw emotions of the morning had been neutered; Brader's time in the witness box drew to a conclusion in a somewhat featureless anticlimax of repeated information.

The approaching evening would offer Laura no comforts, even food was unappetising. On the bus, she dissected her conversation with Iain. Although it had lifted her spirits to know there was somebody to rely on in the jury room, after the trial finished, they would move on; different worlds defined their futures. As for the other newcomer in her quiet life, Sean wasn't texting her, but their plans were set, so why would he? Marco hadn't replied – no surprises there – and her mother was visiting an ancient aunt who lived incommunicado due to a lack of mobile signal. Laura dragged herself upstairs with leaden legs and a splitting headache. Lying stiff on the bed like a stone effigy in the cathedral, she awaited her fate.

'Just give me something definite,' she said to the dark room, accepting fatigue would defeat her in the end.

She wasn't expecting frantic screaming, the pool of scarlet blood trickling through the cracks between the floorboards, the huddled form hiding under a table, and the weeping child calling out for her mother, who never answered. The dream lasted perhaps seconds before Laura woke up, terrorised.

She hugged her knees and wept. It couldn't go on; it had to stop.

Harriet

1872

WHEN I WAS TEN YEARS OLD, James met a girl and courted her. It was then that William started to suspect I wasn't as innocent as he thought.

According to Ma, Harriet was of French descent. James said it was the Huguenots and that was why Ma liked to say Harriet was French. Harriet spoke with a blunt Yorkshire accent, hated croissants, and carried upon her the scent of English roses. Ma described her hair as (silky) chestnuts and her eyes (lukewarm) grey. Her feet must be dainty, because she wore slippers, unlike Ma's clogs or Father's boots. The day she slipped past Ma to find me, she tiptoed up the stairs to my room and opened the door so quietly, I did not hear the creak of the hinges.

I was on the rug, cross-legged under the fan of my skirts and clutching Betty. Ma had made her from an old cotton sheet stuffed with straw and dressed her in a knitted jacket. She had stitched a face on using wool. I chatted to Betty every day (*sotto voce*) and told her stories of magical places filled with blind people who ruled over the sighted. The instant Harriet burst in, I froze, turning myself into a statue, which was my usual means of protecting myself.

'Emma, were you talking?' Harriet closed the door behind her. The floorboards vibrated as she walked towards me.

I held poor Betty tight to my chest and said nothing. Thankfully, Ma had not taught me any useful gestures, such as shaking one's head, and this ensured my ignorance of the invisible language of body and hands. I kept my head naturally still, my lips pressed together, and waited for a touch. A cold draught alerted me to her smell, her particular perfume. Everyone has one.

She moved closer. I felt her warm exhale on my nose. 'Can you hear me?' she whispered into my ear.

The paralysis of fear kept me from flinching. I merely breathed heavily, and slowly unfurled an arm, daring myself to explore. I touched her cheek and recoiled; she was hot, flushed and excited by her discovery.

'What's this?' She tugged on Betty.

I yanked my doll back and grunted in alarm.

She tried to unravel the knot of my fingers, but I held fast. 'Come on, let me look at her.'

I shuffled backwards, squawking and pushing her away with the flat of my hand on her ample bosom. She was already a woman, not a child, although her voice had yet to mature.

'I'm sure I heard you talking,' she said. 'They say the deaf can't talk, though. Am I mistaken? Is this your little secret, Emma?' She laughed, a light airy chuckle that filled the space between us. 'It shouldn't be a secret. Wouldn't your mother like to know? Your father?'

My bones turned cold, curdling the blood in my veins.

'Anyway,' she said. 'I've come to fetch you for dinner. Up you get.' She grabbed my arm and pulled on me, forcing me to my feet.

Ma usually put a spoon in my hand. Then, when I went downstairs, I knew to sit at the table and wait for my bowl to be filled. I hesitated, knowing Harriet would not know of Ma's tricks to keep my hearing concealed. If I ever did speak, used recognisable words, Father sent me to the basket weaver's house where I toiled for countless hours until my fingers were raw. Ma called it slavery. Any wage would go straight into his pocket and not mine, adding to my dependence on his meagre benevolence.

'I'll find you a job, not Bill,' Ma had said to me. 'One where talking will serve a purpose and respect. Nobody will hit you or bully you. Keep your tongue cleaved to your mouth, child. Talk only for somebody worthy of it. Wait until then.'

I had croaked, 'Ma.'

Ma had inhaled sharply and kissed my wet cheek. 'Not me. I've let you down. I haven't the courage to leave him, Emma. My mother won't have me back, and I can't divorce him. What woman can afford to end her marriage when her husband hides his true nature?'

In this matter, I had one thing in common with my father; we both kept secrets. He hid his drunkenness and bitter grief. (I do think he came to be that unkind man after losing James's mother. Ma never made comparisons, but he did frequently.) He kept Ma inconsequential, dependent on him and friendless, although I regret being party to this latter state of affairs; she had no time for companions while she cared for me.

Harriet propelled me towards the stairs. 'Come on. My, you are dumb, aren't you?'

It was the supposed taint of stupidity that protected me from Father's wrath. He would rather ignore me than have to admit that a blind girl had more wits than his uncouth son. If he knew I could read his letter sets and arrange them into words, he would discover he had another hapless female in the house to enslave. Women were not to be raised to any station that purported to intelligence or value; William firmly believed that women should remain chattels. Education was for the man, the provider of sustenance, and even if Ma worked, it was never acknowledged that her wages contributed to food or coal. She was kept busy, because otherwise, her lazy bones would wither and dry up.

This speech he had often delivered after a few beers and when the warmth of the sun had fled the skies. He never knew I heard him berate Ma. 'To be weak-minded is unfortunate, but weak in body, unable to bear children, is a flaw. One that I shall rectify.'

William meant beatings. He believed they instilled strength and fortitude. What he preached was practised regularly but never so far as to leave Ma crippled or unable to work, only sufficiently severe to drive her to tears and cries of pain. Even James cowered in his room on those dreadful nights.

When Harriet joined us at the dining table, politely showing gratitude for a modest meal, she brought with her what she believed was glad tidings, when in fact, she was the harbinger of doom. She ended a life with her little remark.

'I heard Emma talking merrily away to her doll. How's that possible? I thought she couldn't—'

Ma hissed. But it was too late.

The Third Saturday

THE BUS ROUTE WAS CONVOLUTED, taking Laura from her sprawling housing estate in the farthest corner of Lincoln's suburbs, detouring through the other fringe villages, past the university, and over the river. From Broadgate it was a short walk to the county archive. Sean, in his fatigued jeans and a slightly tatty coat, was waiting outside under a rainbow umbrella. Laura had chosen cream chinos and a scallop-neck sweater. She wasn't sure what the dress code was for non-dates involving archives. He raised the umbrella over her head.

'Mornin',' he said cheerfully.

She huddled closer to him for shelter. The rain was the ultra-thin kind that soaked through everything in seconds.

'Hello,' she said.

In close proximity, he scanned her face. She'd tried to hide the hollow shadows under her eyes with a base of foundation. Unsuccessfully, it seemed.

'Okay?' he asked.

She turned, placing herself in profile. 'Yes.'

The scrutiny continued for a couple of seconds, but he had the wits to say nothing. The simple question was sufficient. He understood her nights were miserable.

Sean was familiar with the layout of the building, the staff who greeted him by his name, and where to find the maps set aside for them; a regular researcher and comfortable with the designation.

'There's two maps. One is dated 1855 and the other 1889, so not quite the right age, if we're using the death date on the stone as guidance, but near enough.' He rolled out the oldest map and pegged the curling corners down with weights. The print was dark, the paper, once pulp white, stained with watermarks and, due to light exposure and dust, it had discoloured into a sepia. In an attempt at salvage, the paper had been mounted on linen.

The castle mound and cathedral were easy to find, as was the river. She was surprised to see the railway line established through the city and onwards. Housing was marked by black blocks crammed together in rows of parallel streets, while in the older parts of the city, the roads sprawled in all directions. She was able to pinpoint the location of the bakery.

'Here, this street.'

Sean leaned over, armed with a magnifying glass. 'There's an annotation. Yeah, look for yourself, it's labelled "bakery".'

The blurred outline of a building zoomed out, and she focused on the tiny writing. 'Doesn't give a name. It looks like it extended along this stretch. Must have been bigger than the building I visited.'

'Plenty of hungry mouths to feed.' He took back the magnifier. 'You said you went to the river?'

'A couple of times.' Unfortunately, the flurry of footsteps had been drowned out by the traffic and hubbub of living voices. Nothing on the map resembled the streets she recognised as part of the modern city. A swathe of shops and businesses had obliterated most of the original buildings.

'It's all gone, I think.'

'Tenement housing and rows of terraces were bulldozed. Not much left of that style. The bigger, wealthy properties are scattered about.' He rolled up the map and unfurled the more recent one.

It was in better condition. The paper was whiter, and the text resembled an Ordnance Survey map, the kind she might buy in a shop. What was missing was colour. The housing remained densely packed together, the railway network was extensive, and the road system familiar. Gone were the blocks of housing by the river, replaced by public buildings, such as the one they were standing in.

'It's kind of lost its charm,' she said. 'I mean, the city has grown.'

He nodded, then raised two expectant eyebrows.

She shook her head. 'I just don't see anything. That's the problem; I'm blind, moving through the streets, only hearing and feeling things. The house, or wherever she lives, doesn't have an outside. The prison cell was obvious, but this...' She shrugged.

'Okay, let's move on to the records. Maybe we'll have more luck with computers. I'll look at the assize records, see if I can find an account of a trial that matches the initials on the grave, and you can battle your way through the newspaper articles.'

There were two workstations side by side. He logged her in to an account that had access to the images of scanned newspapers, and there were hundreds of them.

'My God,' she said. 'Don't they have an index?' Or colour coding.

'Nope. You'll have to start at the beginning of the year. One page at a time. It's the *Lincolnshire Chronicle*. It's the only paper they have that covers 1872. Good luck.'

He settled in front of his monitor, eyes focused on document listings.

Laura was accustomed to scanning and pulling up information, however, the material she was familiar with was nothing like the images of an old newspaper. The text was compacted with barely any breathing space between the words or lines. Thick black lettering was packaged into long paragraphs, then separated by horizontal lines and headings. Each page, which was roughly the size of a broadsheet newspaper, was filled with numerous stories and advertising. No pictures. The lack of visual clues was disappointing. She half-expected some pictures, even if they were illustrations or lithographs. It was too early for photos.

Starting in January, she targeted the headlines, then was frequently distracted by the minor stories of life in Victorian Lincoln. The level of detail was astounding. Small day-to-day things were recounted, embellished, and given greater credence. There was a mixture of what might be modern-day tabloid gossip and factual reporting of events at both national and local levels. The bulk of the stories were about people's tragic lives. She quickly discovered that every day there was a list of wrong-doers, people arrested for petty crimes and misdeeds. The reporters peppered their language with harsh words for those caught. Nobody was innocent, it seemed, once they were in the hands of the police.

There were wars happening. She hadn't thought of how the world beyond England was a constant stream of battles. And on top of that, there was the misery of existence. One of the columns regularly referred to outbreaks of disease in parts of the city, whether cholera or typhoid, measles or influenza. By the end of the winter months, the rain had caused the sewers to flood the poorer housing by the river, and the stench was described as beyond human tolerance.

As for E.H., there was no mention of a hanging. She waded on through the pages, picking up speed, her eyes tuned into the font and content.

Sean stretched his hands above his head. 'Nothing so far. Came across dear old Priscilla again. As I suspected, the records for hangings at the prison, the new one, are more extensive. But the old castle ones aren't so good. Most refer to the public hangings on the Cobb Hall roof. Something of a spectator sport.' He grimaced. 'People were after gruesome entertainment back then.'

'Life was hard…' She nearly missed it, listening to Sean. She scrolled back to the page and enlarged the image.

Horry Hanged by "Long Drop" Method
April 1, 1872.

This was no April Fool. There had been a hanging at the castle in that year, a young man who'd shot his wife, Jane Horry, for infidelity. However, his first name was William, and although he was known as Fred, Laura was absolutely sure she'd seen E on the stone and not an F.

Sean picked up on her exclamation. 'Something?'

'I thought it was. Fred Horry was hanged at Lincoln Castle by William Marwood, somebody of notoriety.'

Sean leaned over her shoulder. His warm breath glanced against her neck as he spoke. 'I think I remember the name. Horry. Yep, he's on our list, so I would have discounted him. As for Marwood, something of a celebrity. He came up with the idea of the long drop so that the neck was snapped instead of strangulation. It meant the death was quicker.'

Laura shivered. The thought of a gallows, the jerk of the rope pulling on the neck, was abhorrent.

Jolly Sean was oblivious to her discomfort. 'He worked out the length of rope, the weight of the person. Travelled all over the place hanging people, but mostly in London. Horry was his first, though.'

'But he's not the person I'm looking for.' She scrolled on, preparing herself for disappointment. Had she even touched the headstone? Maybe she had seen Horry's and misread the initials in the shadow of the tree.

'Oh, I should add, Horry's grave is nowhere near the tree,' Sean said. 'Just in case you're wondering. It's one that I know well because people often ask to see it, because it's the first...' He went quiet, then cleared his throat. 'Are you sure you're okay?'

She clicked on another image. 'Fine.'

He returned to his task. They didn't speak again for another hour.

The instant she read "Hanged" in the headline, Laura knew she'd found the grave's occupant. There was a simplicity in the style of writing, as if the reporter was conveying to the reader that something so horrible as an execution was mundane and ordinary. The death of E.H. warranted one solitary column. Laura read through the wretched account of the damned woman rated as trifling and inconsequential, her lifespan cut short by the noose.

The crime was one Laura should have predicted: the murder of her husband. Priscilla wasn't the only woman to despise her husband enough to end his life. She read through the article again. A word stuck out; the implication that the condemned went to her death "weeping" mirrored the despair in Laura's opening nightmare, the overture to what was to follow.

'I found it,' she said. 'I've found her.'

Sean whipped his head around. 'You have?' Using the castors of his chair, he sped across the gap between the two desks. This time, Laura gave him space to read the article.

Woman Hanged at Lincoln Gaol

15 November 1872

Eliza Horton was taken from her prison cell to the place of execution in Lincoln Castle, where she was hanged until dead. The execution was carried out by Hangman William Marwood, who reassured the weeping Horton that her death would be swift.

Mrs Eliza Horton was found guilty of the despicable murder of her husband, Mr William Horton, proprietor of a print shop. She beat him about the head with his walking stick, causing such a grievous injury that his eye did explode from his skull. Mrs Horton pleaded not guilty, claiming her husband was frequently violent towards her and threatened her life that very evening. She presented to the jury that she acted in self-defence and with no intent to commit cold-blooded murder. However, the jury dismissed her claim and found her guilty in less than an hour's worth of deliberation.

The murder took place in the evening during dinner. The only other person present in the house was their daughter, Emma Horton, aged ten years, who, having been born blind, deaf, and mute, was not considered a reliable witness. Mr Horton's older son, James, was not at home and came upon the terrible scene after returning to the house. During the previously reported trial, he described to the court how his father's walking stick was next to his body and covered in blood. Mr James Horton, apprentice, accused his stepmother of lying. The young man refuted the claim she suffered at the hands of her husband. He pointed out that his father had married beneath him and believed Mr Horton had been tricked into wedlock by Eliza, the daughter of a baker. Mr Horton's first wife died of a fever when their son was a young boy.

During the day-long trial, many of Mr Horton's customers came forward to offer their personal admiration for Mr Horton, including the parish priest and police sergeant. The kindness he showed was frequently mentioned, as was his charitable nature and dignified disposition around those less fortunate than himself.

The picture painted by Mrs Horton of a cruel, vindictive husband was not recognised by the court. Her pleas failed to impress the jury or judge, who passed his sentence immediately upon hearing the guilty verdict. The crowd gathered in the public gallery booed the tearful Mrs Horton, and she was removed from the dock still protesting her innocence.

As is the custom, Eliza Horton will be laid to rest in the grounds of the castle, and her name shall not be carved upon any gravestone. The fate of Emma Horton is unknown.

'Eliza Horton,' he said after reaching the last line. 'Well, I never. She's not in our records at the museum, I'm sure of it. Nothing comes to mind. It's like she's vanished.'

Like her grave. A phantom marker that only Laura had seen. 'She was at least hanged by that man, the quick one. So she hopefully didn't suffer,' she said.

Sean rested his hand on Laura's arm; it was only the second time he'd touched her. She held steady, realising it was a subconscious gesture, and brief.

'Her daughter—'

'I know. Blind, deaf, and dumb. Why wonder I'm struggling to make sense of things, if I'm the conduit.' Laura paused, glancing around the reading room; the other visitors were focused on their research. She'd tried not to make a thing of the girl's blindness, but it was becoming harder to ignore the connections. It was as if Laura was being punished, too. Tears formed unhelpfully, and she turned to face Sean, and was startled by his concerned expression.

He hunted her features, wordlessly, for a reason for the sadness, but she wasn't ready to divulge it. Telling Iain, a priest, had happened spontaneously. Sean was filling different shoes, and currently they weren't exactly vacant.

She blinked away the fledging tears; there was something positive to build on, proof that she wasn't acting irrationally and the connections to the past were genuine. 'So… the grave did exist, probably, and if Emma's been haunting me, then she wants me to clear her mother's name. Yes?' Impossible. She gnawed on her lower lip.

Sean shrugged at the suggestion. 'The article doesn't make much of the evidence, does it? Priscilla used poison. This one was violent, driven by rage. Perhaps he, the husband, was having an affair and she found out.'

The impartial discussion helped dissolve the unsettling links of past and present. 'A crime of passion? Or self-defence? There's no evidence of either according to the newspaper. If she is innocent, then who killed him, and why was she blamed?' Laura scrolled back through the pages, fruitlessly looking for the original court case report. Then she noticed the dates of the pages. Two whole months of newspaper articles were missing from the archive's records. She could guess why she'd not seen the original trial report. The story of Eliza Horton was one destined to be forgotten.

Sean returned to his computer. 'At least I know what I'm looking for now.' He typed furiously, bringing up records, then discarding them as unhelpful before trying other ideas.

After ten minutes, he sat back with a satisfied expression. 'This one might help.'

'What?' Laura joined him, peering at the text on the screen. '*The Register of Convicts from the Sessions.*'

'The dates cover our year.' He wrote down the reference number. 'I'll go see if they can access the document for us.'

Laura waited impatiently. She wandered around the room, looking at the notices, which were mostly there to help family history research. There were reference books on display, including trade directories, none of which went back far enough for her investigation. The article referred to Eliza's stepson, James. Was he the real culprit? Had he killed his father because… Laura shook her head. James, if he had any role in the murder, hadn't featured once in Laura's dreams. James wasn't important. She continued to aimlessly browse the shelves, not paying any attention to the contents. How was Laura supposed to give Eliza peace of mind when her own was torn in so many directions?

The two ghosts worked in partnership: a mother and daughter. The mother was trapped in a cell, and occasionally, as if stirred, she gesticulated at the paper shredded on the floor while the child flitted here and there, whispering nonsense from the baker's to the river, and during the night in Laura's dream she bided her time in a bland box room or screamed into the darkness. All those hisses, grunts, and strange whispers fitted what little was known about Emma, but the puzzle remained the same: why was the child desperate to communicate with Laura? To have no sight, hearing, and therefore, minimal speech was unimaginable; Emma was bound by a wall of silence and darkness, ignored and possibly mistreated and neglected. Her mother was the only source of comfort in her life, her only companion: they walked the streets together. The girl playing with miniature letter blocks: what did they represent? Laura had pieced together the braille clue without knowing that Eliza's daughter was blind. Had Emma used braille to communicate something that was subsequently lost? The paper on the cell floor, torn to shreds, had to be representative of something tangible, and real, something broken that needed to be reconstituted.

The visit to the museum in Gainsborough the next day was the only remaining source of hope. She had a name, two names, in fact, and the information provided a renewed sense of purpose.

Sean returned with a ledger bound in crusty tan leather, the boards warped by aging. He lay it on a protective cushion and carefully turned the pages. There were columns straddling both left and right pages, and names listed in rows.

'These are convicts and their descriptions, the location of their trial, not all of them are at Lincoln, and their sentence.' He moved the pages gingerly past the 1840s, 50s and 60s. The order was fixed by date and not name. He slowed up as he approached the 1870s.

Her quick eye was as good as his. They both exclaimed together and pointed at the name.

'Eliza Horton,' they said in unison.

'Twenty-eight years old. She must have married him when she was still in her teens,' Laura said.

The columns detailed her physical appearance. Brown hair. Green eyes. Five foot tall. Born in Lincoln in the same street as the bakery. Married; one child. Profession: shop assistant. Crime: murder. Sentence: death by hanging.

Laura traced her finger along the line, which was written, as were all the pages, in an immaculate copperplate script. 'Pity there isn't a picture of her. I don't know if what I see in my head is her or not.'

'But you do see her in your dreams?'

'If I'm dealing with Emma's memories, the more I think about that, the more the prison dream doesn't make sense. She was a child, blind and deaf, how would she be in a cell?'

He stroked his chin and perched on the edge of the table. 'Maybe that's how she pictured her mother locked up. She must have had an imagination.'

'I suppose.' The dream, or nightmare as it had been when she'd first encountered it, had contained many strange details that were illustrative, like a painting constructed with loose brushstrokes. The scratch marks on the doors, the impossibly high window, the truckle bed…

'They used hammocks in the prison?' she asked.

'Generally. Less trouble with vermin. They were strung widthways and off the floor.'

'There weren't hammocks in my dream because Emma wouldn't know about them. She created that prison scene from guesswork. All the other dreams I've had are minimalist and lacking in details, as you expect from a blind person, because those are her real memories.' Laura was finally in tune with her companion of the night – it was so apparent that dreams were the receptacle for transmitting Emma's memories, those that she perceived through experiences and others that she constructed from hearsay.

Sean took pictures of the pages using his phone before returning the ledger to the archivist. 'I don't think we'll find anything else, but it might be worth just checking the census records. We could find out more about Emma Horton.'

'I'd like that,' she said. Emma was the centre of the story, a blind girl, lost and waiting to be found again.

Sean had access to the census records through his work account and began filling in the search form.

'You've done this lots of times before,' she said.

'At work for research, yeah. I also traced my own family tree a few years back.' He spoke hesitantly, typing at the same time.

'Anything exciting?'

'No. Nothing.' He looked up at her and grinned. 'No royalty, titles, rogues. Not even a workhouse. Very boring. You've not traced your family?'

She shook her head. 'I know the names of my grandparents and great-grandparents, that's good enough for me. Never really seen the point. If there are skeletons in the Naylor closet, they're staying there.'

He laughed that lovely light-hearted chuckle she had come to enjoy hearing. It fizzled out naturally, and he refocused on the monitor, narrowing the search down.

'We'll start with the 1871 census.' He scanned a list of names: Elizabeths, Elspeths, Lizzies, and Elizas. All of them potentially Emma's mother, he explained, because a census wasn't always reliable when it came to the names people went by. 'Let's try her address, too… Bingo. Eliza Horton. Wife and shop assistant. James Horton, apprentice printer. William Horton, printer, and Emma Horton, child of ten years. So that's confirmation. Let's move on to 1882 and see what happened to Emma.'

The same address resulted in only one name: James Horton.

Laura frowned. 'Pity, but not surprising. Eliza and William are dead, and Emma, if she survived, would be twenty and probably living elsewhere. What's James's occupation?'

'Clerk.'

'So he didn't take over his father's printworks.'

Sean searched through the records of all Hortons, but there wasn't an Emma amongst them. Ten years on, in 1891, there was still no trace of her in Lincolnshire. She'd gone, too.

He spoke softly. 'There was an asylum in Lincoln. Maybe—'

'No, don't. What's the point? If nobody cared for her, then I really don't want to think about it, not yet. Maybe she'll tell me in the dreams or she'll keep hassling me to walk somewhere.' The address given in the census record wasn't anywhere near the river.

'It's nearly two o'clock. No wonder my tummy is rumbling. Fancy going somewhere?' His smile was crooked, optimistic on one side, cautious on the other. He played both parts well.

She'd not thought about Marco all morning. 'Sure.'

'What about a film? We can walk down to the Odeon.' He collected their coats off the stand in the corner.

In her handbag were the folded printed pages. They'd taken copies of the newspaper, the ledger, and census records. She was armed with facts. It comforted her to know she wasn't crazy. Perhaps a little celebration was warranted.

'I don't go to the cinema much,' she said.

The last time was a year ago to see some big blockbuster that everyone liked, except her because the noise was unbearable and there were ridiculous amounts of blood, or the fake stuff they used that was too red. As for the fights, surely one substantial blow would do it? There'd been lots of guns, too. Marco had laughed a great deal, saying it was a funny film because it was unbelievable. He'd gone with a friend from the university to see the sequel.

Sean held the door open for her. 'I used to take Maisie all the time, but now she wants to go with her friends. It would be nice to see something other than Disney and ponies.'

'I prefer nothing violent, if you don't mind. Or bad language. It's not my thing.'

'Crap.'

'Oh. You like horror; that kind of thing?' What had she missed?

'No, I wasn't referring to that. I swear all the time, can't help it. Years of living on my own, I've become one of those muttering types, always cursing. Sorry.'

He was pensive. Worried. Her approval mattered to him.

How sweet. 'I meant in films. American type films where they throw it around like confetti.'

'Oh, right.'

'We can have hot dogs, yes? And popcorn. I do like it sweet.'

He blushed, leaned towards her, his face seemingly poised to swoop down. But nothing happened, no follow-through. He rocked back onto his heels, and the moment was lost. The indecision on both their parts was torturous, and she was as much to blame as him.

They watched a family comedy without having to suffer oodles of sickly romance. It was forgettable and fun, two things she needed to brighten her day. In the darkness, she giggled at the slapstick, her positive mood uninhibited, and she enjoyed the pleasure of trivial humour. Sean chuckled, little rumbling belly laughs, and scoffed his way through a bucket of popcorn. The origins of the slight paunch were increasingly apparent. He liked food. She squirted mustard and ketchup on her hot dog and picked off the onions. It was easy dating and juvenile, something she'd never done as a teenager because she was passed back and forth between two warring parents, a shuttlecock in constant flight. It was never too late to catch up with a childhood. Never too late to fill in the missing opportunities.

'I'll get a bus back,' she said on the way out of the cinema.

'I can drop—'

'No, it's fine. I need to stretch my legs and I have a return ticket.'

They were battling a crowd of moviegoers brushing past her shoulders, shouting indiscriminately.

Sean stuffed his hands in his pockets. 'I… it's… I've enjoyed today.'

She admired the simplicity. 'Me, too.'

He pitched forward onto the balls of his feet, expectantly. There was an element of him waiting for her, but what part – why the blinking eyes and nervous twitches?

'Why do you like me?' she asked, followed by a rogue skip of the heart; she'd surprised herself with the abruptness.

The tips of his ears flashed amber under the marigold streetlights, a blush that matched the natural tints in his cropped hair. He glanced around. Thankfully, the teeming throng was thinning.

'Well… it's like the tin, you know, the label. You're exactly what's it says is on the inside.' He grimaced and fiddled with his jacket zip.

An answer far removed from anything she'd anticipated. 'Oh.' Embarrassed for them both, she shrank a tad into the pavement blocks. 'What does that mean?'

He scratched his chin and scuffed his shoe along the base of the streetlamp. 'You're not daft. You're honest.'

And without grace or charm, she thought. 'I'm contrary and too cynical.' She couldn't allow him to bring down her defences, not yet, not while she was uncertain.

He ceased fidgeting. 'Then we complement each other. Which is good, yeah? Anyway you're not cynical. Cautious, perhaps, maybe a bit of an overthinker. Which is okay, cos it balances the flippant types. My mum says I'm unflappable, so I'm not put off by that kind of...' The blush deepened as he picked up on his own hypocrisy. He stepped back to allow a couple to cross in front.

'That's a good thing, too.' In the distance, the double decker's number shone. The sweet-natured conversation was leading her into a quandary; she hadn't intended it to be awkward. But it comforted her in an odd way, seeing him flustered, thinking on his feet.

She pointed at the nearby stop. 'My bus is coming. See you tomorrow,' she said sheepishly.

He'd arranged to pick her up at ten o'clock at her house – there was no bus to Gainsborough on a Sunday morning. She'd run out of excuses.

Laura hugged her knees to her chest and propped her chin on them. Giant emotions assaulted her dwarfed body. She couldn't stop shivering. Unwanted in its inception, the dream had overwhelmed her. The cinema had been a brief distraction, a pleasant one, but ultimately it had failed to prevent the inevitable sense of panic brought on by the re-emergent night terrors.

She had dozed for a while, bite-sized chunks of sleep, until eventually she was too tired to fight it. Then, she'd woken, groped for the light switch with a sweaty hand, and broken free of the gloom. Blinking, bleary-eyed, she waited for her thoughts to coalesce.

She wanted the return of order. If Marco hadn't upped and left her, she would at least have somebody to embrace at night and an offer of physical comfort. He wasn't there, and she had to accept the truth; he wasn't part of her life anymore and was too self-absorbed and lily-livered to tell her. As for Sean, she owed him more than a trip to the cinema for his support and time. But how to pay him back when she had nothing to offer him beyond a curious mystery that stoked his inquisitiveness into action?

The overwhelming emotions of negativity had to do with the return of that dream, the one that had started the whole business of graveyards and prisons – the woman in the cell. Laura had hoped that the blind girl would provide fresh clues, but she hadn't. Wherever she was after that fateful murder, Emma was stuck in a terrifying and lonely loop, unable to move on from her mother's violent past. Poor child. Laura suspected she'd died not long after Eliza's execution. Under what circumstances, she dreaded to find out.

The one thing Laura could do was bring justice to a courtroom. Iain had tried to embolden her with his confession, and he believed the trial was going to redeem the guilt she carried. She hoped he was right about that, the connection to the blind, and that her efforts would end Emma's and Eliza's suffering, too. Eventually, they might give up on Laura and haunt another victim, one with a better imagination.

'Oh, don't be stupid, Laura,' she said. The other jurors weren't going to pay any attention to her, she was the quietest of them all, save Amil. She'd be drowned out. The best she could hope for was no majority, or a hung jury, or, unless the prosecution admitted defeat and left Brader alone, a retrial. At least that would free Laura of the burden of deciding his fate.

The Last Sunday

SEAN DROVE a smoothly contoured Japanese car. With its bright-red exterior, an integrated satnav, and leather steering wheel, the inside was spotless and smelt of oranges. Cars had developed all manner of newfangled things that she might enjoy owning if she was keen on the driving aspect. When she had been behind the wheel, air conditioning was a luxury, keys were necessary to start the engine, and windscreen wipers didn't come on of their own accord. However, the passenger side remained the same, and she coped; not one minuscule flashback.

Sean hadn't asked her why she didn't have a car. He was selective with his curiosity.

'Last night?' he asked.

He was bound to enquire about her dreams. The episodic progress of their investigation was dependent on her updates. She was also surprised how much she wanted to know about braille even though it remained an elusive aspect. She wasn't entirely sure if a visit to an off-the-beaten-track museum would provide any answers; there was no firm evidence a document existed, only Sean's steadfast hunch.

Unfortunately, recalling the strange dream dredged up unpleasant emotions. 'I've come full circle.' She vented her frustration. 'I'm back in the prison cell with Eliza.' At least she had a name, an identity. So did the daughter. 'But no sign of Emma.'

'Just as it was before?' He kept his eyes on the road. The satnav insisted he took the A15. He ignored the instruction and chose a quieter road north to Gainsborough.

'Yes. The same claustrophobic, dark, oppressive hellhole. The air is heavy with something… I can hear her breathing. Throaty noises. A death rattle, almost.'

Sean grimaced in sympathy. 'Can you see her hair? Her green eyes?'

Eliza remained a fixture in the corner of the cell, a murky half-formed figure abandoned by the artist of the dream. 'No. She's in the shadows. It's like a black-and-white drawing. I don't see any colour.' Do people dream in colour? She'd never paid much attention to the shape of dreams, their structural details like colour and sound. She felt emotions during them but couldn't recall ever saying anything herself. What did your own voice sound like in a dream? Was it recognisable? Were her lips moving, her tongue articulating, but her vocal cords silenced by some means?

'And the bits of paper?'

'Shredded on the floor in the dirt. I'm back to square one. I woke up in a terrible state, not because I'm scared by her anymore, I'm over that. It's the fear of not owning my dreams. I'm infected, you know, like a computer virus.'

Sean guffawed. 'Hacked.' He turned on to another road, a busier one. 'I'm sorry. It's not funny. You say the room is exactly the same, the bed—'

'Yes. I'm on the bed. The manuscript I pieced together is shredded again. She's behaving like the dreams are stuck in a loop.'

'Interesting.'

'Why?' She hadn't been thinking of that word. She pressed her hands between her thighs, warming them. It seemed to take forever for the car to heat up.

'You know now that prisoners slept on hammocks. You know more about Eliza, a little bit about what she looked like, but nothing has changed. Aren't dreams a construct of your making, something based on your experiences and subconscious thoughts?'

'I suppose.' She wasn't a psychologist, neither was Sean.

'So why haven't you reconstructed the dream to include new details?' He spoke with growing excitement, glancing in her direction and not at the car in front, whose brake lights Laura considered very twitchy. She'd rather he kept his eyes firmly on the road ahead. Angela called her the worse passenger in the world because Laura saw potential accidents around every corner. She was the lookout and, with her mum in the driver's seat, she often pointed out what could potentially go wrong. She carried with her a morbid sense of fate. With Sean, she had to stay silent. He wouldn't understand the compulsion.

'What do you mean?' she asked.

'We know Emma doesn't know about hammocks, or what the cells actually were like. It confirms you're always experiencing her memories in your dreams.' He scratched his nose. 'Just an idea. My ex is a therapist. Sorry, it rubbed off onto me a bit. She used to irritate me with all the psychobabble.'

Laura appreciated the honest explanation. But he was right. 'Emma doesn't even know what her own mother looks like.'

How sad, and strange. Laura might not see her mother often, her father even less, but she had a clear picture in her head of her mother's blue eyes, chestnut hair, rounded shoulders, and chubby fingers. She hadn't aged much; she was successfully hiding the grey hairs and wrinkles with regular visits to the beauty salon. Her white teeth were suffering the most due to a long phase of incessant smoking, a habit Laura detested. Visualising a caricature of her mother was easy; she hadn't altered particularly over the years. But Laura had never dreamt about her own mother. Only Margery, her stepmother, the bone of contention, and her awful stepbrothers who should have filled the shoes of her unborn siblings but hadn't even tried to know her. Dreams hijacked the worst elements of people and amplified every little fault.

Sean stayed quiet. She liked the thinking space he offered her. She needed to breathe into ideas, allow her own thoughts to coalesce. With the court case, she struggled to keep up with the demands on her thinking time because of the nature of the inquisitional style of the barristers, the constant stream of question and answers; there was never any opportunity to assimilate things. How had Amil made all those notes? It wasn't that she was slow on the uptake, she just preferred the terms methodical and contemplative.

She dismissed the impending last day in court and returned to the dream. 'Doesn't explain why I'm back there.'

'No,' he agreed. He was switching his focus between the windscreen and satnav display, which for some reason he'd muted. He had an idea of where they were going.

'The museum is outside Gainsborough?'

'Yes. It's a private collection in a house. Only opens at weekends. We're lucky to have the museum so nearby.' He turned off the main road into a pot-holed, muddy-verged minor one. He veered the car to the left and right to avoid the craters. The lane navigated an inefficient path around the fields.

Eventually, the satnav took them onto a single-track lane with ample passing spaces. Sean edged cautiously around the blind corners, which pleased Laura. The hedges parted to reveal the entrance to an avenue lined with beech trees. There were two signs, one on either side of the open gate. One simply said *Kestern House* with *Museum of Braille* in small lettering underneath the name of the house. The second sign was large and colourful: *Kestern Caravan Park. Holiday homes for the visually impaired. Provided by Seeside.*

Laura gripped her seat. 'Seeside,' she said quietly.

'What?'

It wasn't appropriate to tell Sean that she was in the process of forming a judgement about Seeside's financial reliability. The leaflet the usher had issued all members of the jury was clear – no talking about the case to anyone, no Googling, no reading newspaper reports. She was in a bubble; a legally required vacuum. In the run-up to their visit, she should have asked Sean more questions. Now she feared the answers might force them to turn back. With nobody to call for advice, she was skirting the confusing legal issues of jury service. However, who would know she'd come to a Seeside holiday park, especially as they had several across the region? Dreams had inspired the reason for their visit, and a caravan park had to be harmless; it wouldn't tell her anything about Brader. She decided Sean knowing was also irrelevant to the reason they were visiting the museum.

'Caravan park,' she said simply. 'Reminds me of family holidays.'

'Yeah. It's over there.' Slowing, he pointed to a barrier of frostbitten evergreen foliage. 'And the museum is part of the house.'

He drove down the lane, and when it forked, he took the one to the left, leading to the house. The sign for the caravan park pointed the other way.

'I gather they've got a sensory garden and an arts centre for the blind,' he said. 'Probably why the occupants of the house have an interest in braille, too.'

The manor house emerged from behind a heavily burdened cedar tree. A silvery stone-built house, it rose three storeys high to touch the slate roof. A grandiose bay window reflected the cotton-wool sky, preventing her from seeing inside. Around the walls, borders had been planted, forming a barrier. The plants had withered for the winter, leaving the soil barren, and only a few low-lying heathers offered colour against the stone backdrop. The drive was interrupted by a lichen-covered dry fountain in the form of a nymph crouched in the middle of a shallow circular pond. Sean navigated around it. A small sign directed him to a gravel parking area. Beyond it was a stable block joined to the side of the house by a red-brick wall. The converted building housed the museum.

Zipping up her coat, she joined Sean outside. He strode up to the blue double door and rattled the door handle, then the letterbox.

'Locked…' He looked at his wristwatch. 'Should be open by now. Shit.' He peered at the note pinned to the inside of the small window by the door. 'Shut. What a bloody idiot. I should have checked.'

Closed for Winter.
Please deliver mail to house.

Laura cupped her hands around her face and pressed her nose against the window. It was still too dark to see anything other than an interior panel of wood. The place seemed empty.

'Maybe they've shut altogether.' Her sigh was laden with disappointment. Even though the purpose of their visit was poorly defined, she'd pinned her hopes on finding something that might explain the existence of a braille document at a time in history when few people had access to braille. Sean had said they kept a rare collection of books and other publications. Not that she expected to find her manuscript in amongst it, but maybe it would point to where hers might have ended up, assuming the document existed at all. Her head throbbed.

'I'm sorry. I've brought you here for no reason.' He thumped his leg, almost brutally, his enthusiasm gone in a blink of an eye.

'Well, I wasn't sure what we might find. It's a very tenuous link.'

Laura's optimism was based on pragmatism, his seemed to ride on hope. She sensed, based on their short time together, that they both relied on diligence, the need to tidy up loose ends and derive satisfaction from a neat, well-done job. While Sean paced in annoyance at his mistake, Laura was already thinking about the return journey home. Perhaps she should tell him about Marco, and her "situation", and the concerns she had about "dating".

'Hello? Are you looking for the caravan park?' The woman's voice came from the side of the house by the open gate in the wall. She carried a basket and waved at them with a small gardening fork. 'The office is back that way.'

Slight, hunched-shouldered and white-haired, the woman wore loose twill trousers and what appeared to be three jumpers piled on top of each other. Her wispy hair was tied up into a bird's nest bun. Clumps of wet grass stuck to her knees, and the gardening gloves crowded her hands. But her boots were clean. She had startlingly grey eyes, moonlit and alert, and ruddy cheeks with threadbare capillaries at the end of her long nose. Once, she'd probably been a handsome woman, but weathering had worn away the finer features.

Sean gestured to the locked door. 'Actually, we came for this, but I foolishly didn't check the opening times.'

'Oh. Have you come far?'

'Lincoln.' Sean glanced at Laura. 'I work in the castle, in the prison museum, I'm a curator. We're putting together a new exhibition, and I found out one of our prisoners might have been blind, so Laura and I thought we'd come out for a look, just something to do.' He smiled. 'Not to worry.'

He painted a picture of a couple out moonlighting on a cold Sunday. Laura was quite content with the scenario if it suited their needs. Sean's patchwork of lies fitted together nicely, too.

'I'm interested in braille,' Laura added. 'How it was printed back in Victorian times and if somebody could put together a manuscript without any sophisticated devices.'

The woman closed the gate behind her and pulled off her gloves. She dropped them in the basket along with the fork.

'Yes, that's entirely possible,' she said. 'We don't get many visitors to the museum. We're thinking of shutting it down and donating things to other archives and museums.'

'It would be a pity to break up the collection,' Sean said with genuine sympathy.

'Yes, but my husband is ill, and my nephew isn't interested. I'm eighty.'

'It's a lovely house,' Laura said.

'Been in the family for a century,' she said. 'Look, I can see you've made a special trip out, so let me go get the key and I'll let you in.'

'Would you? That's very kind of you, thank you... er...'

'Olivia. Olivia Feydon.' She disappeared through the gate, leaving the basket behind on the ground.

Laura's shoes seemed to sink into the loose gravel. She should go. A member of the Feydon family, and probably related to Steven Feydon; Olivia would know all about the trial.

'What's the matter?' Sean asked, catching her sleeve.

But Laura wasn't at the house to talk about Brader. She didn't need to mention him or Seeside at all. 'Nothing.' She leaned towards him. 'Did you know the Feydons lived here?'

He dropped his hand. 'I knew it was their collection. It's listed at the National Archive. Lucky for us to meet with Mrs Feydon in person, hey?'

'Yes.' She returned to the comfort zone of brevity.

A soft-focused frown melted onto his face. He was able to read the tone of her voice too well.

Olivia Feydon returned, carrying a key on a lanyard. She fiddled with the lock, twisting and turning. 'So damn stiff.'

'Here, let me help.' Sean rotated the key, and the lock clicked. 'There.'

'Thank you, young man.'

'Sean,' he said, smiling.

The wood panel Laura had spotted was part of the old stable. On the other side, through a door, was an open space. Olivia flicked a light switch. The old partitions had been removed, the walls plastered and decorated with pin-striped wallpaper, the wooden floorboards covered in Hessian, which muffled their footfalls, and the ceiling fitted with gentle lighting. Arranged in two rows were glass-topped cabinets, and laid out in them were opened books, loose sheets of paper and other intricate items. The papers were embossed rather than printed with text. The exhibition continued along one wall lined with upright glass cabinets displaying various apparatus, many of them similar to typewriters. A larger machine was in a corner, free-standing. Sean was drawn to the back wall and the shelves of the small library.

From old leather-bound books on the left to modern spiral-bound ones on the right, the cases homed an extensive collection. The books ranged from pocket-sized pamphlets to fat tomes with flaking leather spines.

Olivia walked over and touched one of the books, almost caressing it. 'We've over three hundred books, many of them rare; a few are the only ones left in print. Braille books were in short supply for many years and only printed for those who could afford them. The Kestern family were determined to make books available for everyone, young and old, rich or poor.'

Laura moved to one of the cabinets. 'And these are printers?' They were small, hardly any different to a typewriter with their carriage returns and space bars, but only six keys instead of twenty-six letters of the alphabet. Six keys for six dots.

Olivia joined her. 'Yes. That's a Perkins Braillewriter, which David Abraham designed. It took him many years to perfect it. The Perkins model came into general use in the 1950s and is based on much earlier designs that started to appear at the end of the nineteenth century. Unfortunately, those early machines weren't very robust, certainly not suitable for blind children. If you're interested in the earliest forms of writing braille, then these are more appropriate.'

She showed Laura the contents of one of the lower cabinets. 'Louis Braille was blind himself. The idea of using dots wasn't original, but Louis created a new, easy-to-learn code when he was fifteen years old. Braille isn't just for reading, it's for writing.'

The display included a handheld tool with a wooden handle and metal pin, similar to a skewer.

'This is the awl, which later became more like a stylus. Ironic, given Louis was accidentally blinded by an awl. The slate,' she pointed to a hinged metal board with square openings, 'has cells with six indentations for forming the embossed dots. The two metal sheets open up like a book, and the paper is held fast between them.'

Laura bent over the glass. 'The paper is sandwiched between these, and the stylus is pressed down to make the dots.' The cells were evenly spaced.

'That's it,' Olivia said. 'The metal sheet underneath prevents the stylus from pushing through the paper and making unwanted holes. The paper needs to be embossed, raised.'

'It must have been a laborious task writing braille,' she said.

'Indeed, for a beginner. And because the paper is being embossed, the dots are raised on the other side of the paper, not this top side. The writer had to work right to left so that the words could be read left to right.'

'Good grief. This is more complex than I thought.' She already knew that the dots coded for more than letters, numbers, and punctuation marks. They also coded contractions of common words or letter combinations that made up sounds. However, she'd researched the braille from the perspective of the reader and not the writer.

Olivia showed her the next cabinet. There were various hinged sheets, some containing no more than four lines of cells, while the largest was big enough to cover a whole sheet of foolscap paper.

'The beginner would start with a large board, so they didn't have to move the cells down. There are twenty-eight cells on each line.'

'And this would be how it was done in the nineteenth century?' Laura asked.

'It's changed very little. The tools are now plastic, not metal, but the technique remains the same.' Stooping, she circled the cabinet, caressing her palm along the spotlessly clean glass as she pointed out the contents. 'There are other systems, like peg boards, but for simplicity, the stylus remains the best.'

'So, somebody who was blind could have created a document or manuscript of some length using this?'

'Yes. Although braille wasn't standardised much in those days.'

Sean was by the books, leafing through a few. 'Is that why they don't all look the same?' He'd opened up several books, laying them on a counter by the shelves. 'I hadn't realised there was so many different styles of braille. Can I take some pictures?' He removed his mobile from his back pocket.

'You may take photos, but only for personal use. Not all of these forms of coding are called braille. Louis Braille came up with his version in the 1820s, but there were others. The lack of standardisation caused problems for teaching in blind schools. Which did you choose to learn?' Running her hand along the shelf, Olivia picked out one book and opened it.

'This is Moon—'

'I've seen this,' Laura said excitedly. 'I did a little research… it's nothing like Braille.'

Olivia skated her finger along the embossed shapes. 'Feel it.'

Laura closed her eyes and traced the outline of each one. 'I can feel lines, some curves. It's more obvious than just dots.'

'This is the Moon system. Invented by Doctor Moon in the mid-nineteenth century. Some of the shapes resemble letters, like O and C. However, it wasn't quick to read and created bulky books because of the size of the embossed shapes needed to create the code. However, for those who had lost their sight, as opposed to being born blind, this was an ideal compromise. Easier to learn when you know what letters look like. It's still used today.'

'I had no idea,' Sean said. 'So nothing was standardised?'

'It wasn't until this century that there was English Unified Braille.'

'And mass printing?' Laura asked. The enthusiasm lost in the car journey was bubbling to the surface, overtaking Sean's.

Olivia pointed to the larger, free-standing machine. 'Much easier in the world of computers and hi-tech machinery. The Kestern family became involved over a century ago, sometime in the 1880s, when Nicholas Kestern acquired a print shop and converted it into a braille one and used these very techniques to create books for the blind. The printworks was based initially in Lincoln then Gainsborough, where it remained until my husband, Tony, sold it. It was never a commercially successful enterprise. Our money comes from construction design, innovation, and environmental buildings.' Holiday homes, she meant.

There was a reason for Seeside's existence on the grounds of the estate, and that connection to the family's past had begun with one person. The realisation caused a plummeting sensation in Laura's stomach. The threads that had lay loose and separate were now knotting together. She had never foreseen that the court case might be bound directly to her ghostly encounters in the castle.

She closed the book and avoided eye contact with Sean. 'From who did Nicholas get his interest in blindness?' Who, not where or what… she was directing the conversation to an inevitable disclosure.

'From his wife, Emma. She was born blind. She's the reason why…'

Sean inhaled sharply. Laura's hands shook.

'Are you all right?' Olivia asked. 'You've gone quite pale, my dear.'

She should say something, anything to excuse her over-the-top reaction. She glanced over at Sean; he'd stopped examining the spines of the books, and his glasses slipped down the bridge of his nose as he returned her gaze. How studious he'd become since their arrival; he was as comfortable in the past as he was the future. She wished she could join him and make light of the discovery. Sean deserved to see the whole picture. After tomorrow, when the trial concluded, she'd be able to tell him how the pieces of two mysteries linked together to form one.

Laura spoke slowly. 'Are the Kesterns related to the Feydons, to your family?'

Olivia's smile wrinkled her bone-china cheeks. 'Why, yes.'

'And the Hortons?'

The smile evaporated.

The Garden

SEAN SAT LAURA ON A WOODEN CHAIR by the door next to a table that bore a small cash register and a laminated list of exhibits – the only indication that the museum was still in operation. Olivia disappeared into a side room and returned with a glass of water.

The shaking subsided. Laura sipped on the water. 'Thank you. I don't know what came over me.'

'It's a bit chilly in here,' Olivia said politely.

'No, I don't think it's that,' Laura said. She glanced up at Sean.

His eyebrows had drawn together into a curtain of concern for her. She needed his help, and with a small nod, he acknowledged it. He cleared his throat.

'You see, Mrs Feydon. We're actually interested in Eliza Horton. She had a daughter called Emma, who was blind. We read about her in a newspaper report covering her mother's death.'

'Yes, Eliza Horton,' Olivia said, unperturbed. 'Emma's mother and my husband's great-great grandmother.'

'She was hanged for murdering—'

'Her husband. A long time ago. And Emma wasn't involved, so she isn't your blind prisoner. Emma married Nicholas Kestern. They had two sons, one of whom was killed in the First World War, leaving two young children, a girl and boy, and a widow. The children were supported by their uncle, Henry, who never married and bought this house in 1912. Henry's nephew died in the Second World War and was childless. The niece, Frances, married Kevin Feydon, and they are my husband's parents.'

'And your nephew?' Laura asked, rapidly calculating the familial links, the possible generations.

'Steven? Sadly, his father died some years ago when he was a young boy. Tony has been pivotal in his life. Steven is more like a son to us than nephew. Tony and I tried but…' The word died on her lips, and she sighed.

'And Emma lived here?'

'Yes, from 1912. They moved the family out of Lincoln.' A few perplexed furrows formed on Olivia's brow at the return to the past.

Emma hadn't died so young that she was wiped from history; she had lived on as a Kestern, which was why they hadn't found her in the census records. Laura stared at the bank of books. How many of them had Emma touched, run her fingers along and read?

Olivia continued. 'At first, she lived with Nicholas's family in a townhouse they owned.'

Laura's stomach tightened into knots. 'It's by the river, near a park, or what was a park with weeping willows, roses with thorns, and…' Things she'd thought she touched but hadn't. 'When did they get married?'

Olivia maintained a bemused expression. 'They married, oh, I can't remember, they were young, and he did very well. Nicholas inherited a small fortune from his father. She lived here in her later years, after she'd stopped teaching.'

'Teaching?'

'She was a teacher.'

'But.' Laura's lower lip trembled. Nothing made sense, the connection to her dreams was breaking, and what she'd pieced together from the fragments in the archive was proving to be woefully inadequate. 'I thought Emma was congenitally *deaf* and blind.'

'Gracious no.' Olivia exclaimed softly. 'She was a woman of few words, according to Tony's mother. She loved to read and she transcribed braille herself. She created several of the volumes in this library. In the early days of teaching braille to children, the Bible was the standard braille text for schooling. The church paid for them. But Emma wanted the children to enjoy more than religious texts. Nicholas embossed books for her to read to her own children, and later her pupils. She loved Jane Austen and the classics.' Olivia retrieved a heavy book from the shelves and lay it on top of one of the glass cabinets. The leather was disintegrating along the spine, but the paper was clean and intact.

'*Wuthering Heights*.' Olivia touched it reverently and closed her eyes.

'May I?' Laura asked, moving next to her.

Olivia stroked the left-hand page, Laura the right. She shut her eyes and listened. Was Emma here, too? Had she followed her to this house where she'd once lived? Would she whisper in her ears and tell her where the manuscript was…?

Laura opened her eyes. 'Did Emma ever write anything about her life? It must have been a remarkable one, given her upbringing.'

Olivia removed her hand from the page and stiffened. For the first time, she looked pensive, jaded by the unexpected guests in her museum. Her beloved museum, Laura thought.

'You mean about her mother?' Olivia asked.

Sean touched Laura's shoulder, and she ignored it.

'Perhaps it's not a good idea to bring it up,' Laura said.

Olivia blinked at Sean. 'Of course. You work at the castle prison,' she said, as if remembering a distant conversation. 'Forgive me. My memory… yes, Emma's mother was hanged for murdering her father. But beyond that, the family knows little of her past. Nicholas never wrote anything. There are no diaries or photographs that date back to when she was younger. Only after they moved here were records kept of their life together. As for Emma… we believe she wrote her memoir in braille using this very slate.' She pointed to the cabinet with the braille writer and stylus.

Laura held her breath. It was Sean's turn to stiffen.

'Sadly, it's lost,' Olivia said, unmoved.

He deflated immediately. 'But it existed?'

'A rumour, perhaps. Tony's Great-Uncle Henry, Nicholas's second son, thought it might reveal secrets about the Hortons, Emma's parents, things she didn't want anyone to know. There was such a scandal around her father's murder, and I suspect her mother was vilified for killing him in such a cold-blooded manner.'

'But she wrote something down,' Sean persisted.

Laura touched his sleeve. This was her project, not his. She wasn't happy with browbeating an old woman.

'It's gone.' Olivia shrugged, seemingly impervious to Sean's diligence.

'It's not the only thing that's vanished,' Sean said. 'Eliza Horton's headstone is missing from the prison graveyard in the Lucy Tower.'

Olivia's bright eyes twinkled. 'Oh, we know where *that* is.'

'You do?'

The smile broadened. 'It's in our garden here. Every year it's surrounded by new flowers. We tell any visitors it's where a pet is buried. Somebody moved the stone here a long time ago and created a memorial to her.'

'To a woman who murdered her husband?' Sean dodged Laura's scolding glare and removed his glasses.

Olivia offered her own disapproving frown. 'To a mother.'

'Could we see it, please?' Laura asked sweetly.

'I don't see why not, since it's what you're also looking for.' Olivia's acuity was sharp as a razor.

Laura fumbled with her zip. 'We never thought it would turn up. There's no account of her grave.'

'Really?' Olivia's white-crested eyebrows shot up. 'Then how did you know it was missing in the first place?'

'There was no reason for it not to be at the castle,' Sean explained. 'Condemned prisoners were buried in the tower. Laura worked out it was missing.' He avoided embellishing how. The pair of them were neatly tiptoeing around Laura's vision.

'I'd love to see it,' Laura said.

Olivia locked the door behind them and hung the lanyard around her neck. She picked up her basket and led them through the garden gate.

Laura wasn't a gardener. She could appreciate the vision and effort that went into the art of gardening, but it wasn't something that called to her. The landscaped terraces and borders cascaded down the slight incline towards the grassy meadows. Although it wasn't the time of year for blossom or petals, the garden managed to extract colour from the greyness of late autumn. The overhanging trees clung on to the last crumpled leaves, while on the dew-drenched lawn, mulched leaves had been raked into heaps. There was a wheelbarrow filled with exhausted twigs and wilted nettles. The borders were bedded down for the winter with bark shavings and the evergreen shrubs cut back in anticipation of bursting into life in the spring. In the distance, on the other side of a privet hedge, were the rolling banks of fields and the white-topped static caravans in the neighbouring holiday park.

'It's beautiful,' Laura said, pausing to admire the vista.

'Thank you. We have a sensory garden in the corner. Emma established it, and we've kept it going for our blind visitors.'

'The caravan park is popular?' Sean asked, stuffing his hands into his pockets.

'All year round. We keep the numbers up by offering art classes, pottery, and sculpting, and, of course, we teach braille embossing to both sighted and blind. We invite poets and musicians. It's a busy schedule of events.'

None of those activities had been mentioned in court. Only money, raffles, and contracts. The jury had lost sight – Laura thought that ironic – of the purpose of the charity and why it mattered to keep the donations rolling in.

Olivia led them down a mosaic path, though a tunnel of rhododendrons to an opening, and sweeping in a great arc around the dormant flowerbeds, providing them shelter from the breeze, was a yew hedge shaped by topiary. In the middle of the small grove, laid flat, was the roughly hewn headstone. The weeds had tried to inch closer to it but had been beaten back by hoe and trowel. The grey stone was stained by mildew and cracked by numerous frosts, but the lettering remained distinct.

E.H.
Nov 15
1872

Laura crouched and traced her finger along the etching, just as she'd done once before. It felt as real to her as it had done in the Lucy Tower. Except there were anomalies: the stone had aged and…

'I don't recall seeing the date, just the year,' she said, rising to stand over the memorial, pleased that the headstone had been put to good use, and thankful it wasn't a real grave. She had no sense of haunting in the quiet grounds. It was not a place marked with death or suffering – quite the contrary, it was peaceful and calming.

Sean shrugged. 'Maybe she didn't know the exact details.'

By she, Laura knew he meant Emma. It was Emma's memories of the grave that had been recalled to life when Laura visited the tower.

Olivia was close by, plucking at a weed. She lifted her head, straightening her rounded back to a limited extent. 'You've seen this before?' she asked sharply.

Laura took a step back. 'An… account of it,' she stuttered. Although she was relieved to know she hadn't imagined the grave, the original purpose of their visit hadn't been its discovery. 'Would you like to find Emma's memoir?' she asked Olivia.

Olivia pursed her lips. 'If it still exists.' The doubts remained.

Sean, who'd examined the gravestone after Laura, his glasses once again perched on his nose, offered up what Laura was afraid to say. 'It might mention something scandalous.'

Olivia's laughter was surprisingly hoarse. 'I think we're safe from the scandals of our past.'

But not the current ones. Laura kept quiet. Would visitors still come to Kestern if they knew that money had been frittered away by a greedy man?

'Emma died in 1927,' Olivia said proudly. 'Sound of mind. Nicholas lived on for another ten years.'

'She accomplished a great deal,' Sean said, agreeably.

'She's a remarkable woman. Nothing will mar her memory or her good deeds. She brought joy to countless children. Her legacy is why Seeside exists. Nicholas established the charity in her memory.'

If Laura needed to understand the reasons why she'd been chosen to find Emma's missing manuscript, they began with the stone on the ground, then the success of Kestern's braille printworks, Seeside's establishment, and finally and inevitably Brader, the unscrupulous thief. The connections flowed through the dreams and memories of Emma, linking the past and present into one path of discovery and, of all the people on the jury, Laura was the only one with a debt to the blind.

Justice in the crown court depended on jurors acknowledging the imperfections of humanity, which they brought into the courtroom as life experiences. Their judgement was tempered by frailties, and each person carried those flaws whether secretly or openly. However, Laura was the only one with a guilty heart who was likely to attract the attentions of a waiting spirit. Decades had passed since Eliza's death, and perhaps there had been other unsuccessful attempts with visitors to the castle – as illustrated by Sean's accounts of hauntings of the prison chapel – but only Laura had persevered. Or Emma had. Both stubborn, it seemed.

If she was able to give Seeside back its stolen donations, find Emma's manuscript, and return it to her family for safekeeping, she might be able to forgive herself for the accident she hadn't caused but had struggled to live with for fourteen years.

She stood motionless under a bare weeping willow tree and admired the view. Sean and Olivia discussed composting.

Olivia gave Laura her contact details. 'Just in case you find Emma's memoirs.' The wavering belief in the manuscript swung like a pendulum. She also suggested a pub that served Sunday roast for lunch.

Olivia lingered, framed by weathered bricks and golden leaves of honeysuckle, her back slightly stooped and weary, the handle of the wicker basket hooked over the crook of her elbow. Sean reversed out of the dead end, circled the fountain, and when Laura looked back, Olivia had slipped away into the garden.

'Not exactly keen on finding the manuscript, is she?' Sean said.

'I don't think she believes it exists, a family rumour.'

'But they have the headstone displayed like a shrine. And how did it end up in the garden?'

The pub was conveniently at the foot of the hill on the outskirts of the village. They ordered the recommended roast and chose a table in a cramped bay window overlooking the jumbled garden. It wasn't as well-kept as Olivia's.

The food was good, though. She picked at the meat until her appetite arrived, belated and half-formed. The conversation over steaming plates was odd and stilted. While Sean chirped away happily, Laura constructed a mental list of what should happen next; it revolved around the man sitting opposite her. Once the verdict was delivered, she'd tell him about Brader and Seeside, but before that was the accident; she shouldn't let it fester like she had done with Marco. As for Marco, she had to explain to Sean her "situation" and how it would be resolved upon Marco's anticipated return. Instead of listening to Sean, she was doing a thoroughly good job of ignoring the issues that he thought were the point of the conversation.

'We need to find the manuscript,' Sean babbled. 'Perhaps it was deposited with the Lincolnshire Society for the Blind... nah, too obvious. Somebody would have thought of that.' He scooped up a heap of mashed potato, his appetite plain to see.

She needed an injection of his enduring enthusiasm.

'So,' he said, tearing through a slice of beef with a blunt knife. 'I could try the RNIB library. Maybe they've got it... but they would have read it when they catalogued it, and worked out it belonged to the Kestern family. Although, being a charity, they probably haven't got the resources to research the origins of the manuscript. Worth a call.'

'She might have written it anonymously.' Olivia's pessimism was rubbing off on Laura. It seemed unlikely it existed in any form. It was just a dream.

Gravy dripped off his fork. 'Yeah, possibly.' He shrugged off her suggestion. 'Maybe it was sold into private hands.'

'And why would they keep it secret?'

His eyes narrowed. 'Blackmail. Not now, I mean, but back when it was created. Maybe the manuscript was taken by somebody and used against Emma's family.' Sean's rambling imagination outshone Laura's stunted one.

'Olivia would have said something. The past doesn't bother her. She's eighty.' Laura was wilfully adept at shooting down his theories, which was unkind; she should try to maintain their friendship going forward.

He sank a Yorkshire pudding into a puddle of beef juice. 'I think she can read braille.'

Olivia had been overtly tactile when she handled the books. 'Possibly.'

'She's eighty, as you said, but didn't need reading glasses when she looked at the books.' He patted his breast pocket where he kept his glasses, as if to remind himself they were still there.

'Or she knows her library really well.'

'You could tell she doesn't want to break up the collection. It's her baby.'

'So is the garden.'

He nodded. He harried the last remaining peas around the edge of his plate.

Laura placed her knife and fork together. She'd managed half of the giant portion of roast potatoes and some green veg. He eyed her untouched Yorkshire and pointed at it.

'Do you mind?' His cheeks flushed red.

She shook her head, smiling, and he swooped in, filching the flattened pudding onto his plate. His capacity to cheer her up had grown in importance.

The journey to Lincoln was subdued and punctuated by the occasional comment. They batted back and forth his ideas about what to do next, but the reality was that come Monday morning, Sean had other projects waiting his attention and Laura needed to concentrate on Brader.

The mellow warmth generated by the car's heater was comforting. Sean tuned the radio to a sedate channel. The rain held off, and the clouds parted sufficiently to reveal vivid blue in places, but no sun, which had absented itself somewhere near the horizon. Sean hummed to himself tunefully. She didn't recognise the song. He had eclectic tastes; somebody hard to pigeonhole. She'd identified Marco as boyfriend material for the same reason. In retrospect, she hadn't shared enough with Marco, and he certainly hadn't with her. Was she hastening along that familiar path with Sean to another dead end?

Sean parked outside her slender semi-detached house. It was one of many lined up in rows, boxed in by busy roads and cheap amenities. He switched off the engine, and the radio died with it. The silence was acute but for his rapid breathing.

She turned to face him. Those sharp eyes of his were settled on her expectantly. She dropped her gaze to his thin lips, now serious in their directness, and his warm skin tone, vivacious in nature, and attractive. She fidgeted with the hem of her jacket, pinching a loose thread. He paid her hand no attention, his eyes still focused on her face. When he leaned towards her, she held her breath, half closing her eyes. The safety belt snapped around his waist, preventing his approach. Unperturbed, he released it and allowed it to slip off his shoulder.

'Sean,' she said quietly. She couldn't think what else to say.

'Laura.' A dollop of hair flopped over his brow.

Their noses inched closer, and when they were less than an inch to contact, he tilted his chin to one side and brushed his lips against hers. Through the tiny parting he exhaled softly, transmitting his desire in that briefest of caresses, and evoking within her forgotten sensations. The familiar tingling across her scalp was well-developed, and she stiffened involuntarily: a kiss of some sorts. He retreated to his side of the car with no hint of defeat on his face.

'Why don't you pop in?' Speaking before thinking was never a good idea. But it was too late.

Earlier in the day, she'd raced out the front door and greeted Sean by the car. Now, a few hours later, she didn't care about the dregs of Marco in the house. Those things were an unfortunate reminder of his inability to end their relationship properly, but she had sidelined them over weeks into cupboard spaces, the back of shelves, a couple of boxes under a table, and what was left on display was stuff that any occupier might own. Exhilarated by the impromptu decision, she hastened out of the car.

He followed her up the path, waited silently by her shoulder with his hands trapped in his jacket pockets while she fumbled with the key. He walked past her into the narrow hallway, and she leaned her back against the door, closing it with a click. Sizzles of nervous excitement cruised to places that weren't appropriate to describe; she hadn't felt those temptations quite so keenly in a long time. She tossed the key into a cracked ashtray, one purloined from her mother's house, and placed by the entrance for no other purpose than convenience. Sean's eyes sparkled exuberantly, the optimism well-placed for once, and the lack of conversation was perfect; there was something reassuring about physical overtures that helped her ignore the nagging, intrusive thoughts.

She walked backwards into the lounge and collided with the books and papers heaped on the floor. Exclaiming, she pivoted, balancing on her tiptoes by the piles of handwritten notes, then, realising what they were and who was kneeling next to them, she jumped sideways with a yelp of surprise.

'Tesoro. Darling. Where have you been?' Marco excoriated his greeting with a berating glare.

Sean turned on his heel.

Marco tugged on a wire until the earpieces fell off his head and scrambled to his feet. She ignored him and chased after Sean. 'I can explain,' she mouthed.

'You don't have to, Laura,' Sean whispered. 'This is your home. Your life. I've inferred things from what you've said...' Agitated, he combed his fingers through his hair. He hadn't had the chance to undo his jacket buttons or kick off his shoes.

'It's not what you think,' she said breathlessly.

Why hadn't she acted sooner, when she'd had the valid excuses and opportunities to do so? She'd clung on to Marco to ensure she presented some resemblance of normality to those who judged her as quirky, socially awkward, a "tad loopy", as Margery had once said, a loner who couldn't let go of a blameless incident fourteen years ago. She reached out to touch his sleeve, but he was nifty on his feet and slipped past her outstretched hand.

'I should go,' he said, his back to her.

She couldn't convey to Sean that it was over, her and Marco, not while the man was within earshot.

'Laura,' Marco called. 'Is there a problem?'

She wanted to shout an ugly stream of anger at his bad timing. 'Wait,' she said impatiently. She wasn't sure if she meant to say that to Marco or Sean. Probably both, but the tone of her voice was wrong for one of them.

Sean wasn't waiting, though. He opened the door. 'I'll catch up with you sometime. When it suits you.'

Her cheeks were seared with embarrassing heat. Tears might come easily, if she let them. Only the darkness or dead of night were familiar with her weeping.

He walked to the car with sloped shoulders and long strides.

'I'll call you,' she shouted after him. Tomorrow, or the next day. Soon, before he lost all hope. Closing the front door behind her, she stormed into living room.

Marco was watching Sean's departure from the window. 'Who is he?' His English was more accented than usual.

'A friend.' Sean wasn't the issue. 'I wasn't expecting you today.' There was no joy in the reunion, no hugs or kisses, only frowns. She felt nothing, only a cold numbness. She had left her warmth in Sean's car.

He rolled his eyes and gestured to the ceiling with the open palms. 'You have wanted me back for weeks.'

'Your information is out of date.' Her anger was wretched. It wasn't his fault, and if he had let her know in advance, she would have rearranged her trip with Sean. Again, Marco's inability to communicate had unfortunate ramifications.

'I see.' He sat on the armchair and buried his face in his fanned fingers. 'I have a heavy heart, tesoro. Things have not worked out as I would like.'

His melodramatic pose was unnecessary. She was tired of drama. What she understood to be happening was obvious. He was packing. The room was filled with his stuff: a bag of clothes, a couple of boxes of study materials, the half-packed books, a few CDs, and a recipe book, which was in Italian. She'd never used it. Against one wall were three full bin bags.

'You're clearing out.' She folded her arms across her chest.

'Sì... yes.' He knelt back on the floor and picked up a book. 'My things.'

'You're going for good.' She shifted her gaze away from him to the spaces on the bookshelves and the voids he was making; bits of him missing from the house they shared.

He nodded, keeping his head down, his dark eyes hidden.

She slumped into a chair. 'Why, Marco? Why have you kept me guessing for weeks... months? What couldn't you tell me?'

'Nothing went to plan.' He sat back on his haunches.

'To plan? I'm on jury service at the moment, did you know that? I thought not. A lot is going on in my life, and I've managed without you, so I think I'm owed an explanation for your prolonged absence.' Her tongue stuck to her parched palate. In the kitchen, she poured herself a large glass of water and gulped it down. Calmed by the cool liquid, she returned to the lounge.

Marco had finished boxing up his books and was on his feet. He pulled up his jeans. He'd lost weight, and the shadows under his eyes were murky trenches, worse than her own. His hands trembled like hers, and his glassy eyes were primed for tears. He fished out a handkerchief and blew his nose. She'd never seen him cry.

'What?' she asked, equally worried and pacified by his distress. 'Just tell me.'

'Please sit, Laura.' He pronounced her name as "Lara". She used to think it made her sound unique and personal to him. Reassessing many of her presumptions, she knew the pronunciation was simply an inflection, and he wasn't aware he sounded different.

'Remember when I left?'

She recalled the abruptness of his announcement and the two frantic days of preparations. He'd booked a flight from Leeds to Naples, spoken to his tutor, gathered up a bag of clothes, and slipped away early in the morning.

'My father contacted me. He was in a bad way. Upset. Worried.' Marco paced around the boxes. 'My mother has cancer.'

She waited for him to say whether it was curable. The hesitation was the answer. She clutched her shaking hands together and battered away a sympathetic tear with a few blinks. Why hadn't he told her that part?

'I'm so sorry.'

'Babbo panicked. He loves my mother but doesn't always know how to show it. He needed help.' Marco leaned against the mantelpiece.

'And you couldn't come back here, at all, not even to explain?' In her stomach the acid churned. He was too pale, too thin. It wasn't just this one thing that had gone wrong. 'I mean... you've been gone for weeks and weeks—'

'Babbo had a heart attack.' Marco held up a halting hand. 'Minor one. All fixed, but it was a warning to him, and me. And my grandmother took a turn for the worse. She has... that thing... Alzheimer's.'

'Oh, gosh.' Laura covered her mouth.

'It's time consuming, and expensive, looking after sick people.' He smiled briefly, acknowledging her inadequate response.

'Your father's business?'

Marco's gold neck chain was missing. 'He wants to be with my mother... we both do. I went to Rome—'

'I remember the postcard,' she said. Impersonal and hurried, the reason for the brevity unclear.

He blushed. 'That was my second trip. The first time I went, I took money out of my trust fund. I needed my uncle's signature. The second time to ask him to invest in the business.'

'Why couldn't you explain any of this to me? No calls, or texts... a postcard!'

He looked perplexed. 'I didn't know until two weeks ago that my father... everything is different now that Mum needs him, and me... My father has signed over control to me. I am the executive, the director. My uncle didn't want the job.'

The lack of communication, so poorly excused, seemed a distant issue for him. Failing to reveal his family's problems was an oversight Marco couldn't justify; he'd never seen Laura as part of his close-knit family and probably never would.

'You're going back to your parents?' she asked.

'Sì.'

'All this time, I thought you were having an affair.'

He flinched. 'No. No.' He shook his head. 'I love you. I really thought I would be back after a few weeks; I didn't tell you because I thought it would get quickly done, but Babbo wasn't telling me everything about the business situation, the broken contracts, my grandmother's deterioration. By protecting me, he hid too much of his problems. It's taken all this time for him to explain. I wanted to come back.' He stood achingly still, almost dead on his feet. 'Then I wanted you to join me.'

'I felt rejected, abandoned,' she said. Her mistrust of him was justified, but not in any way she could have imagined. 'You must know how that makes me feel after what Dad did to Mum. You could have written me a letter. Told me over the phone.'

He hung his head, chastised. 'I was with my family, my friends. By the time the summer was over, I was too busy to think of coming back. I always was supposed to take over the business – it's why I study.' And he'd never told her that either.

Another confession was there in amongst his rambling explanation. The simple truth was more believable. 'Your family are what matters. You got homesick.'

A flush of colour revived his melancholic face. 'Sì. They matter more than I thought. I love you, Laura. I know you may not think so, but I do. But you deserve better than me, and I shall only make you unhappy. You would not move to Italy, I don't think, and I must make this choice for you.'

She wished he could have kept her informed about his mother's illness. That he hadn't bothered to tell Laura told her plenty about their relationship, regardless of his declarations of love. Either he hadn't wanted to burden her, believing she was emotionally fragile, or that she was too insensitive to handle his needs. Both versions painted a dim picture of herself. She had to try harder to meet people halfway, open up to them, and let them in to her life, too.

She briefly stroked his hand; she was touched by his sadness. 'Go home, Marco. It's for the best.'

'Yes. It is.' He moved away from her, the rejection completed without him acknowledging it.

She caught the shudder of an emotional exhale and quashed it. He must not know how relieved she was. Her freedom was based on his family's misfortunes. She thought it might happen the other way round, that he would come home to her, buoyed by an extended trip away, ready to study and keen to make up for lost time. The explanations for his absence would amount to some trivial situation. She would be the one to weigh up his excuses and dissolve the relationship, like a contract at work. Rescinded.

Before she'd met Sean there had been another version she had developed during Marco's absence where she renewed their romance and they continued, as if nothing had happened. However, the court case and conversations with a priest had shown her that hiding dishonesty never worked out well in the long term. Thankfully, the Sean option had more potential, assuming she could convince Sean to see her again.

'You were expecting me to be in?' she asked Marco as he shuffled the loose sheets of paper into a binder.

He risked a brief smile. 'You never go out on Sunday. You have a routine. I didn't think you would change it. But you have. It is good for you. I think this man will be good for you.' The lack of jealousy was poignant and worth mourning. He was a kind soul and struggling with a string of heartbreaking revelations.

'Assuming you've not scared him off.' She didn't know where Sean lived, or anything about his habits other than what she'd witnessed during three meals and one car journey. He was probably reevaluating things, too. What if he decided to leave her well alone: would she have the courage to walk into a public museum and plead to be heard?

'Sorry if I have complicated things. Tell him, he's a lucky man. You are a thoughtful person, Laura. People think kindness is something you… wear?' He plucked at his sleeve. 'Is that the right expression?'

She laughed. He tried, bless him, to cope with English idioms. 'Yes. I don't show my emotions, do I?'

'No.' A slightly harsh undertone, but then his face softened. 'You are the opposite of the Italian. It is why I like you. I believe in you because you don't pretend.'

But she had kept her emotions too well hidden, and now it was too late to tell him everything about the accident. It didn't matter anymore.

'I'm getting used to the unpredictable.'

He gave her a puzzled expression.

'I'll confess,' she said, and backed out of the room. 'I'm glad we're moving on. I think you'll find somebody, too. You're not as shy as you make out.' She winked at him.

The tension in his shoulders uncoiled.

A couple of hours later, after he'd finished sorting out his things, they were reminiscing about their good times, joking a little, clearing the air sufficiently for him to take away better memories than their last evening together.

She made him a sandwich.

'All this bad luck,' he said, licking his fingers. 'It's all true. Me and my crazy family.' He grinned, but his darting eyes were still anxiously searching her face for reassurances.

'No, you're not crazy, believe it or not.' He hadn't asked what his level-headed girlfriend had been doing in the last few weeks, and she wasn't going to tell him unbelievable stories about haunting dreams and voices in her head, nor how she'd tried to hunt down a gravestone and a missing manuscript; those things wouldn't stand up to his scrutiny. 'Fate has its own purpose.' She left him with that deliberate enigmatic coda.

He piled his bags and boxes into a taxi. He had arranged to give his books to another student, his shabbier clothes to charity – she laughed; 'You don't own any tatty clothes,' – and the rest he would take back home on a flight booked the next day. She didn't ask where he was spending the night.

There were no kisses on the doorstep. But spontaneously, she gave him a swift hug for old time's sake – there was no harm in staying friends. The embrace clearly took him by surprise. Flustered, his marbled eyes darting everywhere but not at her, he waved goodbye. She would miss his animated hands.

Alone in the house, she debated whether to ring Sean or leave a message. He hadn't contacted her, which wasn't surprising. He'd left red-faced and disappointed. She decided that in his shoes she might prefer some breathing space. She wasn't one for hassling; she had been stalked enough over the past couple of weeks to know how creepy it was. In the morning, she'd text him a polite message of enquiry, the kind two friends send when they want to meet up for a coffee. She'd suggest the café and from there she'd explain everything.

She slept fitfully.

Eliza kept her company, her bulging eyes sadder than ever.

Day Fifteen

Monday

THE BRAEBURN was her favourite choice of fruit. She held the apple, uneaten, and stared through the grubby window at the fleeting glimpses of the cityscape, years of the same shops and houses every morning, and she couldn't remember when it had last held her attention.

No message from Sean, and the fiasco of Sunday's unfortunate encounter with Marco had dented her hopes for a new friendship. Perhaps, given the degree of mutual awkwardness, she should initiate contact with Sean and enliven his optimism; hers surely needed it. How long was a "breathing space" anyway? Was it an actual measure of time or one of those ambiguous expressions that never translated into real situations?

She'd intended to use the time on the bus – sitting at the back on her own – for jury preparation, but instead dredged up her mistakes. In hindsight, the situation with Marco exposed her skewed motives more than she would've liked. She'd allowed the pretext of an absent boyfriend to impose artificial rules and voluntarily create an impasse with Sean. Her past had shaped her opinions. Her father had been married when he'd cheated; Laura wasn't. When her mother found out about Margery, she hadn't begged him to stay or let him stew, wondering if things would work out between them. She'd booted him out of the house, bolted the door, and gave the young Laura the option of going with him or staying. A mother's tear-streaked face, bubbling with unsuppressed rage, effortlessly illustrated the consequences of a broken heart. Laura had taken about two seconds to make up her mind. Much later, a still painfully shy teenager finally plucked up the courage to confront her father and say all the things that a ten-year-old couldn't say because they hurt too much.

Neither she nor Marco had engaged in an affair, but she'd acted as if one of them had, probably because she'd overthought things and embroiled herself in weeks of playing hurt. The reasoning had a logical path: over the waning summer, she'd gone into denial, refusing to believe he might be cheating on her; by the autumn, she'd feared the consequences of his possible deceit might break her heart, like her mum's, so best not know (was she actually in love?); then, because she was sure she wasn't in love with Marco, she'd been (perhaps cruelly?) using Sean to define what cheating actually meant by way of "dating" him. She hadn't come out of that experiment well.

Crushed between her fingers, the flesh of the apple bore the brunt of her silent recriminations, and by the time the bus reached her stop, the fruit had suffered enough. She tossed it in the waste bin.

The bus arrived late. She hurried to the castle grounds and the ivy-clad courthouse. High above on the escarpment, the buildings were swathed in a pewter mist. Grey hazy droplets blended with stone to form a blanket that eclipsed the top of the trees and walls. She pulled her hood over her ears; a futile attempt at deafening herself.

Emma ran alongside her. A child still with her smaller strides, she struggled to keep up with Laura. Nearly drowned out by her own heavy breathing, Laura heard something new. It brought her up sharply because she recognised its purpose. A repetitious *tap-tap* on the cobbles. Emma was carrying a stick, feeling her way, like she must have done for years after her mother's death. Where the path forked, the combination of footfalls and stick veered from Laura's side. She wanted Laura to go to the prison. The obsession with the terrible cell irked Laura. She had done everything to free Eliza from that hellhole and the last thing she wanted to do was go back there, mentally or physically. She and Sean had to talk first.

She checked her watch. There was no time anyway.

'Later, please,' she hissed.

A disappointed, desperate wail drifted by her ear. They both knew, she and her familiar, that they were running out of time. Today, Brader would find out his fate, and Laura would finish jury service. She wanted it to be over, and at the same time, for things to drag on sufficiently longer for her to help Emma find peace. Resolving the potential standoff in the jury room meant stepping up to a soapbox, something she was loath to do; however, if she bottled it, she would regret the consequences.

The barristers presented their closing arguments. Mr Waverly went first. The lawyer was swift, portraying Brader as the arrogant thief of the blind who'd orchestrated years of fraud, until, cocksure, he took too many risks and was caught. He reminded the jury that committing mistakes, then knowingly not correcting them, counted as dishonesty.

'Mr Brader has had ample opportunities over the years to put right his shortcomings but has chosen to let them lie.' He ended with a flourish of his black-caped arm. 'Why? Because it made him rich.'

A detached house, holidays abroad, kids in private schools, and silk suits were unaffordable for most people. Laura's definition of wealth was simpler: not having to account for every penny spent.

Mr Calm, his voice level and hypnotic, weaved a different picture of the accused. 'Mr Brader was perhaps not the best man to do the accounts; he made errors and demonstrated incompetence...'

Laura admired his quiet destruction of dishonesty.

Behind him Brader baulked silently at the harsh words. His eyes darted between his lawyer and the judge, who kept his head down, taking notes. He mouthed something to the woman in the public gallery. She shrugged, wide-eyed. They hadn't been expecting a character assassination.

Laura had been. It was the only sensible defence left. Brader was downgraded from a semi-retired engineer of good repute to a recalcitrant man who shunned advice. It was a last-ditch attempt to make him out to be unsuitable for his post, but not dishonest. Foolish, but not criminal.

'Being honest does not mean that a person can't make mistakes and fail to spot them or underestimate their significance. Did Mr Brader knowingly strive to defraud his employer? Was he devious or clever in his deception? There is nothing to indicate he was actively seeking to defraud. Surely, somebody intent on reaping a rich reward from embezzling and creating false documents wouldn't leave a trail of evidence leading back to himself?'

The judge summoned up the case, running through the charges, and explaining the burden of proof for each one in his familiar, monotonous voice. The jury by now were restless, fidgeting with papers and eyeing the clock on the wall. They wanted to finish today. Everyone did, it seemed. The haste was unseemly, Laura thought, and undeserving of the gravity of the case. She, and perhaps Iain and Beryl, were the only ones thinking of Seeside's fate.

They were dismissed to the jury room. Between them, they gathered up the heaps of documents they'd accumulated over the weeks and were finally allowed to take them out of the courtroom. The usher warned them about leaving the room, how to contact the judge if needed, then she asked for their mobile phones.

Laura grabbed hers and swiped the screen. Distracted by Emma's badgering and the rushed queue through the security gates, she'd forgotten to send Sean a message.

She tapped it out, fingers and thumbs working against each other.

Can we meet up? I want to explain.

The usher held out her hand. Laura switched the phone off and handed it over. Even if he replied, she wouldn't see it until the end of the day. The devices were stacked inside a wooden box nailed to the wall. The usher locked the safe with a key and pocketed it. Seemingly satisfied that everything was in order, she slipped out of the door.

Jodi peered at the sheet of paper in front of Laura.

'What's that?' she whispered.

Laura's list of couplets represented three weeks of notetaking.

Printing invoices.
Raffle tickets.
Missing builder?
Cash payments.
Tax evasion?
Friends first.
No references.
Bad acting.
Desperate measures.
Smug bastard.
Blind faith.

Laura covered it with her hand. 'Just thoughts.'

Silky-voiced, Jodi whispered her approval. 'It's a very good list. Poetic in construction; the shift from exploratory facts to exposed emotions. That kind of involvement happens to us all.'

Laura wished the teacher wasn't smiling so keenly.

With little preamble, Brian engineered himself a show of hands and announced himself foreman. Nobody else contested the choice; he had the loudest voice, one that was tailored to deliver the verdicts of guilty or not guilty. Another show of hands was requested.

'Who thinks he's innocent of all charges?'

Five hands shot up. Laura wasn't surprised, she thought it might be more. Naturally, Brian was one of them.

'That he's guilty.'

'All the charges?' Iain asked.

'Well, that for starters.'

Nobody put their hand up, including Laura, because she knew that some of the charges were a waste of time trying to prove.

'Okay, so that leaves a few of us floating in the middle, I guess.' Brian scratched his head. 'If you think he's guilty of at least one of them, then stick up your hand.'

Four hands rose. Amil's, Iain's, Haden's, and Laura's.

She glanced at Beryl, who shrugged. 'Don't know one way or the other,' she said.

Laura admired her honesty. She wasn't alone. Jodi hadn't lifted her arm, nor had Pauline the post office worker, or Deborah the dentist, who was staring at the locked box with an anxious expression. Laura only remembered their names because of the alignment with their jobs.

'Okay,' Brian said with a grumpy mouth. 'We should go through the indictments alongside the documents, and... go from there.'

Laura clasped her hands on the table and watched, silently and with an increasing sense of desperation, as the jury disintegrated into the fiasco she'd feared from the outset. None of them had a clue how to interrogate the data, the reams of numbers, the statements of the witnesses, the hours of interviews with Brader by the police, during which he'd denied everything. They messed up the piles, confused which was the defence's evidence with the prosecution's, talked over each other, until Brian barked, irritated and dismissive.

'It's bloody obvious. He screwed up, but it doesn't prove anything.' He tossed his pen across the table.

Beryl retrieved a sandwich from her bag and started to eat. Haden pushed his chair aside and propped his elbow on the windowsill. Laura stared beyond his hewed body-builder's shoulders and the striated muscles of his neck to the castle walls outside. Only a few hundred years away was the no-nonsense man she really wanted to be talking to. She squeezed her eyes tight shut and attempted to school her thoughts. Fortunately, the hubbub of undulating conversation drowned out any opportunity to listen out for Emma.

'Things would have happened a lot quicker if they hadn't kept sending us in and out like a bloody rabbit in a hole,' Derek said, scratching his bald patch.

Haden shifted. 'It's because of disclosure issues. The prosecution has to disclose all their evidence to the defence. If they don't, it can end the trial. I guess the judge ruled in the prosecution's favour.'

'And you know this because?' Derek's eyebrows furrowed. Derek the bin man. She hadn't paid that much attention to the other jurors for three weeks, and only now regretted the lack of insight.

Haden sighed. 'I studied law for a year. I dropped out. Wasn't for me, all that debating and sitting around. Should have joined the police.'

Laura's bubble of detachment burst with Haden. Mired by personal prejudice and entirely to Haden's detriment, she'd heeded his appearance in isolation. Haden, along with Amil, was probably the sharpest of them all.

Iain, on Laura's other side, lay his hand on her note sheet. 'It's time, don't you think?' he said. 'We'll be here forever, otherwise, or he'll get away scot-free.'

She couldn't, though. Her mouth was glued shut. She'd not said a word. Her heart was racing so fast, she was convinced the pounding against her breastbone would alert the others to her crisis of confidence. She was already close to absenting herself – in a mental capacity since the physical wasn't possible – from the whole process. She wasn't the only one. Deborah was doodling. The two men whose names she couldn't recall at all, the ones who'd cold-shouldered Brian, were yawning in tandem, as if joined at the hip.

But what about Seeside? She'd made a promise.

'I'll help,' Iain said. 'So will Amil. Look at him, he's chomping to say something but won't, not unless you take the lead. As for Haden, he made his mind up ages ago. One year of law school, and he knows the system.'

'You say something, Iain,' Laura said.

Iain shook his head. 'This is your chance to shine, Laura. It's why you're here.'

The beats of her heart grew louder, deafening; her hearing was now so sensitive it was edging on painful. She looked at her poetic list. Could she live with herself if the "Smug Bastard" went free?

She had to pick the right moment to launch into the debate.

'These bonuses,' Brian said at the other end of the table. 'The board approved them, so why the fuss?'

The moment was now. Laura forced out the first syllable, and it stumbled into the next. 'Th-ey… they approved them, then later retracted one of them. However, the prosecution failed to come up with robust supporting evidence. Same goes for the pension top-up, so we should discard them; there's no indication he inflated the amounts.' Her voice dropped off. Everyone was staring at her. It was the first time she'd said anything all morning. 'The invoices, on the other hand, are more incriminating.'

Brian folded his arms across his chest. 'You think so,' he said, not even trying to hide the snark.

Amil's quiet voice filled the vacuum. 'Knocking off the pension and bonuses removes fourteen-thousand pounds from the total embezzled.' He didn't look up from his notes.

'Thank you, Amil.' Iain leaned forward, monopolising Brian's view. 'I think we should listen to Laura. She works for the council in the finance division.'

'Really?' Beryl said. 'You never said.'

Laura stuck her trembling hands under the table. She could do this. All she had to do was pretend it was a meeting at work with her boss: Michael with eleven different faces.

'I assist the financial controller. I deal with tendering, quarterly reports, and help manage the budgets.'

'But not accounts,' Brian smirked.

Laura no longer liked Brian. Nobody else on the jury had presented themselves in such a multifaceted way. Friendly one minute, brusquely dismissive the next; sympathetic, then condescending. He was the same age as Brader and probably believed that men having reached middle-age were inscrutable and beyond reproach. He'd made his mark, running his canning business, and was at the peak of his career. The fear of failing was what blinkered his mind.

'Not at the council. However, prior to that job I worked in a different capacity for an accountancy firm that conducted forensic audits. I helped compile the reports.'

Iain pivoted, his eyes widening. The news had taken him by surprise, too. 'So,' he said, calmly, his lips twitching with amusement. 'What about the invoices?' He cocked his head at her hushed audience.

She rummaged through the scattering of documents until she found what she needed: a sample invoice submitted by the prosecution.

Taking a deep breath, she held up sheet. 'Brader used one builder who specialised in adapting holiday homes for the disabled.'

'Everything is subcontracted these days,' Derek said sweepingly.

She nodded. 'A special relationship, which is fine. If you have a good builder, why switch to another? The work is carried out, an invoice is received, and Brader authorises payment to a subcontractor via the builder. Except, the defence never managed to show that the money passed through the builder's account and, surprise, surprise, the builder has liquidated its business and vanished.'

'So what do you think happened?'

'Look at this invoice, look at the others, they're for refurbishments and minor alterations which are totally unnecessary. Ramps, handrails, and bath fittings.' She pointed to the one-line description.

Beryl let out the tiniest of gasps. She picked up another invoice. 'This one is for knocking down a wall to create an "open-plan living space for access".'

'So?' Brian said, tilting back in his chair.

Beryl removed her reading glasses. 'They're blind. Why would they need any of this? Do you think they're incapable of walking up steps or moving around furniture?'

The others muttered. The sample invoices were distributed around the table. Laura, her heartbeats now racing to an imaginary finishing line, continued her explanation. She had won their attention from puff-cheeked Brian, whose arms were still pinned across his broad chest.

'What do they need?' Pauline with the letterbox glasses asked. 'If Seaside provide specialist holiday homes for the blind, what alterations are needed?'

'Gadgets,' Beryl said. 'I've seen these things in kitchens that tell somebody when a cup of hot water is full to the brim, and alarms that go off when a window is left open. And talking things that read out messages.'

Haden swung his feet back around and under the table. 'Exactly.'

'Much of the work carried out by the builder is going to be legit,' Laura said. 'Seaside state in their brochure' – she waded into the pile and extracted the glossy pamphlet – 'that they buy up cheap, run-down houses and turn them into simple, practical homes for the blind. They want to make their customers as independent as possible. But no ramps or handrails. Just a new coat of paint and renovated kitchens. The bigger building projects, Brader couldn't possibly fabricate the invoices for those; somebody probably inspected the property to check the quality of the work. But the little things listed on these invoices don't require the same level of scrutiny.'

'What about the payments?' The question was asked by one of the twins, finally engaged and curious, his little eyes focused on the papers.

'He issues false invoices, enters the details on Seeside's payment system, which is pretty basic from what I can deduce, then arranges the transfer of funds. Except, he's set up accounts to receive the payments—'

'Wait,' Deborah said, her pearly white teeth biting down on her lower lip. 'What accounts?'

'Ah.' Laura knew if it had been that easy, Brader would have pleaded guilty straightaway. 'The payee details aren't on the invoice, which is odd.'

'Where are these accounts?' Brian asked, raising his palms. He wasn't giving up yet.

Beryl's nose twitched. She was on to something. 'That woman in the gallery – she's his wife? He's always looking at her. What if she set up accounts for him, he takes the money from there, shifts it around, and then she closes the account to cover their tracks. The text messages were pretty dodgy.'

Laura stared at Beryl. 'What did you do before you retired, Beryl?'

'My husband and I ran a fish and chip shop.' She shrugged. 'We got tired of the long hours and sold it. The smell turned me off. The fat burns, too.'

Laura smothered a smile. Beryl's talents were more hidden that her own.

Iain chuckled gently, his shoulders bobbing up and down. 'You missed your true vocation, Beryl. Should have been a copper.'

'Anyway,' Laura said, 'lady friend or wife, the money ended up in his hands. He's crafty. He had to keep the amounts small and he didn't do it too often. But eventually, he got greedy. He kept the evidence off his computer, which the police confiscated, and printed the invoices off site somewhere. It's too late to find out where. When the fake invoices arrived on his desk, he paid them into bogus accounts, then filed the hard copies in the office, believing that would reconcile the payments. But the forensic accountant spotted them.'

She rested her hands on the table, allowing them to settle. The trembles shooting down her arms into her fingers were less about the anxiety of speaking and more about losing respect. She waited for the disputes and criticism.

'Well, I don't know about you, but that has changed my mind completely,' Jodi said. 'How much did this amount to?'

The money mattered. The original, and substantial, total claimed by the prosecution had been whittled down; each charge lost impacted the summation.

'The specimens submitted—' Laura began.

'Five thousand two hundred pounds over five years.' Amil lifted his head slightly, his opaque eyes brimming with delight. 'The subcontracting stopped after the forensic accountant flagged up discrepancies.'

'Amil has compiled that total just from the specimens. If you look through Seeside bank accounts, there'll be more than that; start with the smaller historical amounts as a guide.' Laura held her breath and waited.

Nobody contradicted her.

Brian fidgeted with his pen while the others examined the invoices and bank balances and checked their own notes for validation. Nearly three weeks had passed since the prosecution started their case against Brader. Laura only needed her simple couplet – printing invoices – to recollect the reasoning behind the indictment. She listened to the conversations circulating the table and smiled. They were working it out for themselves.

'What else, Laura?' Iain asked after the chatter died down.

All eyes turned to her. This time, the trembling held off. She reached over to the document pile, rifled through it, and retrieved the sample batch of raffle tickets, one of many printed and submitted as evidence.

'These,' she said. 'If you want to sell raffle tickets in advance of the draw and the proceeds are less than twenty thousand, you need to register for a Small Society Lottery licence.'

The prosecution had laboured this point to emphasise that Brader appeared to play by the rules when he wasn't actually doing so behind the scenes.

'Ten thousand of these were printed for a draw; the main prize was cash. Seeside had three months to sell the tickets. Brader wrote to the trustees a few weeks before the draw date and told them not enough had sold, so the draw date was put back. The defence argued the delay was notified in emails to Seeside's sponsors, newsletter recipients, and volunteers, who do most of the sales. Three months later, the new draw happens, the winner is paid.'

'Seems feasible,' Deborah said.

'By delaying the draw, he then had ample opportunity to pocket the extra cash raised, and still have enough money to pay out. Look at the ticket numbers and what he put through the charity's accounts. He only declared the first batch of numbers.'

'I can't believe nobody checked,' Brian said gruffly.

'Who does?' Iain said. 'Who actually checks what you say or do is correct when you're a small charity with limited resources and staff? He tells them the sales are poor, when in fact they're selling well. Why wouldn't they trust him?'

Laura silently thanked Iain for reminding her that the real question of Brader's guilt revolved around his honesty. 'When Brader arranged for the raffle tickets to be printed, he made a serious error and never corrected it. The police picked up on it.'

'Sorry, love, I'm confused,' Beryl said, examining one of the sold raffle tickets.

Iain whispered in Laura's ear. 'Tell a story.'

Laura's confidence continued to wax and wane regardless of the extra support she'd gained from a couple of the jurors. It simply wasn't enough unless she swung the whole lot of them behind her. She backtracked and told the story she'd worked out days ago.

Brader had the idea quite early on, she assumed. He'd spotted the weakness in the way Seeside ran their raffles and how little supervision he was given. He tried the scam out once on a smaller lottery with a two-week delay, and it was successful. The second time, he went for a three-month sales period with the intention of extending it to six. He printed the raffle tickets, and after three months he reported to the trustees that they weren't selling enough to cover the costs or prize money. The email he'd sent was on the table; she read it back to the other jurors. There was no mention of the batch numbers on the tickets sold.

The trustees agreed to putting the date of the draw back. The charity's website was updated, and a plea was issued to sponsors and donors to buy more tickets. So they did, and in far greater numbers than Brader had claimed. The cash rolled in, usually in envelopes, a few inconvenient people transferred the money directly into the charity's account, but mostly it was cash. What the trustees didn't know was that he'd secretly printed another consignment of raffle tickets and sent them out, augmenting the first lot.

'He made a stupid mistake.' She held up two sold tickets, both acquired by the police and presented in evidence by the detective assigned to the case. 'One of these was sold before the delay, the other after. Note the dates of the draw.'

'What about them?' Brian shrugged. 'They're the same.'

'They're the same original draw dates. Now if Brader was an honest man, and the sales had genuinely picked up after an initial slow start, and he decided to print more tickets to boost sales further, why isn't the correct date on the second batch? If the wrong date was an honest mistake, why not correct the error and get the batch reprinted? He ordered two batches prior to the original draw date. He planned it, took the risk the dates would be overlooked. That's dishonesty. And by then, Brader had pocketed a fair-sized sum of cash. Nobody knew he had sold close to twenty thousand tickets.'

'Based on the return of unsold tickets, an estimate according to the auditor's report,' Amil said, 'he declared roughly nine thousand, eight hundred ticket stubs to the charity and kept the proceeds of the tickets sales from the rest for himself.'

Deborah picked up the two sample tickets. 'Why didn't he tell them he printed twenty thousand to begin with and simply apologise for the mistake?'

'The experienced admin assistant told him not to print too many in the first place; she anticipated fewer sales. If he hadn't made mistakes,' Haden said, flexing his back muscles, 'he might not have got caught. That's why he's facing charges.'

'Where did Brader put the money?' Derek asked.

The mood in the room was shifting. A reinvigorated Haden provided the answer, not Laura. He, too, had obviously thought that the verdict was going to be in Brader's favour. 'In the accounts he set up. And he uses his now deceased great-aunt as a backup story – she gifted him money at pretty convenient moments, don't you think?'

'Which leads me to the cheques he cashed.' Laura had left the easiest kind of fraud to last. Writing cheques to yourself was the simplest way to skim off money.

They took a break, refuelled themselves from their packed lunches, stretched stiff legs, and drank tepid water from the dispenser. Brian was subdued. Haden bounced on his toes and stretched up to the ceiling. Deborah copied him. Laura avoided looking out of the window; she didn't want to think about Sean. Or Emma waiting by the yew tree – for what to happen? Or Eliza in her dungeon, perpetually dying a gruesome death. Triggered by a familiar sense of coldness, she shivered. Food proved unappetising, again.

'Keep going,' Iain said. 'You've got them hooked.'

She had; they were keen to continue and tie up the last few loose ends. She walked them through the specimen of cheques he'd cashed over the years and the strange lack of receipts – lost, he'd claimed. What might have seemed unfortunate during his testimony was now treated as a blatant lie. There never had been receipts.

'Small amounts, just a few pounds here and there. Mainly expense claims or cash floats for fundraising stalls, which are easy to justify. Many will be real, but in amongst them, he cashed cheques for himself. Then he upped the stakes by claiming for bigger trips, visits to Seaside's centres around the region, and then fed fake reports to the trustees.'

Iain stirred next to Laura. 'Did he ever actually go that often? Given how little he seems to know about what the blind need, I doubt it. I don't think he cared one jot about the blind. He joined the charity because he knew it was a sweet place to scam.'

'He got cocky,' Derek said, smirking.

'Yes,' Brian murmured. For half an hour, he'd sat and said nothing.

Laura hoped he'd take some useful lessons away from jury service. She certainly would.

She settled back, letting the others go through the external auditor's report, the one that had been tediously read out in court and understood in varying degrees by the jury. Now that she had them focused on specific issues, she had to give them free rein to draw their own conclusions. Too much leading was wrong. From the cheques, they quickly decided that tax evasion was likely – he had claimed nothing of what he'd stolen.

'How much?' she asked Amil, who remained content to sit on the sidelines with his notes and numbers.

He totted up a column of figures. 'About eighty-two thousand pounds.'

It was enough – she was pleased. She hoped Olivia would be, too. Eventually most of it would make its way back into Seeside's coffers, recouping what they'd lost through Brader's greed by way of compensation and refunds from his assets.

Laura relaxed, only speaking when asked a direct question. She wasn't challenged; her expertise was accepted. The clock ticked closer to four. Brian asked for a show of hands on each indictment. There were no waverers this time. Everyone was either in the guilty or not guilty camp, and each vote was unanimous.

Brian summoned the usher.

He delivered the verdicts in a bombastic tone as if he alone had decided Brader's fate. The first three responses to the usher were not guilty. The charges related to events that had happened nearly eight years ago. Laura never expected them to be proved, and they merely set the tone leading up to the more serious offences. Brader smiled at the woman in the gallery, her hands clasped in a position of prayer.

The usher read out the next indictment covering the false invoicing.

'Guilty,' Brian boomed.

Laura admired how the colour washed out of Brader's face in the same way the dirty water swirled down a plughole. His savage display of arrogance vanished somewhere around his flared nostrils, then his cheek muscles twitched, randomly and awkwardly, and the line of his eyebrows drew together into an overarching bridge. He glanced first at the judge, followed by the woman, who had buried her face in her hands, before dispatching daggers at the back of his barrister. Laura witnessed barely contained anger, the kind that accompanied defiance, not despair or bewilderment. The next indictment related to the pension top-up, and he was declared not guilty on abuse of position, followed by a similar charge for the bonuses. Again, a robust not guilty.

Brader's alarmed face relaxed a fraction; he tucked his hands behind his back and focused on the coat of arms behind the judge's head. Mr Calm remained calm, executing his supportive role with professional detachment; he merely ticked off each charge like a shopping list. Laura read much into his lack of reaction; he had struggled to manufacture a line of defence compatible with the charges. Mr Waverly exchanged a wide-eyed stare with his clerk. The surprise turned to muted delight when Brian called out, 'Guilty,' to the charge of conspiracy to commit fraud.

The transformation in Brader upon hearing this verdict was conclusive. Next to Laura, Iain sucked in his breath; he saw it, too, and winced at the change. Brader hardened his features into whitewashed granite, stopped sharing embarrassed smiles with the now weeping woman, and settled himself into a pose of indifference. He wasn't going to break down in public. Laura kept staring at Brader as Brian said 'Guilty' with an unpleasant degree of relish. Guilt was something she thought she understood, and although she'd been told countless times she wasn't responsible for any wrongdoing that day, it seemed natural that she wanted Brader to crack apart and show some humanity or remorse. Instead, he was rapidly sinking into a state of resignation. It dawned on her that he hadn't been that confident at the start of the trial. The slouching was a feeble attempt at arrogance and disinterest in the proceedings, and it reminded her of a petulant child hoping nobody had noticed them steal a sweet from the jar when it was so obvious they had.

Thanked and dismissed by the judge for the last time, the twelve vacated their seats and left the courtroom. The tension that had surrounded them for fifteen days evaporated in the few steps it took them to walk from oak-panelled chamber to the cramped deliberation room. They could talk normally and unrestrained by protocols. The secrecy was over, although they were reminded by the usher not to speak of their experiences in the jury room. She unlocked the secured box. Deborah was the first to collect her mobile.

As they were escorted to the waiting area and advised to fill in their expenses claim form, Laura switched on her phone. She tottered up the bus fares, while keeping one eye on the message app. There was nothing from Sean. Just one text from her mother wanting an update on the trial, and several from Michael hoping she'd be back in work on Tuesday.

She signed the claims form with a spidery signature which was nothing like her usual sturdy one. The trial was over, but the tension was stitched into her body, refusing to go.

'I'm off,' Jodi said. 'Bye, everyone. You,' she said to Laura, 'write poetry or something.' With that tossed remark, she was gone.

Haden left next, chatting to somebody on the phone. He waved at Laura, grinned, and strode off using his long legs to great effect.

Amil wasn't far on his heels. Laura caught his eye, he nodded, and she returned the minute gesture of mutual respect.

'Job done,' Derek said with satisfaction and left with Pauline.

Brian called her a dark horse. 'Should have said something about your jobs,' he said, grumpily.

'The video didn't mention providing a biography,' she said sharply.

He picked up his briefcase, which he'd used to carry his packed lunch and nothing else. 'Anyway. Well done.'

Infuriated, she nearly retorted something less than complimentary about his contribution. But he wasn't worth salvaging.

'I'm glad it's over,' Beryl said. 'It was doing my head in, all them numbers. Couldn't see what they were on about. So thanks, pet, for setting me straight.' She touched Laura's arm, then picked up her oversized handbag, smiled generously at Iain and left.

Laura sidled up to Iain. 'Did I unduly influence her? Or anyone else.'

He looked surprised. 'No, of course not. You did what needed doing. Be proud of yourself.'

'Proud?'

They walked out of the building together.

'Yeah,' he said, 'You went head-to-head with booming Brian, contained babbling Beryl, made use of quiet Amil, and engaged the distracted dentist and dreamy teacher into offering opinions. You championed the cautious thinkers while soothing the confident contributions of Brian, Haden, and Derek. Nobody was left voiceless, and the decision was unanimous.'

His summary stunned her. 'I did?' Had she done all that in the space of a few hours? 'You'd make me sound praiseworthy to anybody. Is that how you delivered your sermons?'

He laughed joyfully.

Hovering on the path where it forked into different directions, she realised there wasn't anything left to say to Iain. But she wanted to say something poignant.

'Will you go back to it?' She gestured to the cathedral's steeple, boldly lit up against the dusky sky.

He lifted his head. 'No. Moving on. Been thinking of going abroad to do charity work. Somewhere that doesn't need technology to make a difference. Just kindness.'

'Good luck.'

'Will you come back for the sentencing?' he asked.

Brader had been released on bail until the sentencing day, and they were probably his last days of freedom for a while.

'No. It will be in the papers, I assume.' Which would be unfortunate for Seeside.

'I'll come back.' He glanced over his shoulder at the courthouse. 'I have to know what penance he'll get. As I said, can't let go of that Catholic upbringing. It isn't going to be a few Hail Marys, though.'

'I hope they recover the money.' It was a pity atonement was all about money.

He lowered his chin to her level. 'Well, your debt is paid. Don't let what happened to you shape the rest of your life.'

She was pleased he didn't add the "accidents happen" line that many people thought would make her happier. 'I'll try.'

He shook her hand, which pleased her even more. Then with his head born proudly, he strolled away.

Her debt was almost paid off.

The prison museum was closed. Sean would be on his way home. It was worth one last try, for both of their sakes.

Please don't ignore me. I'm sorry if I hurt you. It wasn't my intention. I wasn't expecting company. He's gone for good. Laura.

She put the mobile away. Staring at it wouldn't make things any easier.

Walking on, she listened for footsteps, whispers, anything that might provide company. Her companion of the castle, Emma Horton, was quiet, not even the flutters of breathless whispers or the *tap-tap* of her stick penetrated the expanse that existed between her and Laura. Emma's life, and all that had happened when she was a young child, remained a mystery, Eliza's motive for murder was a secret that stayed locked in her cell, and Emma's memoir was still missing. Passing under the portcullis, Laura realised it was still there – a sharpness, the thing that made her acutely aware. It didn't matter now because the melancholic, nonsensical murmuring had ceased. Nobody followed her.

'Oh, well.' Laura sighed and walked to the bus stop.

By the time she was in bed, earlier than usual due to mental exhaustion, there was only one message from Marco saying goodbye from the airport.

She fell asleep. She dreamt about nothing. Absolute emptiness. Eliza was gone, too.

Tuesday

THERE WAS AMPLE WORK TO CATCH UP ON; nobody had tackled her colour-coded to-do list. She waded through the in-tray, determined to put the trial behind her, which meant fending off the intrusive questions about the verdict from her normally diffident colleagues.

'You can read about it in the newspaper.' Her pat answer stalled most of the enquiries. She dodged one meeting that morning with the excuse she was too busy and, thankfully, Michael backed her up since it was his workload she was supporting.

However, misery stalked her in other ways, and she failed to distract herself from interruptions of the self-inflicted variety. She had lost both Marco and Sean. As well as frustration, there was anger blended into the hopelessness. If she'd ignored Marco and chased after Sean, the situation might be different. There were no regrets about Marco's departure. Lost in a protracted bout of homesickness, Marco had simply forgotten her, and the emergent realisation was that they wouldn't ever have had a workable relationship. On the other hand, she thought she and Sean gelled really well and had potential. Unfortunately, just one whiff of competition, and he'd scarpered. And so had the troubling dreams that had haunted her for three weeks; Emma had abandoned her, too. Maybe the trial, the guilty verdict, was all that mattered, and the memoir was a figment of Laura's overactive analysis.

Restless and bored – strangers, both of them, to her usual frame of mind – Laura glanced at her watch. A lunchbreak was due. She couldn't let Emma go that easily. The final dream, the revival of the cell scene, was the key to unlocking the cycle; why was that horrible place important? The walk to the castle was an uphill trek, but if she was quick on her feet, she hoped to visit the Lucy Tower and give Emma one last chance to offer up any other clues, something that might tempt inquisitive Sean into responding to Laura's messages.

At one o'clock, the couple with the giggling child – her sequin mittens had pawed every single one of the gravestones – left the Lucy Tower. Laura leaned against the yew's tangled ribbons of bark and closed her heavy eyelids. She inhaled, drawing breath down into her lungs and held it, lips pressed together. She listened, waited, and wished for companionship. The wait ended with a lonesome exhale; her ghostly familiar had truly gone. The sounds reaching Laura's ears were those she expected to hear and nothing else: the breeze weaving its way through the creaking branches, birds singing tuneful repetitive snippets, a party of schoolchildren somewhere below shouting to each other.

Opening her eyes, she scanned the small graveyard. The mystic presence that had drawn her there in the first place was gone. Somebody had trimmed the grass at the foot of each stone and raked the leaves into a heap. Glimpses of sunlight touched the solitary markers and created a bright halo of warmth around them. The tendrils of fog had vanished to reveal a crisp scene with its structured landscape, confined as it was, seemingly tranquil and forgiving. What might be a hopeless, unkind place to bury the bodies of the condemned was less austere now that the haunting had ceased, and what she had seen and felt seemed a dream in itself. If it wasn't for the headstone lying in Olivia's garden, Laura's imagination could have concocted everything: the vanishing stone, the footfalls, the whispering voice.

While there was success with Brader's conviction, for Emma and her mother's tortured soul, there was no relief or salvation. Emma's descendants still believed Eliza was a cold-hearted killer who, although remembered as a mother, was quietly given sanctuary away from prying, unsympathetic eyes. What redemption the Horton women sought was buried in the manuscript, an object of dubious providence and untraceable.

'Sorry,' Laura whispered to the mossy grass and trampled soil where once she'd seen a gravestone.

'Laura!'

The cry brought a thump to her heart, in the same way a hammer struck an anvil. Over by the gateway, catching his breath, Sean raised one hand in a signal that might be a wave or an instruction to stay put.

'I saw you...' he panted, 'walk past the museum... and I ran up the bleedin' steps... wanted to speak to you...'

'I sent you text messages.' She walked towards him but stopped short within a few metres of reaching him.

He lifted his head, groped for the wall, and sagged against it. 'Phew,' he gasped, red-faced. 'I am so unfit.'

'Didn't you get them?' she asked.

'Yes... probably... I lost my phone.' He straightened up. 'I was going to call you but couldn't find my mobile, which obviously has your number stored in it, and I don't have a landline either.' The excuses were expelled between snatches of breath. He held up his palm again, and she closed her mouth. 'I know, it's Tuesday, but it's taken me this long to track it down. I thought it was in the car. But no. It wasn't there.'

She recalled exactly the last time she'd seen it. 'You took photos.'

He grinned comically. 'I completely forgot. Idiot. But by then, it was too late to try to reach Olivia. Spent Monday ringing the museum number. Nobody answered, obviously.'

'The caravan park—'

'They don't deal with the house. Separate thingies.' He took out his hanky and wiped his brow. He had no coat on, only the sweatshirt with the museum's logo. He stuffed his handkerchief back in his trouser pocket. 'They said, that is the woman in the office, she'd try to track down Olivia for me, give her my work number.'

Laura left her arms loose by her sides. There were other ways to reach out to people. Was Sean another Marco? 'You know my address; it would have been okay to call on me.'

'I know.' He shrugged. 'But… things were so awkward on Sunday. I could see you were embarrassed—'

'Embarrassed!'

'I'd caused it, I'm sure, I didn't want to make you feel uncomfortable, but I realised later, I probably had, unintentionally.' He gnawed a little on his lower lip. 'I admit, I was a bit embarrassed for you, too. Didn't know what to say. But I shouldn't have dashed off.'

'I thought…' She crept closer to him, avoiding the last gravestone. 'I texted you. I said sorry. He's gone – Marco – gone back to Italy.'

'I knew you'd hinted at something on previous occasions. I shouldn't have assumed you were—'

'I invited you in, led you on—'

'He's your friend—'

'Ex-boyfriend. He came back to pack—'

'Oh.' He paused. 'I thought he was like a houseshare mate—'

'Really?' She was sure she'd told him she was on her own in the house. They'd only known each other for a couple of weeks, though. She'd held back on so much.

'Well, no,' he said sheepishly. 'I was thinking of excuses for you.'

'For me…' Laura was confused. He hadn't expected an apology, only an explanation. 'I can explain—'

'Only if you want to. As for my phone, I finally got hold of Olivia this morning. The mobile was in the museum where I left it. She found it. She was out on Monday; she's not been back into the museum since we left.'

'So my messages to you—'

'Bleeped into the silence.' He smiled long enough for her to register it, then was serious again. 'I'll delete the messages, if you don't want me to read them.'

'It's okay. They didn't say much.' She fumbled with the strap of her handbag. 'You'll get the phone back?'

'Going to Kestern House after work.' He hugged his chest. He'd recovered sufficiently to feel the cold and pay attention to their surroundings. 'You came here… is the trial finished?'

'Yes. Convicted on five counts. I suspect it's enough to put him away.'

'Sweet justice?'

'Yes.' But she couldn't say why. 'I thought I'd come for one last time. The dream has stopped. Emma has gone.' She turned to face the graves. 'Looks pretty tranquil, doesn't it?'

'I suppose.' He was disappointed.

Perhaps she was, too. She wouldn't miss the nightmares.

She wandered back to where Eliza's stone once marked the site of her grave. 'I had one more on Sunday, same old cell, then last night I slept like a log. A lumberyard full of logs.'

'You probably needed it.' He stood next to her.

She leaned on his arm, and he stretched his around her waist. The small act of comfort was welcome. She didn't need anything else from him. Not yet.

'We'll never know if they were working as one or in parallel,' she said. 'Emma's sensory-deprived childhood memories; Eliza's grim final place.' The combination had been effective.

'Oh, I forgot to mention. I went to the archive this morning.'

She lifted her weight from his shoulder to allow him to retrieve a folded piece of paper from his back pocket.

'I thought about that stone,' he said, 'why it was moved, and realised there was only a limited window of opportunity after Eliza's execution to retrieve it.'

'Why?'

'The castle prison closed in 1878; the prisoners were transferred to the new Lincoln prison, which is still in use. So I went back to the archive and searched the newspapers and found this… it's a report of the gravestone's theft.' He unfolded the single sheet and passed it to Laura. 'I guess the stone was taken not long before the prison closed its doors to both convicts and visitors. The court kept going, of course. I made a photocopy of the article.'

Lucy Tower: Missing Gravestone

16th March 1878

The warden of Lincoln's old prison, Mr Obadiah Grey, has expressed outrage at the removal of a headstone from the graveyard in the Lucy Tower. The tradition of burying the prison's deceased, including those executed, dates back many years and provides a suitable resting place for the condemned away from the hallowed grounds of the parish churchyard. The graves bear only the initials and date of death and are simple memorials that ensure the buried are not given high esteem or lauded by peddlers of tales who seek gratuitous delight in selling the stories of the executed.

On Sunday morning, a visitor to the tower noticed the missing headstone, which was ripped out of the ground, leaving a small hole. The gravestone missing is that of Eliza Horton, the last woman to be executed in the castle. The stone, that bore her initials and date, was extracted from the loose soil. Carrying the heavy stone would have required effort. The warden is perplexed as to why any person would choose to remove the marker of a murderess, especially as the body remains intact in the grave itself.

The family of Mr William Horton, the victim of the murderess, are still mourning his loss and refuse to countenance the speculation they have destroyed the grave in an act of revenge. The grievous murder of Mr Horton has left the family business in a dire financial situation, and the parish has offered Mr James Horton funds to assist him during his period of grief. As for Mrs Eliza Horton's relatives, they have shown surprise at the theft. They prefer for her to be left in peace and have no wish for further publicity.

The police believe it is the actions of a fantasist with a fascination for the macabre and have decided not to investigate further. Mr Grey agrees that it is an unusual crime, and one that probably does not warrant much consideration, commenting that the grave is nothing of consequence to decent people who honour the laws of the land. Eliza Horton will be forgotten, as she should be, he said. She is not the victim.

If the gravestone is found, Mr Grey asks that it be returned to the prison. However, he states it is unlikely that it will be replaced, due to lack of funds, and drawing attention to the small graveyard is not in the interest of the prison.

Laura folded the sheet. 'This means that the gravestone went missing years before it arrived at Kestern House. Whoever took it wanted to hide it, not put it on display. It was nice of you to take the effort, tidies things up, but I don't think it tells us anything more about Emma's manuscript, only that Eliza never actually left this place.' She pointed down. 'The headstone's purpose is simply a belated memorial placed in friendlier soil.'

'And Eliza remains where she is: in the earth and unmarked.' Sean stubbed the point of his shoe into the earth, and it easily picked up dirt. She nearly told him off for disturbing the graves. Nobody had disturbed the ground since 1878.

And there it was, an idea popping into her head, so simple in its conception but sufficiently plausible to generate a burst of adrenaline. No wonder Eliza had persisted in her dream. 'Oh my God. Sean, I know where to find the manuscript. Can I come with you to Kestern House? I need to speak to Olivia.'

By the time he'd picked her up outside the council offices it was already getting dark; the streetlights flickered on in sequence. The traffic was worse than their previous trip – they were impinging on the end-of-day escape. However, the crawling stream of cars opened up an opportunity for Laura.

'I have to tell you a couple of things,' she said, removing the ID lanyard from around her neck.

'If that's what you'd like to do,' he said cautiously.

'It is.' She folded her hands into her lap and stared ahead. She began with Marco, their swift courtship and subsequent cohabitation, but with scant information about actual events, just enough for Sean to know they had been lovers up until Marco left in the summer. She merely referred to a family crisis. Maybe she'd never been in love because what she felt towards Sean was different. However, she shouldn't compare, it wasn't fair. She left those bits out, too.

Throughout her uncharacteristic splurge of speech, he hadn't interrupted, giving her space to pause and think about appropriate words, especially the emotionless ones. 'We're still friends. We fell out of love, but not into hate.'

'Sounds familiar.' Sean curled his fingers around the steering wheel. 'Better end it now then later, eh? What was the other thing you wanted to tell me?' He'd put Marco to one side just like that; a wise move and appreciated.

Laura was less keen on the second subject. She started with, 'When I was nineteen—'

Telling a lapsed priest was easier.

They were on the minor roads by then. Unlike her unromantic tale of Marco and Laura, this story was fraught with emotion. It made her realise how little Marco's departure had upset her and how telling Sean something she'd held back from many people in her life, was more significant and cathartic. With no cars behind them, Sean pulled over and dug out a packet of tissues from the glove compartment. He touched her thigh, squeezed it slightly, then withdrew his hand.

She hiccoughed and blew her nose. 'I am so sorry. I didn't mean for you to witness that.'

'I'm glad you told me. It's something that's had a major impact on your life. Thank you for letting me… in.' He started the engine. 'I did wonder about the buses. I assumed you couldn't afford a car.'

'I can, if I really want to. Maybe one day… I feel my guilt has run its course, like the river reaching the sea, a destination. I'm working towards forgiving myself. You see… I know he had a wife and kid. I grieve for them; that accident ruined their lives.' She hadn't told Iain the full facts, and definitely not Marco, only her parents, and following that, her mother had stepped up and taken Laura to a qualified grief counsellor. That consultation had paved the way for a painful recovery.

'We're nearly there. Are you up to this?'

'Yes,' she said hoarsely.

He turned off the road into the driveway and slowed. There were low lights hidden in the bushes, illuminating the avenue. They reminded her of Christmas.

'We're about to ask Olivia to do something strange. She might not agree to help,' Sean said pensively, his chin leaning over the steering wheel.

Laura wondered about Olivia's commitment, too. 'Well, if she refuses, at least we'll get your phone back.'

He parked where the drive diverged. Between the naked branches, the bay windows of the house were visible. The curtains were drawn, but lamplight crept through the gaps in the drapes and projected slivers of light across the gravel. They were home. Anthony, Olivia, and possibly Steven.

She hadn't told Sean the third tale she wanted to tell, the one about a trial, as the correct audience for that were the Feydons. If they knew her real motive for finding Brader guilty was born out of a sense of duty, she might convince them to look for the manuscript.

Sean walked around to her side of the car and held open the passenger door. He slid his fingers between hers, weaving them into a gentle lock, and with his back to the house, he drew her up, stooped, and approached her mouth with tender persuasion. The kiss, unlike the previous cursory brush of two nervous pairs of lips, was confident and executed without flourish. A sojourn, not a long visit, a taste of each other that promised more. He withdrew, leaving her lips parted, her tongue tingling and hopes high.

'Don't be embarrassed,' he whispered.

'I'm not. Not this time.'

The Yew Tree

OLIVIA OPENED THE FRONT DOOR of the house, her shoulders bunched under a fawn wrap bearing the imperfections of homemade knitting.

'Come in. I'll get the phone.'

At the end of the hallway, a grandfather clock, ornately carved, chimed the hour of their arrival – six o'clock – with a melancholy set of dongs. The interior of the house was nothing on the scale of the vast salons and painted ceilings of a stately mansion. Kestern House represented an unpretentious foray into wealthy property; the generous rooms easily eclipsed a modern detached house but fell comfortably short of immodestly splendid.

Olivia directed them to the front room with the bay window. Laura's eye for detail remained accentuated, super-sensed like Emma's. She immediately tuned in to the subtleties, a trait which she now accepted as a permanent gift and not a nuisance. The house had the hallmarks of a bygone era – oil paintings in gilt frames (tarnished), a walnut roll-top bureau (scratched), the limping carriage clock on the mantel. And alongside those antiques were the trappings of modern life – a flat-screen television (dusty), and (disparately coloured) scatter cushions arranged neatly on a plain cream sofa. Parked in the arc of the bay was a wheelchair occupied by an elderly man with groomed whiskers and a face speckled with sunspots.

Anthony Feydon had lost the use of one side of his body. The paralysed leg was tucked up while the unaffected limb was stretched out lazily with the heel resting on the carpet. Anthony was lanky and angular like a matchstick man. His right arm lay on a cushion on his lap, the fingers of his hand twisted around a tennis ball. Laura walked up to him, touched his good hand, and gave it a gentle shake.

'I'm Laura. It's very kind of you to let us visit.'

The lopsided smile took several seconds to accomplish. She waited. He chewed, rocking his jaw from side to side, but said nothing. His grey eyes, punished with cataracts, were alert and watchful.

'He can't talk,' Olivia said, entering the room. 'We were at the rehab centre yesterday; it's why you couldn't reach me.' She handed the mobile to Sean. 'Probably lots of messages.'

He checked the screen. 'Battery's flat. It needed a recharge on Sunday. My fans will have to wait for my replies… I've dealt with the most pressing matters.' He glanced over to Laura.

She accepted his silent blue-eyed apology with a nod.

'Would you like a cup of tea or coffee before your drive back to Lincoln?' Olivia asked.

The invitation saved Laura from forcing an excuse on Olivia. She needed to stay a while longer.

'Tea, please—'

'Thank you,' they said in unison.

Laura sat on the sofa, straight-backed with tension, her hands cupped around her kneecaps, her jaw aching from clenching her teeth. Sean, seated next to her, settled against the cushions and crossed his legs. He was quite unaware of her impending revelation.

With Olivia out of the room fetching the tea, Anthony pointed to two portraits on the wall opposite. The good side of his face was twitching; the frozen side remained droopy and unresponsive.

Laura went to inspect the paintings. The man had a Charles Darwin beard big enough to hide a bird's nest, rugged jowls, and dark eyes. He wore a white cravat tie and a severe expression. The woman next to him was of the same period – nineteenth century. Her hair was hidden by a prim bonnet, her dress modest and lacking frilly lacework. A proud woman and happy, Laura decided, because a trace of a faint smile had been captured by the artist.

Olivia reappeared carrying a tray with a floral teapot (chipped) and matching cups and saucers (flaking gold rims).

'They're Nicholas Kestern's parents.' She placed the tray on the low coffee table in front of the fireplace.

Laura resumed her seat. 'Must be lovely to be surrounded by family portraits.' There were contemporary framed photographs on top of the bureau.

'It's the Kestern family home. The Feydons married into the family, just as I did.' Olivia perched on a low-slung armchair; her old bones were hidden by loosely fitted slacks and the wrap. 'But it is nice to have so much history in your home. Although, the damp and the leaking roof aren't so friendly.' She smiled. 'Shall I be Mum and pour?'

Laura accepted the cup and saucer, a milky tea with no sugar. The china rattled, and she immediately put the saucer down on the table.

'I wanted to tell you something I couldn't talk about previously during our last visit. It wasn't appropriate or permissible for me to speak,' Laura said.

Sean sat up and uncrossed his legs. He'd assume she was bringing up the manuscript.

'Sean is also unaware,' she said.

'Laura?' Sean said apprehensively. 'You don't have to mention—'

'No, not that,' she said swiftly. The accident was too personal and a step that involved exposing all of her frailties in one go. 'I've been on jury service for the past few weeks, and the trial finished yesterday.'

Olivia pivoted in her seat and stared at Laura with her glassy eyes, sharply focused, and her lips cresting into a pucker of bemusement. The lump wedged in Laura's throat refused to budge.

'It's a trial,' she croaked, 'with which you're probably going to be familiar.' She took a swig of lukewarm tea and swallowed painfully.

'I didn't attend,' Olivia said. 'Steven was called... of course, you know that.'

'Laura?' Sean's confusion was understandable.

She offered an explanation for his benefit. 'I've been hearing the case of Craig Brader. He was charged with defrauding Seeside. He was their finance director. We, the jury, found him guilty of five charges. He's waiting for sentencing.'

Sean's mouth formed a perfect, silent "Oh". He glanced again at the portraits, then to Anthony, whose body was twitching, his blazing eyes a muted emotional outburst. Laura shifted uncomfortably, and her flimsy aplomb evaporated, leaving her tongue stuck to the inside of her mouth and the thrumming pulse in her throat quickening. She had misjudged the situation. Steven was Craig's childhood friend, and the Feydons had known Craig for years. The shock and disappointment of the accusation, followed by a public trial and resulting unwanted publicity, was bad enough, but now Laura had rolled up and was making a meal of explaining herself.

'I'm sorry,' she stuttered, braced against the settee. She was about to batter their already bruised loyalties. 'I can't talk about what the jury said, but I had no doubts about his guilt.' She hung her head, strangely ashamed of the verdict. She'd been proud of it yesterday.

Olivia's face softened, the wrinkles creasing her marble complexion. 'Gracious, my dear, don't upset yourself. We're not cross with the jury. The verdict was what we expected.'

Laura gasped, relieved and confused in equal measure. 'You knew he was guilty? But Steven—'

'Is devastated and struggling with the truth. He was cheated out of a friendship. Tricked and used most cruelly. Eventually, he'll see that.' Olivia sipped on her tea. Her china cup didn't rattle on the saucer. Steady and calm wasn't what Laura had expected. Anthony, on the other hand, was red-faced with bubbly froth drooling out of his mouth, the words he wanted to say locked inside.

Olivia continued. 'Tony had his suspicions, especially when Craig cosied up to the building company he'd contracted, brought in against Tony's advice. The other trustees weren't prepared to deal with the issue, not until things became too difficult to ignore.'

'The builder liquidated—'

'Tony asked awkward questions. Craig was decidedly cagey about his relationship with them. Tony ended the contract, something Craig had convinced Steven not to do.' Olivia lowered the saucer, resting it on her knee. 'Craig was furious, but by then, he was facing a criminal investigation.'

'I work in finance,' Laura said, 'so I had the advantage of seeing the flaws and holes put forward by the defence.'

'He's done Seeside huge damage,' Olivia said mournfully.

'You'll get the money back.'

'It will take time, our solicitor says. He'll have to dissolve his assets. He won't cooperate.' Olivia frowned. 'Deceitful, two-faced man. He told me he had a blind niece to gain my sympathies, to imply he was suited to working for the charity. But when I met his wife – frivolous woman and hawkish – she couldn't recall any member of Craig's or her family being blind. He'd made it up. He showed little interest in meeting the beneficiaries.'

'That was his downfall.' Laura bit on her lip; she was drifting dangerously close to the private debates of the jury members.

'Yes, I suppose. Although, to his credit, in the beginning, he was successful in raising funds. It doesn't matter now. He's lazy, arrogant, and controlling. I tolerated him because Steven adored him. Craig has the charisma Steven lacks.'

'Anthony fired him, I gather?'

'When the police became involved, Steven was distraught.' Olivia's eyelids flickered, batting away tears, and her shoulders bowed under the invisible weight of memories, something that Laura understood. 'Days later, Tony had a stroke. Steven is torn between loyalties. He's dealing with the guilt, as if he was in the dock himself. He called me last week, after he'd given evidence, and broke down. He's wretched, grieving almost. Steven was his best man... twice!' She brushed aside a tear with a flick of her hand. 'Mustn't burden you with our troubles.'

They could end the conversation there, say their goodbyes, draw a line under Seeside and the Feydons. And the Hortons. In the real world, everything had reached its natural conclusion. But Laura had an obligation she couldn't discard out of convenience for the living, or herself. Sean, who'd sat patiently, listening without interrupting, which he must have wanted to do, was the reason she was still there. He would back her up, ensure she didn't come across as a lunatic.

'Olivia,' she started, with a cautious smile, then it fragmented, losing its confidence. There was no easy way to explain the bizarreness; she had to keep it plain and simple, as if she was in the witness box giving evidence. 'The whole time I was on the jury, sitting in the courtroom, walking around the castle, I was never alone, I was followed by—'

'Somebody Craig sent?' Olivia asked, aghast.

'Oh no.' Laura shook her head. 'Nothing like that.'

Olivia's puzzled expression rested on Sean. 'You work in the museum.' She thought Laura meant him, his company.

'Not Sean. We only met three weeks ago. He's been helping me. What I'm trying to say, and very badly because it's so weird, I've been kind of haunted, having strange dreams. Visitations—'

'Like borrowing memories,' Sean interjected. 'That's how I see it. Memories and dreams. Laura's like a vessel.' He gave a nod of encouragement, mouthing, 'Go on'.

'Somebody wanted, wants, me to find the truth about the fate of the Horton women, Eliza and Emma.'

Olivia put her cup down on the tray and smoothed out the creases in her linen trousers. 'I thought you were assisting Sean with museum work.'

There it was again, Laura recognised it from their first visit, the edginess in her voice that meant Olivia preferred to tread warily around the issue of the Hortons.

'It's more the other way around,' Sean said, taking Laura's hand and squeezing it. 'Laura has developed a unique, somewhat amazing connection to the past, in particular to Tony's ancestors. I don't claim to understand how, but I believe what she's experiencing is very real to her—'

'It stopped. Yesterday. It's only happened while I've been on jury service,' Laura said. 'When the trial concluded, it stopped.'

'I think,' Sean weighed in with a serious voice, 'that the trial, centred on a charity for the blind, Emma's disability, and Laura's… natural openness to finding the truth, has created a conduit, from her to the past.'

He held on to his sturdy poker face. Olivia searched his then Laura's.

'What is it that you think you've found?' Olivia asked, her skin still pasty.

Laura took a deep breath and exhaled. 'I know where Emma's manuscript is. I thought you should know.'

'Emma's memoirs,' Olivia murmured, staring at the frozen features of her husband.

Anthony grunted and attempted to spit out sounds. He pointed a juddering hooked forefinger at Laura and grunted again. Laura closed her eyes to prevent the tears from tumbling out. Anthony's mutterings, incomprehensible and understandably frustrated by his disability, were familiar in their nature. The only difference between his and Emma's whispers was his baritone pitch.

'Where is it?' Olivia asked softly.

'In my dream, my recurring nightmare, I'm in a cell with Eliza. She wears the marks of her execution.' Laura touched her own neck. 'The floor of the cell is covered in pieces of paper embossed with braille. Took me a while to work that out. I pieced them together to make the pages. Clean, white pages. But on the floor they were covered in dirt, sawdust and debris, as if...' Sean offered her encouragement in the form of a stream of tiny nods. 'I think the manuscript is buried under the headstone in your garden.' From out of her handbag, which was resting by her feet, she retrieved the newspaper article about the gravestone's theft and handed it to Olivia.

'What is this?' Olivia peered at the small print. 'My glasses—'

'I found it,' Sean said. 'This newspaper article reports the gravestone as going missing in March 1878. Dug up and carried off. There's speculation as to why, but no accusations. Given the date, it's apparent that Nicholas, in support of Emma, removed it and kept it out of sight until such time as it could serve an actual purpose.'

'The thing is, why not create a memorial there and then?' Laura's question had bothered Sean as much as her. 'Why wait for forty-plus years? I believe once she had completed the manuscript, they decided to bury it. The gravestone finally had a use, not as a memorial but a marker. What remains unclear, is why bury the manuscript? Why write it, then hide it?'

'If there were rumours in the family about its contents, they'd petered out long before Tony was born in the 1930s,' Olivia said.

'It's up to you, if you want to look,' Sean said. He placed his empty cup on the tray and rose to his feet. 'We'll leave you. Probably taken up enough of your time. You don't have to pay any attention to this or us, but Laura wanted to be honest about her experiences. She's been having a challenging time. I didn't even know about the trial.' He held out his hand to Laura.

She was blushing, she knew it.

'No wait.' Olivia looked up from her diminutive chair. 'You deserve an answer, Laura. I'll get a torch and spade. We'll deal with this right now.'

'You... believe me?' Laura said incredulously, her throat tightening.

'You knew where the Kesterns lived in Lincoln. I never mentioned where the house was, but you described it by the river.'

Laura recalled the details of her walk with Emma through an imagined park to the river. Emma's stuttering footsteps had led her to the site of the Kestern's townhouse and not Eliza's home. It made sense, given where the gravestone ended up. 'Emma took me there,' she said softly. 'We walked, I followed, down streets, places I don't go. I thought she was seeking the house she was born in, which is gone. That part of the city has changed completely. Sean and I checked the old city maps.'

Olivia fetched a hefty torch. Sean carried the shovel. Laura pushed the wheelchair. Together, relying on moonlight and a torch beam, they converged on the gravestone sheltered beneath the bowers of a yew tree, whose branches were contained in the shape of an umbrella.

'Well,' Olivia said, 'this is quite something. If you dig up any bulbs, please put them to one side. I'll replant them later.'

The keen gardener was more concerned with flowers than finding a manuscript. She wasn't expecting there to be anything down there. She was humouring Laura, treating her kindly, as the sane might with the mad, if they cared enough. If Sean dug up nothing, Laura wanted to disappear into the empty hole with shame and declare herself well and truly fucked up, something she'd avoided acknowledging for years. Sean would admire the honest vulgarity. She despised it.

It took surprisingly little time to loosen the small misshaped slab of stone, but it needed two pairs of hands to lift it. Sean leveraged one end of it under the steel spade, then he and Laura crouched, wriggled their fingers under one end, and heaved in unison, their frosty breath mingling into a cloud. Together, they carefully lowered the stone onto a patch of damp grass. Blotched on one side with weathered piebald lichen and stained on the other with chalk-streaked clay, it weighed less than she'd anticipated. Given a sturdy bag, it would have been entirely possible for Nicholas to steal it away without garnering attention.

Olivia shone the torch beam into the shallow trench. Woodlice and earwigs scurried around the dead roots of the surrounding plants in a frantic search for cover. A hairy spider ambled unperturbed along the alluvial veins left by ingresses of rainfall. Sean picked up the spade and dug into the trench, shovelling the soil onto a stretch of path. A dancing stripe of light reflected off the aluminium spade.

The chilled air was a blessing, although the exertions left him breathless and red-faced. He removed his fleece jacket and handed it to Laura, who hooked it around her shivering shoulders. Her teeth were chattering ferociously. Nerves or the cold? The symptoms were indistinguishable. Before leaving the house, Olivia had replaced her woollen wrap with an ankle-length overcoat. Anthony was obliterated from slippers to chin in a swathe of blankets. There was little to see of any of their faces, especially Olivia's, whose expression was sheltered in a silhouette, her hooded head nothing more than a black outline set against the moonlit sky.

How preposterous, keeping two old people out in the cold in the hope of finding something that may not exist. Worse perhaps, Laura had encouraged them to dismantle a cherished sanctuary. As Sean continued to dig fruitlessly, Anthony grunted and gestured in agitation, and Olivia's unguarded, 'Oh dears' reeked of pity. Whether Olivia wanted the memoir found or not, it was increasingly likely that Laura's theory was hogwash, a figment of her imagination and a giant leap of blind faith from dream to supposed braille manuscript, which must be a concoction of her mind and nobody else's. She was cruel and selfish, acting thoughtlessly.

She touched the Sean's arm. 'Perhaps it's time—'

'Whoa,' Sean exclaimed, but not at her. The spade had jolted against something below. 'There's something hard down here.'

'Probably a stone,' Laura said, defeated.

Sean crouched and, using his hand, swept away the granules of clay and humus, the fractured roots of distant plants that lay tangled under the headstone. Olivia focused the beam on his hands.

Anthony's leg jerked, nearly kicking Laura. She moved to one side so he could see. His opaque eyes squinted, and he said something; not a word, only a sound, but to Laura it was an obvious noise of delight.

'I think you're right,' Laura said, peering closer. 'Is it sacking? No, tarpaulin, and a bit smelly.'

Sean gingerly touched it. 'Feels quite stiff.' He used the spade to work around the buried object, until an outline was excavated.

Laura joined him, feeling with her fingertips. There was something hard and unyielding within the tarpaulin parcel.

'Help me,' he said.

They dug it out with their hands, rather than risk damaging it with the metal shovel. Gradually, they freed the object, which was box-shaped, no more than a couple of inches deep and a foot square.

With bent knees, Sean grasped the two opposing ends and heaved. He staggered backwards, nearly falling. 'Wow. It's quite light.' The extraction created a trail of loose crumbs of soil that had cascaded from out of the tarpaulin wrapping. He gently wiped off the filth and slipped his hand between the layers of covering.

'Well?' Laura asked pensively.

'Feels like a tin. Some kind of metal box with a lid.'

Olivia flooded the discovery with light. The tarpaulin was ripped in places but otherwise intact. 'It's waxy,' she said.

'Waterproof, relatively speaking,' Sean said.

'Let's take it into the kitchen.'

They trooped behind her, Laura pushing Anthony's wheelchair, Sean carrying the covered box. Once indoors, Olivia cleared a space on the kitchen table and protected the surface with sheets of old newspapers. Unlike the units, which were contemporary and shiny, featuring all the latest appliances, the chubby pinewood table and chairs belonged in a countrified cottage.

Sean apologised for the dirt that had followed him. He and Laura washed their hands in the sink. Gathering around the table, blinking eyes still adjusting to the bright lights, the four of them maintained a moment of silent reverence for the unearthed object. It had been protected from the elements, supporting Laura's theory that Emma wanted it to be found again. Its purpose remained unknown, but being forgotten for an eternity wasn't it.

'Please would you…' Olivia said to Sean.

'Sure, if you're okay with that.' He leaned over the table and began to unwrap the box. More detritus fell away. A worm wriggled out of the sacking.

Laura squealed, childishly. Olivia expertly picked it up and dropped it outside the back door. Anthony, no longer swamped by blankets, was pushed closer to the table, allowing him a better view.

The box appeared plain, because if it had been decorated, the pattern had rusted away. The lid was sealed tight.

'Might be a bit of a vacuum,' Sean said. He clawed with his fingers and tried to prise it off. 'Certainly in good nick, probably galvanised steel.'

Which Laura took to be a good sign. Paper wouldn't survive underground if it got wet.

With a ping, the lid flew off and clattered onto the tabletop. A fleeting, musty aroma of arrested decay wafted past her nostrils. Laura peeped over Sean's shoulder, daring herself to look, and with fingers crossed behind her back – such superstitions she would have previously sneered upon, but now, after dallying with ghosts, she was open to adventurous beliefs. Inside was another bundle of canvas, treated with a wax coating, and as stiff as cardboard. Sean lifted it with experienced hands. He was the ideal person to unravel the material and he did so cautiously and with surprisingly nimble fingers for a man who couldn't handle contact lenses.

Laura swayed, dizzy and overcome with relief. Olivia murmured, 'Gracious!' Anthony grunted his exclamation. Sean beamed. He held the bound manuscript aloft, as if in worship, and then, with gravity, he offered it to Olivia.

'I think you should sit down,' he said softly. 'Take your time.'

Olivia nodded and pulled out a chair. 'My glasses, they're by the bed. The room opposite the sitting room. We live downstairs.'

Sean hastened out of the room.

Laura chose the chair next to Olivia and refrained from looming over her slight shoulder. The manuscript belonged to the Feydons, not Laura. The shabby cover was sawdust yellow and fashioned out of suede cloth rather than buffed leather. Olivia pinched the corner and slowly folded it back. The bound manuscript flopped open, and its spine creaked like a rheumatic backbone awoken from a long sleep. The binding used thread, not glue, and was intact. Blotched and warped along the edges, the title page appeared blank, but as Laura focused in on the tiny shadows and patterned texture, she recognised the familiar embossed dots.

Olivia stroked her fingertips over the sheet as if to savour the hidden words. Laura fought off her growing impatience; it was a private moment of reflection and to be respected. Sean returned with the reading glasses, and Olivia perched them on the end of the nose, then she turned to address not Laura, but her husband, recognising what Laura had forgotten; this was his family's legacy.

'It's an older style of braille,' she said simply. 'What you'd expect Emma to have learnt at the end of the nineteenth century.' She spoke to Laura. 'Remember the lack of standardisation?'

'Can you arrange for it to be transcribed?' Sean asked.

Olivia glowed. 'Oh, my dear, that's not necessary. I can read it.' She slid her finger along a line of dots. 'Quite quickly.'

'But... you're not—'

'Blind?' She laughed softly. 'Gracious, it's not a skill that requires blindness, only sensitivity of touch. I can read it with my eyes shut, but like most sighted readers of braille, I read it faster if I combine touch and sight. I can decipher the patterns with my eyes in step with my fingers.'

'You can read it,' Laura said in amazement. 'I never... how thoughtless of me.'

'There's nothing to suggest you are. You've come a long way for us,' Olivia said.

Laura didn't think Lincoln was that far away. Then it dawned on her that Olivia meant metaphysically, like a knight's quest. Laura said nothing, acknowledging the effort she'd undertaken on behalf of others with nothing more than an ironic smile. Her motives were best kept to herself.

'Would you like me to read this to you?' Olivia asked.

'What, now?' Laura said. 'Don't you need to read it through first?'

'I trust you. I don't think what Emma has written will likely cause our family grief. We're dealing with plenty of issues as it is. This is an echo, is it not, of her grief and anguish for her mother's crime, and it's likely to give the reason why her father was killed, a man we know next to nothing about. It has travelled through the years, waiting for the opportunity to be found again.'

'If you're able to read it, then please, I would very much like to know what Emma wrote,' Laura said.

'Would you fetch me a glass of water,' Olivia asked Sean. 'You'll have to be patient with my reading. It's not something I do very often these days. I'm out of practice.'

After taking a sip of water, adjusting her glasses, and laying the book flat on the table so that she could use both hands, she traced her fingers from left to right.

'There's a heading... It says... Bronte.'

Laura gasped.

'Yes, Bronte,' Olivia repeated.

'Crikey.' Sean dropped into the chair opposite Laura with a thump.

'Is there a reason for your stunned expressions?' Olivia asked.

'Only,' Laura said, 'that's the name I first heard whispered in the court. But Sean couldn't find anything about a Bronte in the prison. It didn't make sense. It was the enigma of the grave that helped us track down Eliza, then Emma.'

Olivia read the first paragraph aloud, her voice clear and undeterred by the intense concentration needed. The first mystery was solved: Bronte was the name by which Emma knew her mother. Then the story mentioned a bakery…

'I know where the bakery is,' Laura interrupted, unable to contain her advantageous position. 'She took me, Emma took me there.'

Olivia paused, took another sip of water. 'It still exists?'

'Not as a bakery. A rather dull café. But I smelt bread… I'm sorry, please read on. My reflections should come later.' Laura closed her eyes and listened as Olivia grew in confidence, deciphering the braille with increasing speed, so by the time she'd finished the first chapter up to Emma's birth, she was able to read fluently and with infrequent hesitations.

The clock ticked in the background. Anthony breathed heavily, sometimes as if in pain. The reason for the distress was obvious. William Horton was not the upstanding person portrayed in the newspaper report. Eliza had suffered at the hands of a vile husband yet managed at the same time to single-handedly raise a disadvantaged child using techniques that would have impressed any qualified modern teacher.

'Remarkable,' Olivia murmured. She refreshed her dry mouth with another sip. 'She taught Emma how to use her senses to great effect. Such a tragedy the girl was too afraid to speak. A selective mute, I suppose.'

The chapters shifted forward in time, closer to the crucial year of Eliza's death. When Harriet had mistakenly revealed to William that Emma possessed the ability to hear and speak, the four of them in the kitchen acknowledged the impending tragedy with deep sighs.

Olivia turned the page. 'Heading: William.'

'This reaches the point when Eliza must have killed William to protect Emma,' Laura said. 'The guilt must have been crippling, knowing her mother died saving her from a violent man.'

'Indeed, and probably why she hid the manuscript. It implicates her mother.' She cleared her throat. 'When Harriet revealed in her eagerness the truth…'

William

1872

WHEN HARRIET REVEALED in her eagerness the truth that I had speech, and consequently hearing, James had the wits to remove his sweetheart from the house with a speed that he rarely showed on any other occasion.

'Come, Harriet. Let us take a walk in the moonlight,' he said in his recently broken voice. Nearly sixteen years old, he was desperate to marry and escape his father's house. Fortunately, Harriet's parents were blessed with both money and property.

'But, James,' Harriet said witheringly, 'there is a chill in the air.'

'You have your mittens. We can warm ourselves in a public house, can we not?' He stomped his feet, as if to march, and escorted Harriet out of the house.

My spoon rattled against the bowl. I had no appetite. Ma's breaths were rapid and ragged.

The front door slammed shut.

William picked me up by the shoulders and shook me. 'Talk!' His poisonous spittle sprayed my face.

I screamed, kicked, and squirmed as worms do. My head was tossed from side to side; my arms were painfully pincered by his grip. The nothingness of my vision gave me no means to guess how far from the floor my feet dangled.

'Bill, please.' Ma's voice was stretched thinner than a thread.

'Shut it, woman.'

He flung me aside, and, like a ragdoll, I landed in a heap by the sideboard. A plate smashed, then another. I felt around, hoping to find a path to the door. I crawled, caught my sleeve on the edge of a chair in my desperate escape, and cowered there among the table legs. The blows were repetitive, and the worst kind. William aimed not for Bronte's face – he avoided marks – but thumped her back, knocked the breath out of her lungs until she gasped in pain.

'Where's my stick?' he seethed. 'I'll give a good hiding to the pair of you. You kept her mute, didn't you? Tricked me.'

'Bill, you don't know the truth.' Ma's desperate pleading cut into my heart. 'She's special. God's creature, like all children. Like James.'

The naming of his precious son unleashed fresh rancour. 'I should've left her at a foundling hospital or an orphanage. But you wanted her here. You made me keep her. Feed her. Clothe her. Is she a wicked child? Tell me, bitch. Is she the spawn of some devil? I bet she's not even mine.'

'She's just a bairn, Bill. Ours, I swear.' Ma sobbed, and I cried into my fists, pressing them to my pointless eyes.

'A brainless one, but if she hears, then I'll put her out to that basket maker on Brewer Street. He'll pay a fair wage for her hands. Eyes aren't needed. Just a good pair of ears that can listen and learn.' He placed a value on our lives, and it was pitiful.

'No, Bill. Don't. She's gifted, I'm sure. I know she can learn. She'll learn so much if we let her—'

The slap was vicious. I scrambled to my feet and fled into the parlour, tripping over this and that in my zeal. I spun around, held out my arms, and tried to judge the distances between sofa, armchair, and the mantel of the unlit fireplace – Ma never moved things; James liked to tease me. I bent, hunting for the poker, and failed. The bellows were missing, too. Next door, William's rabid curses continued. He was not dissuaded by Ma's use of meekness to defend herself. It was her usual strategy to endure his tirade until she could soothe him with affectionate words and deeds. William yearned for love but had not the capacity to requite it. As a child I did not understand this necessity for marriage – love equally partnered and shared – I only heard the selfish needs of a man's greed. William's rage was not dulled by begging, and I feared for Bronte.

'She's a half-wit. An incurable. She should never have been born. And where are the sons you promised me? What have you done to me? You're hysterical, woman, so I shall beat it out of you until you're cured.'

She choked back a cry. Pleading turned to cries, then they weakened until I thought she had no breath left in her.

He kept the stick in the umbrella stand by the front door. It was made from oak, capped with a weighty brass knob, and polished by his gloved hand. I shook off my fear, orientated myself, and slowly, so as not to trip or crash into the furniture, I edged my way along the wall to the door, feeling the peeling wallpaper between my fingers, and the splinters of the doorframe. I had to save my mother, prove I was no weakling, no half-formed human. I would fight back for the both of us. Although my body might have been of tender years, I was filled with rage, resilience and courage, and with strength born from this place, I grabbed the cold staff, lifted it high, and charged back into the room with it above my head.

'No, Emma!' Ma rasped.

I lashed out, swung the walking stick with both hands; the brass found its target. I make this clear – I was acting with intent and wanted to disable him. He must have been bent over her whilst her belly was flat against the table, her legs kicking. He perhaps glanced over his shoulder, not expecting to see his milky-eyed daughter raising aloft his preferred weapon. The accuracy of my swing was fortuitous and entirely by chance. I can only conclude that being occupied by his frenzied beating, he had not the wherewithal to raise his hands to protect his head. It would have not surprised me if he had looked upon me with disbelief and saw no threat. William's heavy weight struck the floor with a thunderous crash. Ma's whimpers intensified.

'Bill,' she said, a soft bleat of despair. 'Bill.'

I smelt the blood, the familiar ooze of red. My nostrils flared, and my stomach churned. I dropped the stick, letting the hateful thing clatter by my feet. Its purpose was now to be indelible evidence.

'He's dead,' Ma said, aghast.

She was right; I tasted death in the air. I had killed my father. My knees started to buckle, and I tore at my hair. I had set in motion an unstoppable sequence of events. I had not meant to end his life, but within seconds of his death, my guilt was established in my bones, the fault entirely mine. For those not acquainted with the emotion, guilt born out of an unintended crime at first instils feelings indistinguishable from fear and denial. Remorse takes time to feel, a passage of time beyond the years of a child and many beyond that. What fate awaited me then?

'Where can we go?' Ma muttered. The stench of blood mingled with fear.

Ma on her own might be able to run and hide, but with me tied to her, unable to see and fend for myself, fleeing would not take her far before she was captured.

'Go,' I croaked, forcing the "Oh" out between dry lips. I was the murderess not her, and I should bear the punishment alone. She was free of him, and me, too. As a half-wit child and a mute, I offered her a means to escape her fate. But Bronte foresaw things differently: in court, the jury would not believe a child of ten had the strength to crack open a man's skull with one fatal blow. Consequently, my perceived weaknesses would bring the prosecutor's case to rest once more upon my mother's role, especially if she absconded and left me behind, hardly the actions of a sympathetic mother.

'No,' she said. 'No, no. I shall not. I shall not leave you. My life was in danger, yours, too. You had to do this... I shall protect you...' Her voice faltered.

I held out my hand, hopeful that she was in reach, only to feel the expanse between us.

A key turned in the door. Harriet entered the room. She screamed. James retched. I sat still, a statue, unsure if I should break my silence and acknowledge my part in Father's death.

'Hush,' Ma murmured. 'Say nothing.'

The blame was all hers, she decided, and I had not the words or the means to tell anyone otherwise. It mattered not what a judge or jury believed, because they would never be presented with the truth. Instead, Bronte, the lover of romances and tragedy combined, planned to offer them a different version of events to the truth. (Her pleas of self-defence fell on deaf ears; no jury of men had the capacity to imagine why a woman would stay with a man who abused her so. Inconceivable! She was a wicked woman who had taken a respectable man and dashed his life with one angry blow.)

While a hysterical James ran down the street shouting for the constables, Harriet, having ceased her ear-piercing screams, stayed with us.

'What happened?' she whispered.

Ma said nothing. My teeth chattered, and I rocked back and forth in the chair. The shock disabled me further. From then on, I trusted no one in authority.

'You poor thing,' Harriet said, stroking my hair. The specks of blood had dried and stuck in the strands.

Ma must have more of it on her dress; she was closer to him when I struck out. The evidence mounted.

'She'll need somebody to look after her,' Ma said thinly.

Would she ever forgive me for ruining her life? She might have survived her beating. The lethal blow had denied us any chance of knowing what might have befallen us.

The shouts outside grew louder; boots pounded the pavements; a crowd would soon gather. 'Why did you do it?' voices repeated endlessly.

Do I regret killing him? That particular question should have been mine to answer, for Bronte and I were destined to end our lives in an early grave at the hands of that monster, a terrible phantom who I never saw yet always feared. Sadly, Ma carried my voice within hers, and I was mute.

'Marriage changed him. He is not the man I thought he was.' Bronte's warning was met with silence by Harriet and a low moan of despair from me.

The doctor summoned by the police declared my father dead. The chaos surrounding his body was confusing. Voices were raised, accusations were made and, in the midst of it, I hunted for Ma with my hands, reaching out and grabbing anyone who passed close to my side. They, those voyeurs of death, pushed my hands away, some kindly, others with a force as if I was diseased. In the commotion, while boots trampled in and out of the house, a hand touched mine and gave my fingers a swift squeeze. I recognised its print, the finer details of calluses and cracked skin, and I hung my head, hoping she might kiss my crown. Her hand was ripped away by a stronger, crueller force.

James's shrill voice reached my ears. 'She did it, she did it.'

I croaked and grunted, unable to shape the words that were stuck in my head – *Me, he means me.* But James did not point the finger at his half-sister. Why would he? I was a weakling, a child with no voice, sight, or hearing. I was locked in my own little world, my guilt kept secret so that my innocence was assured from the outset.

Ma never said yay or nay to his accusation. All I heard was her pleading with Harriet and James, and my name was repeated until she was told to shut up. The police handcuffed Bronte, issued their arrest, and removed her from the house. She went so quietly, so obediently to her fate. I never heard or touched my mother again. That loss haunts me still. She bravely carried my burden of guilt out of the house.

(In court, the police inspector described Ma as cold and calculating, lacking any remorse, and by then, she had no friends left to support her claim that her husband was a violent man with a temper. A motive was never elucidated by the prosecutor. He depended on a portrait of William that neither I nor Bronte would have recognised. As for James, he had not been in the house to bear witness to the murder and refused to offer any mitigation on behalf of his stepmother.)

As the clock ticked on the mantelpiece, my fate was being decided by those who barely knew me. Somebody mentioned the workhouse. I sobbed louder and rocked faster.

'No. She's not going there,' Harriet overruled James.

Harriet pressed Betty into my hands, wrapped a cloak around my shoulders, and took me to her house. On the doorstep, she introduced me to her parents and younger brother, Nicholas.

'This is Emma Horton. We must help her, please.'

'Then… It wasn't Eliza,' Laura said, sharing a stunned, wide-eyed exchange with Sean.

She had listened carefully, experiencing vicariously the distressing guilty feelings that Emma had written into her vivid account as if the events she described had only happened recently and not forty, nearly fifty years ago in Emma's lifetime. Blurry eyed, Laura looked across at Sean and locked into his gaze. He maintained a genuinely sombre expression. He reached over and patted the back of her hand, offering her his handkerchief, as he done once before. She declined. The tears were held back by willpower and the wish to hear the story to its conclusion.

Olivia, her eyes now closed, her sight not necessary to read the braille, had stumbled over some of the words, losing fluency.

'How sad,' she said in an understated yet dignified way. 'Eliza took the blame to ensure her daughter wasn't put in some ghastly asylum.' Everything that Eliza had striven to do had been on behalf of Emma, especially the education provided in secret; it would have been wasted if Emma was nothing to William other than a pair of working hands, a tyrannical father who planned to turn his daughter into his slave for the rest of her days.

'She sacrificed herself and stayed silent,' Laura said. 'The guilt Emma felt was doubled, don't you think? She murdered her father, and no matter how cruel he was, she must have known it was wrong, then stayed silent so that her mother took the blame, the pleas of self-defence dismissed.'

'Wow,' Sean said softly. 'Thank goodness for Harriet. Is there more?'

'Yes. The last chapter is headed,' Olivia's fingers caressed the dots, 'Nicholas.'

Nicholas

1872

HARRIET TREATED ME LIKE A DOLL for those first few weeks after my father's death. I was too shocked to break out of my self-imposed shell, too afraid to even whisper to Betty. The impending court case attracted the attention of neighbours, and I was kept indoors, only occasionally allowed out into the modest garden. My naivety appealed to Harriet, and she tolerated my ignorance; she had been tutored and sent to school. I had no understanding of femininity or proper deportment. Bronte had never bothered with ribbons in my hair or bows around my waist.

Harriet eventually coaxed out of me fragments of words by tempting me with promises of boiled sweets or a slice of cake. Utilising her natural stubbornness, she helped me learn how to string sounds together, then words into sentences. She confirmed what she had suspected – I had perfectly good hearing. In truth, I am extremely sensitive to the quietest sounds. She was also blessed with a kind heart, something that I had misunderstood upon our first encounter. She was genuinely pleased I possessed the faculty of hearing, and to my relief, she never applied that knowledge retrospectively to the night my father died. She never asked me, then or later, as if she had some inkling as to the true nature of events.

Harriet's parents, Mr and Mrs Kestern, were cautious at first, not wishing to become emotionally attached to me. I was an encumbrance to their purse, and although their spacious house could accommodate me, they had not anticipated another child joining their household. Nicholas was their youngest.

The outcome of Bronte's trial was reported in the newspaper. The Kesterns spoke of it in hushed voices. My acute hearing deduced that my mother's pleas for mitigation had been crushed by the cold counterarguments of the prosecution. Her impending execution attracted unwanted attention, and the Kesterns wished the matter was finished so that they might return to their quiet way of life. I had no ability or influence to plead on behalf of my poor mother.

I wept for Bronte during those last brutal days as she waited in that cold cell for her execution. Emboldened by my new circumstances and faith in decent people, I decided I had to tell the truth about that evening and save my mother from the noose. I practised my speech alone, often tripping over my tongue in my haste to combine syllables into words, but to my horror, the newspaper reported that Bronte had suffered her fate and I was too late. Grief-stricken, I barricaded myself in my room and refused to come out.

It was Nicholas, not Harriet, who convinced me to emerge and embrace life once more.

Nicholas, a studious child, had freckles – spots that covered his face, which moved and shifted from his nose to his forehead. He let me poke those little dots.

'Horrible, aren't they?' He laughed. 'You've such smooth skin, Emma.'

I snatched my hand back and picked up Betty, looping her woolly hair around my finger.

'James came to visit Harriet today. They had a terrible argument. She accused him of rejecting you, his only sister. He thinks you're an idiot and should be locked away in an asylum for your own protection.'

My mouth went dry.

'Don't worry,' he said quickly. 'Papa and Mama are livid that he would treat you so abhorrently. It's not your fault what happened to your parents.'

Nicholas touched the back of my hand, and I flinched. The air seemed thinner, harder to suck into my lungs.

'Are you all right? You're very pale.'

Like milk, Ma would say. I have no means to see why milk is pale, nor why clouds are fluffy and the cold sea is blue, and so on. But these curious descriptions stick in my head and remain forever memories of Bronte's soft voice.

Nicholas clucked his tongue. 'You're not to blame. Harriet has booted your brother out of our house and refused to see him again.'

Now my heart was pounding frantically. Would James insist I went home with him? He was my kin. Or would he force me upon my grandmother and the oppressive heat of the bakery where I would toil until broken?

'Don't worry.' Nicholas stroked my knuckles, soothing my nerves. 'Mama won't let you go.' He lowered his voice. 'She's quite taken to you.'

I wanted to tell him everything, blurt it out and make my confession. Nicholas was my priest, the soul mate who might help me carry my burden and find the path to forgiveness. I opened my mouth.

'Yes?' he asked.

I brought my jaw up, halting the beginnings of a word. Nobody should carry my sin but me. I would have to suffer the consequences of my guilt for all eternity, on this earth and beyond, where my soul would suffer in perpetuity.

He chuckled. 'You're so sweet, Emma. Pretty. If only you could write things down. I believe that it's much easier to write about feelings than say them. Papa says it is how men do things. Mama chatters away to Harriet. The pair of them are like this.'

I had no clue what "this" was. I grunted.

He took my fingers and crossed two of them. 'Best friends are close, knotted together.'

'Friends,' I repeated.

Nicholas taught me gestures. The shake of my head for no, a nod for yes, and a tap of my finger on his palm to count out numbers. I used these props until, like a small child, I fully grasped the fundamentals of proper speech and not the gibberish I whispered to Betty.

When he placed a pencil in my hand and a piece of paper on the table, he gasped with astonishment. I had not forgotten the rudimentary patterns of letters or the shapes Ma had taught me. He called for his parents and sister.

'Look, look. She can write,' he said. 'Harriet, she knows how to hold a pencil.'

'Well, almost,' Harriet said, slightly deflating my achievement. 'We can help her, can't we?'

'I suppose,' Mr Kestern said. 'But we can't afford a tutor—'

'I'll teach her,' Nicholas said. 'Please, Papa, let me.'

'Pl-ease,' I said, in the sweet voice that Ma might have called an angel's. But she never had the chance to hear it.

I acquired a new mother and father who generously permitted me to call them Mama and Papa, a necessary distinction from Ma and Father. Mama was kind, calm and, due to the presence of servants, able to spend time with me. She had wrinkles on her forehead and satin cheeks. Papa had a bird's nest on his chin, which tickled. He let me stroke it and told me stories about how the phoenix rises out of his fiery whiskers to live again. He gave me great hope.

Mama designed a sensory garden for me. We chose the flowers and herbs together. She hung tinkling bells from the branches of trees and secured a guide rope along the length of the garden path for me to follow. As for Papa, he and Nicholas devised a yard stick for me to carry. Light and straight in construct, so that the vibrations travelled its length and into my hand. The stick bounced off things, producing sounds that my cunning ear learnt to distinguish. Through it, I discovered the intricate world of objects that lay in my path: the jetty of a kerbstone and the parallel railings of a fence, the splash of a puddle, and the tangled twigs of a shrub.

Over the months that followed, Nicholas and I spent many hours together. We exchanged the habits of our lives, and I offered him a different view of the world. He wore a blindfold, and I introduced him to the power of senses, just as Bronte had shown me. Of course, my heart ached at first as I recalled those early lessons in the park, but by sharing them, I came to terms with the enormity of my loss. There is a hole in my heart, an emptiness, and nothing will fill it, but in sharing my blindness, Nicholas opened my mind to other emotions – the awakenings of love for an equal.

I told him about the letter blocks in William's drawers; I described how I traced them with my fingers.

'Wouldn't it be wonderful if you could read letters with your fingers,' he said as we sat side by side at the table. He was writing an essay on the history of Lincoln Castle. Soon he would finish school and start to work for his father, who was a successful architect and builder.

I rubbed the tips of my fingers with my thumb. 'Yes, it would.' My manners have always remained politely taciturn and my use of speech minimal. What good are thousands of words when a few suffice?

'I shall find you some of those letter blocks.'

'You will need many.'

He sighed. 'I shall ask Mr Golding what is used to teach the blind to read.'

Mr Golding was Nicholas' favourite schoolmaster.

'The blind do not read,' I said.

'Who says?' He tapped his pen on the table. 'Just doesn't seem right that there isn't anything to help you.'

'Ma liked to read.'

'Did she?' Nicholas shuffled the papers around. 'I assumed she wasn't... that's unfair of me, isn't it? A baker's daughter has every right to read and enjoy books.'

'Yes,' I agreed fervently. 'Blind girl also.'

He laughed heartily. 'Emma. If I can, I shall make you a book to read.'

He made that promise in jest, but little did I realise that one day he would make it real.

One day, when we are both adults and holding hands for everyone to see, he'd ask me to marry him and I would say yes. One day, when James's philandering ways and drunkenness brought him ruination, Nicholas, my attentive husband, would buy out his printing business. And out of that printworks, he might create something unheard of – story books for the blind. So successful a venture it would become that he sent books far and wide, even to the farthest reaches of the Empire. I would use them not only for pleasure, but to read to our children, and later, to the pupils I taught in our little school for the blind.

Then one day, many years later, in the hope my troubled soul might find peace before it retired for eternity, I would finally compose my confession and tell Nicholas the truth of what I know he and Harriet have always suspected but never spoke aloud. He'd acknowledge the existence of my guilt but never use it to judge me. By then, we will both be old and prefer the company of our grandchildren to tiresome adults.

The events I predicted began on my twelfth birthday. Nicholas discovered the one word that would entwine our lives together forever.

He raced home from school and stampeded up the stairs.

'Emma, Emma...' he said, panting. 'Mr Golding says it's called braille. What we're looking for is braille.'

Olivia, her voice suffering, had managed to croak her way to the final page where Emma recalled the beginnings of a better life and her future husband's enthusiasm for a new form of communication: braille.

'Sweet.' Sean punched the air with his fist, his sadness easily dispelled. 'I like that ending. It's good to know that she found her true family in the end.'

Laura sniffed and dabbed at the corners of her eyes. 'Just ignore me. I'm not sad, far from it. You're right, it explains how she came to be living here, the memorial, and everything in my dreams, all those details I didn't understand. I thought she was in a pitch-black coffin, but she was locked in the attic. The tiny blocks were used for typesetting, and she knew they were letters. The days spent in the bakery, the walks to the park, listening to the organ in the cathedral. Even the things I smelt were her memories come to life. I'm just so relieved that I'm not crazy.' Vindicated, too. Laura was unshackling herself from guilt as much as remorseful Emma had, and the wrongly accused Eliza.

Sean squeezed her hand. 'Laura, aren't you pleased? She'll rest now, surely? No more haunting anyone. And Eliza, too. What a courageous lady. She brought Emma up to be an amazing, strong woman.'

Olivia removed her glasses. 'With a wish to educate, just like her aspiring mother. I shall always think of her as Bronte now, reborn like the phoenix and free.' She closed the manuscript and pressed her palms flat on the surface; her arthritic fingers must ache badly.

'What will you do with it?' Sean, the curator of artefacts, raised his one mobile eyebrow expectantly.

'I don't know.' Olivia rubbed the shadowy lines beneath her eyes. 'It has implications I can't yet fathom. I admit, the manuscript's existence wasn't something I greatly believed in. The rumours about Emma's memoir were weakened by time and a lack of enthusiasm. Where it is kept was well-conceived – right under our noses. As for our family,' she covered her husband's gnarled fingers, 'we're the last Feydons. Our legacy is Seeside and the small museum next door, which I hope will survive. I don't think Steven cares for such things in the same way you do, Laura. I guess that we know all we need to know about Emma.'

Nearly all. The strange theft of the gravestone remained a mystery, as was the reason why the manuscript was buried.

Olivia took her husband's hand in hers and held it. The pair exchanged meaningful glances, practising some kind of silent communication that they'd learnt since his stroke. Anthony looked down, his eyes sinking lower, his chin tucked onto his chest, his whole body pointing downward.

Laura understood. She suspected Sean would be disappointed, but it wasn't his decision.

'Like Nicholas, I can't destroy it. We'll rebury it,' Olivia said. 'Put the headstone back.'

'But, but,' Sean stuttered. 'It *belongs* in your library, where others can read it. It proves Eliza was wrongfully hanged.'

Laura withdrew her arm sharply. 'I think it's for the best, too,' she said pointedly. 'Eliza has been forgotten for decades. Who will go looking for her and why? Do you want to make her the object of some exhibit? Dredge up the reasons why her grave is gone from the Lucy Tower? The first woman hanged by a notorious executioner! None of these things will give Emma peace, or Olivia and Tony.'

She covered her mouth, stopping herself from saying things she might regret. Her hot face betrayed her shame. She'd belittled Sean's authentic wish to present the past correctly. Laura's dreams and borrowed memories might have tickled his interest, but he yearned to tell the truth using genuine artefacts and not fantastical tales.

Sean scratched his chin and shrugged, but he smiled, too, unhurt by her chastising. 'Okay, you're right. It's not my decision. It's just a pity that it can't be kept somewhere else, even secretly.'

Olivia laughed. 'Like secretly buried in the ground?'

Laura slipped her hand back under Sean's, and he embraced it with a warm palm and a gentle squeeze. She'd judged Sean too quickly. From now on, she'd try to let others cautiously influence her, and not rely too heavily on comfortable facts to guide her decisions.

Sean offered to rebury the box that night, but Olivia was clearly exhausted, and she wanted to find a new container to put the manuscript in, something that would keep it dry and safe. 'Like a time capsule.'

Olivia hugged Laura on the doorstep. 'Thank you for being a bit crazy. I hope you can find your own peace now,' she whispered into Laura's ear.

'I can give you some advice if you like about how to protect the manuscript, keep it in good condition,' Sean offered, shaking Olivia's hand. 'Here's my business card.'

Laura watched incredulously as he whipped out a laminated card from his back pocket. He'd planned this intervention; he had his eye on the vulnerable braille collection.

'I never got one of those,' she said dryly.

'Well, you know where to find me,' he said with mock haughtiness.

Olivia laughed. 'Children, play nicely.' She turned on the sweeping security light, and the illuminated dry fountain shimmered into view. 'We should really get that working again. So much still to do.'

She and Sean said goodbye, waved to Anthony, who was parked in the bay window with the curtain drawn back, then they walked over to the car.

Sean checked for his phone. 'Still in my pocket.'

'It wouldn't be a bad thing to come back again, would it?'

'To the house or the museum?' He unlocked the car door.

'Both. I feel there's still something for us to do, don't you?' She wasn't sure what, but there was a purpose to everything, she'd decided.

'Us?' He tipped her shy chin upwards. 'I think we can do lots of things together. Why not come to my place tonight, and we can start thinking about it?'

She caught sight of his twitching lips just as the security light gave out. Only the moonlight braved the wintery skies. She left her face tilted up, her brazen lips parted, and waited. To her delight, she had his undivided attention.

Beyond

LAURA TURNED THE PAGE of the recipe book and examined the photograph of the chicken and leek pie. Hers almost looked like the one in the picture. She was chuffed with the outcome; the purchase of the book was vindicated. Steam rose out of the hole in the top of the pastry crust, and a little gravy trickled down the side of the dish. Otherwise, it had the same golden colour as the photo and, more importantly, it hadn't burnt. She hoped it tasted good. Placing it on a tray, she carried the pie into the next room.

Sean had set the dining table and opened the wine. Another classic cheap vintage on offer at the supermarket and warmed on the radiator – his suggestion. The aroma (frisky plums) caught her nostrils as she inhaled a glassful of red liquid. She'd not lost the ability. More time had passed since she'd last entwined with Emma's sensory world, and the nuances of hypersensitivity lingered on. She didn't resent the peculiar trait. She'd adapted, and still was practising the art of opening up. Before the trial, she had engineered a self-possessed cocoon to protect herself; breaking out meant braving hurtful emotions. She had promised to visit her father and extend an olive branch. Angela accepted it was Laura's choice and said nothing unkind.

Sitting opposite Sean, Laura raised her wine glass in a toast. 'Here's to pie, wine, and us.'

He smiled and clinked her glass. He cut into the pie and served it onto the plates, and she added a dollop of mashed potato to each. Breath held, she waited for him to taste it.

He smacked his lips and nodded. 'It's good. Really good.' His fork sank into the crust.

She didn't have to keep pace with him. Sean had slowed himself down and done so without losing that enthusiasm she loved. The hungry haste brought on by nerves was now unnecessary for either of them. After unearthing the manuscript, they had spent several evenings together and three whole nights. She was suitably happy with how things were progressing, and it helped that Sean was an honest communicator and she was learning how to show him frivolity without worrying about the consequences.

His mobile vibrated. He hesitated. 'You don't mind...'

She shook her head.

He examined the screen. 'Interesting. We've had an invite.'

'Oh, who? Where?'

'Kestern House.' He returned the phone to his jacket pocket.

'Olivia's ready for the time capsule?' Laura grinned.

Sean had acquired a steel box to replace the old tin. 'She says there's something else to show us. This Saturday?' He raised an eyebrow.

'Okay. Did she say what?'

'Only that we'd be interested to know before reburying the manuscript.'

She sipped on her wine. 'Well, Olivia's full of intrigue.' Just when Laura had thought such things were over.

Once more they settled around Olivia's generous kitchen table. Centre stage was the manuscript, wrapped in a crushed-velvet cloth and treated with ongoing reverence. Olivia unfolded the covering under the watchful eyes of her husband.

Laura pushed aside the cup and saucer, the arabica flavour suddenly unappealing. The reason for their visit was about to be unveiled.

'I kept it by the boiler,' Olivia said, 'like you suggested, Sean, so that it's ready for your box, when I spotted this.' She turned to the back cover and poked at the corner of the binding. 'There's something here.' Olivia passed the book to Sean. 'Something stuck under the flap between the binding sheets. See it?'

'Yes.' He peeled the cover away, revealing tissue-thin paper. 'It's another sheet. Loose, and handwritten in ink.' He carefully extracted the yellowing paper, which was packed with neat lettering, and glanced at the signature at the bottom. 'This is signed by Nicholas in 1921. It's a coda to Emma's journal.'

'Please, you read it.'

Laura hoped it wasn't anything that would change the optimism of Emma's final chapter. She closed her eyes and listened to Sean's even baritone, clutching his hand throughout.

There is nothing more precious than the words of your beloved. I hold them to my heart every day.

The pages of this memoir are a legacy to one woman's brave determination to keep her daughter safe. If, in years to come and in reading this, you judge Eliza harshly, please remember how few opportunities were granted to women. The estate of a man included his wife. The well-being of his family was entirely at his disposal. To deny him was unheard of and against the law. It still is and must not be so.

After Emma finished this account and told me the contents, I could not countenance it falling into the wrong hands. For it is a confession to murder and one that should not be made public even in these modern times. Realising the danger, and fearing for her grandchildren's future, Emma wanted to destroy it. But having spent painful hours creating the pages of braille, it would be a great pity to do so. Within these leaves are decent memories that should be kept alive. I suggested that we hide the manuscript until such time that society will treat my wife and mother-in-law kindly and with understanding.

But where shall we place it, and at what point will it be rediscovered?

It is Emma's idea, and bemused as I am by her thinking, I will carry out her wishes obediently.

I must therefore explain about the gravestone. After Eliza died, Emma and I would visit her grave in the Lucy Tower. The warden at the time took pity on a blind child and allowed her to visit upon the anniversary of Eliza's death each year. Flowers were arranged, sweet-smelling roses, and Emma would stroke the letters carved into the stone.

The announcement of the prison's closure brought panic to the girl who had already stolen my heart. We feared the headstones would be removed, even the graves dug up and the bones placed in a communal pit. The thought of Eliza tossed into a hole with heartless murderers was an abhorrence to her memory, which had already suffered greatly.

I confided in my sister, Harriet, older and wiser than I, and we both agreed to take responsibility for our actions. Emma knew nothing until the task was completed. Upon visiting the assizes and sitting in the public gallery, we waited until the business of the court was concluded, then crept out and hid behind the storehouses. When darkness fell, we went up to the Lucy Tower, and by the light of a weak candle, using half-staffed shovels, we dug out the grave marker. Poor Eliza herself could not be moved as it was too risky and likely to result in accusations of grave robbing, but the stone itself will serve as a good memorial when Emma and I have the freedom to honour Eliza's devotion and self-sacrifice. We carried the roughly hewn slab away, grateful for the cloudy night and bitter cold, which kept the foot patrols by their braziers.

From the castle, I took the stone and hid it under a bed at my parent's house where I lived with Emma. Later, after we married, I told her where it was kept and that one day we would fashion a more suitable memorial out of it. In 1912, we moved out of Lincoln into the peaceful countryside. At Kestern House, Emma continued to transcribe and teach braille. It was after our son died in 1917, his remains buried at Etaples, that Emma regretted missing the opportunity to explain to her son what had occurred on that dreadful night in 1872. She hid herself away for many weeks and wrote this account of her mother.

One summer's evening, we will dig a new grave; above it we will plant flowers and lay the headstone. Into this shallow nook I shall place this manuscript, wrapped to protect it from the elements, and there it shall remain until an era when justice is safer, and the evidence is scrutinised by equals and appeals heard by cautious ears. When these pages come to light, women will have continued to make great strides towards equality, and the blind will be gainfully employed along with the sighted. I can only hope that the future with its wondrous modern contraptions (Emma does love the telephone) will bring joy to the handicapped.

Emma assures me she believes this time will come and I should have faith, for sometimes I am at a loss at the wickedness of this world.

How this manuscript will be discovered is a mystery. It will be buried out of sight and mind. Whomever finds it must have an adventurous nature, or may be simply curious, or perhaps they might be able to conjure a connection to the deceased. Emma keeps her own memories alive by visiting many of the places known to her mother, including those that bring anguish: the courthouse, the old prison building with its peculiar chapel, and the overgrown graveyard, where Eliza lies, still forgotten. It is not for me to guess, Emma tells me. As long as its discovery is long after her death.

She does not know that I've written a coda to this memoir. I do not think she will mind. Her quietness, her softly spoken words and gentle touch are a reminder of her kind heart, one that guilt cannot destroy or consume.

Nicholas Kestern
August 1921

'Good.' The finality in Olivia's voice was clear. The story of Emma and Nicholas ended where her understanding of their relationship began. They were, and always would be, in the minds of Olivia and Anthony, a loving couple.

'Does this change anything?' Sean asked, laying the paper flat. 'I mean your plans to rebury it?'

'This coda I will keep above ground and safe. It reveals nothing of her guilt, only the devotion of a husband. I do like love letters.' She winked at Anthony with youthful acuity. 'Did you bring it?'

Sean nodded. He left the kitchen to retrieve the special box from his car.

Olivia released the brakes on the wheelchair. 'Laura, why don't you visit the sensory garden with Anthony while Sean and I ready the manuscript. We can meet by the yew tree.'

Snug inside a fleece jacket, her bare hands gripping the silicone handles, Laura wheeled Anthony along a paved path to the farthest corner where the garden was situated next to a boxed laurel hedge. She'd read about such gardens, and this one didn't disappoint.

He pointed with a shaky arm to a guide rope strung alongside a smooth footpath, and after she left him secured in the centre on a round patch of lawn, she followed its route, smiling with joy. Anthony laughed with her. While speech eluded him, laughter hadn't, and she listened to his grunts and sighs, the mutterings of a different language, and answered him with the odd whoop of surprise or giggle of appreciation.

She sniffed the plants in the raised boxes, and, knowing it was best to rely on every sense but sight, she closed her eyes. 'This smells minty... and this one like malt whisky or old peat.'

There were brass bells hanging from tree branches, whooshing bamboo chimes and twirling metallic spirals that whistled in the breeze. Boisterous starlings hurtled across the path, while birds, tempted into the garden by nest boxes and bird baths, sang hidden from view. There was a trickle of a fountain, and she dipped her hands under the icy water and inhaled sharply. Beneath the surface were smooth pebbles to roll between her fingers.

She brushed her hand against the rigid grooves of tree bark, and read the sign beneath, the words next to the braille, that explained the good luck brought from touching wood, then she stroked the velvet lamb's ears that formed a silvery carpet of leaves. Unlike other visitors, she did have the advantage of sight to see the granite rock garden, purple heathers, and the ochre soil harbouring the dying foliage. In winter, few flowers were hardy, and the emerald leaves belonged to the evergreens. She picked up stray pinecones and placed them on the dwarf walls for others to discover.

Utilising all the senses she was blessed with, she tasted damp moss floating on the air, yesterday's rain, and... sage. 'It must be beautiful in the summer, all those petals releasing their aroma.'

She played with a wooden xylophone mounted on a bench. The melodies were poorly defined compared to the easy rhythm she hammered out.

Anthony laughed again at her attempt at music making.

'I know. Everyone does *We Will Rock You.*' She giggled childishly, enjoying a carefree moment, something she'd often avoided. For the last fourteen years, she'd been stuck in the time warp of guilt and misgivings, and there was no way to wind back the clock; Emma had proved that point; time alone healed the broken spirit.

The visit ended with the arrival of Sean, who fetched them both up to the top end of the garden where the yew tree sheltered the little hole in the ground. Sean peeled back the canvas that had protected it from rainwater.

'I'll dig a bit deeper.' He'd read up on time capsules, the closest procedure for burying objects for longevity. He picked up the spade and dug. 'Who exactly is going to find this…' He panted. 'Is Emma likely to re-haunt the castle now that you've read her memoir?'

He'd directed his question to Olivia because every subsequent visit to the castle by Laura had been devoid of any supernatural encounters. She was truly free.

Olivia shrugged and smiled amiably. 'I know you'd like it out in the open, but I'm convinced it belongs here. There's nothing stopping you from telling her story, if that's what you want to do.'

Laura, holding the lightweight box in her arms, shook her head. 'No. Definitely not. How will we explain any of this without making me look silly?'

Sean took the box from her. 'Then only the very inquisitive might ever stumble upon this. After all, gravestones are markers, and this is a gravestone.'

Eliza's headstone lay waiting on the grass. A determined snail had glued itself to the surface.

Sean crouched and eased the square container into the hole. It had been labelled at his insistence with the date of the reburial and the names of those present crudely etched in the metal casing – witnesses in case of questions. Standing straight, he hunted for Laura's frozen hand and warmed it in his.

Laura wondered if words were appropriate. It wasn't as if this was a true grave. All they were burying were memories, and most people's memories were forgotten with time. Photographs might stay in albums, diaries shoved into the backs of drawers, and videos stored on old computer drives or ethereal data clouds, but ultimately, the substances of people's lives were lost long after their earthly presence. So, it didn't really matter that Emma and Nicholas might never be remembered beyond a few simple facts and family anecdotes. Olivia had the coda, and it alone was sufficient. And that was fine.

Everything was fine. Olivia was smiling contentedly, and Anthony was still.

After Sean had shovelled soil over the top of the container, Laura helped him lift the cover stone, and they repositioned it exactly as before. Other than a ring of dirt around it, there was nothing to indicate it had been moved.

'Thank you,' Olivia said with an air of deep satisfaction. She tapped the handles of the wheelchair. 'Let's get in the warmth. There's one more thing to give you.'

The heat of the kitchen welcomed them indoors. Laura uncoiled her scarf and loosened the buttons of her coat.

Olivia bustled energetically from the back door to a cupboard and fetched something from a drawer. She brought it to Sean: a key on a familiar lanyard. 'Here, take it.'

The museum key rested on his palm. Frown lines formed on his forehead. 'I don't understand.'

'I can't do this on my own, and I think you're the kind of person who can and wants to help. And I know Laura is interested in learning braille.'

Laura had said nothing to anyone. It was Olivia's intuition and it was perfectly correct. She did want to learn to read and write braille. Why, she wasn't sure. Perhaps a residue of Emma's memories was lodged in her mind.

Sean's eyes brimmed with emotion. 'You're giving me a museum?'

'I can't pay you. It's not to replace your job. It's just so you can advise us, about its future. We're at a loss, Tony and me. We need galvanising. You're that type of person. Laura can help you, I'm sure.'

Olivia sat on a chair and rested her rheumatic fingers on her lap.

Laura swept a lock of hair out of her blurry eyes with an unsteady hand. 'Both of us?'

'Naturally. You are a couple, after all. It's very obvious, you know. Take it from a happily married pair.' Olivia's face glinted under the lights.

Laura took the lanyard from Sean's palm, reached up, and draped it around his neck. The key settled next to his chest. 'She's right. I want to do this.'

Sean stooped to kiss the top of her head. 'Then we shall, together.'

Epilogue

LincolnOnline – Latest News

An application for an appeal hearing for Craig Brader (52), who was found guilty of five counts of conspiracy to commit fraud and sentenced to three years and two months, has been turned down. He has appointed a new solicitor, his third. A family member has reported that Brader's estranged wife has absconded overseas having abandoned her lover, Ben Cardwell, a discredited accountant linked to a building company used extensively by Brader during his tenure as finance director of the charity Seeside. Mrs Brader has always insisted there is no connection between her husband's trial and her decision to divorce him.

The police have arrested Cardwell in connection with accusations of falsifying accounts of several construction and engineering companies, including the one used by Seeside. Cardwell is accused of masterminding a conspiracy to commit fraud in conjunction with Brader, his longtime associate.

Brader has been instructed to return £88,000 to the Seeside charity. The trustees have appointed a new finance director to replace Brader. Steven Feydon has stepped down from the board, stating that, going forward, no member of the Feydon family will have operational control of the charity's fundraising activities.

Following the death of its patron, Anthony Feydon, the Museum of Braille, which is housed at Kestern House, will be closed indefinitely. Appeals have been made for a new home for the collection. Mrs Olivia Feydon is optimistic it will be handed over to a suitable organisation and reopened to the public. Any enquiries should be made to Sean and Laura Pringle, volunteer helpers who are coordinating the re-homing of the historically valuable collection of early braille publications, braille writers and printers.

Author's Note

Not everyone is granted the opportunity to do jury service, and if you are called up to serve, criminal trials can be any number of things: daunting, fascinating, distressing, tedious. But ultimately it is a responsibility not forgotten. My two weeks of jury service involved charges that bear no resemblance to the trial Laura heard. The subject of the trial wasn't what motivated me to write her story, it was the courthouse, an old, creaky courtroom that belonged to another century and that has changed little over the decades. The seats were extremely uncomfortable, the air cold, and the acoustics appalling. And, like Laura, I experienced something alien to my everyday life.

Inspired by the physical characteristics of the courthouse, and setting aside the evidence presented during the trial, I realised my memories of jury service are sensory, and that evocative awakening was the first step in writing this book. What if my juror was haunted while she sat in a courtroom, and what if those supernatural encounters took her out of the courtroom and on a journey, meeting new people, and exploring her own trials and tribulations?

Laura had to be ordinary in her daily life, and yet also unusual in her perceptions of the world around her. A challenging character to develop, and fun, too. Following Laura's footsteps, I had to do some research to help understand the past, especially regarding braille and its historical development. I'm particularly grateful to the staff at RNIB who answered my questions enthusiastically and pointed me in the direction of useful websites and contacts.

A special thanks to Alison, Emmy and Richie for their invaluable contributions, advice and hard work. This book wouldn't exist without them.

I also have to give a big thank you to Lincoln for providing me with the perfect location – the prison, graveyard, and courthouse are all there together within the castle walls, and the cathedral next door. Executed prisoners are buried in the Lucy Tower, including William "Fred" Horry and Priscilla Biggadike, both hanged by the long drop method. However, I took some liberties, too. You won't find a yew tree in the tower quite like I describe, and there are no publicly available images of the courtroom interiors, so I brought along my local courthouse and superimposed it on Lincoln's. I have visited the chapel in the prison museum but never met a ghost there. However, there are real tales of hauntings, so you never know…

If you enjoyed my book, please leave a review; it helps keep me inspired and full of ideas for my next project. If you want to sign up for my occasional newsletter (by visiting rachelwalkley.com), you'll have the opportunity to read about what I read, and what other stories I'm shaping, whether long or short.

Rachel Walkley's Books

The Last Thing She Said

It was a gripping story of family dealing with loss and love with an added sprinkle of magic for good luck! ~ Amazon Reviewer

**A sister and her lover bring turmoil to a family.
Was her grandmother's prophetic warning heeded?**

"Beware of a man named Frederick and his offer of marriage."

Rose's granddaughters, Rebecca, Leia and Naomi, have never taken her prophecies seriously. But now that Rose is dead, and Naomi has a new man in her life, should they take heed of this mysterious warning? Naomi needs to master the art of performing. Rebecca rarely ventures out of her house. She's afraid of what she might see. As for Rebecca's twin, everyone admires Leia's giant brain, but now the genius is on the verge of a breakdown.

Rebecca suspects Naomi's new boyfriend is hiding something. She begs Leia, now living in the US, to investigate.

Leia's search takes her to a remote farm in Ohio on the trail of the truth behind a tragic death.

Just who is Ethan? And what isn't he telling Naomi?

In a story full of drama and mystery, the sisters discover there is more that connects them than they realise, and that only together can they discover exactly what's behind Rose's prophecy.

Three sisters. Three gifts. One prophecy.

Available Now.

The Women of Heachley Hall

The house itself is almost a breathing entity with its own personality and I loved this about it. A cleverly written plot that drew me in and had me wandering the rooms of Heachley Hall along with Miriam. A story about love, regret and the secrets families keep. ~ Brooks Cottage Reviews

Only women can discover Heachley's secret.

The life of a freelance illustrator will never rake in the millions so when twenty-eight-year-old Miriam discovers she's the sole surviving heir to her great-aunt's fortune, she can't believe her luck. She dreams of selling her poky city flat and buying a studio.

But great fortune comes with an unbreakable contract. To earn her inheritance, Miriam must live a year and a day in the decaying Heachley Hall.

The fond memories of visiting the once grand Victorian mansion are all she has left of her parents and the million pound inheritance is enough of a temptation to encourage her to live there alone.

After all, a year's not that long. So with the help of a local handyman, she begins to transform the house.

But the mystery remains. Why would loving Aunt Felicity do this to her?

Alone in the hall with her old life miles away, Miriam is desperate to discover the truth behind Felicity's terms. Miriam believes the answer is hiding in her aunt's last possession: a lost box. But delving into Felicity and Heachley's long past is going to turn Miriam's view of the world upside down.

Does she dare keep searching, and if she does, what if she finds something she wasn't seeking?

Has something tragic happened at Heachley Hall?

Miriam has one year to uncover an unimaginable past.

Available from online retailers.

Printed in Great Britain
by Amazon